Bunyip Land
A Story Of Adventure
In New Guinea

By

George Manville Fenn

Bunyip Land
A Story Of Adventure In New Guinea
by George Manville Fenn

ISBN: 978-93-60463-64-9

Published by

DOUBLE 9 BOOKS

2/13-B, Ansari Road
Daryaganj, New Delhi – 110002
info@double9books.com
www.double9books.com
Tel. 011-40042856

ABOUT THE AUTHOR

George Manville Fenn was a very productive author of novels, a writer, an editor, and an educator from England. He was born on January 3, 1831, in Pimlico, London. He mostly learned on his own; he taught himself Italian, French, and German. During the years 1851–1854, he went to Battersea Training College for Teachers and then became the head of a state school in Alford, Lincolnshire. In the early 1850s, Fenn started to write short stories and pieces for newspapers and magazines. The Old Forest Ranger, his first book, came out in 1856. Afterward, he wrote more than 100 books, many of them for teenagers and young adults. He was one of the most famous writers of his time, and his books were well-liked and read by many people. He also worked as a reporter and writer for Fenn. Among the newspapers and magazines, he worked for was The Boy's Own Paper, which he ran from 1866 to 1874. He worked hard to make children's books better and was a strong supporter of education and reading. The Englishman Fenn passed away on August 26, 1909, in Isleworth.

CONTENTS

Chapter One
How I made my Plans and they were Endorsed

"Now, Master Joseph, do adone now, do. I'm sure your poor dear eyes'll go afore you're forty, and think of that!"

"Bother!"

"What say, my dear?"

"Don't bother."

"You're always running your finger over that map thing, my dear. I can't abear to see it."

Nurse Brown looked over the top of her spectacles at me and shook her head, while I bent lower over the map.

Then the old lady sighed, and went on making cottage windows all over my worsted stockings, giving vent to comments all the time, for the old lady had been servant to my grandmother, and had followed her young mistress when she married, nursing me when I was born, and treating me as a baby ever since. In fact she had grown into an institution at home, moving when we moved, and doing pretty well as she liked in what she called "our house."

"Bang!"

"Bless the boy! don't bang the table like that," she cried. "How you made me jump!"

"It's of no use talking, nurse," I cried; "I mean to go."

"Go!" she said. "Go where?"

"Go and find my poor dear father," I cried. "Why, nurse, am I to sit down quietly at home here, when perhaps my poor father is waiting for me to come to his help?"

"Oh, hush! my dearie; don't talk like that I'm afraid he's dead and gone."

"He isn't, nurse," I cried fiercely. "He's a prisoner somewhere among those New Guinea savages, and I mean to find him and bring him back."

Nurse Brown thrust her needle into the big round ball of worsted, and held it up as if for me to see. Then she took off her glasses with the left hand in the stocking, and shaking her head she exclaimed:

"Oh, you bad boy; wasn't it enough for your father to go mad after his botaniky, and want to go collecting furren buttercups and daisies, to break your mother's heart, that you must ketch his complaint and want to go too?"

"My father isn't mad," I said.

"Your father *was* mad," retorted Nurse Brown, "and I was surprised at him. What did he ever get by going wandering about collecting his dry orchardses and rubbish, and sending of 'em to England?"

"Fame," I cried, "and honour."

"Fame and honour never bought potatoes," said nurse.

"Why, four different plants were named after him."

"Oh, stuff and rubbish, boy! What's the good of that when a man gets lost and starves to death in the furren wilds!"

"My father was too clever a man to get lost or to starve in the wilds," I said proudly. "The savages have made him a prisoner, and I'm going to find him and bring him back."

"Ah! you've gone wandering about with that dirty black till you've quite got into his ways."

"Jimmy isn't dirty," I said; "and he can't help being black any more than you can being white."

"I wonder at a well-brought-up young gent like you bemeaning yourself to associate with such a low creature, Master Joseph."

"Jimmy's a native gentleman, nurse," I said.

"Gentleman, indeed!" cried the old lady, "as goes about without a bit of decent clothes to his back."

"So did Adam, nursey," I said laughing.

"Master Joseph, I won't sit here and listen to you if you talk like that," cried the old lady; "a-comparing that black savage to Adam! You ought to be ashamed of yourself. It all comes of living in this horrible place. I wish we were back at Putney."

"Hang Putney!" I cried. "Putney, indeed! where you couldn't go half a yard off a road without trespassing. Oh, nurse, you can't understand it," I cried enthusiastically; "if you were to get up in the dark one morning and go with Jimmy—"

"Me go with Jimmy!" cried the old lady with a snort.

"And get right out towards the mountain and see the sunrise, and the parrots in flocks, and the fish glancing like arrows down the silver river—"

"There's just how your poor dear pa used to talk, and nearly broke your poor ma's heart."

"No, he didn't; he was too fond of her," I said; "only he felt it his duty to continue his researches, the same that brought him out here, and—oh, I shall find him and bring him back."

"Don't, don't, don't! there's a good boy; don't talk to me like that. You're sixteen now, and you ought to know better."

"I don't want to know any better than that, nurse. I know it's my duty to go, and I shall go."

"You'll kill your poor ma, sir."

"No, I sha'n't," I said. "She won't like my going at first, because it will seem lonely for her out here; but she'll be as pleased as can be afterwards. Look here: my mother—"

"Say *ma*, Master Joe, dear. Doey, please; it's so much more genteel."

"Stuff! it's Frenchy; mother's old English. Mother don't believe father's dead, does she?"

"Well, no, my dear; she's as obstinate as you are about that."

"And she's right. Why, he's only been away four years, and that isn't so very long in a country where you have to cut every step of the way."

"Cooey—cooey—woo—woo—woo—woo—why yup!"

"Cooey—cooey!" I echoed back, and nurse held he hands to her ears.

"Now don't you go to him, Master Joseph; now please don't," said the old lady.

"Mass Joe! hi Mass Joe! Jimmy fine wallaby. Tick fass in big hole big tree."

Just then my first-lieutenant and Nurse Brown's great object of dislike, Jimmy, thrust his shiny black face and curly head in at the door.

"Go away, sir," cried nurse.

"Heap fis—come kedge fis—million tousand all up a creek. Jimmy go way?"

He stood grinning and nodding, with his hands in the pocket holes of his only garment, a pair of trousers with legs cut off to about mid-thigh.

"If you don't take that nasty black fellow away, Master Joseph, I shall be obliged to complain to your poor ma," said nurse.

"Get out!" I said; "Jimmy won't hurt you; and though it don't show, he's as clean as a new pin."

"He isn't clean; he can't be, dear. How can any one be clean who don't wear clothes, Master Joseph? and look at his toes."

Nurse Brown always fell foul of Jimmy's toes. They fidgeted her, for they were never still. In fact Jimmy's toes, which had never probed the recesses of a pair of boots, were more like fingers and thumbs, and had a way of twiddling about when he was supposed to be standing still—stand perfectly still he never did—and these toes belonged to feet that in climbing he could use like hands. More than once I've seen him pick stones off the ground—just like a monkey, nurse said—or stand talking to any one and keep his attention while he helped himself to something he wanted with his feet.

"There, be off Jimmy," I said, for I wanted to stop indoors.

"Come kedge fis."

"No, not to-day."

"Hi—wup—wup—wup!"

Jimmy threw himself into an attitude, snatching a small hatchet from the waistband of his trousers, and made believe to climb a tree, chop a hole larger, and draw out an animal, which he seemed to be swinging round by its tail.

"No, not to-day, Jimmy," I cried.

"Sleep, sleep," said Jimmy, imitating a kangaroo by giving a couple of hops into the verandah, where he chose a sunny place, well haunted by flies, curled up, and went to sleep.

"Good morning!" cried a hearty voice, and I ran out to welcome our neighbour the doctor, whose horse's hoofs had not been heard, and who was now fastening the rein to the hook in one of the verandah posts.

"Well, Joe," he said as I shook hands and looked up admiringly in his bold well-bearded face.

"Well, doctor, I'm so glad you've come; walk in."

"Ah! nurse," he cried; "how well you look!"

"Yes, yes; but I am glad you're come," she said. "I want you to look at Master Joseph."

"I did look at him."

"Isn't he feverish or something, sir? He's that restless as never was."

"Sign he's growing," cried the doctor. "How's mamma?"

"Oh, she's pretty well," I said. "Gone to lie down."

"That's right," said the doctor. "I had to come and look at Bowman's broken arm, so I came on here to beg a bit of dinner."

"I'm so glad!" I said: for Jimmy, the half-wild black, was my only companion, there being no boys within miles of our run; "stop a week and have some fishing."

"And what's to become of my patients?"

"You haven't got any," I said. "You told me so last time."

"True, O King Joseph! I've come to the wrong place; you don't want many doctors in Australia. Why, nurse, how this fellow grows!"

"I wish he'd grow good," cried the old lady. "He's always doing something to worry away his poor ma's and my life."

"Why, what's the matter now, nurse?"

"Matter, sir! Why, he's took it into his head to go looking for his poor dear dead-and-gone pa. Do, do please tell him he mustn't think of such things."

"Why, Joe!" cried the doctor, turning sharply round to me, and ceasing to beat his high boots with his long-thonged whip.

"I don't care what anybody says," I cried, stamping my foot. "I've made up my mind, and mean to go to New Guinea to find my father."

"There, doctor, did you ever hear any one so wickedly obstinate before?" cried nurse. "Isn't it shocking? and his ma that delicate and worried living all alone, like, here out in these strange parts, and him as ought to be a comfort to her doing nothing but hanker after running away to find him as is dead and gone."

"He's not dead, nurse; he's only gone," I cried; "and I mean to find him, as sure as I live. There, that I will."

"There, doctor, did you ever hear such a boy?" cried nurse.

"Never," said the doctor. "Why, Joe, my boy," he cried as I stood shrinking from him, ready to defend myself from his remonstrances, "your ideas do you credit. I didn't think you had it in you."

"Then you don't think it is wrong of me, doctor?" I said, catching his hand.

"No, my boy, I do not," he said gravely; "but it is a task for strong and earnest men."

"But I am strong," I said; "and if I'm not a man I'm in real earnest."

"I can see that, my lad," said the doctor, with his brown forehead filling with thoughtful wrinkles; "but have you counted the cost?"

"Cost!" I said. "No. I should get a passage in a coaster and walk all the rest of the way."

"I mean cost of energy: the risks, the arduous labours?"

"Oh, yes," I said; "and I sha'n't mind. Father would have done the same if I was lost."

"Of course he would, my lad; but would you go alone?"

"Oh, no," I replied, "I should take a guide."

"Ah, yes; a good guide and companion."

"There, Master Joseph, you hear," said nurse. "Doctor Grant means that sarcastical."

"No, I do not, nurse," said the doctor quietly; "for I think it a very brave and noble resolve on the part of our young friend."

"Doctor!"

"It has troubled me this year past that no effort has been made to find the professor, who, I have no doubt, is somewhere in the interior of the island, and I have been for some time making plans to go after him myself."

Nurse Brown's jaw dropped, and she stared in speechless amazement.

"Hurray, doctor!" I cried.

"And I say hurray too, Joe," he cried. "I'll go with you, my lad, and we'll bring him back, with God's help, safe and sound."

The shout I gave woke Jimmy, who sprang to his feet, dragged a boomerang from his waistband, and dashed to the door to throw it at somebody, and then stopped.

"You'll break his mother's heart, doctor," sobbed nurse. "Oh! if she was to hear what you've said!"

"I did hear every word," said my mother, entering from the next room, and looking very white.

"There, there," cried nurse, "you wicked boy, see what you've done."

"Mother!" I cried, as I ran to her and caught her—poor, little, light, delicate thing that she was—in my arms.

"My boy!" she whispered back, as she clung to me.

"I must go. I will find him. I'm sure he is not dead."

"And so am I," she cried, with her eyes lighting up and a couple of red spots appearing in her cheeks. "I could not feel as I do if he were dead."

Here she broke down and began to sob, while I, with old nurse's eyes glaring at me, began to feel as if I had done some horribly wicked act, and that nothing was left for me to do but try to soothe her whose heart I seemed to have broken.

"Oh, mother! dear mother," I whispered, with my lips close to her little pink ear, "I don't want to give you pain, but I feel as if I must—I must go."

To my utter astonishment she laid her hands upon my temples, thrust me from her, and gazing passionately in my great sun-browned face she bent forward, kissed me, and said:

"Yes, yes. You've grown a great fellow now. Go? Yes, you must go. God will help you, and bring you both safely back."

"Aw—ugh! Aw—ugh! Aw—ugh!" came from the verandah, three hideous yells, indicative of the fact that Jimmy—the half-wild black who had attached himself to me ever since the day I had met him spear-armed, and bearing that as his only garment over the shoulder, and I shared with him the bread and mutton I had taken for my expedition—was in a state of the utmost grief. In fact, he had thrown himself down on the sand, and was wallowing and twisting himself about, beating up the dust with his boomerang, and generally exciting poor old nurse's disgust.

"Mother!" I cried; and making an effort she stood up erect and proud.

"Mr Grant," she exclaimed, "do you mean what you say?"

"Most decidedly, my dear madam," said the doctor. "I should be unworthy of the professor's friendship, and the charge he gave me to watch over you in his absence, if I did not go."

"But your practice?"

"What is that, trifling as it is, to going to the help of him who gave me his when I came out to the colony a poor and friendless man?"

"Thank you, doctor," she said, laying her hand in his.

"And I go the more willingly," he said smiling, "because I know it will be the best prescription for your case. It will bring you back your health."

"But, doctor—"

"Don't say another word," he cried. "Why, my dear Mrs Carstairs, it is five years since I have had anything even approaching a holiday. This will be a splendid opportunity; and I can take care of Joe here, and he can take care of me."

"That I will—if I can," I cried.

"I know you will, Joe," he said. "And we'll bring back the professor with all his collection of new plants for that London firm, on condition that something fresh with a big red and yellow blossom is named after me—lay the Scarlet Grantii, or the Yellow Unluckii in honour of my non-success."

"You're never going to let him start, Miss Eleanor?" cried nurse.

"Would you have me stand between my son and his duty, nurse?" cried my mother, flushing.

"Dearie me, no," sighed the old lady; "only it do seem such a wild-goose chase. There'll be no one to take care of us, and that dreadful black, Jimmy"—nurse always said his name with a sort of disrelish—"will be hanging about here all the time."

"Iss, dat's him, Jimmy, Jimmy, here Jimmy go. Hi—wup—wup—wup, Jimmy go too."

"Nonsense, Jimmy!" I said; "I'm going to New Guinea to seek my father."

"Iss. Hi—wup—wup—wup, Jimmy going to look for his fader."

"Why, you said he was dead," I cried.

"Iss, Jimmy fader dead, little pickaninny boy; Jimmy go look for him, find him dere."

"Be quiet," I said, for the black was indulging in a kind of war-dance; "you don't understand. I'm going across the sea to find my father."

"Dat him. Jimmy want go 'cross sea find him fader bad. Hi! want go there long time."

"Why, you never heard of the place before," I said.

"No, never heard him fore; want to go long time. Jimmy go too."

"Why, what for?" I said.

"Hunt wallaby—kedge fis—kill black fellow—take care Mass Joe—find um fader. Hi—wup—wup—wup!"

"He would be very useful to us, Joe," said the doctor.

"And I should like to take him," I said eagerly.

"Iss, Jimmy go," cried the black, who contrived, in spite of his bad management of our language, to understand nearly everything that was said, and who was keenly watching us all in turn.

"He would be just the fellow to take," said the doctor.

"Hi—wup—wup! Jimmy juss a fellow to take."

"Then he shall go," I said; and the black bounded nearly to the ceiling, making nurse utter a shriek, whereupon he thrust his boomerang into his waistband, and dragged a waddy from the back, where it had hung down like a stumpy tail, and showing his white teeth in a savage grin, he began to caper about as if preparing to attack the old lady, till I caught him by the arm, and he crouched at my feet like a dog.

"Come long," he said, pointing out at the sun, "walk five six hour—all black dark; go sleep a morning."

"All in good time, Jimmy," I said. "Go out and wait." The black ran out, and crouched down upon his heels in the verandah, evidently under the impression that we were about to start at once; but Europeans bound on an expedition want something besides a waddy, boomerang, and spear; and with nurse shaking her head mournfully the while, my mother, the doctor, and I held a council of war, which, after a time, was interrupted by a curious noise between a grunt and a groan, which proved to be from Jimmy's throat, for he was preparing himself for his journey by having a nap.

Chapter Two
How we prepared to start, and started

You will have gathered from all this that my father had been missing for pretty well three years, and that he, a well-known botanist, had accepted a commission from a well-known florist in the neighbourhood of London to collect new plants for him, and in his quest he had made his last unfortunate trip—which had followed one to Carpentaria—to New Guinea.

We had heard from him twice, each time with a package of seeds and plants, which we had forwarded to London. Then there was an utter cessation of news; one year had become two—then three—and it would soon be four.

Quite a little fellow when he started, I had cried with disappointment at being left behind. Now I had grown into a big fellow for my age; I had dreamed incessantly of making the attempt to find my father, and now at last the time had come.

I believe I was quite as excited over the proposed journey as Jimmy, but I did not go about throwing a spear at gum-trees, neither did I climb the tallest eucalyptus to try if I could see New Guinea from the topmost branches. Moreover I did not show my delight on coming down, certain of having seen this promised land, by picking out a low horizontal branch and hanging from it by my toes.

All of these antics Jimmy did do, and many more, besides worrying me every half-hour with—

"Come long—time a go find him fader."

Of course now I know that it would have been impossible for me to have carried out my plans without the doctor, who was indefatigable, bringing to bear as he did the ripe experience of a man who had been all over the world pretty well before he came to Australia to make a practice; and every day I had from him some useful hint.

He was quite as eager as I, but he met all my impatient words with—

"Let's do everything necessary first, Joe. Recollect we are going to a far more savage land than this, and where we can renew nothing but our store of food. Don't let's fail through being too hasty. All in good time."

But the time did seem so long, for there was a great deal to do.

Jimmy—who by the way really bore some peculiar native name that sounded like Wulla Gurra—was fitted out with a serviceable sailor's suit, of which he was very proud, and never prouder than when he could see it to its best advantage.

This was in the wool barn, where, upon every opportunity, the black used to retreat to relieve himself of the unwonted garb, and hang it up against the shingle wall. Then he would show his teeth to the gums and squat down, embrace his knees, and gaze at the clothes.

When satisfied with the front he would rise deliberately, go to the wall, turn every article, and have a good look at the other side.

We ran some risks at this time, for our henchman was given his first lessons in the use of a rifle, and for a long time, no matter how the doctor tried, it seemed as if it was impossible for the black to hold the piece in any other direction than pointed straight at one of his friends. By slow degrees, though, he got over it, and wanted lessons in loading and firing more often than his master was prepared to give them.

Jimmy had heard the report of a gun hundreds of times, but his experience had never gone so far as holding the piece when it was fired; and when, after being carefully shown how to take aim, he was treated to a blank charge and pulled the trigger, the result was that I threw myself on the ground and shrieked with laughter, while the doctor seated himself upon a stump and held his sides, with the tears rolling down his cheeks.

For at the flash and report Jimmy uttered a yell, dropped the rifle, and turned and ran as hard as he could for the barn, never once looking behind him.

A couple of minutes were, however, sufficient to let his fear evaporate, and he came back waddy in fist, half shamefaced, half angry, and rubbing his right shoulder the while.

"Don't do dat," he cried fiercely. "Don't do dat. Play trick, Mass Joe. Play trick, Jimmy."

"I didn't," I cried, laughing. "Here; see me."

I took the rifle, put in a charge, and fired.

"There," I said, reloading. "Now, try again."

Jimmy had on only his curtailed trousers, into whose waistband he cautiously stuck the waddy, the knob at the end stopping it from falling through, and gingerly taking the rifle once more to show that he was not afraid, he held it loosely against his shoulder and fired again.

The gun kicked more than ever, for it was growing foul, and, uttering a yell, Jimmy dashed it down, snatched the waddy from his waistband, and began belabouring the butt of the piece before we could stop him, after which he stood sulkily rubbing his right shoulder, and scowling at the inanimate enemy that had given him a couple of blows.

One or two more experiments with the piece, however, taught the black its merits and demerits to such an extent that he was never so happy as when he was allowed to shoulder the formidable weapon, with which he would have liked to go and fight some native tribe; and his constant demand to me was for me to put in an extra charge so that he might have what he called "big-bang."

The doctor took care that we should both be well furnished with every necessary in arms, ammunition, and camp equipments, such as were light and would go into a small space. He got down from Sydney, too, a quantity of showy electro-gilt jewellery and fancy beads, with common knives, pistols, guns, and hatchets for presents, saying to me that a showy present would work our way better with a savage chief than a great deal of fighting, and he proved to be quite right in all he said.

Taken altogether we had an excellent outfit for the journey, my mother eagerly placing funds at the doctor's disposal. And then came the question of how we were to get to the great northern island, for as a rule facilities for touching there were not very great; but somehow this proved to be no difficulty, all that we undertook being easily mastered, every obstacle melting away at the first attack. In fact the journey to New Guinea was like a walk into a trap—wonderfully easy. The difficulty was how to get out again.

Perhaps had I known of the dangers we were to encounter I might have shrunk from the task—I say might, but I hope I should not. Still it was better that I was in ignorance when, with the doctor, I set about making inquiries at the harbour, and soon found a captain who was in the habit of trading to the island for shells and trepang, which he afterwards took on to Hongkong.

For a fairly liberal consideration he expressed himself willing to go out of his way and land us where we liked, but he shook his head all the same.

"You've cut out your work, youngster," he said; "and I doubt whether you're going to sew it together so as to make a job."

"I'm going to try, captain," I said.

"That's your style," he said heartily, as he gave me a slap on the shoulder. "That's the word that moves everything, my boy—that word 'try.' My brains and butter! what a lot 'try' has done, and will always keep doing.

Lor', it's enough to make a man wish he was lost, and his son coming to look after him."

"Then you have a son, captain?" I said, looking at him wistfully.

"Me? Not a bit of it. My wife never had no little 'uns, for we always buys the boats, they arn't young ships. I married my schooner, my lad; she's my wife. But there, I'm talking away with a tongue like an old woman. Send your traps aboard whenever you like, and—there, I like you—you're a good lad, and I'll help you as much as ever I can. Shake hands."

It was like a fierce order, and he quite hurt me when we did shake hands, even the doctor saying it was like putting your fist in a screw-wrench.

Then we parted, the doctor and I to complete our preparations; the various things we meant to take were placed on board, and now at last the time had come when we must say *Good-bye*!

For the first time in my life I began to think very seriously of money matters. Up to this money had not been an object of much desire with me. A few shillings to send into Sydney for some special object now and then was all I had required; but now I had to think about my mother during my absence, and what she would do, and for the first time I learned that there was no need for anxiety on that score; that my father's private income was ample to place us beyond thought for the future. I found, too, that our nearest neighbour had undertaken to watch over my mother's safety, not that there was much occasion for watchfulness, the days gliding by at our place in the most perfect peace, but it was satisfactory to feel that there were friends near at hand.

I was for saying *good-bye* at the little farm, but my mother insisted upon accompanying us to Sydney, where I noticed that in spite of her weakness and delicate looks, she was full of energy and excitement, talking to me of my journey, begging me to be prudent and careful, and on no account to expose myself to danger.

"And tell your father how anxiously I am looking forward to his return," she said to me on the last evening together; words that seemed to give me confidence, for they showed me how thoroughly satisfied she was that we would bring my father back.

We were too busy making preparations to the very last for there to be much time for sadness, till the hour when the old skipper came, and was shown up to our room.

He came stamping and blundering up in a pair of heavy sea-boots, and began to salute me with a rough shout, when he caught sight of my pale delicate-looking mother, and his whole manner changed.

"Lor', I didn't know as there were a lady here," he said in a husky whisper, and snatching off his battered Panama hat, sticking out a leg behind, and making a bow like a school-boy. I beg your pardon for intruding like, mum, but I only come to say that the schooner's warped out, and that youngster here and Mr Grant must come aboard first thing in the morning.

He sat down after a good deal of persuasion, and partook of refreshment—liquid, and copiously. But when, on leaving, my mother followed him to the door, and I saw her try to make him a present, he shook his head sturdily.

"No, no," he growled; "I asked my price for the trip, and the doctor there paid me like a man. Don't you be afeared for young chap there while he's aboard my craft. While he's with me I'll look after him as if he was gold. I don't like boys as a rule, for they're a worrit and wants so much kicking before you can make 'em work, but I've kind of took to youngster there, and I'll see him through. Good night."

The captain went clumping down the stairs, and we could hear him clearing his throat very loudly down the street. Then the doctor, with great delicacy, rose and left us alone, and I tried to look cheerful as I sat for an hour with my mother before going to bed.

Did any of you who tried to look cheerful when you were going to leave home for the first time ever succeed, especially with those wistful, longing eyes watching you so earnestly all the time? I'm not ashamed to say that I did not, and that I almost repented of my decision, seeing as I did what pain I was causing.

But I knew directly after that it was pain mingled with pleasure, and that I was about to do my duty as a son.

Twice over, as I lay half sleeping, I fancied I saw, or really did see, somebody gliding away from my bedside, and then all at once I found that it was morning, and I got up, had a miserable breakfast, which seemed to choke me, and soon after—how I don't know, for it all seemed very dream-like—found myself on the wharf with my mother, waiting for the boat that was to take us three travellers to the ship.

Jimmy was there, looking rather uncomfortable in his sailor's suit, which was not constructed for the use of a man who always sat down upon his heels. The doctor was there, too, quiet and cheerful as could be, and I made an effort to swallow something that troubled me, and which I thought must be somehow connected with my breakfast. But it would not go down, and I could do nothing but gaze hard as through a mist at the little delicate woman who was holding so tightly to my hands. There was a dimness and an unreality about everything. Things seemed to be going on in a way I did not understand, and I quite started at last as somebody seemed to say, "Good-bye," and I found myself in the little boat and on the way to the schooner.

Then all in the same dim, misty way I found myself aboard, watching the wharf where my mother was standing with a lady friend, both waving their handkerchiefs. Then the wharf seemed to be slowly gliding away and getting more and more distant, and then mixed up with it all came the sound of the bluff captain's voice, shouting orders to the men, who were hurrying about the deck.

Suddenly I started, for the doctor had laid his hand upon my shoulder.

"We're off, Joe," he said heartily; "the campaign has begun. Now, then, how do you feel for your work?"

His words electrified me, and I exclaimed excitedly:

"Ready, doctor, ready. We'll find him and bring him back."

Chapter Three
How I made my first Charge with a Lance

We had not been a day at sea before our black follower was in trouble. As a matter of course the men began joking and teasing him about the awkward manner in which he wore his sailor's suit, asking him if it wouldn't be better to have a coat of white paint over him instead, as being cooler and less trouble, and the like.

All this Jimmy took with the greatest of equanimity, grasping the men's meaning very well, and very often throwing himself flat on the deck and squirming about, which was his way of showing his delight. But it was absolutely necessary that all this banter should come from the Englishmen. If one of the Malay sailors attempted such a familiarity, Jimmy was furious.

"Hi—wup—wup!" he exclaimed to me after one of these bouts; "dirty fellow, brown fellow no good. Not white fellow, not black fellow. Bad for nothing."

One afternoon the doctor and I were sitting forward watching the beautiful heaving waves, and talking over the plans we intended to follow when we landed, and we had agreed that a small party was far more likely to succeed than a large one, being more suitable for passing unnoticed through the country. We had just arrived at the point of determining that we would engage six natives at a friendly shore village to carry our baggage and act as guides, when the noise of some trouble aft arose, and we turned to see a Malay sailor lying upon the deck, and Jimmy showing his teeth fiercely, waddy in hand, after having given the man what he afterwards called "a topper on de headums."

We ran up, fearing more mischief, for Jimmy could fight fiercely when roused; and we were just in time, for as the doctor reached the Malay the man had scrambled up, drawn his knife, and rushed at the black. But before he could strike, the doctor showed me what wonderful strength of arm he possessed, by seizing the Malay by the waistband and arm and literally swinging him over the low bulwark into the sea.

"That will cool his passion," said the doctor, smiling. "I'm sorry I did it though, captain," he said the next minute; "these men are very revengeful."

"Too late to say that," cried the captain roughly. "Here, hi! man overboard! Never mind the boat: he swims like a fish."

This was plain enough, for the Malay was making his way swiftly through the water, and the captain ran aft with a coil of rope to throw to him from the stern.

I ran too, and could see that as the man struck the water in a peculiar fashion, he held his knife open in his hand, and was thinking whether he would use it when the captain threw the rope, the light rings uncoiling as they flew through the air and splashed the water.

"Here, look out!" cried the captain; but the man did not heed, but began to beat the water furiously, uttering a strange gasping cry.

"Look, doctor!" I cried, pointing, and leaning forward.

A low hiss escaped his lips as he, too, saw a dull, indistinct something rising through the transparent sea.

"Yah, hi! Bunyip debble fis!" shouted Jimmy excitedly. "Bite sailor, brown fellow. Hoo. Bite!"

The black gave a snap and a shake of the head, and then taking the long sharp knife the doctor had given him from his belt, he tore off his shirt and, it seemed to me, jumped out of his trousers. Then the sun seemed to flash from his shiny black skin for an instant, and he plunged into the sea.

The exciting incidents of that scene are as plain before me now I write as if they had taken place yesterday. I saw the body of the black strike up a foam of white water, and then glide down in a curve in the sunlit sea, plainly crossing the course of the great fish, which had altered its course on becoming aware of the second splash.

The Malay knew what he was doing, for ignoring the help of the rope he allowed himself to drift astern, seeing as he did that the shark's attention had been drawn to the black.

"He knows what he's about," said the captain. "If he laid hold of that there rope, and we tried to draw him aboard, that snipperjack would take him like a perch does a worm in the old ponds at home. Here, lower away that boat, and I'll go and get the whale lance."

Away went the skipper, while the men lowered the boat; and I was so intent upon the movements of the great fish that I started as the boat kissed the water with a splash.

The shark was about ten feet long and unusually thick; and as it kept just below the surface the doctor and I could watch its every movement, guided by the strange but slow wave of the long, curiously-lobed tail.

"Now, you brown fellow, you come on. Knife, knife!"

As Jimmy shouted out these words he raised himself in the water and curved over like a porpoise, diving right down, and at the same moment the shark gave a sweep with its tail, the combined disturbance making so great an eddy that it was impossible to see what took place beneath the surface. Then all at once there was a horrible discoloration in the sea, and I drew back, holding on by the bulwarks with both hands to keep myself from falling. For, as the water grew discoloured, so did the air seem to glow before my eyes. I was sick and dizzy; the deck seemed to rise in waves, and a curious kind of singing noise in my ears made everything sound distant and strange. There was a strange despairing feeling, too, in my heart, and my breath came thick and short, till I was brought partly to myself by hearing a voice shouting for a rope, and then the mist gradually cleared away, and I became aware of the fact that the boat was moving before me, and that the round, shiny black face of Jimmy was close at hand.

A few minutes later both Jimmy and the Malay were aboard, the former throwing himself flat on his back to rest, for he was panting heavily after his exertions.

"Big bunyip debble, Mass Joe," he sputtered; "swim more stronger Jimmy, but no got knife. Tick black fellow knife in um lot o' time. Tick it in him frontums, tick it in ums back ums tight, and make um dibe down and take Jimmy much long ways."

"Why didn't you leave go of the knife, my man?" said the doctor.

"Leave go dat big noo knife?" cried Jimmy sharply. "Let bunyip fis have dat noo knife?"

Jimmy did not finish, but shook his head from side to side, so that first one black ear went into the puddle of water on the deck, then the other, while his lips parted in a tremendously long grin, which seemed to say, "Black fellow knows better than to do such a stupid thing as that."

Then, as if made of india-rubber, Jimmy drew his heels in, gave a spring, and leaped to his feet, running to the side, and then throwing up his arms with delight.

"Dere um is, Mass Joe; turn up him under frontums like fis on hook an' line."

For there was the monster making an effort to keep in its normal position, as it swam slowly round and round, but always rolling back, and rising helplessly every time it tried to dive.

"Jimmy sorry for you," cried the black. "Plenty good to eat like much muttons. Go down boat bring him board."

"Well, I don't know about good meat, blackee, but we may as well have his head to boil out his jaws," said the captain, who was standing looking on, whale lance in hand.

"Go down and put him out of his misery, captain," I said, "and take me too."

"Oh! all right, my lad," he said, laughing. "You may do the job if you like."

"May I?"

"To be sure," he said; and I jumped down into the boat, after he had lowered himself, bear fashion, on to one of the thwarts.

"Here, send out one of the sailors," said the doctor. "I'll go too."

One of the men returned to the deck, looking rather glum, and the doctor took his place, while I sympathised with that sailor and wished that the doctor had not spoken, for I felt sure that he had come down into the boat to take care of me, and it made me feel young and childish.

But I did not show my annoyance, I am glad to say; and a minute later the men gave way, and the boat glided slowly towards where the shark had drifted—I all the while standing up in the bows, lance in hand, full of the desire to make use of it, and feeling a cruel, half savage sensation that it would be exceedingly pleasant to drive that lance right home.

"Now my water Saint George the Second," cried the doctor banteringly; "mind you slay the sea-dragon."

"Mind what you're after, youngster," said the captain. "Give it him close below the gills; a good dig and then draw back sharp."

"All right!" I cried back to the captain, for I was offended by the doctor's chaff; it made me feel small before the men. Then, recalling what I had read that a harpooner would do under such circumstances, I shouted: "Give way, boys!"

I'd have given something to have been back on board the schooner just then, for a roar of laughter greeted my command, and I felt that I was very young, and had made myself rather ridiculous, while to add to my discomfiture the men obeyed my order with such energy that the boat gave a jerk, and I was nearly sent back in a sitting position on the foremost man.

There was another laugh at this, and the doctor said drily:

"No, no, my lad; the lance is for the shark, not for us."

I recovered my balance without a word, and planting my feet firmly wide apart, remained silent and looking very red, while I held my weapon ready.

It was an old rusty affair, with a stiff pole about eight feet long, and was used by the captain for killing those curious creatures which no doubt gave rise to the idea of there being such things as tritons or mermen—I mean the manatees or dugongs that in those days used to swarm in the warmer waters of the Eastern Australian coast.

"Keep it up, my lads; pull!" said the captain, who had an oar over the stern to steer. "We must get back soon."

I thought this was because the shark, which had ceased to swim round and round, was now laboriously making its way with the current at the rate of pretty well two miles an hour; but as the captain spoke I could see that he was scanning the horizon, and I heard the doctor ask if anything was wrong.

"Looks dirty," he growled; and I remember wondering half-laughingly whether a good shower would not wash it clean, when the skipper went on: "Gets one o' them storms now and then 'bout here. Now, my lads; with a will!"

The water surged and rattled beneath my feet, and I was forgetting my annoyance and beginning to enjoy the excitement of my ride; and all the more that the shark had once more stopped in its steady flight, and was showing its white under parts some fifty yards away.

"Ready, my lad!" cried the captain. "I'll steer you close in. Give it him deep, and draw back sharp."

I nodded, and held the lance ready poised as we drew nearer and nearer, and I was ready with set teeth and every nerve tingling to deliver the thrust, when *whish*! *splash*! the brute gave its tail a tremendous lash, and darted away, swimming along with its back fin ploughing the water, and apparently as strong as ever.

"Only his flurry, my lad. Pull away, boys; we'll soon have him now."

The men rowed hard, and the boat danced over the swell, rising up one slope, gliding down another, or so it seemed to me.

"He'll turn up the white directly," cried the captain. "Take it coolly and you'll have him. I'll put you close alongside, and don't you miss."

"Not I, sir," I shouted without turning my head, for it seemed such a very easy task; and away we went once more, getting nearer and nearer, till the back fin went out of sight, came up again, went out of sight the other way, and then there was the shining white skin glistening in the sun.

There was another swirl and the shark made a fresh effort, but this time it was weaker and the boat gained upon it fast.

"Now, boys, pull hard, and when I say 'In oars,' stop, and we'll run close up without scaring the beggar. Pull—pull—pull—pull! Now! In oars!"

The men ceased rowing, the boat glided on from the impetus previously given, and I was just about to deliver a thrust when the wounded creature saw its enemy, and as if its strength had been renewed, went off again with a dart.

"Look at that," cried the captain. "Never mind, he's not going to get away. We'll have him yet."

"We seem to be getting a long way from the schooner," I heard the doctor say, and I turned round upon him quite angrily.

"Oh!" I cried, "don't stop. We nearly had him that time."

"Well, you shall have another try, my boy," said the captain. "Pull away."

We were going pretty fast all the time, and again and again we drew near, but always to be disappointed, and I stamped my foot with anger, as, every time, the brute darted off, leaving us easily behind.

"Better let me have the lance, Joe," said the doctor smiling.

"No, no," I cried. "I must have a try now."

"Let him be," growled the captain; "nobody couldn't have lanced him if he'd tried. Now look out, lad! Steady, boys! In oars! Let's go up more softly. That's the style. We shall have him this time. Now you have him, lad; give it him—deep."

All these words came in a low tone of voice as the boat glided nearer and nearer to where the shark was swimming slowly and wavering to and fro, and in my excitement I drew back, raising the lance high, and just as the monster was about to dash off in a fresh direction I threw myself forward, driving the point of the lance right into the soft flesh, forgetful of my instructions about a sharp thrust and return, for the keen lance point must have gone right through, and before I realised what was the matter I was snatched out of the boat; there was a splash, the noise of water thundering, a strangling sensation in my nostrils and throat, and I was being carried down with a fierce rush into the depths of the sea.

Chapter Four
How I was not drowned, and how
we chased that Schooner

I don't remember much about that dive, except that the water made a great deal of noise in my ears, for the next thing that occurred seemed to be that I was lying on my back, with the back of my neck aching, while the doctor was pumping my arms up and down in a remarkably curious manner.

"What's the matter?" I said quickly; and then again in a sharp angry voice, "Be quiet, will you? Don't!"

"Are you better, young 'un?" said the captain, who seemed to be swollen and clumsy looking.

"Better? Here!" I cried as a flash of recollection came back, "where's the shark?"

"Floating alongside," said the doctor, wiping the great drops of perspiration from his forehead.

I pulled myself up and looked over the side, where the great fish was floating quite dead, with one of the sailors making fast a line round the thin part of the tail.

"Why, I know," I cried; "he dragged me down."

It was all plain enough now. The captain had fitted a lanyard to the shaft of the lance, so that it should not be lost, and I had got this twisted round one of my wrists in such a way that I was literally snatched out of the boat when it tightened; and I felt a strange kind of shudder run through me as the doctor went on to say softly:

"I had begun to give you up, Joe, my boy."

"Only the shark give it up as a bad job, my lad. That stroke of yours finished him, and he come up just in time for us to get you into the boat and pump the wind into you again—leastwise the doctor did."

"The best way to restore respiration, captain."

"When you've tried my plan first, my lad," replied the captain. "What is it drowns folks, eh? Why, water. Too much water, eh? Well, my plan is to hold up head down'ards and feet in the air till all the salt-water has runned out."

"The surest way to kill a half-drowned person, captain," said the doctor authoritatively.

"Mebbe it is, mebbe it isn't," said the captain surlily. "All I know is that I've brought lots back to life that way, and rolling 'em on barrels."

I shuddered and shivered, and the men laughed at my drenched aspect, a breach of good manners that the captain immediately resented.

"There, make fast that shark to the ring-bolt, and lay hold of your oars again. Pull away, there's a hurricane coming afore long."

As he spoke he looked long at a dull yellow haze that seemed to be creeping towards the sun.

"Had we not better let the fish go?" said the doctor anxiously.

"No, I want the oil," said the captain. "We've had trouble enough to get him, and I don't mean to throw him away. Now, my lads, pull."

The men tugged steadily at their oars, but the dead fish hung behind like a log, and our progress was very slow. Every now and then it gave a slight quiver, but that soon ceased, and it hung quite passively from the cord.

I was leaning over the stem, feeling rather dizzy and headachy when, all at once, the captain shouted to me to "cut shark adrift; we're making too little way. That schooner's too far-off for my liking." I drew my knife, and after hauling the fish as closely as I could to the side I divided the thin line, and as I did so the boat seemed to dart away from its burden.

It was none too soon, for the yellow haze seemed to be increasing rapidly, and the wind, which at one minute was oppressively calm, came the next in ominous hot puffs.

"Why, the schooner's sailing away from us," cried the captain suddenly. "Hang me if I don't believe that scoundrel of a Malay has got to the helm, and is taking her right away out of spite."

"Don't begin prophesying evil like that, captain," cried the doctor sharply. "Here, man, I can pull; let's take an oar apiece and help."

"I wasn't croaking," growled the captain; "but whether or no, that's good advice. No, no, youngster, you're not strong enough to pull."

"I can row," I said quickly; and the captain making no farther objection, we three pulled for the next half-hour, giving the men a good rest, when they took their turn, and we could see that while the haze seemed nearer the schooner was quite as far-off as ever. There was a curious coppery look, too, about the sun that made everything now look weird and unnatural, even to the doctor's face, which in addition looked serious to a degree I had never seen before.

"There'll be somebody pitched overboard—once I get back on deck, and no boat ready to pick him up. Here, what does he mean?"

He stood up in the boat waving his hat to those on board the little vessel; but no heed was paid, and the captain ground his teeth with rage.

"I'll let him have something for this," growled the captain. "There, pull away, men. What are you stopping for?"

The men tugged at their oars once more, after glancing uneasily at each other and then at the sky.

"If I don't give him—"

"Let's get on board first, captain," said the doctor, firmly.

"Ay, so we will," he growled. "The brown-skinned scoundrel!"

"That's land, isn't it, captain?" I said, pointing to a low line on our left.

"Ay, worse luck," he said.

"Worse luck, captain? Why, we could get ashore if we did not overtake the schooner."

"Get ashore! Who wants to get ashore, boy? That's where my schooner will be. He'll run her on the reefs, as sure as I'm longing for two-foot of rope's-end and a brown back afore me."

"A crown apiece for you, my lads, as soon as you get us aboard," cried the doctor, who had been looking uneasily at the men.

His words acted like magic, and the oars bent, while the water rattled and pattered under our bows.

"That's the sort o' fire to get up steam, doctor," said the captain; "but we shall never overtake my vessel, unless something happens. I'd no business to leave her, and bring away my men."

"I'm sorry, captain," I said deprecatingly. "It seems as if it were my fault."

"Not it," he said kindly. "It was my fault, lad—mine."

All this while the mist was steadily moving down upon us, and the captain was watching it with gloomy looks when his eyes were not fixed upon the schooner, which kept on gliding away. The doctor's face, too, wore a very serious look, which impressed me more perhaps than the threatenings of the storm. For, though I knew how terrible the hurricanes were at times, my experience had always been of them ashore, and I was profoundly ignorant of what a typhoon might be at sea.

"There," cried the captain at last, after a weary chase, "it's of no use, my lads, easy it is. I shall make for the land and try to get inside one of the reefs, doctor, before the storm bursts."

"The schooner is not sailing away now," I said eagerly.

"Not sailing, boy? Why she's slipping away from us like— No, no: you're right, lad, she's— Pull, my lads, pull; let's get aboard. That Malay scoundrel has run her on the reef."

Chapter Five
How we found Jack Penny

The captain's ideas were not quite correct. Certainly the little trading vessel had been run upon one of the many reefs that spread in all directions along the dangerous coast; but it was not the Malay who was the guilty party.

As far as I was concerned it seemed to me a good job, for it brought the schooner to a stand-still, so that we could overtake it. No thought occurred to me that the rocks might have knocked a hole in her bottom, and that if a storm came on she would most likely go to pieces.

Very little was said now, for every one's attention was taken up by the threatened hurricane, and our efforts to reach the schooner before it should come on.

It was a long severe race, in which we all took a turn at the oars, literally rowing as it seemed to me for our lives. At times it was as if we must be overtaken by the fierce black clouds in the distance, beneath which there was a long misty white line. The sea-birds kept dashing by us, uttering wild cries, and there was overhead an intense silence, while in the distance we could hear a low dull murmuring roar, that told of the coming mischief.

Every now and then it seemed to me that we must be overtaken by the long surging line, that it was now plain to see was pursuing us, and I wondered whether we should be able to swim and save our lives when it came upon us with a hiss and a roar, such as I had often heard when on the beach.

"We shall never do it," said one of the men, who half-jumped from his seat the next moment as the captain leaned forward from where he was rowing and gave him a sound box on the ears.

"Pull, you cowardly humbug!" he cried. "Not do it? A set of furriners wouldn't do it; but we're Englishmen, and we're going to do it. If we don't, it won't be our fault. Pull!"

This trifling incident had its effect, for the men pulled harder than ever, exhausted though they were. It was a struggle for life now, and I knew it; but somehow I did not feel frightened in the least, but stunned and confused, and at the same time interested, as I saw the great line of haze and foam coming on. Then I was listening to the dull roar, which was rapidly increasing into what seemed a harsh yell louder than thunder.

"Pull, my lads!" shouted the captain, with his voice sounding strange and harsh in the awful silence around us, for, loud as was the roar of the storm, it seemed still afar off.

The men pulled, and then we relieved them again, with the great drops gathering on our faces in the intense heat; and my breath came thick and short, till I felt as it were a sense of burning in my chest. Then I grew half-blind with my eyes staring back at the wall of haze; and then, as I felt that I should die if I strained much longer at that oar, I heard the captain shout:

"In oars!" and I found that we were alongside the schooner, and close under her lee.

There was just time to get on board, and we were in the act of hauling up the boat, when, with an awful whistle and shriek, the storm was upon us, and we were all clinging for life to that which was nearest at hand.

Now, I daresay you would like me to give you a faithful account of my impressions of that storm, and those of one who went through it from the time that the hurricane struck us till it passed over, leaving the sky clear, the sun shining, and the sea heaving slowly and without a single crest.

I feel that I can do justice to the theme, so here is my faithful description of that storm.

A horrid wet, stifling, flogging row.

That's all I can recollect. That's all I'm sure that the doctor could recollect, or the captain or anybody else. We were just about drowned and stunned, and when we came to ourselves it was because the storm had passed over.

"What cheer, ho!" shouted the captain, and we poor flogged and drenched objects sat up and looked about us, to find that the waves had lifted the schooner off the rocks, and driven her a long way out of her course; that the sails that had been set were blown to ribbons; and finally that the schooner, with the last exception, was very little the worse for the adventure.

"She ain't made no water much," said the captain, after going below; "and—here, I say, where's that Malay scoundrel?"

"Down in the cabin—locked in," said an ill-used voice; and I rubbed the salt-water out of my eyes, and stared at the tall thin figure before me, leaning up against the bulwark as if his long thin legs were too weak to support his long body, though his head was so small that it could not have added very much weight.

"Why, hallo! Who the blue jingo are you?" roared the skipper.

The tall thin boy wrinkled up his forehead, and did not answer.

"Here, I say, where did you spring from?" roared the captain.

The tall thin boy took one hand out of his trousers' pocket with some difficulty, for it was so wet that it clung, and pointed down below.

The skipper scratched his head furiously, and stared again.

"Here, can't you speak, you long-legged thing?" he cried. "Who are you?"

"Why, it's Jack Penny!" I exclaimed.

"Jack who?" cried the captain.

"Jack Penny, sir. His father is a squatter about ten miles from our place."

"Well, but how came *he*—I mean that tall thin chap, not his father—to be squatting aboard my schooner?"

"Why, Jack," I said, "when did you come aboard?"

"Come aboard?" he said slowly, as if it took him some time to understand what I said. "Oh, the night before you did."

"But where have you been all the time?"

"Oh, down below there," said Jack slowly.

"But what did you come for?"

"Wanted to," he said coolly. "If I had said so, they wouldn't—you wouldn't have let me come."

"But why did you come, Jack?" I said.

"'Cause I wanted," he replied surlily. "Who are you that you're to have all the fun and me get none!"

"Fun!" I said.

"Yes, fun. Ain't you goin' to find your father?"

"Of course I am; but what's that got to do with fun?"

"Never you mind; I've come, and that's all about it," he said slowly; and thrusting his hands back into his trousers' pockets as fast as the wet clinging stuff would let him, he began to whistle.

"But it arn't all about it," cried the captain; "and so you'll find. You arn't paid no passage, and I arn't going to have no liberties took with my ship. Here, where's that Malay chap?"

"I told you where he was, didn't I?" snarled Jack Penny. "Are you deaf? In the cabin, locked in."

"What's he doing locked in my cabin?" roared the captain. "I say, are you skipper here, or am I? What's he doing in my cabin locked in?"

"Rubbing his sore head, I s'pose," drawled Jack Penny. "I hit him as hard as I could with one o' them fence rails."

"Fence rails!" cried the captain, who looked astounded at the big thin boy's coolness, and then glanced in the direction he pointed beneath the bulwarks. "Fence rails! What do you mean—one of them capstan bars?"

"I don't know what you call 'em," said Jack. "I give him a regular wunner on the head."

"What for, you dog?"

"Here, don't you call me a dog or there'll be a row," cried Jack, rising erect and standing rather shakily about five feet eleven, looking like a big boy stretched to the bursting point and then made fast. "He was going to kill the black fellow with his knife after knocking him down. I wasn't going to stand by and see him do that, was I?"

"Well, I s'pose not," said the captain, who looked puzzled. "Where is the black fellow? Here, where's Jimmy?"

"Down that square hole there, that wooden well-place," said Jack, pointing to the forecastle hatch. "He slipped down there when the yaller chap hit him."

"Look here—" said the captain as I made for the hatch to look after Jimmy. "But stop a minute, let's have the black up."

Two of the men went below and dragged up poor Jimmy, who was quite stunned, and bleeding freely from a wound on the head.

"Well, that's some proof of what you say, my fine fellow," continued the captain, as the doctor knelt down to examine poor Jimmy's head and I fetched some water to bathe his face. "What did you do next?"

"Next? Let me see," drawled Jack Penny; "what did I do next? Oh! I know. That chap was running away with the ship, and I took hold of that wheel thing and turned her round, so as to come back to you when you kept waving your cap."

"Hah! yes. Well, what then?"

"Oh, the thing wanted oiling or greasing; it wouldn't go properly. It got stuck fast, and the ship wouldn't move; and then the storm came. I wish you wouldn't bother so."

"Well, I *am* blessed," cried the captain staring. "I should have been proud to have been your father, my young hopeful. 'Pon my soul I should. You are a cool one, you are. You go and run the prettiest little schooner there is along the coast upon the rocks, and then you have the confounded impudence to look me in the face and tell me the rudder wants greasing and it stuck."

"So it did!" cried Jack Penny indignantly. "Think I don't know? I heard it squeak. You weren't on board. The ship wouldn't move afterwards."

"Here, I say; which are you?" cried the captain; "a rogue or a fool?"

"I d'know," said Jack coolly. "Father used to say I was a fool sometimes. P'r'aps I am. I say, though, if I were you I'd go and tie down that yaller Malay chap in the cabin. He's as vicious as an old man kangaroo in a water-hole."

"Your father's wrong, my fine fellow," said the captain with a grim smile; "you ar'n't a fool, for a fool couldn't give such good advice as that. Here, doctor, p'r'aps you'll lend me one of your shooting things. You can get into your cabin; I can't get into mine."

The doctor nodded, and in the excitement of the time we forgot all about our drenched clothes as he went down and returned directly with his revolver, and another for the captain's use.

"Thank'ye, doctor," said the captain grimly, cocking the piece. "I don't want to use it, and I daresay the sight of it will cool our yaller friend; but it's just as well to be prepared. What! are you coming too? Thought your trade was to mend holes and not make 'em."

"My trade is to save life, captain," said the doctor quietly. "Perhaps I shall be helping to save life by coming down with you."

"P'r'aps you will, doctor. Here, we don't want you two boys."

"We only want to come and see," I said in an ill-used tone; and before the doctor could speak the captain laughingly said, "Come on," and we followed them down below, the men bringing up the rear, armed with bars and hatchets.

The captain did not hesitate for a moment, but went straight down to the cabin door, turned the key, and threw it open, though all the while he knew that there was a man inside fiercer than some savage beast. But had he been a little more cautious it would have saved trouble, for the Malay had evidently been waiting as he heard steps, and as the door was opened he made a spring, dashed the doctor and captain aside, overset me, and, as the men gave way, reached the deck, where he ran right forward and then close up to the foremast, stood with his long knife or kris in his hand, rolling his opal eyeballs, and evidently prepared to strike at the first who approached.

"The dog! he has been at the spirits," growled the captain fiercely. "Confound him! I could shoot him where he stands as easy as could be; but I arn't like you, doctor, I don't like killing a man. Never did yet, and don't want to try."

"Don't fire at him," said the doctor excitedly; "a bullet might be fatal. Let us all rush at him and beat him down."

"That's all very fine, doctor," said the captain; "but if we do some one's sure to get an ugly dig or two from that skewer. Two or three of us p'r'aps. You want to get a few surgery jobs, but I'd rather you didn't."

All this while the Malay stood brandishing his kris and showing his teeth at us in a mocking smile, as if we were a set of the greatest cowards under the sun.

"Look here, Harriet," cried the captain; "you'd better give in; we're six to one, and must win. Give in, and you shall have fair play."

"Cowards! come on, cowards!" shouted the Malay fiercely, and he made a short rush from the mast, and two of the hatchet men retreated; but the Malay only laughed fiercely, and shrank back to get in shelter by the mast.

"We shall have to rush him or shoot him," said the captain, rubbing his nose with pistol barrel. "Now then, you dog; surrender!" he roared; and lowering the pistol he fired at the Malay's feet, the bullet splintering up the deck; but the fellow only laughed mockingly.

"We shall have to rush him," growled the captain; "unless you can give him a dose of stuff, doctor, to keep him quiet."

"Oh, yes; I can give him a dose that will quiet him for a couple of hours or so, but who's to make him take it?"

"When we treed the big old man kangaroo who ripped up Pompey, Caesar, and Crassus," drawled Jack Penny, who was looking on with his hands in his pockets, "I got up the tree and dropped a rope with a noose in it over his head. Seems to me that's what you ought to do now."

"Look'ye here," cried the captain, "don't you let your father call you fool again, youngster, because it's letting perhaps a respectable old man tell lies. Tell you what, if you'll shin up the shrouds, and drop a bit of a noose over his head while we keep him in play, I won't say another word about your coming on board without leave."

"Oh, all right! I don't mind trying to oblige you, but you must mind he don't cut it if I do."

"You leave that to me," cried the captain. "I'll see to that. There, take that thin coil there, hanging on a belaying-pin."

The tall thin fellow walked straight to the coil of thin rope, shook it out, and made a running noose at the end, and then, with an activity that surprised me, who began to feel jealous that this thin weak-looking fellow should have proved himself more clever and thoughtful than I was, he sprang into the shrouds, the Malay hardly noticing, evidently believing that the boy was going aloft to be safe. He looked up at him once, as Jack Penny settled himself at the masthead, but turned his attention fiercely towards us as the captain arranged his men as if for a rush, forming them into a semicircle.

"When I say ready," cried the captain, "all at him together."

The Malay heard all this, and his eyes flashed and his teeth glistened as he threw himself into an attitude ready to receive his foes, his body bent forward, his right and left arms close to his sides, and his whole frame well balanced on his legs.

"Ready?" cried the captain.

"All ready!" was the reply; and I was so intent upon the fierce lithe savage that I forgot all about Jack Penny till I heard the men answer.

There was the whizzing noise of a rope thrown swiftly, and in an instant a ring had passed over the Malay's body, which was snatched tight, pinioning his arms to his side, and Jack Penny came down with a rush on the other side of the fore-yard, drawing the savage a few feet from the deck, where he swung helplessly, and before he could recover himself he had been seized, disarmed, and was lying bound upon the deck.

"I didn't mean to come down so fast as that," drawled Jack, rubbing his back. "I've hurt myself a bit."

"Then we'll rub you," cried the captain joyously. "By George, my boy, you're a regular two yards of trump."

The excitement of the encounter with the Malay being over, there was time to see to poor Jimmy, who was found to be suffering from a very severe cut on the head, one of so serious a nature that for some time the poor fellow lay insensible; but the effect of bathing and bandaging his wound was to make him open his eyes at last, and stare round for some moments before he seemed to understand where he was. Then recollection came back, and he grinned at me and the doctor.

The next moment a grim look of rage came over his countenance, and springing up he rushed to where the Malay was lying upon the deck under the bulwarks, and gave him a furious kick.

"Bad brown fellow!" he shouted. "Good for nothing! Hi—wup—wup—wup!"

Every utterance of the word *wup* was accompanied by a kick, and the result was that the Malay sprang up, snatched his kris from where it had been thrown on the head of a cask, and striking right and left made his way aft, master of the deck once more.

"Well, that's nice," growled the captain.

"I thought them knots wouldn't hold," drawled Jack Penny. "He's been wriggling and twisting his arms and legs about ever since he lay there. I thought he'd get away."

"Then why didn't you say so, you great, long-jointed two-foot rule?" roared the captain. "Here, now then, all together. I'm skipper here. Rush him, my lads; never mind his skewer."

The captain's words seemed to electrify his little crew, and, I venture to say, his passengers as well. Every one seized some weapon, and, headed by the skipper, we charged down upon the savage as he stood brandishing his weapon.

He stood fast, watchful as a tiger, for some moments, and then made a dash at our extreme left, where Jack Penny and I were standing; and I have no doubt that he would have cut his way through to our cost, but for a quick motion of the captain, who struck out with his left hand, hitting the Malay full in the cheek.

The man made a convulsive spring, and fell back on the edge of the bulwarks, where he seemed to give a writhe, and then, before a hand could reach him, there was a loud splash, and he had disappeared in the sea.

We all rushed to the side, but the water was thick from the effects of the storm, and we could not for a few moments make out anything. Then all at once the swarthy, convulsed face of the man appeared above the wave, and he began to swim towards the side, yelling for help.

"Ah!" said the skipper, smiling, "that's about put him out. Nothing like cold water for squenching fire."

"Hi—wup! hi—wup!" shouted Jimmy, who forgot his wound, and danced up and down, holding on by the bulwarks, his shining black face looking exceedingly comic with a broad bandage of white linen across his brow. "Hi—wup! hi—wup!" he shouted; "bunyip debble shark coming— bite um legs."

"Help!" shrieked the Malay in piteous tones, as he swam on, clutching at the slippery sides of the schooner.

"Help!" growled the captain; "what for? Here, you, let me have that there kris. Hitch it on that cord."

As he spoke the captain threw down the thin line with which the Malay had been bound, the poor wretch snatching at it frantically; but as he did so it was pulled away from his despairing clutch.

"I could noose him," drawled Jack Penny coolly. "I've often caught father's rams like that."

"Yes, but your father's rams hadn't got knives," said the captain grimly.

"No, but they'd got horns," said Jack quietly. "Ain't going to drown him, are you?"

"Not I, boy; he'll drown himself if we leave him alone."

"I don't like to see fellows drown," said Jack; and he left the bulwarks and sat down on the hatchway edge. "Tell a fellow when it's all over, Joe Carstairs."

"Help, help!" came hoarsely from the poor wretch; and my hands grew wet inside, and a horrible sensation seemed to be attacking my chest, as I watched the struggles of the drowning man with starting eyes. For though he swam like a fish, the horror of his situation seemed to have unnerved him, and while he kept on swimming, it was with quick wearying effort, and he was sinking minute by minute lower in the water.

"For Heaven's sake, throw the poor wretch a rope, captain," said the doctor.

"What! to come aboard and knife some of us?" growled the captain. "Better let him drown. Plenty of better ones than him to be had for a pound a month."

"Oh, captain!" I cried indignantly, for my feelings were too much for me; and I seized a rope just as the Malay went down, after uttering a despairing shriek.

"Let that rope alone, boy," said the skipper with a grim smile. "There, he's come up again. Ketch hold!" he cried, and he threw his line so that the Malay could seize it, which he did, winding it round and round one arm, while the slowly-sailing schooner dragged him along through the sea. "I'm only giving him a reg'lar good squencher, doctor. I don't want him aboard with a spark left in him to break out again: we've had enough of that. Haul him aboard, lads, and shove him in the chain locker to get dry. We'll set him ashore first chance."

The Malay was hauled aboard with no very gentle hands by the white sailors, and as soon as he reached the deck he began crawling to the captain's feet, to which he clung, with gesture after gesture full of humility, as ha talked excitedly in a jargon of broken English and Malay.

"That's what I don't like in these fellows," said Jack Penny quietly; "they're either all bubble or else all squeak."

"Yes; he's about squenched now, squire," said the captain. "Here, shove him under hatches, and it's lucky for you I'm not in a hanging humour to-day. You'd better behave yourself, or you may be brought up again some day when I am."

As the captain spoke to the streaming, shivering wretch he made a noose in the rope he held, manipulating it as if he were really going to hang the abject creature, in whom the fire of rage had quite become extinct. Then the sailors took hold of him, and he uttered a despairing shriek; but he cooled down as he found that he was only to be made a prisoner, and was thrust below, with Jimmy dancing a war-dance round him as he went, the said dance consisting of bounds from the deck and wavings of his waddy about his head.

As the Malay was secured, Jack Penny rose from his seat and walked to the side of the vessel, to spit into the water with every sign of disgust upon his face.

"Yah!" he said; "I wouldn't squeak like that, not if they hung me."

"Well, let's see," cried the captain, catching him by the collar; "hanging is the punishment for stowaways, my fine fellow."

"Get out!" said Jack, giving himself a sort of squirm and shaking himself free. "You ain't going to scare me; and, besides, you know what you said. I say, though, when are we going to have something to eat?"

The captain stared at Jack's serious face for a few moments, and then he joined with the doctor and me in a hearty laugh.

"I don't well understand you yet, my fine fellow," he said; "perhaps I shall, though, afore I've done. Here, come down; you do look as if a little wholesome vittles would do you good. Are you hungry then?"

"Hungry!" said Jack, without a drawl, and he gave his teeth a gnash; "why, I ain't had nothing but some damper and a bottle o' water since I came on board."

Chapter Six
How Jimmy was frightened by the Bunyip

"Oh, I don't know that I've got any more to say about it," said Jack Penny to me as we sat next day in the bows of the schooner, with our legs dangling over the side. "I heard all about your going, and there was nothing to do at home now, so I said to myself that I'd go, and here I am."

"Yes, here you are," I said; "but you don't mean to tell me that you intended to go up the country with us?"

"Yes, I do," he said.

"Nonsense, Jack! it is impossible!" I said warmly.

"I say!"

"Well?"

"New Guinea don't belong to you, does it?"

"Why, of course not."

"Oh, I thought p'r'aps you'd bought it."

"Don't talk nonsense, Jack."

"Don't you talk nonsense then, and don't you be so crusty. If I like to land in New Guinea, and take a walk through the country, it's as free for me as it is for you, isn't it?"

"Of course it is."

"Then just you hold your tongue, Mister Joe Carstairs; and if you don't like to walk along with me, why you can walk by yourself."

"And what provisions have you made for the journey?" I said.

"Oh, I'm all right, my lad!" he drawled. "Father lent me his revolver, and I've got my double gun, and two pound o' powder and a lot o' shot."

"Anything else?"

"Oh, I've got my knife, and a bit o' string, and two fishing-lines and a lot of hooks, and I brought my pipe and my Jew's-harp, and I think that's all."

"I'm glad you brought your Jew's-harp," I said ironically.

"So am I," he said drily. "Yah! I know: you're grinning at me, but a Jew's-harp ain't a bad thing when you're lonely like, all by yourself, keeping sheep and nobody to speak to for a week together but Gyp. I say, Joe, I brought Gyp," he added with a smile that made his face look quite pleasant.

"What! your dog?" I cried.

"Yes; he's all snug down below, and he hasn't made a sound. He don't like it, but if I tell him to do a thing he knows he's obliged to do it."

"I say, I wonder what the captain will say if he knows you've got a dog on board?"

"I sha'n't tell him, and if he don't find it out I shall pay him for Gyp's passage just the same as I shall pay him for mine. I've got lots of money, and I hid on board to save trouble. I ain't a cheat."

"No, I never thought you were, Jack," I said, for I had known him for some years, and once or twice I had been fishing with him, though we were never companions. "But it's all nonsense about your going with us. The doctor said this morning that the notion was absurd."

"Let him mind his salts-and-senna and jollop," said Jack sharply. "Who's he, I should like to know? I knowed your father as much as he did. He's given me many a sixpence for birds' eggs and beetles and snakes I've got for him. Soon as I heard you were going to find him, I says to father, 'I'm going too.'"

"And what did your father say?"

"Said I was a fool."

"Ah! of course," I exclaimed.

"No, it ain't 'ah, of course,' Mr Clever," he cried. "Father always says that to me whatever I do, but he's very fond of me all the same."

Just then the captain came forward with his glass under his arm, and his hands deep down in his pockets. He walked with his legs very wide apart, and stopped short before us, his straw hat tilted right over his nose, and see-sawing himself backwards and forwards on his toes and heels.

"You're a nice young man, arn't you now?" he said to Jack.

"No, I'm only a boy yet," said Jack quietly.

"Well, you're tall enough to be a man, anyhow. What's your height?"

"Five foot 'leven," said Jack.

"And how old are you?"

"Seventeen next 'vember," said Jack.

"Humph!" said the captain.

"Here, how much is it?" said Jack, thrusting his hand in his pocket. "I'll pay now and ha' done with it."

"Pay what?"

"My passage-money."

"Oh!" said the captain quietly, "I see. Well, I think we'd better settle that by-and-by when you bring in claim for salvage."

The captain pronounced it "sarvidge," and Jack stared.

"What savage?" he said. "Do you mean Joe Carstairs' black fellow?"

"Do I mean Joe Carstairs' grandmother, boy? I didn't say savage; I said salvage—saving of the ship from pirates."

"Oh, I see what you mean," replied Jack. "I sha'n't bring in any claim. I knew that Malay chap wasn't doing right, and stopped him, that's all."

"Well, we won't say any more about stowing away, then," said the captain. "Had plenty to eat this morning?"

"Oh yes, I'm better now," drawled Jack. "I was real bad yesterday, and never felt so hollow before."

The captain nodded and went back, while Jack turned to me, and nodding his head said slowly:

"I like the captain. Now let's go and see how your black fellow's head is."

Jimmy was lying under a bit of awning rigged up with a scrap of the storm-torn sail; and as soon as he saw us his white teeth flashed out in the light.

"Well, Jimmy, how are you?" I said, as Jack Penny stood bending down over him, and swaying gently to and fro as if he had hinges in his back.

"Jimmy better—much better. Got big fly in um head—big bunyip fly. All buzz—buzz—round and round—buzz in um head. Fedge doctor take um out."

"Here, doctor," I shouted; and he came up. "Jimmy has got a fly in his head."

"A bee in his bonnet, you mean," he said, bending down and laying his hand on the black's temples.

"Take um out," said Jimmy excitedly. "Buzz—buzz—bunyip fly."

"Yes, I'll take it out, Jimmy," said the doctor quietly; "but not to-day."

"When take um out?" cried the black eagerly; "buzz—buzz. Keep buzz."

"To-morrow or next day. Here, lie still, and I'll get your head ready for the operation."

The preparation consisted in applying a thick cloth soaked in spirits and water to the feverish head, the evaporation in the hot climate producing a delicious sense of coolness, which made Jimmy say softly:

"Fly gone—sleep now," and he closed his eyes, seeming to be asleep till the doctor had gone back to his seat on the deck, where he was studying a chart of the great island we were running for. But as soon as he was out of hearing Jimmy opened first one eye and then another. Then in a whisper, as he gently took up his waddy:

"No tell doctor; no tell captain fellow. Jimmy go knock brown fellow head flap to-night."

"What?" I cried.

"He no good brown fellow. Knock head off. Overboard: fis eat up."

"What does he say; he's going to knock that Malay chap's head off?" drawled Jack.

"Yes, Jimmy knock um head flap."

"You dare to touch him, Jimmy," I said, "and I'll send you back home."

"Jimmy not knock um head flap?" he said staring.

"No. You're not to touch him."

"Mass Joe gone mad. Brown fellow kill all a man. Jimmy kill um."

"You are not to touch him," I said. "And now go to sleep or I shall go and tell the captain."

Jimmy lifted up his head and looked at me. Then he banged it down upon his pillow, which was one of those gooseberry-shaped rope nets, stuffed full of oakum, and called a fender, while we went forward once more to talk to the doctor about his chart, for Jack Penny was comporting himself exactly as if he had become one of the party, though I had made up my mind that he was to go back with the captain when we were set ashore.

All the same, at Jack Penny's urgent request I joined him in the act of keeping the presence of the other passenger a secret—I mean Gyp the dog, to whom I was stealthily introduced by Jack, down in a very evil-smelling part of the hold, and for whom I saved scraps of meat and bits of fish from my dinner every day.

The introduction was as follows on the part of Jack:

"Gyp, old man, this is Joe Carstairs. Give him your paw."

It was very dark, but I was just able to make out a pair of fiery eyes, and an exceedingly shaggy curly head—I found afterwards that Gyp's papa had been an Irish water spaniel, and his mamma some large kind of hound; and Jack informed me that Gyp was a much bigger dog than his mamma—then a rough scratchy paw was dabbed on my hand, and directly after my fingers were wiped by a hot moist tongue. At the same time there was a whimpering noise, and though I did not know it then, I had made one of the ugliest but most faithful friends I ever had.

The days glided by, and we progressed very slowly, for the weather fell calm after the typhoon, and often for twenty-four hours together we did nothing but drift about with the current, the weather being so hot that we were glad to sit under the shade of a sail.

The doctor quite took to Jack Penny, saying that he was an oddity, but not a bad fellow. I began to like him better myself, though he did nothing to try and win my liking, being very quiet and distant with us both, and watching us suspiciously, as if he thought we were always making plots to get rid of him, and thwart his plans.

Gyp had remained undiscovered, the poor brute lying as quiet as a mouse, except when Jack Penny and I went down to feed him, when he expressed his emotion by rapping the planks hard with his tail.

At last the captain, who had been taking observations, tapped me on the shoulder one hot mid-day, and said:

"There, squire, we shall see the coast to-morrow before this time, and I hope the first thing you set eyes on will be your father, waving his old hat to us to take him off."

Just then Jimmy, whose wound had healed rapidly, and who had forgotten all about the big bunyip fly buzzing in his head, suddenly popped his face above the hatchway with his eyes starting, his hair looking more shaggy than usual, and his teeth chattering with horror.

He leaped up on the deck, and began striking it with the great knob at the end of his waddy, shouting out after every blow.

"Debble, debble—big bunyip debble. Jimmy, Jimmy see big bunyip down slow!"

"Here, youngster, fetch my revolver," shouted the captain to me. "Here, doctor, get out your gun, that Malay chap's loose again."

"A no—a no—a no," yelled Jimmy, banging at the deck. "Big bunyip—no brown fellow—big black bunyip debble, debble!"

"Get out, you black idiot; it's the Malay."

"A no—a no—a no; big black bunyip. 'Gin eat black fellow down slow."

To my astonishment, long quiet Jack Penny went up to Jimmy and gave him a tremendous kick, to which the black would have responded by a blow with his war-club had I not interposed.

"What did you kick him for, Jack?" I cried.

"A great scuffle-headed black fool! he'll let it out now about Gyp. Make him be quiet."

It was too late, for the captain and the doctor were at the hatchway, descending in spite of Jimmy's shouts and cries that the big bunyip—the great typical demon of the Australian aborigine—would eat them.

"Shoot um—shoot um—bing, bang!" *whop* went Jimmy's waddy on the deck; and in dread lest they should fire at the unfortunate dog in the dark, I went up and told the captain, the result being that Gyp was called up on deck, and the great beast nearly went mad with delight, racing about, fawning on his master and on me, and ending by crouching down at my feet with his tongue lolling out, panting and blinking his eyes, unaccustomed to the glare of daylight.

"You're in this game, then, eh, Master Carstairs?" said the captain.

"Well, yes, sir; Penny here took me into his confidence about having brought the dog, and of course I could not say a word."

"Humph! Nice game to have with me, 'pon my word. You're a pretty penny, you are, young man," he added, turning to Jack. "I ought to toss you—overboard."

"I'll pay for Gyp's passage," said Jack coolly. "I wish you wouldn't make such a fuss."

The captain muttered something about double-jointed yard measures, and went forward without another word, while Gyp selected a nice warm place on the deck, and lay down to bask on his side, but not until he had followed Jimmy up the port-side and back along the starboard, sniffing his black legs, while that worthy backed from him, holding his waddy ready to strike, coming to me afterwards with a look of contempt upon his noble savage brow, and with an extra twist to his broad nose, to say:

"Jimmy know all a time only big ugly dog. Not bunyip 'tall."

Chapter Seven
How we stopped the Blackbird Catchers

The captain was right, for we made the south coast of New Guinea the *very* next morning, and as I caught sight of the land that I believed to be holding my father as in a prison, a strange mingling of pain and pleasure filled my breast I looked excitedly and long through the doctor's double glass, and he shook hands with me afterwards, as if he thoroughly appreciated my feelings in the matter.

It was a lovely morning, with a pleasant breeze blowing, and as we drew nearer we made out a vessel very similar in build to our own going in the same direction.

"Why, they are for the same port, I should think!"

"I don't know," said the skipper rather oddly. "We're for a little place I know, where the savages are pretty friendly, and I've been talking it over with the doctor as to its being a good starting-place for you, and he thinks it will be. There it lies," he said, pointing north-east. "We can soon make it now."

"Looks a nicer place than our land," said Jack Penny, as I stood with him gazing wonderingly at the forest and mountain scenery that hour by hour grew more clear. "I think I shall like Noo Guinea."

The day glided on with the look-out growing more and more interesting; and at last, when we were pretty near, we could see the other schooner had outsailed us, and was within a short distance of a scattered collection of huts; while a little crowd of the natives was on the sandy beach busily launching their canoes, in which they paddled out towards the other vessel.

"I don't like that," said the skipper suddenly, as he was using his glass. "That's bad for us."

"What is?" I said eagerly.

"That there schooner going before us. They're blackbird catchers, or I'm a Dutchman."

"Blackbird catchers?" I said. "Why, I thought there were no blackbirds out of Europe."

"Just hark at him," said the captain, turning to the doctor. "Blackbirds, boy, why, there's thousands; and it's them varmint who go in for the trade of catching 'em as makes the coast unsafe for honest men."

"What do you mean?" I cried, and I became aware of the fact that Jack Penny was bending over me like a bamboo.

"Mean, boy? just you take the doctor's little double-barrelled telescope and watch and see."

I took the glass and looked intently, watching through it the scene of the blacks paddling up to the schooner, and holding up what seemed to be fruit and birds for sale.

All at once I saw something fall into one of the canoes, which immediately sank, and eight of its occupants were left struggling in the water.

To my great relief I saw a small boat rowed round from the other side of the little vessel, evidently, as I thought, to go to the help of the poor creatures; but, to my horror, I saw that two men stood up in the boat, and, as it was rowed, they struck at the swimming men with heavy bars, and dragged them one by one into the boat.

I saw four saved like this, and then the boat was rowed rapidly in pursuit of the other four, who were swimming as hard as they could, as they tried to overtake the canoes, whose occupants were making for the shore.

The noise of the shouts reached our ears faintly, and I saw one of the men picked up by the last canoe, and the other three were literally hunted by the schooner's boat, diving like ducks and trying every feat they could think of to avoid capture; but oars beat hands in the water, and I saw two of the fugitives struck on the head by a fellow in the bows of the boat, and then they were dragged over the side.

There was one more savage in the water, and he swam rapidly and well, besides which, he had gained some distance during the time taken up in capturing his fellows. As he had changed his direction somewhat I had a better view of the chase, and I felt horrified to see how rapidly the boat gained upon him till it was so near that it could be only a matter of minutes before he would be worn out and treated in the same way as his unfortunate fellows.

At last the boat overtook the poor wretch, but he dived down and it passed over him, the blow struck at his head merely making a splash in the water, when up he came, his black head just showing above the surface, and he struggled in another direction for his liberty.

To add to the excitement of the scene the sandy shore about the huts was lined with savages, who were rushing about in a tremendous state of excitement, shaking their spears and yelling, but showing plainly that they were a very cowardly race, for not one of them made an effort to launch a canoe and try to save his brother in distress.

There could be but one end to this cruel tragedy, so I thought; but I was wrong. Again and again the boat overtook the poor fellow, but he dived and escaped even though blows were struck at him with a boat-hook; but it was evident that he was growing weaker, and that he stayed below a shorter time.

All at once, as if the men had become furious at the length of the chase, I saw the boat rowed rapidly down upon him; but the savage dived once more, evidently went right under the boat, and came up full thirty yards astern, swimming now straight for the shore.

Then all at once I saw him throw up his arms and disappear, as if he had been snatched under.

"Out of his misery," said a deep voice beside me; and turning I found that the captain had been watching the scene through his long glass.

"What do you mean?" I said.

"Sharks took him down, poor chap," said the captain. "Sharks is ignorant, or they would have grabbed the white fellows instead."

As I still watched the scene, with my brow wet with perspiration, I saw the boat make now for the schooner, and quite a dozen canoes put off from the shore.

"Lor', what a thing ignorance is, and how far niggers are behind white men in pluck! Why, if these fellows knew what they were about, they might easily overhaul that little schooner, take their brothers out of her, and give the blackbird catchers such a lesson as they'd never remember and never forget, for they'd kill the lot. There ain't a breath o' wind."

"But they will take them, won't they, captain?" I cried.

"No, my lad, not they. They'll go and shout and throw a few spears, and then go back again; but they'll bear malice, my lad. All white folks who come in ships will be the same to them, and most likely some poor innocent boat's crew will be speared, and all on account of the doings of these blackbird catchers."

"But what do they do with the poor fellows?" I cried.

"Reg'larly sell 'em for slaves, though slavery's done away with, my boy."

"But will not the blacks rescue their friends?" I said.

"No, my lad."

"Then we must," I cried excitedly; and Jack Penny threw up his cap and cried "Hooray!" Gyp started to his feet and barked furiously, and Jimmy leaped in the air, came down in a squatting position, striking the deck a tremendous blow with his waddy, and shouting "Hi—wup, wup—wup," in an increasing yell.

The captain, hardened by familiarity with such scenes, laid his hand upon my shoulder, and smiled at me kindly as he shook his head.

"No, no, my lad, that would not do."

"Not do!" I cried, burning with indignation. "Are we to stand by and see such cruelties practised?"

"Yes, my lad; law says we musn't interfere. It's the law's job to put it down; but it's very slow sometimes."

"But very sure, captain," said the doctor quietly. "And when it does move it is crushing to evil-doers. The captain is quite right, Joe, my boy," he continued, turning to me. "We must not stir in this case. I've heard of such atrocities before, but did not know that they were so common."

"Common as blackguards," said the captain, "It's regular slavery. There, what did I tell you, my lad?" he continued, as he pointed to the canoes, which were returning after making a demonstration. "These poor blacks are afraid of the guns. It's all over—unless—"

He stopped short, scratching his head, and staring first at the schooner and then at us in turn.

"Unless what, captain?" I said excitedly.

"Here, let's do a bit o' bounce for once in our lives," said the bluff old fellow. "Get out your revolvers and shooting-tackle, and let's see if we can't frighten the beggars. Only mind, doctor, and you too, my young bantam, our weapons is only for show. No firing, mind; but if we can bully those chaps into giving up their blackbirds, why we will."

The boat was lowered, and with a goodly display of what Jack Penny called dangerous ironmongery, we started with three men, but not until the captain had seen that the Malay was safely secured. Then we started, and the people aboard the other schooner were so busy with their captives that we got alongside, and the captain, Doctor Grant, and I had climbed on deck before a red-faced fellow with a violently inflamed nose came up to us, and, with an oath, asked what we wanted there.

"Here, you speak," whispered the captain to Doctor Grant. "I'm riled, and I shall be only using more bad language than is good for these youngsters to hear. Give it to him pretty warm, though, all the same, doctor."

"D'yer hear?" said the red-faced fellow again. "What do you want here?"

"Those poor wretches, you slave-dealing ruffian," cried the doctor, who looked quite white as he drew himself up and seemed to tower over the captain of the other schooner, who took a step back in astonishment, but recovered himself directly and advanced menacingly.

"Come for them, have you, eh?" he roared; "then you'll go without 'em. Here, over you go; off my ship, you—"

The scoundrel did not finish his speech, for as he spoke he clapped a great rough hairy paw on the doctor's shoulder, and then our friend seemed to shrink back at the contact; but it was only to gather force, like a wave, for, somehow, just then his fist seemed to dart out, and the ruffianly captain staggered back and then fell heavily on the deck.

Half a dozen men sprang forward at this, but Doctor Grant did not flinch, he merely took out his revolver and examined its lock, saying:

"Will you have these poor fellows got into our boat, captain?"

"Ay, ay, doctor," cried our skipper; and the slave-dealing crew shrank back and stared as we busily handed down the blackbirds, as the captain kept on calling them.

Poor creatures, they were still half-stunned and two of them were bleeding, and it must have seemed to then? that they were being tossed out of the frying-pan into the fire, and that we were going to carry on the villainy that our ruffianly countrymen had commenced. In fact had we not taken care, and even used force, they would have jumped overboard when we had them packed closely in.

"Here, shove off!" the captain said, as we were once more in our boat; and just then the leader of the ruffians staggered to his feet and leaned over the side.

"I'll have the law of you for this," he yelled. "This is piracy."

"To be sure it is," said our captain; "we're going to hyste the black flag as soon as we get back, and run out our guns. Come on, my red-nosed old cocky-wax, and we'll have a naval engagement, and sink you."

He nudged me horribly hard with his elbow at this point, and turning his back on the schooner winked at me, and chuckled and rumbled as if he were laughing heartily to himself in secret; but he spoke again directly quite seriously.

"I haven't got no boys of my own," he said, "but if I had, I should say this was a sort o' lesson to you to always have right on your side. It's again' the law, but it's right all the same. See how we carried all before us, eh, my lads! The doctor's fist was as good as half a dozen guns, and regularly settled the matter at once."

"Then we may set these poor fellows free now?" I said.

"Well, I shouldn't like to be one of them as did it," said the captain drily. "Look at the shore."

I glanced in that direction and saw that it was crowded with blacks, all armed with spears and war-clubs, which they were brandishing excitedly.

"They wouldn't know friends from foes," said the doctor quietly. "No; we must wait."

I saw the reason for these remarks; and as soon as we had reached the side of the schooner and got our captives on board I attended the doctor while he busied himself bandaging and strapping cuts, the blacks staring at him wondering, and then at Jimmy, who looked the reverse of friendly, gazing down at the prisoners scornfully, and telling Jack Penny in confidence that he did not think much of common sort black fellow.

"Jimmy xiv all o' men waddy spear if try to kedge Jimmy," he said, drawing himself up and showing his teeth. "No kedge Jimmy. Killer um all."

It was hard work to get the poor prisoners to understand that we meant well by them.

"You see they think you're having 'em patched up," said Jack Penny, "so as they'll sell better. I say, Joe Carstairs, give your black fellow a topper with his waddy; he's making faces at that chap, and pretending to cut off his legs."

"Here, you be quiet, Jimmy, or I'll send you below," I said sharply; and as I went to the breaker to get a pannikin of water for one of the men, Jimmy stuck his hands behind him, pointed his nose in the air, and walked forward with such a display of offended dignity that Jack Penny doubled up, putting his head between his knees and pinning it firm, while he laughed in throes, each of which sent a spasm through his loose-jointed body.

The black to whom I took the water looked at me in a frightened way, and shook his head.

"He thinks it is poisoned, Joe," said the doctor quietly; and I immediately drank some, when the prisoner took the pannikin and drank with avidity, his companions then turning their eager eyes on me.

"It is the feverish thirst produced by injuries," said the doctor; and as I filled the pannikin again and again, the poor wretches uttered a low sigh of satisfaction.

The schooner lay where we had left it, and all seemed to be very quiet on board, but no movement was made of an offensive nature; and the day glided by till towards sundown, when there was less excitement visible on the shore. Then the captain ordered the boat to be lowered on the side away from the land, while he proceeded to sweep the shore with his glass.

"I think we might land 'em now, doctor," he said, "and get back without any jobs for you."

"Yes, they seem pretty quiet now," said the doctor, who had also been scanning the shore; "but there are a great many people about."

"They won't see us," said the captain. "Now, my blackbirds, I'm not going to clip your wings or pull out your tails. Into the boat with you. I'll set you ashore."

For the first time the poor fellows seemed to comprehend that they were to be set at liberty, and for a few minutes their joy knew no bounds; and it was only by running off that I was able to escape from some of their demonstrations of gratitude.

"No, my lad," said the captain in response to my demand to go with him. "I'll set the poor chaps ashore, and we shall be quite heavy enough going through the surf. You can take command while I'm gone," he added, laughing; "and mind no one steals the anchor."

I felt annoyed at the captain's bantering tone, but I said nothing; and just at sunset the boat pushed off quietly with its black freight, the poor fellows looking beside themselves with joy.

"I say, skipper," said the captain laughingly to me, "mind that Malay chap don't get out; and look here, it will be dark directly, hyste a light for me to find my way back."

I nodded shortly, and stood with Jack Penny and the doctor watching the boat till it seemed to be swallowed up in the thick darkness that was gathering round, and the doctor left Jack Penny and me alone.

"I say," said Jack, who was leaning on the bulwarks, with his body at right angles; "I say, Joe Carstairs, I've been thinking what a game it would be if the captain never came back."

"What!" I cried.

"You and I could take the ship and go where we like."

"And how about the doctor?" I said scornfully.

"Ah!" he drawled, "I forgot about the doctor. That's a pity. I wish he'd gone ashore too."

I did not answer, for it did not suit my ideas at all. The adventure I had on hand filled my mind, and I felt annoyed by my companion's foolish remark.

We had tea, and were sitting with the doctor chatting on deck, after vainly trying to pierce the darkness with our eyes or to hear some sound, when all at once the doctor spoke:

"Time they were back," he said. "I say, Skipper Carstairs, have you hoisted your light?"

"Light!" I said excitedly. "What's that?" for just then a bright red glow arose to our right in the direction of the shore.

"They're a making a bonfire," said Jack Penny slowly.

"Or burning a village," said the doctor.

"No, no," I cried; "it's that schooner on fire!"

"You're right, Joe," said the doctor excitedly. "Why, the savages must have gone off and done this, and—yes, look, you can see the canoes."

"Here, I say, don't!" cried Jack Penny then, his voice sounding curious from out of the darkness; and the same moment there was a rush, a tremendous scuffle, Jimmy yelled out something in his own tongue, and then lastly there were two or three heavy falls; and in a misty, stupefied way I knew that we had been boarded by the savages and made prisoners, on account of the outrage committed by the other captain.

What followed seems quite dream-like; but I have some recollection of being bundled down into a boat, and then afterwards dragged out over the sand and hurried somewhere, with savages yelling and shouting about me, after which I was thrown down, and lay on the ground in great pain, half sleeping, half waking, and in a confused muddle of thought in which I seemed to see my father looking at me reproachfully for not coming to his help, while all the time I was so bound that I could not move a step.

At last I must have dropped into a heavy sleep, for the next thing I saw was the bright sunshine streaming into the hut where I lay, and a crowd of blacks with large frizzed heads of hair chattering about me, every man being armed with spear and club, while the buzz of voices plainly told that there was a throng waiting outside.

Chapter Eight
How I ran from the Whitebird Catchers

Yes, I may as well own to it: I was terribly frightened, but my first thoughts were as to what had become of my companions. Jack Penny and the doctor must have been seized at the same time as I. Jimmy might have managed to escape. Perhaps his black skin would make him be looked upon as a friend. But the old captain, what about him? He would return to the schooner with his men and be seized, and knocked on the head for certain. The fierce resistance he would make certainly would cause his death, and I shuddered at the thought.

Then I began to think of my mother and father, how I should have failed in helping them; and I remember thinking what a good job it was that my mother would never know exactly what had happened to me. Better the long anxiety, I thought, of watching and waiting for my return than to know I had been killed like this.

"But I'm not killed yet," I thought, as the blood flushed to my face. "I'll have a run for it, if I can."

I had not much time given me to think, for I was dragged to my feet, and out into a large open place where there were huts and trees, and there before me lay the sea with our schooner, but the other was gone; and as I recalled the fire of the previous night I knew that she must have been burned to the water's edge and then sunk.

I began wondering about what must have been the fate of the other schooner's crew, and somehow it seemed that they deserved it. Then I began thinking of my own friends, and then, very selfishly no doubt, about myself.

But I had little time for thought, being hurried along and placed in the middle of a crowd of the savages, all of whom seemed to be rolling their eyes and looking at me as if enjoying my position.

"Well," I thought to myself, "it is enough to scare anybody; but I'll try and let them see that I belong to a superior race, and will not show what I feel."

My eyes kept wandering about eagerly, first to look where my companions were placed, but as I saw no sign of them I began to hope that they might have escaped; secondly, to see which would be the best course to take if I ran for my life. For I could run, and pretty swiftly, then. The hardy life I had led out in the bush, with Jimmy for my companion, had made me light of foot and tolerably enduring.

But for some little time I saw not the slightest chance of escape. There were too many savages close about me, and they must have divined my ideas, for they kept a watchful eye upon every act.

At first I had felt numbed and cold. My legs and arms ached, and when the blacks took off the rope that they had bound about my limbs every nerve seemed to throb and burn; but by degrees this passed off, and to my great joy I felt more myself.

At last, after a great deal of incomprehensible chatter, it seemed that a decision had been come to about me, and a tall black armed with a war-club came dancing up to me, swinging his weapon about, chattering wildly, and after a few feints he made a blow at my head.

If that blow had taken effect I should not have been able to tell this story. But I had been too much with my friend Jimmy not to be well upon the alert. We had often played together—he like a big boy—in mimic fight, when he had pretended to spear me, and taught me how to catch the spear on a shield, and to avoid blows made with waddies. Jimmy's lessons were not thrown away. I could avoid a thrown spear, though helpless, like the black, against bullets, which he said came "too much faster faster to top." And as the savage made the blow at me I followed out Jimmy's tactics, threw myself forward, striking the wretch right in the chest with my head, driving him backward, and leaping over him I ran for my life, making straight for the forest.

"It's all because of those wretches in the other schooner yesterday," I thought, as I ran swiftly on with a pack of the enemy shouting in my rear; and though I could run very fast, I found, to my horror, that my pursuers were as swift of foot, and that though I was close upon the forest it was all so open that they would be able to see me easily, and once caught I knew now what was to be my fate.

I began thinking of the hunted hare, as I ran on, casting glances behind me from time to time, and seeing that though some of my pursuers lagged, there were four who were pretty close upon my heels, one of whom hurled his spear at me, which came whizzing past my ear so closely that it lightly touched my shoulder, making me leap forward as if struck by the weapon.

I was panting heavily, and a choking sensation came upon me, but I raced on, since it was for life.

How long the pursuit lasted I cannot tell. Perhaps a minute. It seemed half an hour. Twice I leaped aside to avoid blows aimed at me, and each time ran blindly in a fresh direction; but all at once the idea occurred to me in a flash that in my unnerved stupefied position I must have been going backward and struck my head violently against a tree, for it seemed as if there was a violent shock like thunder with a flash of lightning to dazzle my eyes, and then there was nothing at all.

Chapter Nine
How I was not made into Pie

When I came to, it was as if all the past was a dream, for I heard voices I knew, and lay listening to them talking in a low tone, till, opening my eyes, I found I was close to the doctor, the captain, Jimmy, and the sailors, while Jack Penny was sitting holding my hand.

"What cheer, my hearty?" said the captain, making an effort to come to me; but I then became aware of the fact that we were surrounded by savages, for one great fellow struck the captain on the arm with his club, and in retort the skipper gave him a kick which sent him on his back.

There was a loud yell at this, and what seemed to threaten to be a general onslaught. My friends all prepared for their defence, and Jimmy took the initiative by striking out wildly, when half a dozen blacks dashed at him, got him down, and one was foolish enough to sit upon his head, but only to bound up directly with a shriek, for poor Jimmy, being held down as to arms and legs, made use of the very sharp teeth with which nature had endowed him.

We should have been killed at once, no doubt, had not one tall black shouted out something, and then begun talking loudly to the excited mob, who listened to him angrily, it seemed to me; but I was so dull and confused from the blow I had received upon my head that all seemed misty and strange, and once I found myself thinking, as my head ached frightfully, that they might just as well kill us at once, and not torture us by keeping us in suspense.

The talking went on, and whenever the tall chief stopped for a moment the blacks all set up a yell, and danced about brandishing their spears and clubs, showing their teeth, rolling their eyes, and behaving—just like savages. But still we were not harmed, only watched carefully, Jimmy alone being held, though I could see that at a movement on our part we should have been beaten to death or thrust through.

At last, after an interminable speech, the big chief seemed to grow hoarse, and the blacks' yells were quicker and louder.

Then there was a terrible pause, and a dozen sturdy blacks sprang towards us as regularly as if they had been drilled, each man holding a spear, and I felt that the end had come.

I was too stupid with my hurt to do more than stare helplessly round, seeing the bright sunshine, the glittering sea, and the beautiful waving trees. Then my head began to throb, and felt as if hot irons were being thrust through it.

I closed my eyes, the agony was so great; and then I opened them again, for all the savages were yelling and clapping their hands. Two men had seized me, and one of them had his head bandaged, and in a misty way I recognised him as one of the poor wretches to whom I had given water. He and the others, who were easily known by the doctor's patches of sticking-plaster, were talking with all their might; and then all the blacks began yelling and dancing about, brandishing their spears and clubs, frantic apparently with the effect of the injured men's words.

"They ar'n't going to kill us, my lad," said the captain then; "and look ye there, they are going to feast the doctor."

For the latter was regularly hustled off from among us by a party of blacks, led by two of the sticking-plastered fellows, while two others squatted down smiling at us and rubbing their chests.

"Are we to be spared, then?" I said.

"Spared? Well, I don't know, my lad," said the captain. "They won't be so ungrateful as to kill us, now these blacks set ashore have turned up and told 'em what sort of chaps we are; but I don't think they'll free us. They'll keep us here and make the doctor a physic chief. Eh! go there? All right; I can understand your fingers better than your tongue, my lad. Come on, all of you."

This last was in response to the gesticulations of the injured men who were with us, and soon after, we were all settled down in a very large open hut, eating fruit and drinking water, every drop of which seemed to me more delicious than anything I had ever tasted before.

A curious kind of drink was also given to us, but I did not care for it, and turned to the water again; while the doctor set to work to dress and strap up my injury as well as he could for the pressure of the people, who were wonderfully interested in it all, and then gathered round the doctor's other patients, examining their injuries, and listening to the account of the surgical treatment, which was evidently related to them again and again.

"Well, this is different to what you expected; isn't it, squire?" said the captain to me the first time he could find an opportunity to speak. "I was beginning to feel precious glad that I shouldn't have a chance to get back and meet your mother after what she said to me."

"Then you think we are safe now?" said the doctor.

"Safe!" said the captain; "more than safe, unless some of 'em, being a bit cannibal like, should be tempted by the pleasant plumpness of Mr Jack Penny here, and want to cook and eat him."

"Get out!" drawled Jack. "I know what you mean. I can't help being tall and thin."

"Not you, my lad," said the captain good-humouredly. "Never mind your looks so long as your 'art's in the right place. We're safe enough, doctor, and I should say that nothing better could have happened. Niggers is only niggers; but treat 'em well and they ain't so very bad. You let young Squire Carstairs here ask the chief, and he'll go with you, and take half his people, to try and find the professor; ah, and fight for you too, like trumps."

"Do you think so?" I said.

"Think! I'm sure of it; and I'm all right now. They'll be glad to see me and trade with me. I'm glad you made me set those chaps free."

"And what has become of the crew of the other schooner?" I said anxiously.

"Nobbled," said the captain; "and serve 'em right. Tit for tat; that's all. Men who plays at those games must expect to lose sometimes. They've lost—heavy. Change the subject; it's making young Six-foot Rule stare, and you look as white as if you were going to be served the same. Where's the doctor?"

"He said he was going to see to the injured men," I replied.

"Come and let's look how he's getting on," said the captain. "It's all right now; no one will interfere with us more than mobbing a bit, because we're curiosities. Come on."

I followed the captain, the blacks giving way, but following us closely, and then crowding close up to the door of the great tent where the doctor was very busy repairing damages, as he called it, clipping away woolly locks, strapping up again and finishing off dressings that he had roughly commenced on board.

During the next few days we were the honoured guests of the savages, going where we pleased, and having everything that the place produced. The captain moored his vessel in a snug anchorage, and drove a roaring trade bartering the stores he had brought for shells, feathers, bird-skins, and other productions of the island.

Gyp was brought on shore, and went suspiciously about the place with his head close up to his master's long thin legs, for though he had tolerated and was very good friends with Jimmy, he would not have any dealings with the New Guinea folk. It did not seem to be the black skins or their general habits; but Jack Penny declared that it was their gummed-out moppy heads, these seeming to irritate the dog, so that, being a particularly well-taught animal, he seemed to find it necessary to control his feelings and keep away from the savages, lest he should find himself constrained to bite. The consequence was that, as I have said, he used to go about with his head close to his master's legs, often turning his back on the people about him; while I have known him sometimes take refuge with me, and thrust his nose right into my hand, as if he wished to make it a muzzle to keep him from dashing at some chief.

"I hope he won't grab hold of any of 'em," Jack Penny said to me one day in his deliberate fashion; "because if he does take hold it's such a hard job to make him let go again. And I say, Joe Carstairs, if ever he's by you and these niggers begin to jump about, you lay hold of him and get him away."

"Why?" I said.

"Well, you see," drawled Jack, "Gyp ain't a human being."

"I know that," I replied.

"Yes, I s'pose so," said Jack. "Gyp's wonderfully clever, and he thinks a deal; but just now, I know as well as can be, he's in a sort of doubt. He thinks these blacks are a kind of kangaroos, but he isn't sure. If they begin to jump about, that will settle it, and he'll go at 'em and get speared; and if any one sticks a spear into Gyp, there's going to be about the biggest row there ever was. That one the other day won't be anything to it."

"Then I shall do all I can to keep Gyp quiet," I said, smiling at Jack's serious way of speaking what he must have known was nonsense. After that I went out of the hut, where Jack Penny was doing what the captain called straightening his back—that is to say, lying down gazing up at the palm-thatched rafters, a very favourite position of his—and joined some of the blacks, employing my time in trying to pick up bits and scraps of their language, so as to be able to make my way about among the people when we were left alone.

I found the doctor was also trying hard to master the tongue; and at the same time we attempted to make the chiefs understand the object of our visit, but it was labour in vain. The blacks were thoroughly puzzled, and I think our way of pointing at ourselves and then away into the bush only made them think that we wanted fruit or birds.

The time sped on, while the captain was carrying on his trade, the blacks daily returning from the ship with common knives, and hatchets, and brass wire, the latter being a favourite thing for which they eagerly gave valuable skins. My wound rapidly healed, and I was eager to proceed up the country, our intention being to go from village to village searching until we discovered the lost man.

"And I don't know what to say to it," said the captain just before parting. "I'm afraid you'll get to some village and then stop, for the blacks won't let you go on; but I tell you what: I shall be always trading backwards and forwards for the next two years, and I shall coast about looking up fresh places so as to be handy if you want a bit of help; and I can't say fairer than that, can I, doctor?"

"If you will keep about the coast all you can," said the doctor, "and be ready, should we want them, to supply us with powder and odds and ends to replenish our stores, you will be doing us inestimable service. Whenever we go to a coast village we shall leave some sign of our having been there—a few words chalked on a tree, or a hut, something to tell you that English people have passed that way."

"All right, and I shall do something of the kind," said the captain. "And, look here, I should make this village a sort of randy-voo if I was you, for you'll always be safe with these people."

"Yes; this shall be headquarters," said the doctor. "Eh, Joe?"

I nodded.

"And now there's one more thing," said the captain. "Six-foot Rule; I suppose I'm to take him back?"

"If you mean me," drawled Jack Penny, entering the hut with Gyp, "no, you mustn't take him back, for I ain't going. If Joe Carstairs don't want me, I don't want him. The country's as free for one as t'other, and I'm going to have a look round along with Gyp."

"But really, my dear fellow," said the doctor, "I think you had better give up this idea."

"Didn't know you could tell what's best here," said Jack stoutly. "'Tain't a physicky thing."

"But it will be dangerous, Jack. You see we have run great risks already," I said, for now the time for the captain's departure had arrived, and it seemed a suitable occasion for bringing Jack to his senses.

"Well, who said it wouldn't be dangerous?" he said sulkily. "Gyp and me ain't no more afraid than you are."

"Of course not," I said.

"'Tain't no more dangerous for me and a big dog than it is for you and your black fellow. I don't want to come along with you, I tell you, if you don't want me."

"My dear Jack," I said, "I should be glad of your company, only I'm horrified at the idea of your running risks for your own sake. Suppose anything should happen to you, what then?"

Jack straightened up his long loppetty body, and looked himself all over in a curious depreciatory fashion, and then said in a half melancholy, half laughing manner:

"Well, if something did happen, it wouldn't spoil me; and if I was killed nobody wouldn't care. Anyhow I sha'n't go back with the captain."

"Nonsense, my lad!" said the latter kindly. "I was a bit rough when I found you'd stowed yourself on board, but that was only my way. You come back along with me: you're welcome as welcome, and we sha'n't never be bad friends again."

"Would you take Gyp too?" said Jack.

"What! the dog? Ay, that I would; wouldn't I, old fellow?" said the captain; and Gyp got up slowly, gave his tail a couple of wags slowly and deliberately, as his master might have moved, and ended by laying his head upon the captain's knee.

"Thank'ye, captain," said Jack, nodding in a satisfied way, "and some day I'll ask you to take me back, but I'm going to find Joe Carstairs' father first; and if they won't have me along with them, I dessay I shall go without 'em, and do it myself."

The end of it all was that we shook hands most heartily with the captain next day; and that evening as the doctor, Jack Penny, Jimmy, Gyp, and I stood on the beach, we could see the schooner rounding a point of the great island, with the great red ball of fire—the sun—turning her sails into gold, till the darkness came down suddenly, as it does in these parts; and then, though there was the loud buzzing of hundreds of voices about the huts, we English folk seemed to feel that we were alone as it were, and cut off from all the world, while for the first time, as I lay down to sleep that night listening to the low boom of the water, the immensity, so to speak, of my venture seemed to strike me, giving me a chill of dread. This had not passed off when I woke up at daybreak next morning, to find it raining heavily, and everything looking as doleful and depressing as a strange place will look at such a time as this.

Chapter Ten
How we saw Strange Things

"You rascal!" I exclaimed; "how dare you! Here, doctor, what is to be done? How am I to punish him?"

"Send him back," said the doctor; "or, no: we'll leave him here at the village."

Jimmy leaped up from where he had been squirming, as Jack Penny called it, on the ground, and began to bound about, brandishing his waddy, and killing nothing with blows on the head.

"No, no," he shouted, "no send Jimmy back. Mass Joe leave Jimmy — Jimmy kill all a black fellow dead."

"Now look here, sir," I said, seizing him by the ear and bringing him to his knees, proceedings which, big strong fellow as he was, he submitted to with the greatest of humility, "I'm not going to have you spoil our journey by any of your wild pranks; if ever you touch one of the people again, back you go to the station to eat damper and mutton and mind sheep."

"Jimmy no go back mind sheep; set gin mind sheep. Jimmy go long Mass Joe."

"Then behave yourself," I cried, letting him rise; and he jumped to his feet with the satisfaction of a forgiven child. In fact it always seemed to me that the black fellows of Australia, when they had grown up, were about as old in brains as an English boy of nine or ten.

That morning we had made our start after days of preparation, and the chiefs of the village with a party of warriors came to see us part of the way, those who stayed behind with the women and children joining in a kind of yell to show their sorrow at our departure. The chief had offered half-a-dozen of his people for guides, and we might have had fifty; but six seemed plenty for our purpose, since, as the doctor said, we must work by diplomacy and not by force.

So this bright morning we had started in high spirits and full of excitement, the great band of glistening-skinned blacks had parted from us, and our journey seemed now to have fairly begun, as we plunged directly into the forest, the six men with us acting as bearers.

We had not gone far before our difficulties began, through the behaviour of Jimmy, who, on the strength of his knowledge of English, his connection with the white men, and above all the possession of clothes, which, for comfort's sake, he had once more confined to a pair of old trousers whose legs were cut off at mid-thigh, had begun to display his conceit and superiority, in his own estimation, over the black bearers by strutting along beside them, frowning and poking at them with his spear. At last he went so far as to strike one fine tall fellow over the shoulders, with the result that the New Guinea man threw down his load, the others followed suit, and all made rapid preparations for a fight.

Humble as he was with me, I must do Jimmy the credit of saying that he did not turn tail, but threw himself into an attitude as if about to hurl his spear; and blood would undoubtedly have been shed had I not taken it upon myself to interfere, to the great satisfaction of our bearers.

Order then was restored, the loads were resumed, and Jimmy, who did not seem in the slightest degree abashed by being degraded before the men he had ill-treated, strutted on, and the journey was continued, everyone on the look-out for dangerous beast or savage man.

The doctor and I carried revolvers and double-barrelled guns, one barrel being charged with ball. Jack Penny was delighted by being similarly furnished; and in addition he asked for an axe, which he carried stuck in his belt.

We were each provided with a similar weapon, ready to hand at times to the blacks, who were always ready to set down their burdens and make short work of the wild vines and growth that often impeded our path.

We had determined—I say we, for from the moment of starting the doctor had begun to treat me as his equal in every sense, and consulted me on every step we took; all of which was very pleasant and flattering to me; but I often felt as if I would rather be dependent upon him—we had then determined to strike into the country until we reached the banks of a great river, whose course we meant to follow right up to the sources in the mountains.

There were good reasons for this, as a moment's thought will show.

To begin with, we were in a land of no roads, and most of our journey would be through dense forest, whereas there was likely to be a certain amount of open country about the river banks.

Then we were always sure of a supply of water; game is always most abundant, both birds and beasts, near a river, and, of course, there is always a chance of getting fish; fruit might also be found, and what was more, the villages of the natives not upon the coast are nearly always upon the rivers.

Of course, on the other hand, there were plenty of dangers to be risked by following a river's course: fever, noxious beast and insect, inimical natives, and the like; but if we had paused to think of the dangers, we might very well have shrunk from our task, so we put thoughts of that kind behind us and journeyed on.

At first, after getting through a dense patch of forest, we came upon open plains, and a part of the country that looked like a park; and as I trudged on with fresh objects of interest springing up at every turn, I found myself wondering whether my poor father had passed this way, and as I grew weary I began to take the most desponding views of the venture, and to think that, after all, perhaps he was dead.

That we were in a part not much troubled by human beings we soon found by the tameness of the birds and the number of deer that dashed frightened away from time to time, hardly giving us a glimpse of their dappled skins before they were lost in the jungly growth.

The walking had grown more difficult as the day wore on, and at last the great trees began to give place to vegetation of a different kind. Instead of timber we were walking amongst palm-like growth and plants with enormous succulent leaves. Great climbers twined and twisted one with another, unless they found some tree up which they seemed to force their way to reach the open sunshine, forming a splendid shelter from the ardent rays when we wished to rest.

There was no attempt during the morning to make use of our guns, for at first we moved watchfully, always on the look-out for enemies, seeing danger in every moving leaf, and starting at every rustling dash made by some frightened animal that crossed our path.

By degrees, though, we grew more confident, but still kept up our watchfulness, halting at mid-day beside a little clear stream in a spot so lovely that it struck me as being a shame that no one had a home there to revel in its beauties.

The water ran bubbling along amongst mossy rocks, and overhung by gigantic ferns. There were patches of the greenest grass, and close by, offering us shade, was a clump of large trees whose branches strewed brightly coloured flowers to the earth. A flock of gorgeously plumaged birds were noisily chattering and shrieking in the branches, and though they fled on our first coming, they came back directly and began climbing and swinging about so near that I could see that they were a small kind of parrot, full of strange antics, and apparently playing at searching for their food.

"We'll have two hours' rest here," said the doctor, "a good meal, and perhaps a nap, and our feet bathed in the cool water, and the rest of the day's journey will come easier."

"But hadn't we better get on?" I said anxiously.

"'Slow and sure' must be our motto, Joe," said the doctor. "We have hundreds of miles to tramp, so we must not begin by knocking ourselves up. Patience, my boy, patience and we shall win."

As soon as he saw that we were going to stop for rest and refreshment, Jimmy began to rub the centre of his person and make a rush for the native basket that contained our food, from which he had to be driven; for though generally, quite unlike many of his fellow-countrymen, Jimmy was scrupulously honest, he could not be trusted near food.

There was no stopping to lay the cloth and arrange knives and forks. We each drew our heavy knife, and filled the cup of our little canteen from the stream before setting to at a large cold bird that we had brought with us, one shot by the doctor the day before, and cooked ready for the expedition. I cannot give you its name, only tell you that it was as big as a turkey, and had a beautiful crest of purple and green.

We had brought plenty of damper too, a preparation of flour that, I dare say, I need not stop to describe, as every one now must know that in Australia it takes the place of ordinary bread.

The native carriers were well provided for, and my depression passed off as the restful contented feeling induced by a good meal came over me. As for Jack Penny, he spread himself out along the ground, resting his thin body, and went on eating with his eyes half shut; while Gyp, his dog, came close alongside him, and sat respectfully waiting till his master balanced a bone across his nose, which Gyp tossed in the air, caught between his jaws, and then there was a loud crunching noise for a few minutes, and the dog was waiting again.

Jimmy was eating away steadily and well, as if he felt it to be his bounden duty to carry as much of the store of food neatly packed away inside him as it was possible to stow, when he suddenly caught sight of Gyp, and stopped short with his mouth open and a serious investigating look in his eyes.

He saw the dog supplied twice with what he evidently looked upon as dainty bits, and a broad smile came over his countenance. Then he looked annoyed and disappointed, and as if jealous of the favour shown to the beast.

The result was that he left the spot where he had been lying half-way between us and the carriers, went to the stream, where he lay flat down with his lips in the water, and drank, and then came quietly up to my side, where he squatted down in as near an imitation of Gyp as he could assume, pouting out his lips and nose and waiting for a bone.

The doctor burst out laughing, while I could not tell whether to set it down to artfulness or to simple animal nature on the poor fellow's part.

However, I was too English at heart to lower my follower, so I did not treat him like a dog, but hacked off a good bone and sent him to his place.

We thoroughly enjoyed our meal, and, as the doctor said, somewhat lightened our loads, when all at once it seemed to me that a spasm ran through Jack Penny where he lay. Then, as I watched him, I saw his hand stealing towards his gun, and he looked at me and pointed towards where a dense patch of big trees formed a sort of buttress to the great green wall of the forest.

For a few moments I could see nothing; then I started, and my hand also went towards my piece, for peering round the trunk of one of the trees, and evidently watching us, was one of the most hideous-looking faces I had ever seen. The eyes were bright and overhung by dark wrinkled brows, and, seen in the half light, the head seemed as large as that of a man. In fact I was convinced that it was some fierce savage playing the spy upon our actions.

I felt better when I had fast hold of my gun—not that I meant to fire, only to protect myself—and I was reaching out a foot to awaken the doctor, who had thrown himself back with his hat over his face, when I found that Gyp had caught sight of the hideous countenance, and, with a fierce bay, he dashed at the creature.

Jack Penny and I started to our feet, Jimmy went after the dog, waddy in hand, and his yell awakened the doctor, who also sprang to his feet just in time to see the creature leap up at a pendent branch, swing itself up in the tree, and disappear amongst the thick leafage, while Gyp barked furiously below.

"Big monkey that, my lads," said the doctor. "I did not know we should see anything so large."

Jack Penny was all eagerness to follow and get a shot at the animal; but though he looked in all directions, and Gyp kept baying first at the foot of one tree then at the foot of another, he did not see it again. Where it went it was impossible to say; perhaps it travelled along the upper branches, swinging itself from bough to bough by its long arms; but if it did, it was all so silently that not so much as a leaf rustled, and we were all at fault.

I was not sorry, for the idea of shooting anything so like a human being, and for no reason whatever, was rather repugnant to my feelings, so that I did not share in my companion's disappointment.

"Depend upon it, he has not gone far," said the doctor, when Jack Penny stood staring at the tree where we saw the ape first. "There, lie down, my lad, and rest, and—hallo! what's the matter with Jimmy?"

I turned to see the black standing close by, his waddy in one hand, his boomerang in the other, head bent, knees relaxed, an expression of the greatest horror in his face, as he shivered from head to foot, and shook his head.

"Why, what's the matter, Jimmy?" I cried.

"Bunyip," he whispered, "big bunyip debble—debble—eat all a man up. Bunyip up a tree."

"Get out!" I said; "it was a big monkey."

"Yes: big bunyip monkey. Come 'way."

For the sudden disappearance of the ape had impressed Jimmy with the idea that it was what the Scottish peasants call "no canny," and as it was his first interview with one of these curious creatures, there was some excuse for his apparent fear, though I am not certain that it was not assumed.

For Jimmy was no coward so long as he was not called upon to encounter the familiar demons of his people, the word bunyip being perhaps too often in his mouth.

The black's dread went off as quickly as it came, when he found that he was not noticed, and for the next two hours we lay resting, Jack Penny and I seeing too many objects of interest to care for sleep. Now it would be a great beetle glistening in green and gold, giving vent to a deep-toned buzzing hum as it swept by; then a great butterfly, eight or nine inches across, would come flitting through the trees, to be succeeded by something so swift of flight and so rapid in the flutter of its wings that we were in doubt whether it was a butterfly or one of the beautiful sunbirds that we saw flashing in the sunshine from time to time.

It proved afterwards to be a butterfly or day-moth, for we saw several of them afterwards in the course of our journey.

Over the birds Jack Penny and I had several disputes, for once he took anything into his head, even if he was wrong, he would not give way.

"These are humming-birds," he said, as we lay watching some of the lovely little creatures that were hovering before the flowers of a great creeper, and seemed to be thrusting in their long beaks.

"No," I said, "they are not humming-birds;" and I spoke upon my mother's authority, she in turn resting on my father's teaching. "There are no humming-birds here: they are found in America and the islands."

"And out here," said Jack, dictatorially. "There they are; can't you see 'em?"

"No," I said, "those are sunbirds; and they take the place of the humming-birds out here in the East."

"Nonsense! Think I don't know a humming-bird when I see one. Why, I saw one at Sydney, stuffed."

"When you two have done disputing," said the doctor, "we'll start."

"Look here, doctor; ain't those humming-birds?" said Jack.

"No, no, doctor," I cried; "they are sunbirds, are they not?"

"I don't know," said the doctor; "let's make haste on and ask the professor."

I sprang to my feet as if stung by a reproach, for it seemed to me as if I had been thinking of trifles instead of the great object of my mission.

Chapter Eleven
How Jack Penny was not satisfied with himself

It was intensely hot when we started again, the heat seeming to be steamy, and not a breath of air to fan our cheeks; but we trudged on for a time without adventure, till all at once a butterfly of such lovely colours flashed across our path, that it proved too much for Jack Penny, who laid down his gun, snatched off his hat, and went in pursuit.

We could not go on and leave him; so we stopped to rest, and watch him as he was hopping and bounding along through a tolerably open sunlit part, full of growth of the most dazzling green. Now he neared the insect; now it dashed off again, and led him a tremendous chase, till, just as the doctor shouted to him to return, we saw him make a dab down with his hat and then disappear.

"He has got it," I said; for I could not help feeling interested in the chase; but I felt annoyed again directly, as the doctor said coldly:

"Yes: he seems to have caught his prize, Joe; but we must defer these sports till our work is done."

Just then we saw Jack Penny rise up and turn towards us. To hide my vexation I shouted to him to make haste, and he began to trot towards us, his long body bending and swaying about as he ran.

Then he jumped and jumped again, and the doctor shaded his eyes with his hands.

"He has got into a swampy patch," he said. "Of course. There's a bit of a stream runs along there, and — "

"Ow!" came in a dismal yell, followed by a furious barking, as we saw Jack make a tremendous jump, and then disappear.

"Help, help!" came from among some dense green growth, and hurrying forward we at last came in sight of our companion, at least in sight of his head and shoulders, and we could not approach him, for the ground gave way beneath our feet, the bright green moss almost floating upon a treacherous bog.

"Hold on!" shouted the doctor; "we'll help you directly;" and taking out his big knife he began to hack at some small bamboos which grew in thick clumps about us.

"Make haste," moaned Jack, "I'm sinking;" and we could see Gyp, who was howling furiously, tearing at the soft moss as if to dig his master out.

"Give Jimmy knife," said the black, who was grinning and enjoying Jack Penny's predicament.

I handed him mine, and he too cut down armfuls of the young green bamboo, the carriers coming up now and helping, when, taking a bundle at a time, Jimmy laid them down, dancing lightly over them with his bare feet, and troubling himself very little about danger, as he made a sort of green path right up to Jack.

"His black fellow pull up," shouted Jimmy; but I ran up to where he was, and each taking one of Jack's hands he gave a wriggle, floundered a bit, and then we had him out covered with black mud; and though we were standing up, he would not trust himself just then erect, but crept after us on hands and knees, the soft bog beneath us going up and down like a wave.

As soon as he was quite safe there was a hearty laugh at Jack Penny's expense; and the doctor drily asked for the butterfly.

"Oh, I caught him," said Jack; "but I lost him when I trod on that great beast."

"What great beast?" I said.

"Crocodile fifty foot long," drawled Jack.

"Say sixty," said the doctor.

"Well, I hadn't time to measure him," drawled Jack. "I trod upon one, and he heaved up, and that made me jump into a soft place, and—ugh! what's that?"

I was very doubtful about Jack's crocodile, but there was no mistake about the object that had made him utter this last cry of disgust.

"They're pricking me horrid," he shouted; and we found that he had at least twenty large leeches busily at work banquetting upon his blood.

The blacks set to work picking them off, and scraping him clear of the thick vegetable mud that adhered to him; and with the promise that he was to have a good bathe in the first clear water we encountered, we once more started, Jack looking anything but cheerful, but stubbornly protesting that it was wonderful how comfortable his wet clothes made him feel.

Master Jack had to listen to a lecture from the doctor, in which the latter pointed out that if success was to attend our expedition, it would not do for the various members to be darting off at their good pleasure in search of butterflies, and at first Jack looked very grim, and frowned as if about to resent it all. To my surprise, however, he replied:

"I see, doctor; we must be like soldiers and mind the captain. Well, all right. I won't do so any more."

"I'm sure you will not," said the doctor, holding out his hand. "You see we must have discipline in our little corps, so as to be able fully to confide in each other in cases of emergency. We must be men."

Jack scratched his head and looked ruefully from one to the other.

"That's just what I want to be, doctor," he drawled; "but I'm always doing something that makes me seem like a small boy. I'm grown up a deal, but somehow I don't feel a bit older than I used to be years ago."

"Ah, well, wait a bit, Penny," replied the doctor; "and we will not say any more about the butterfly hunt."

Jack's brow seemed to grow as wrinkled as that of an old man, and he was very solemn for the rest of the day, during which we tramped on through the forest, its beauties seeming less attractive than in the freshness of the early morning, and the only striking thing we saw was a pack of small monkeys, which seemed to have taken a special dislike to Jimmy, following him from tree to tree, chattering and shrieking the while, and at last putting the black in a passion, and making him throw his boomerang savagely up in return for the nuts that were showered down.

"Bad black fellow," he said to me indignantly. "Come down, Jimmy fight twenty forty all a once."

He flourished his club and showed me how he would clear the ground, but the monkeys did not accept the challenge, and that night we halted under a great tree covered with a scarlet plum-like fruit, and proceeded to set up our tent as a shelter to keep off the heavy dew.

Chapter Twelve
How Watch was kept by Night

The sheet which I have called our tent was stretched over a low bough, and secured to pegs at the four corners, being all open at the sides, so that as I lay I could gaze right away in any direction.

On one side there was gloom, with the tall pillar-like tree trunks standing up grey and indistinct; on the other side there was the bright fire, which was as dangerous, I thought, as it was useful, for though it served to keep off wild beasts it was likely to attract savage men, just as moths fly to a flame.

As I lay there I could see the doctor keeping watch, and beside him one of the natives, whose black face looked curious and ghastly with the bandage he wore round his head, for this was one of the men who had been seized by the captain of the other schooner, and who had eagerly volunteered to be of our party.

This man was gazing intently at the doctor, as if eager to catch the slightest indication of a wish, and so still and misty did he look in the weird light that but for the flaming of the fire from his eyes it would have been hard to tell that he was a living being.

Though it was not cold our black followers all slept close about the fire, Jimmy the nearest—so close, in fact, that he seemed as if he were being prepared for a feast on the morrow; and this idea of roasting came the more strongly from the fact that we were in a land whose inhabitants were said to have certain weaknesses towards a taste for human joints.

Jack Penny was sleeping heavily close to me, and at regular intervals seeming to announce that he was dreaming of eating, for his lips gave vent over and over again to the word *pork*!

Sometimes this regular snoring sound annoyed me, but I forgot it again directly as I lay sleepless there, now watching the gloom of the forest, now the flickering and dancing light of the fire as the wood crackled and burned and the sparks and smoke went straight up, till they were lost on high amid the densely thick branches overhead.

It was a curious sensation to be there in that awful solitude, thinking of my past adventures, and wondering what the next day might bring forth. I wanted to sleep and rest, so as to rise refreshed when the doctor called me two hours after midnight, when I was to relieve guard; but sleep would not come, and I lay fidgeting about, wondering how it was possible that such a small twig could set up so much irritation beneath my back.

Then, just as I thought I was going off there would be the sensation as of some creeping insect crawling about over my face and in amongst the roots of my hair. Then after impatiently knocking it away, something seemed to be making its way up my sleeve, to be succeeded by something else in the leg of my trousers, while I had hardly got rid of this sensation when a peculiarly clammy cold touch taught me that either a lizard or a snake was crawling over my feet.

This last I felt constrained to bear, for a movement might result in the bite of some poisonous creature, while by lying still I might escape.

At last I really was dropping off into a sound sleep, when all at once I started into wakefulness, fascinated as it were by the sight of something shining in the black darkness to the left of our fire.

With a shudder running through me I rose to my elbow, at the same moment seizing my gun, when a single intent glance convinced me that I was right, for certainly some creature was watching the doctor, and probably crouching before making a deadly bound.

I cocked the piece softly, holding the trigger the while, so that there should be no sharp click, and in another moment I should have fired, after careful aim, between the two bright glaring eyes, when the doctor made a movement, and the animal darted aside and went bounding off, just giving me a glimpse of its form, which was that of a small deer.

I saw the doctor shade his eyes and stand watching the flying creature. Then stooping down he picked up a few branches that had been gathered ready, and made the fire blaze more brightly.

As the glow increased I saw something which there was no mistaking for a harmless deer, for not ten yards away there was a large cat-like creature crouching close to the ground, while, to make assurance doubly sure, there came from between its bared and glistening white teeth a low angry snarl.

I took aim, and tried to get a good sight at its head, but hesitated to draw trigger, for the glow from the fire made appearances deceptive, the body of the cat-like beast seeming to waver up and down; and directly after the creature moved, and its head was covered by a low bush.

But the doctor and his companion had both seen the animal, which uttered a menacing roar as the former stepped forward, snatched a piece of burning wood from the fire, and hurled it towards the beast, his example being followed by the New Guinea man.

The result was a furious roar, and the great cat bounded away towards the forest.

This brought Gyp to his feet with a fierce volley of barking, and he would have been off in pursuit but for his master, who woke up and ran out exclaiming:

"Dingoes after the sheep! dingoes after the sheep! Here, Gyp, boy! here, Gyp—here—eh! I say, is anything the matter?"

"No, no; all right!" cried the doctor.

"I—I thought I was at home," said Jack, rubbing his eyes; "and—oh! how sleepy I am."

"Lie down again, then," said the doctor; and Jack obeyed, Gyp following and curling up close by his master, who very soon resumed his heavy breathing, in so objectionable a manner that I felt over and over again as if I should like to kick him and wake him up.

For there is nothing on earth so annoying as to be unable to sleep when some one close by is snoring away in happy oblivion.

As I lay there with my face turned from the fire, so that it should not keep me awake, I felt more and more the sensation of awe produced by being there in the midst of that wild place. While I was perfectly still my eyes were directed upwards in amongst the branches of the great tree, now illumined by the bright flame of our fire, and by degrees I made out that these boughs were peopled by birds and what seemed to be squirrels, and all more or less excited by the unaccustomed light.

I lay gazing up at them, seeing the different objects very indistinctly in the dancing light, and then all at once it seemed to me that one particular branch was rising and falling slowly with a peculiar movement. It was a strange wavy motion, which was the more remarkable from the fact that there was no wind; but after a moment or two's thought I fancied I had found the cause in the heated air produced by the fire.

But that did not explain what next took place in the smoky obscurity above the fire, for the branch seemed to wave about more and more, and to lengthen; and then I made sure that it was the shadow I saw; but directly after, a thrill ran through me as I recalled that these creatures were fond of nestling high up in branches, where they captured birds and monkeys, and I said in a low hoarse whisper:

"Why, it's a snake!"

There was no doubt about the matter, for as it swung lower, holding on by its tail, I could see that it was indeed a snake, evidently of considerable length, and about as thick as my arm. It had been aroused from probably a torpid state by the fumes of the fire, and was now descending from bough to bough to reach the earth, and I paused for a time, asking myself what I had better do.

The result was that I overcame the unwillingness I felt to move, and crept so softly towards the doctor that I was able to lay my hand upon his shoulder before he heard me approach.

"Why, Joe!" he exclaimed, starting, "I thought it was an enemy."

"Yes; there he is!" I said with a shudder, and I pointed up among the branches.

The black who was the doctor's fellow-watcher had seen me approach, and following with his eyes the direction pointed to by my hand, he too looked up into the tree, where, glistening in the fire-light, there was the reptile swinging slowly to and fro with a pendulum-like motion.

In spite of the horror inspired by such a creature, free and within a few yards of where I was standing, I could not help noticing the beauty of the scales, which shone in the fire-light as if of burnished bronze. But I had little time for examination; one moment I was noting the head and curved neck of the reptile, the next there was a sharp twanging noise, and I saw the serpent's head jerk upwards, and then what seemed to be a mass of thick rope fell near the fire; there was a tremendous lashing and tossing about, and when the doctor and I approached the spot cautiously with our guns, it was to find that the reptile had glided off into the forest depths.

"A good shot for a bow and arrow," said the doctor, turning to our black companion, who smiled complacently, our manner plainly showing him that we were admiring his skill.

"You are getting a poor night's rest, Joe," said the doctor smiling. "Now go and lie down again."

"It is of no use," I said fretfully. "I can't sleep, and I only lie thinking about home and him. I shall stay and watch."

The doctor protested, but finding at last that I was unwilling to lie down again, he said:

"Well, I am quite different, for I am so tired that I cannot keep awake. I will go and lie down then, if you promise to come and wake me as soon as you are drowsy. Mind and keep up a good blaze."

I replied that he might be sure of that.

"Don't fire unnecessarily," he continued. "If any wild animal comes near, a piece of burning wood will scare it away at once."

"As it did that great cat!" I said.

"Did you see, then?" he said.

"I have not been asleep for a single minute," I replied. "What was it—a tiger?"

"Tiger! No, my lad," he said, laughing; "I don't think we shall see any tigers here. There, I shall yawn my head off if I stop here talking. Good night!"

He walked to the shelter, and I went and sat down next our black companion, who smiled a welcome; and thinking this a favourable opportunity, I set to work to try and increase my knowledge of the language, by lifting up different objects and making the black give them their native name, which I tried to imitate as well as I could.

He was very intelligent, grasping my meaning at once, and repeating the words again and again, till I was nearly perfect, when he laughed with childlike pleasure.

The time passed so quickly in this occupation that I was quite startled by hearing a wild resonant cry that seemed to echo through the forest arcades. Then there was a succession of piercing screams, followed by loud whistling and muttering. A monkey started a chattering noise, which was answered from a distance with a hundredfold power; and looking about me I found that the day was breaking and the night-watch at an end.

The change from night to morning is very rapid near the equator, and soon the sun was making bright and attractive places that had looked awful and full of hidden dangers in the night; while, in place of the depression produced by the darkness, I felt eager sensations and desires springing up within my heart, and a strong inclination to get forward once more upon our journey.

We made a very hearty meal before the sun was much above the horizon; our simple packing was soon done, and we were not long before we were well on the road of discovery.

I expected to be very tired and sleepy, but to my surprise I did not feel in the least the worse for my restless night, and we trudged along pretty swiftly when the land was open, slowly and toilsomely when tangled growth obstructed our way.

I was too much occupied with thoughts of my father to pay much heed to the fruits and flowers that we came upon in many spots; besides, I was on before with Jack Penny, and Gyp in front of us very intelligently leading the way. There was, I knew, always the chance of meeting some danger, and on this account we kept a very sharp look-out ahead, till suddenly we were stopped by a strange noise as of water being struck a succession of heavy blows; and as Gyp set up his ears, threw up his nose, and uttered a low whimper, there was the click, click of gun-locks, and every one prepared for some coming danger, the blacks remaining quiet, and looking wonderingly at our strange proceedings.

The sound ceased as suddenly as it had begun, and though we listened intently we heard it no more for that time, so we continued our journey with every one thoroughly on the alert.

Chapter Thirteen
How Jack Penny put his Foot in a Trap

We had made our plans, but they were very elastic, for it was impossible for us to keep to any hard-and-fast line.

"No, Joe," the doctor said, "we cannot say that we will do this or that; we must be governed by circumstances. We have one object in view—to find your father, and so far we have determined to follow the course of the first big river; when we shall be diverted from it time must prove."

We slept that night under the shade of another tree, and as the mist rolled off the next morning we started once again.

It was so glorious a morning that, in spite of the serious nature of our position, it was impossible not to feel in the highest of spirits. The way lay through dense forest, but we had fallen into a track which I at first thought was a regular pathway, and so it proved to be, but not of the kind I imagined as I eagerly called the doctor's attention to it, and the ease with which we were now getting along.

"No, Joe," he said; "this is not a path used by human beings. Look down at the footprints."

I looked down to see the hoof-marks of innumerable wild creatures, and said so.

"Yes," replied the doctor, "it is a track down to the river, followed by the animals that go to drink, and we shall not be long before we get to the water side."

Our way did not seem wearisome, for there was so much to see, the birds in particular taking my attention greatly. One moment a flock of black cockatoos would fly screaming by, then a cloud of brilliantly-coloured parroquets, and in one opening we came upon what looked at first like a gigantic beech-tree completely alive with tiny blue-and-green parrots about the size of sparrows, climbing, fluttering, chattering, and chirping, now with their heads up, now heads down, and forming one of the prettiest sights I had ever seen.

I could have shot twenty or thirty together as they sat in rows upon the bare branches, so little did they heed our presence; but it was unnecessary to destroy their little lives, and we passed on.

I was less merciful an hour later, for food was a necessity, and I was fortunate enough to bring down at the first shot a beautiful little deer that started up in our very path.

My shot seemed to alarm the whole forest and set it in an uproar: birds shrieked, monkeys chattered, and to right and left there was a rushing crackling noise, as of big creatures seeking flight. There was a deep-mouthed howl, too, away on our right that made me look anxiously at the doctor.

"I don't know, Joe," he replied, as if in answer to a spoken question. "There may be tigers here, and leopards, and old men of the woods, big as ourselves. It is new land, my lad, so don't look to me for information."

"Dat big bunyip," said Jimmy in a scared whisper. "Take black fellow— kill um, eatum."

Just then we heard the same beating noise that had fallen upon our ears the previous day.

"Dat big bunyip beat um gin," whispered Jimmy, with a curious awe-stricken look in his countenance.

"'Taint," said Jack Penny slowly. "I don't believe in bunyips. If it was a bunyip beating his gin, she'd holloa out like hooray, and squeak the leaves off the trees."

"'Fraid squeak," said Jimmy eagerly, as he caught Jack's meaning.

"Well, perhaps Jimmy's right," said the doctor slowly; "and as I've never seen a bunyip the present is a favourable opportunity, and we can interfere to stop him from too severely castigating his wife. Come, Jimmy, lead on."

Jimmy's jaw dropped, but his hand stole to his waistband, from which he drew his waddy, talking slowly the while, till, seeing the doctor make a movement towards him, he turned round and darted into the bush.

"He won't stop till he gets back to the village," drawled Jack.

"He won't go farther than the first big tree," I said, laughing. "He's watching us now, I'll be bound."

"Then you and I will have to meet the bunyip, Joe," said the doctor. "Are you coming, Penny?"

"Yes, I'll come," said Jack quietly. "I should like to see a bunyip. Come along."

Jack went on—not first, for Gyp started before him and, guided by the noise, we pushed on amongst the dense growth, finding the earth grow moister beneath our feet; and then all at once it seemed as if the big trees had come to an end and we were in a lighter place.

"There's the water," I cried, as I caught sight of a flash.

"You'll be in it here directly, same as I was," drawled Jack. "I say, doctor, ain't this the sort of place big snakes like?"

"Hush!" whispered the doctor; and pressing back the thick growth we advanced cautiously, and following his example I, too, stepped from tuft to tuft, listening to the beating noise and to the other sounds that arose.

First there was the loud rustle of wings as some water birds flew up, long-legged creatures with far-stretching necks. Then on my left there was an ominous noise, as of something crawling amongst the reeds, and I shuddered as I saw that Jack Penny was holding his gun ready, and that Gyp's hair was bristling all about his neck, while his teeth were bared.

The doctor was some distance before us now, and I could see him peering between some bushes and waving his hand to me to come forward; so, forgetting the danger, if danger there was, I went cautiously to my companion's side, to gaze with astonishment at the scene before me.

There was no bunyip or native Australian demon there, but a great shallow, muddy pond or lake, which seemed as if it must be swarming with fish and crocodiles, for every here and there, as the great rugged backs of the horrible lizards were seen pushing towards the shore, shoals of silvery fish leaped out, flashing in the sunshine before they splashed back into the water.

Here, then, was the secret of the mysterious noise which was being produced before my eyes. For the crocodiles were driving the shoals of fish into the little bays and creeks, and then stunning them by beating the water heavily with their tails, the result being that the paralysed fish were easily devoured.

I felt as if I could never tire of gazing at the monsters so busy before us. There must have been at least five-and-twenty, and all of large size; and it was not a pleasant thought to consider what would have been the consequences if we had attempted to wade across the lagoon.

Before leaving, however, the doctor took out his glass and swept the shore of the great pond, to nod with satisfaction.

"This is only a sort of bay belonging to the river we are seeking, Joe," he said. "Look there to the left, and you can see the entrance choked up with reeds."

We crept back cautiously, to find Jimmy awaiting our return; and then making a détour towards the lake, we soon reached the river, along whose bank was a well-trodden path, in whose softer parts, besides those of deer, it was plain to see the ugly toes of crocodiles, and the long trail they made as they dragged themselves along.

We did not halt until we had left the crocodile pond a long way behind; but a fine dry, open spot, close to the flashing water of the swift river, was so tempting that we did not go so far as we had intended.

Here a fire was soon lit, and Jimmy sat watching the roasting of the buck with an indescribable look of satisfaction in his countenance; while, eager to try whether it would be possible to add to our provision store at any time from the river, I went on down to the water's edge. For if there were fish in such abundance in the lagoon, I felt sure that if they would bite there must be plenty in the stream.

My first idea had been to have a bathe in the cool-looking water, but, seeing my intention, the black who had been my companion in the watch, took my hand, led me cautiously along for a short distance, and then pointed to where there was lying, dimly outlined in the thickened water, one of the hideous creatures such as I had seen in the lagoon.

The black then put his wrists together, spread wide his hands, and closed them sharply upon my arm like a pair of jaws, and snatched me sidewise with a good tug.

I was quite satisfied, and nodding and shuddering I joined the doctor, who was ready enough to help me fish.

We soon had our lines ready, and baiting the hooks with pieces of raw meat, we threw out and waited, after the manner of fishermen at home, for a bite.

After a time I examined my bait and threw in again. Then the doctor examined his and threw in again, but neither of us had the slightest touch, and growing weary we went back to the fire to find the buck sufficiently roasted and Jimmy's eyes standing out of his head with hunger; so we made a hasty meal, left the blacks to finish it, and Jack Penny to rest his long body, while we had another try at the fishing.

But Jack Penny did not care to rest when anything was going on, and after we had been fishing without result for about half an hour he joined us.

"Caught anything?" he said; and on our replying in the negative, "Here, let me try," he said.

I handed him my line, and he twisted it well round his hand.

"Fish run big, sometimes," he said, nodding his head sagaciously. "Don't leave your line like that, doctor," he added; "make it fast to that bough."

The doctor obeyed, and leaving Jack looking very drowsy and dreamy we two took our guns and started along the river bank, thinking that perhaps we might find something useful for the larder, the heat of the climate rendering it necessary for a supply to be obtained from day to day.

It was a glorious walk past quiet bends of the river that were as still as ponds, and full of red and white lotus plants which shot up their lovely blossoms from amidst their floating liliaceous leaves. Trees in places overhung the water, and great wreaths of blossom or leaves of dazzling green were reflected on the surface. Insect life was abundant: burnished beetles and lovely coloured butterflies flitting from flower to flower. Birds, too, especially waders and great creatures that I took to be pelicans, were busy in the shallows, where now and then a great crocodile wallowed through the mud, evidently roused by our approach, for though we saw several of these creatures, not one gave the slightest sign of a disposition to attack.

"There, we are not likely to see deer before evening when they come down to drink," said the doctor. "Let's get back, Joe, my lad, the sun is not so powerful as it was, and we may as well make a fresh start."

We were about three parts of the way back, finding some fresh object of interest at every turn, when I suddenly caught hold of my companion's arm, for a peculiar cry fell upon my ear.

"Something wrong!" exclaimed the doctor, and we set off at a sharp run where the undergrowth would allow.

A curious sensation of dread came over me, and a cold damp feeling was on my brow and in the palms of my hands as the cry rose once more—a singularly doleful cry, as of some one in great peril.

"Are you loaded?" said the doctor, as we ran on, and his voice sounded hoarse with emotion.

I nodded, for I could not speak, and, full of the idea that our little camp had been attacked by savages and that some of our followers were being killed, I ran on.

It was hard work and like running in a nightmare to get back to our starting-place, for there was always some thorn or tangle that we had not noticed in our careful advance seeming to stop us on our way; but at last we came within sight of the spot where we had left Jack Penny, but he was not there.

"There's something wrong at the camp," I panted.

"Be cool," replied the doctor, "we may have to fire. Try and keep your nerve. Ah!"

This ejaculation was consequent upon our simultaneously catching sight of Jack Penny, up to the armpits in the river, holding on by the branch of a tree.

As he saw us he shouted lustily for help. It was no drawl now, but a sharp quick shout.

I ran down the bank and the doctor following, we joined hands, when, catching at Jack's wrist, I held on tightly.

"Now, then," I said, as I gazed wonderingly in his ghastly face and staring eyes, "let go, and we'll draw you ashore."

"No, no," he cried hoarsely. "Got hold of me—drag me in."

"Got hold? Of course," I said, "we'll drag you in."

"One of those brutes has got him, Joe," cried the doctor excitedly, and his words sent such a thrill through me that I nearly loosed my hold. "Here, pull both together," he said, as he got down by my side and seized Jack Penny by the other arm.

We gave a fierce drag, to find that it was answered from below, Jack being nearly drawn out of our hands, his head going down nearly to the eyes, and for the moment it seemed as if we were to be drawn in as well.

But fortunately Jack still had tight hold of the branch, to which he clung in the agony of desperation, and he uttered such a piercing cry that it served to arouse the sleeping blacks, the result being that, as we were holding on, and just maintaining our ground, Jimmy and Ti-hi, the black who had attached himself to me, came running down.

They saw what was wrong, and Jimmy seized me, the black doing the same by Jimmy, with the effect of dragging poor Jack Penny farther and farther from the water in spite of the struggles of the reptile that was trying to haul him back. First we had him out to the chest, then to the hips, then nearly to the knees, and I never till then thoroughly realised what a lot there was of him, for it seemed as if he would never end.

"Hold on!" cried the doctor suddenly. "I'm going to loose him."

"No, no!" panted Jack, with a horrified look; but the doctor did loose his hold and caught up his gun.

"Now, then," he cried. "All together. Haul with all your might."

We obeyed, and though we were for the moment mastered we gave a good swing again, and it seemed as if Jack Penny must be dragged in two.

It was like playing a game of French and English, and we were in danger of getting the worst of it. We saw what the doctor wanted, and that was to get the reptile so near the surface that he could fire; but as soon as we got poor Jack nearly ashore the creature gave a tremendous tug, making the water swirl and the mud and sand from the bottom rise in clouds.

This went on for five minutes, during which we were striving with all our might, when I nearly loosed my hold, for Jack said in a low despairing tone of voice:

"Joe Carstairs, don't let him have me till you've shot me first."

I held fast though, and the fight went on, till, just as we were beginning to despair, the reptile came nearer to the surface, the ugly protuberances over its eyes were level with the water, and, bending down, the doctor reached out with his gun in one hand, held the muzzle close to the creature's eye, and fired.

There was a tremendous sputter and we were nearly forced to leave go, but the next moment there was no resistance but weight, and we drew Jack and his aggressor, a crocodile about ten feet long, right up to the bank, the monster's jaws, which had closed over one of Jack's stoutly booted feet, remaining fast, though the upper part of its head was all blown away.

"Dat a big bunyip," cried Jimmy, forcing the end of his spear through the reptile's jaws and trying to push them open, which he did with his companion's help, and Jack Penny was free to limp feebly for a few yards, and sink down amongst the reeds.

Jimmy did not seem in the least afraid of the bunyip now, for hacking off a long lithe cane he put it over the reptile's jaw, and, twisting it tightly rope-fashion, he and Ti-hi dragged it right away from the water, and, avoiding the frantic lashings of its tail, they turned it over with their spears, used like levers, and kept on stabbing it in its tender underparts until it ceased to struggle, when Jimmy turned it over again and began to perform a triumphant war-dance on its back.

Meanwhile poor Jack Penny, who had been nearly speechless, began to revive.

"That's better," said the doctor. "Now let me look at your foot."

"Has he bit it right off?" said Jack faintly. "I can't feel it. Just when I needed it so badly, too!"

"Bit it off! No!" I cried. "Is it much hurt, doctor?"

"I can't tell till I have unlaced his boot," he replied. "Tell me if I hurt you much, my lad."

"It don't hurt," said Jack faintly. "I can't feel at all."

It was rather hard work to get the boot off; but at last it was free, and the doctor inspected a double row of red spots, two of which bled a little, but not much.

"I'm beginning to feel now," said Jack dolefully. "Why, he ain't bit it off!" he said, raising himself so that he could look down at the injured member. "I thought it was gone."

"No; your foot has only had an ugly pinch; the stout boot saved it. Let it bleed a little, my lad; it will save you pain."

"What! had he only got hold of my boot?" said Jack excitedly.

"And the foot in it," said the doctor. "See, here are the marks of the teeth."

"I thought he'd bit it right off, Joe Carstairs," said Jack dolefully. "An' I say, what a coward I am!"

"Coward!" I exclaimed. "Why?"

"To be so frightened as I was," replied Jack, with a dismal sigh.

"Well, I don't know about being a coward, Master Jack Penny," said the doctor quietly; "but I do know that if I had had my foot in that reptile's mouth I should have been in a most horrible state of fear. There, my lad," he continued kindly, "don't think any more about it, only to be thankful for your escape."

"But he ought to tell us first how he was caught like that," I said.

"Oh, there ain't much to tell," said Jack, sitting up and raising his leg, and softly rubbing his injured foot. "I was fishing, and the fish wouldn't bite, and I got a little nearer to the river side and threw in again and fished; and the sun seemed to get hotter, and I suppose I fell asleep, for I remember dreaming that the dingoes had got among father's sheep again, and that he flicked his whip-lash round my wrist. Then I tried to start up, but a big fish had hold of the line, and it tugged away so hard that I was overbalanced, and took a header off the bank right into the river; and when I came up, pretty tidy astonished like, and began to swim for the bank, the fish on the line, which I had twisted round my wrist, began tugging me out into the stream. It took me out ever so far before I could get the line off my wrist; and then I swam easily back, feeling awful popped like at having lost the fish and the line; and I was just wondering what you would say, when all at once there was a regular rush in the water, and something shut on my foot, giving me such an awful nip that I yelled out as I caught hold of that branch, and held on, shivering all the while with fear, for I forgot about the crocodiles, and thought it must be a shark."

"Well!" I said, excitedly; for he stopped.

"Well, what?" said Jack.

"What next? What did you do?" I said.

"Hollered!" replied Jack laconically. "So would you if you had been me."

"Yes," I said, "of course; but what took place next?"

"Oh, nothing; only that I held tight and he held tight, and as often as he tugged at me it jumped the bough up and down like a see-saw, and it was very horrid."

"Most horrible!" said the doctor.

"Then I hollered again," said Jack.

"Yes; go on!" I cried impatiently.

"I did go on," he replied. "I went on hollering, but them chaps at the camp were asleep, and I began to feel that I should have to let go soon; only I wouldn't, because I wanted to find out first what had become of the professor. Then at last you came, and that's all; only I don't feel much like walking very far to-day, so I shall sit still and fish."

"Fish! what, with things like that in the water?" I exclaimed.

"Oh! they won't hurt me," said Jack; "because I shall be on the look-out now, and won't go in after the next fish that takes my line. I say, where's Gyp?"

"I don't know," I said. "I have not seen him."

"Crocodiles are very fond of dogs," said Jack quietly. "I hope one of 'em hasn't got Gyp."

"Oh, no! he'd be too sharp for one of the reptiles," said the doctor reassuringly.

"I don't know," said Jack in his quiet drawl. "I thought I was much too clever for crocodiles; but they're sharp—precious sharp about the teeth. Perhaps he's gone hunting something. He often used at home."

"Oh, yes; he'll come back," I said.

"Well, we shall see," said Jack. "I'm better now. Lend me another line, Joe Carstairs. I want to see if I can't catch a fish."

I looked about first to see if I could trace my line, but it was hopelessly gone. To my surprise and pleasure, though, I found the doctor's where he had left it, tied to a root and drawn out tight, evidently with a fish at the end.

I imagined that I could easily draw this out, and I did get it close up to the bank, but as soon as it was in the shallow water it sprang right out and darted away again, making the line rush through my hands so rapidly that it burned my skin.

As it leaped out I had a good opportunity of seeing that a great silvery fellow, fully a yard long, had hooked itself, and meant to have some playing before it turned over upon its side in token of submission.

I kept on playing the fish, which seemed to grow stronger instead of weaker as I went on at give and take with it, till I was almost tired. At least six times did I draw it in and try to bring it within reach of Ti-hi's fingers, but in vain, for it always darted off as if refreshed.

At last, though, I drew it well in, and once more it was about to repeat its tactics; but this time it was too late, for the black pounced down upon it, thrust his hooked finger into its gills, and pulled it up on to the bank.

Just then Jimmy came trotting up, hauling away at a line, and to my great delight I found that he had hunted out the one we had left with Jack Penny.

"Fastum round big wood!" he cried; and then he tried to explain how the fish had entangled the line round what an American would call a snag; and the result was that we had two fine fish to carry back to the camp, Jimmy's being tired out and readily yielding as he hauled on the line.

"I don't think I'll fish to-day," said Jack Penny then. "I say, I feel as if that buck warn't good enough to eat."

Hardly had he spoken before he softly sank down sidewise, and lay looking very white, and with his eyes shut.

"Is it the venison?" I said in a whisper to the doctor.

"No. He is a little faint, now the reaction has set in," replied the doctor; and we had to carry poor wet Jack Penny as well as the fish into camp, and of course we got no farther on our journey that day.

Chapter Fourteen
How a strange Visitor came to Camp

Jack seemed very little the worse after a good night's rest, that is to say bodily. He was a little white, and his breakfast did not disappear so rapidly as usual, for, probably on account of his great length, and the enormous amount of circulation and support to keep up, Jack Penny used to eat about as much as two ordinary boys. He was, however evidently a little bit upset in his mind, and he laid this open to me just before starting once more.

"I say," he said in a low tone, "did I seem such a very great coward yes'day, Joe Carstairs?"

"Coward! No," I said; "not you. Any one would have been frightened."

"But I hollered so," whispered Jack. "I don't think a young fellow ought to holler like a great girl."

"I know I should," I replied. "There, never mind now. They're all ready to start. Come on!"

Jack Penny shook his head rather thoughtfully, and then, in a dissatisfied dreamy way, he walked on with me, shouldering his gun, and stooping more than ever, so that it seemed as if he were looking for something which he could not find.

We had to pass pretty close to the crocodile, so close that Jack nearly stumbled over it, and a cry of horror involuntarily escaped him as he jumped aside.

Then, turning scarlet with annoyance, he gave the monster a kick, and darted back holding his nose, for it was exhaling a most offensive musky odour.

I looked at the creature closely and with some curiosity, thinking the while how much smaller it was than those we had seen in the lagoon. All the same, though, it was fully as big in body as a man, though double the length.

It was not going to poison the air long, for already it was covered with something red, and a long red line extended from it right away into the jungle. Each tiny red object was an ant, and from experience I knew that very soon every particle of flesh would be devoured.

Keeping within easy reach of the river we journeyed steadily on, finding the country grow more beautiful at every step. The trees were bigger, the bamboos taller and more feathery. In the sunny patches flowers were in abundance, and we had no want of opportunities for supplying our larder, large pheasant-like birds, with long tails and crests, and plumage of the most beautiful tints, being plentiful.

It seemed a pity to shoot them, but it was a necessity, for our supply of powder, shot, and ball was looked upon by us as so much condensed meat, ready to be expanded when opportunity served.

We encountered nothing particular that day except Gyp, who turned up all at once with a piece of furry skin in his mouth, all he had been able to carry of some deer that he had run down; and at the sight of his friend Jack Penny became more himself, throwing off a good deal of his gloom. In fact I saw the tears stand in his eyes as he saw him once more; but catching sight of me looking at him he scowled, and, running to the dog, kicked him over and over again quite savagely.

"Just you run away again," he drawled angrily, "and I'll 'bout kill yer. That's what I'll do with you."

Gyp closed his eyes and winced and crouched down close to the ground till his master had ceased punishing him, and then he rose dejectedly, and followed quite in the rear of our party with drooping head and tail.

I noticed at the time that Jimmy had watched all this with sparkling eyes, wonderfully intent, but I thought no more of it till I saw the black glance at us all in turn, and then begin to slink back.

"What is he after now?" I said to myself; and stepping aside among the thick leafage, I let our party go by and stopped to see what Jimmy was about to do.

I had not long to wait, for the fact was that the black had snatched at the opportunity to tyrannise over something. He had been summarily checked when amusing himself by sticking his spear into the New Guinea men, and, as we have seen, one of them resented it; but here was a chance. Gyp had been beaten, and had cowered down under his master's blows, so Jimmy took out his waddy, and after glancing forward to see that he was not observed, he waited until Gyp came up slowly, and casting sidelong looks at the Australian, who gave him a heavy thump on the ribs with the war-club.

"Bad bunyip dog. Good for nothing, dirty dingo dog," cried Jimmy. "Go long, bad for good dog. Get—yah!"

This last was a terrific yell of fear and pain, for instead of cowering down and suffering himself to be beaten and kicked, Gyp knew that this was not his master. For one moment he had stood astonished at the blow, and then seemed puzzled by the strange broken English objurgations; then with a fierce snarl he darted at the black and tried to seize him by the legs, an attack which Jimmy avoided by making a tremendous spring, catching at a horizontal branch above him, and swinging himself up into a tree, where he crouched like a monkey, showering down angry epithets upon the dog as it yelped and barked at him furiously.

I came out of my hiding-place laughing till the tears ran down my cheeks; and the noise made by Gyp brought back the doctor and Jack Penny, the latter taking in the situation at a glance and indulging in a broad grin.

"Take away bunyip dog; take um way or Jimmy killum," cried the black.

"All right!" said Jack Penny; "come down and kill him then."

But Jimmy showed no disposition to move, and it was not until Jack had ordered the dog away that the black dropped down, looking at me very sheepishly and acting like a shamefaced child.

As we proceeded farther into the interior, wild creatures grew more abundant, and we saw fewer traces of man having traversed these regions. As I noted the various objects I could not help feeling how my father must have revelled in exploring such a naturalist's paradise as this, and I grew more hopeful as the idea gained ground in my mind that very likely he was busy in the interior still pursuing his researches.

We travelled very little way now without catching glimpses of some of the occupants of these wilds. Perhaps it was but a glimpse, but generally we were able to distinguish what it was that darted through bush, tree, or shadowy glade. Once or twice we caught sight of the spots of leopards; then a graceful deer would stand at gaze for a moment before going off like the wind. Once a herd of heavy buffaloes started up before us and crashed through the undergrowth; and at last, as we drew near a great tree, the doctor said, pointing upward:

"No fear of our wanting food, Joe, while there are such birds as these."

As he spoke, with a noise like a whirlwind a flock of great pigeons took flight—great fellows, three times as big as ordinary pigeons, and, as we knew from those shot in Australia, splendid eating.

The great tree offered so pleasant a camping place that we decided to pass the night there, and after a look round to see if there was likely to be danger lurking near, the fire was lit, the blacks setting to work at once to collect wood when they had put down their burdens. Then food was prepared and a hearty meal enjoyed, the restful sensation that came over us after the day's exertion being most delicious. Then one by one our followers dropped asleep, Jack Penny, who was still rather grumpy, last.

The doctor and I were sitting together by the fire that night, talking in a low voice about our plans, and agreeing that we could not do better than wander on and on through the wilds until we learned some tidings of the lost man, when suddenly my companion laid his finger on his lips and bent forward as if listening.

I listened too, thinking the while how strange it all looked about us, with the fire casting weird shadows all around, while the silence now was almost appalling.

"Nothing, Joe," said the doctor, dropping his hand. "I thought I heard something."

"I'm sure I did," I whispered, with a strange feeling upon me that it would be dangerous to speak aloud.

"There are curious sounds heard sometimes in forests," he said thoughtfully. "There, go on—what were we talking about?"

As he spoke there was a strange rushing noise, then a peculiar whining sound not far distant among the trees.

"What can that be, doctor?" I whispered.

"Can't say, Joe. Sounds as if some animal had been climbing along a branch, or had bent down a sapling and then let it fly up again with a loud whish among the trees."

"That is just how it sounded to me," I said, gazing full in his eyes.

He remained silent for a few moments, not listening but thinking.

"We must take a lesson from our friend Jack Penny, there," he said, smiling in my face as he stroked his broad beard. "I must confess, Joe, to feeling a curious sensation of awe as we sit out here in this primeval forest, surrounded by teeming savage life; but Jack Penny coolly sleeps through it all, and, as I say, we must take a lesson from him, and get used to these strange sounds."

"There it is again!" I said, catching his arm, and unable to control the feeling that at any moment something might spring out of the darkness upon my back.

For the same curious rustling of leaves came whispering from among the trees, and then there was a low expiration of breath, as if some great beast had yawned.

Click-click, click-click sounded loudly on the night air, and I followed the doctor's example, cocking both barrels of my piece.

"It's coming nearer, whatever it is," said the doctor in a low tone, "and that strange noise means, I think, that it is some great serpent."

"But would serpents be out at night?" I said.

"That one was the other night, Joe, and we must not reckon upon the regular habits of animals if we light great fires in their lairs."

We sat listening again, and the rustling sound began once more.

"It's just as if the thing were climbing along trees that are not strong enough to bear it," I said in an excited whisper, "and they keep flying up after it passes."

"Hush!" said the doctor.

We listened, and from out of the darkest part before us there arose a loud tearing noise as if bark was being scratched from a tree trunk.

"Some kind of beast of the cat family, I should say," whispered the doctor. "Pst! be ready; but don't fire unless we are attacked."

Just then there was a rush, a scramble, a dull thud, and some creature uttered a sound that seemed like the word *Howl* in a hollow echoing tone.

Again and again there was the low rustling, and then that word *Howl* that seemed to come from some great throat; and in imagination I saw in the darkness a pair of fiery eyes and a set of great sharp teeth.

"Yes; some kind of cat, leopard, or panther," said the doctor; but, low as his utterance was, it seemed to irritate the creature in our neighbourhood, as it kept on the rustling, for there was a harsh exclamation and the earth seemed to be torn up.

Then all at once the sound ceased, and it was perfectly still for quite a quarter of an hour, which seemed an endless time; and then, tired of staring intently into the darkness, and too much excited to be silent, I whispered:

"This night-watching is the hardest part of our work, doctor."

"Oh! no, my boy. It makes you a little creepy at first, but as soon as you feel your own power and how you must alarm these creatures, you will get used to it."

"But the fire makes them see us, and we can't see them," I said, in an ill-used tone.

Just then there arose from what seemed to be just the other side of the fire one of the most awful cries I ever heard, and my hair felt as if a tiny cold hand were stirring it about the roots, while a curious sensation ran down my back.

As the fearsome howl rang out the doctor levelled his piece, ready to fire, and as the fire shone full upon him in his half-kneeling position there was something terribly earnest in his face, and he looked so brave that it seemed to give me a little courage just when I seemed to have none.

"Pick up some of those thin branches and throw them on the fire," said the doctor; and I hurried to obey his command, when there was another awful howling roar, and the creature, whatever it was, charged at me; but I threw on the branches all the same, when the fire leaped up with a tremendous blaze, lighting the forest all round.

"See it, doctor?" I whispered.

"No," he answered; "it keeps in amongst the trees."

The doctor's voice sounded so hoarse and strange that it added to my trepidation. He stopped, and I wanted him to go on talking, but he remained silent, while once more the forest resounded with the hideous cry of the beast.

The wood blazed well, so that I could see, as it were, a circle of light, and behind us our black shadows were thrown upon the trees, quite startling me as I looked round.

"Keep up the fire," whispered the doctor; "whatever it is it will not attack while there is this blaze."

I obeyed him and kept on throwing twigs and boughs that had been laid in a heap ready, but with a curious sensation of dread the while, for it seemed to me that if the fire consumed all our wood we should be left at the creature's mercy.

All at once it seemed to me that the rustling and snuffling noise was coming round to our left, and as if I had drawn his attention to the fact, the doctor exclaimed:

"Yes, it is coming on here; keep round this way."

We edged round the fire so as to keep it between us and the animal that seemed to be watching us, when all at once the sound came from close behind us, and, as if moved by one impulse, we bounded past the fire, the pieces I had held in my hand making a crackling blaze and shower of sparks.

This seemed to excite our assailant, which uttered three hideous roars at intervals, and each seemed nearer than the last, so that we were driven to keep on edging round the fire so as to keep it as our shield.

We walked slowly round the fire three times, fully aware of the fact that the creature was regularly stalking us, for it kept up the scratching rustling noise, and howled at intervals.

This was trying enough to our nerves; but when, all at once, every sound ceased, and we stood there by the ruddy blaze, it seemed terrible to know that our enemy was close at hand, but not to know exactly where. At any moment we felt that it might spring upon us, and I turned a wistful look upon the doctor, which he responded to by saying:

"Throw on more wood."

I obeyed him, and the blaze flashed up higher once again, spreading a cloud of sparks on high to rise among the leaves and tinge the broad branches with a ruddy golden glow.

I gazed in all directions for the danger, and started with nervous trepidation every time the doctor spoke, his words being generally— "Throw on more wood." But at last, after a terrible period of anxious silence, he whispered my name.

"Yes," I said.

"This can't go on much longer. I'm afraid the beast is coming nearer. Can you see anything your side?"

"Yes—no—yes, I think so," I whispered back. "There's a shadowy something just at the edge of the light. I think it is some kind of wild beast."

"Is it the dog?" he whispered back.

"No," I said. "Gyp always sleeps close to his master."

"Do you think you could take steady aim at it, my lad?" he said.

"I don't know," I replied, "but I will try. Shall I fire at it?"

"Let me think," he answered. "I don't know whether it would be wise to fire, and perhaps only wound the creature."

"But perhaps I shall kill it," I said.

"It is doubtful, Joe," he replied, "and the noise of your piece would bring out our people, perhaps into danger. Let us wait. Here," he said, "I have it! This beast has been cautiously following us round, always keeping out of our sight. I think now that the best way will be for you to continue the retreat round the fire while I stop here on one knee. The beast will then follow you, and I shall get a good certain shot at him."

I did not like the idea at all, for it seemed like setting a trap and making me the bait; but I said nothing beyond intimating that I would do as he wished, and he went on:

"I shall be certain to hit the brute, but I may not kill, so be ready to fire in turn; you will get a good chance for a sure hit, the animal will be less cautious."

"Stop a moment," I said. "I thought at first that it would be very dangerous for me; now I see that it will be more dangerous for you. Let's keep together."

"Do as I bid you," he replied sternly. "Now go on round, as if trying to keep the fire between you and danger. Fire quickly if you have a good chance, and don't miss. But first of all let's try the effect of a firebrand or two in the direction you think you saw the brute."

He picked up a piece of blazing wood and gave it a whirl round his head.

The result was to bring a fierce roar from the wood close behind us, and we involuntarily sprang to the other side of our fire.

"There's no knowing where to have the beast," muttered the doctor, as he realised the cunning sneaking habits of our enemy.

As he spoke he stooped and picked up another blazing piece of wood, for he had dropped the first to bring his gun to bear. Now, holding the gun in his left hand, he gave the blazing wood a whirl round his head and threw it in the direction from which the fierce roar had come.

To my horror and consternation it was answered by a savage yell, and something charged out nearly to the fire but dashed back directly, so quickly, indeed, that we had no time to get more than a sharp shot apiece at the fierce creature.

"Load again quickly," whispered the doctor; and I obeyed him, listening the while to the rustling crackling noise at a little distance.

"Do you think we hit it?" I said softly. I was afraid to speak aloud lest it should bring down a charge upon us.

"I'm afraid not," he replied, as he reloaded and then stood scanning the edge of the circle of light formed by the fire's glow.

There was nothing visible but what seemed to be a dark opening amongst the trees, through which it appeared to me that our enemy must have passed.

Then we waited, watching so excitedly for the next attack that the fire was for the moment forgotten. Then, seeing the glow it cast become less, we both seized upon armfuls of wood and threw them on, deadening the flame so that the space around was comparatively dark.

That was the most anxious time of all, for, do what we would, the fire sent forth huge volumes of smoke, but would not blaze. At any moment it seemed that the great beast might take advantage of the gloom and spring upon us, and we shook the ends of the burning branches and half-consumed pieces of wood, but in vain. Instead of the light glow there was comparative darkness, and in despair, as if again moved by the same impulse, we ceased troubling about the fire, and stood with hand on trigger, ready to pull at the first chance.

Then all at once there was a vivid tongue of flame cutting right through the thick smoke, another and another, and I uttered a sigh of relief as the heap of smouldering boughs and leaves burst once more into a blaze.

"Now while the light lasts let's have a good shot at the brute," said the doctor, speaking as if nerved to desperation by the torture under which we both writhed. "I'm going to kneel here, Joe; you walk on, and that will make the tiger, or whatever it is, show itself in watching you."

"It isn't a tiger," I whispered. "I caught sight of it, and it looked more like a man."

The doctor gave me a quick look, and then said sharply, "Go on!"

I obeyed him, walking backwards round the fire, my piece ready, so as to get a shot if I saw the creature again; but this time all remained perfectly still, and though I went right round the fire, no sound came from among the trees.

"Take a piece of burning wood and throw it opposite to where you stand, Joe."

I did so, and the blazing wood described an arc, fell in a tuft of dry undergrowth which burst out into a vivid column of light for a few minutes and died out, but there was no charge, no roar from our enemy, not even the rustling of the bushes as it passed through.

"It's very strange, Joe," whispered the doctor. "Pile on more wood."

I obeyed him, and this time it caught directly and there was a tremendous blaze, but no attack followed; and we stood listening for some sound of the enemy in vain.

"You must have shot it," I said, speaking with some confidence.

"Or else you did, Joe," said the doctor.

I shook my head, and we remained listening for quite a quarter of an hour, but still in vain. The silence in the forest was now awful, and though we strained our eyes till the fire across which we looked dazzled them, we could see nothing to cause alarm.

"Either it's dead or it has gone off, scared by our fire," said the doctor at last. And now that we found time to think, he continued, with a smile, "I hope we are not going to have many such night-watches as this on our expedition. I say though, my lad, how some people can sleep! I should have thought that those howls would have wakened anything. Why, hallo! Gyp, didn't you hear anything? Where's your master?"

He stooped and patted the dog, which came trotting up to us, and then yawned and stretched himself out.

"Here I am," said Jack Penny, involuntarily imitating his dog. "Here, where's that chap Jimmy? He was to watch with me, wasn't he? Is it time?"

"Time! Yes," I said impatiently. "You ought to have been here two hours ago. He'll have to look out, won't he, doctor, for that tiger or wild man."

"Yah! stuff!" said Jack with a sneer. "I sha'n't see no— hullo! what has Gyp found? Look, there's something there."

We all turned to see the dog, which had picked up some scent about half-way between the fire and the edge of the circle of light. He ran at once to the thick bushes, barked angrily, and then followed the scent round and round the fire at the distance of about twenty yards, ending by dashing right off into the forest depths, his bark growing fainter as we listened.

"I say, ought we to follow Gyp?" said Jack Penny.

"If we wish to lose our lives," replied the doctor. "You see, Joe, it has gone right off."

"But I don't like Gyp to go off after anything and not follow him," cried Jack Penny. "He's a good dog, you know. What is it he's after?"

"Some savage beast that has been haunting us all night," cried the doctor. "I should like to follow Gyp, but it would be madness, my lads, and—hark, what's that?"

I felt cold as a most unearthly howl came from a long distance away.

"Is—is that him?" said Jack, whose eyes looked round and large.

"Dat big bunyip," said a voice that made us start, for Jimmy had come up from the dark camp unperceived. "Eat black fellow, white man, anyfing."

No one replied to Jimmy's piece of information, and we listened for some minutes till a faint rustling, heard first by the black, who stood ready to hurl his spear, made us all place a finger on the trigger.

But it was only caused by the dog, who soon after came into sight, with his tail between his legs, and his hair bristling with terror.

He ran right to his master and stood behind him, shivering and whining, as he stared in the direction from which he had come.

"Gyp see big bunyip!" cried Jimmy. "Gyp find a bunyip!"

"I say," said Jack; "it's my watch now. I s'pose you two are going to lie down."

"Frightened, Jack?" I said maliciously.

"P'r'aps I am, and p'r'aps I ain't," said Jack stoutly. "I should say I felt frightened if I was; but if you two were going to watch I wouldn't go away and leave you with a big beast like that about. He must be a big one or he wouldn't have frightened Gyp, who'll tackle old man kangaroos six-foot high. You can go if you like, though."

This was a long speech for Jack Penny, who rubbed one of his ears in an ill-used way.

"Jimmy, black fellow 'fraid um bunyip; oh, yes!" said my follower; "but Jimmy no run away."

"We shall not leave you alone, Penny," said the doctor, smiling. "It would not be fair."

So we stayed with him till day broke, and not having heard the slightest sound to intimate the neighbourhood of danger, and the dog lying quite still and content by his master, the doctor and I went to get a couple of hours' rest, just as the forest glades were beginning to echo with the screaming of birds of the parrot family, Jimmy bending over me and poking me with the butt end of his spear, almost directly, so it seemed to me, that I had lain down.

"Jimmy hungry," he said; "gimmy damper—brackfass. Come long."

"Did you hear the bunyip any more, Jimmy?" I said, yawning.

"No. Bunyip go sleep all a morning—all a day! Come a night. How-wow!"

He put his head on one side and gave so marvellous an imitation of the terrible cries I had heard during the night that I felt sure he must know the creature.

"What is it makes that noise, Jimmy?" I said eagerly.

"Bunyip—big ugly fellow bunyip!" he exclaimed; and I felt so cross and annoyed with his eternal bunyip that I was ready to kick him; but I refrained, and went instead to the fire, where the doctor was waiting breakfast, after sending Jimmy to wake me up.

Chapter Fifteen
How Jack Penny was persecuted by Pigs

I have often thought since what a wild journey ours was, and how ignorant we must have been to plunge recklessly and in such a haphazard way into a country that, though an island, is a long way on towards being large enough to be called a continent.

Still we made the venture, and somehow as soon as a peril was passed we all looked upon it as belonging to yesterday, and troubled ourselves about it no more.

I had risen on the morning after our nocturnal adventure feeling despondent and sleepy; but the bright sunshine and the tempting odour of roasting bird stuck on a stick close to the flame, soon made me forget the troubles of the night, and an hour later, with every one in the best of spirits, we made a fresh start, keeping near the river, but beneath the shade of the trees, for the sun seemed to be showering down burning arrows, and wherever we had to journey across the open the heat was intense.

In the shady parts the green of the undergrowth looked delicate and pale, but in the sunshine it was of the most vivid green; and bathing in it, as it were, flies and beetles hummed and buzzed, and beat their gauzy wings, so that they seemed invisible, while wherever there was a bare patch of stony or rocky earth lizards were hurrying in and out, and now and then a drab-looking little serpent lay twisted up into a knot.

The bearers stepped along lightly enough beneath their loads, and I observed that they never looked to right or left, or seemed to admire anything before them, their eyes being always fixed upon the earth where they were about to plant their feet.

Ti-hi in particular tried to warn me to be on the look-out, pointing over and over again to the spade-headed little serpents we saw now and then gliding in amongst the grass.

"Killum," said Jimmy upon one of these occasions, and he suited the word to the action by striking one of these little reptiles with his spear and breaking its back. After this he spat viciously at the little creature, picking it up by its tail and jerking it right away amongst the trees.

"No killum kill all a body," said Jimmy nodding; and he went through a sort of pantomime, showing the consequences of being bitten by a viper, beginning with drowsiness, continuing through violent sickness, which it seemed was followed by a fall upon the earth, a few kicks and struggles, and lastly by death, for the black ended his performance by stretching himself out stiffly and closing his eyes, saying:

"Jimmy dead; black fellow dig big hole and put um in de ground. Poor old Jimmy!"

Then he jumped up and laughed, saying: "Killum all um snake! No good! No!"

"I say, Joe Carstairs," said Jack Penny, who had watched the performance with a good deal of interest; "don't that chap ever get tired?"

"Oh yes; and goes to sleep every time he gets a chance," I said.

"Yes! but don't his back ache? Mine does, horrid, every day, without banging about like that;" and as if he felt his trouble then Jack Penny turned his rueful-looking boy's face to me and began softly rubbing his long man's back just across the loins.

It was very funny, too, when Jack was speaking earnestly. In an ordinary conversation he would go on drawl, drawl, drawl in a bass voice; but whenever he grew excited he began to squeak and talk in a high-pitched treble like a boy, till he noticed it himself, and then he would begin to growl again in almost an angry tone; and this was the case now.

"Here, you're laughing!" he said savagely. "I can't help being tall and thin, and having a gruff voice like a man, when I'm only a boy. I don't try to be big and tall! I grew so. And I don't try to talk gruff."

"Oh yes! you do, Jack," I said.

"Well, p'r'aps I do; but I don't try to talk thin, like I do sometimes."

"I couldn't help laughing, Jack," I said, holding out my hand. "I did not mean to ridicule you."

He gave my hand quite an angry slap and turned away, but only to come back directly.

"Here, I say; I beg your pardon, Joe Carstairs," he said, holding out his hand, which I shook heartily. "I wish I hadn't got such a beastly bad temper. I do try not to show it, but it makes me wild when people laugh at me."

"Well, I won't laugh at you any more, Jack," I said earnestly.

"No, don't; there's a good chap," he said, with the tears in his eyes. "It's partly why I came away from home, you know. I wanted to come and find the professor, of course, and I like coming for the change; but it's principally that."

"Principally *that*!" I said. "I don't understand you, Jack."

"Why, I mean about being laughed at! Everybody has always been laughing at me, because I grew so thin and long and weak-looking, and I got tired of it at last, and was precious glad to come out to New Guinea to stop till I had grown thicker. For I said to myself, I don't s'pose the savage chaps will laugh at me, and if they do I can drop on 'em and they won't do it again."

"It must have been unpleasant, Jack," I said.

"It's horrid, old fellow," he said confidentially; "and all the more because you are obliged to laugh at it all when you feel as if you'd like to double 'em up and jump on 'em."

"Well, there, Jack; I give you my word I won't laugh at you again."

"Will you?" cried Jack, with his face beaming, and looking quite pleasant. "Well, that is kind of you. If the doctor wouldn't laugh either I should be as happy as the day's long."

"I'll ask him not to," I said.

"Oh, no; don't do that!" he cried quickly then; "he'd leave off laughing at me just out of pity, and I'd rather he laughed at me than pitied me, you know. Don't ask him not."

"All right!" I said. "I will not."

"I'd rather he laughed at me," said Jack again thoughtfully; "for I like the doctor; he's such a brave chap. I say, Joe Carstairs, I wish I could grow into a big broad-chested brave chap with a great beard, like the doctor."

"So you will some day."

"Tchah!" he cried impatiently. "Look there—there's long thin arms! There's a pair of legs! And see what a body I've got. I ain't got no looking-glass here, but last time I looked at myself my head and face looked like a small knob on the top of a thin pump."

"You let yourself alone, and don't grumble at your shape," I said sturdily, and to tell the truth rather surprising myself, for I had no idea that I was such a philosopher. "Your legs are right enough. They only want flesh and muscle, and it's the same with your arms. Wait a bit and it will all come, just as beards do when people grow to be men."

"I sha'n't never have any beard," said Jack, dolefully; "my face is as smooth as a girl's!"

"I daresay the doctor was only a little smooth soft baby once," I said; "and now see what he is."

"Ah! ain't he a fine fellow?" said Jack. "I'm going to try and do as he does, and I want to have plenty of pluck; but no sooner do I get into a scrape than I turn cowardly, same as I did over that little humbug of a crocodile."

"Don't talk nonsense, Jack!" I said.

"'Tisn't nonsense! Why, if I'd had as much courage as a wallaby I should have kicked that thing out of the water; and all I did was to lay hold of a bough and holler murder!"

"I didn't hear you," I said.

"Well, *help*! then. I know I hollered something."

"And enough to make you. The doctor said he is sure he should not have borne it so bravely as you."

"No: did he? When?"

"To be sure he did, when we were sitting watching last night."

"Bah! it was only his fun. He was laughing at me again."

"He was not," I said decidedly. "He was in real earnest."

"Oh!" said Jack softly; and there was once more the pleasant light in his countenance that quite brightened it up.

I was going to say something else, but he made a motion with his hand as if asking me to be silent; and he walked on to the front to go behind Ti-hi, who was first man, while I went and marched beside the doctor, and chatted with him about the country and our future prospects.

"It seems, almost too lovely," I said; "and it worries me because I feel as if I ought to be sad and unhappy, while all the time everything seems so beautiful that I can't help enjoying it."

"In spite of perils and dangers, Joe, eh?" he said smiling; and then we went on threading our way amongst the magnificent trees, and every now and then coming upon one standing all alone, its position having allowed of its growing into a perfect state.

Again we came upon one of these, literally alive with parrots; and, as I stopped to admire them, I could see that when they opened their vivid green wings the inner parts were of a brilliant flame colour, and there was a ruddy orange patch upon the little feathers at the inset of their tails.

Then we came upon monkeys again, quite a family of them, and instead of running away and leaping from branch to branch they began to chatter and shriek and dash about in the greatest excitement, just as if they were scolding us for coming among them, chattering among themselves directly after as if meditating an attack.

Before another hour had passed, after noting the beauty of the butterflies, which seemed to increase in number as we penetrated farther into the interior, we came next upon an enormous tree full of gaudily-tinted parroquets, which were nearly as numerous as the parrots of an hour before.

"We sha'n't want for food, Joe," the doctor said, "so long as we have plenty of powder; parroquets and parrots are fruit birds, and splendid eating. Look there."

As he spoke he raised his gun, fired, and directly the report had struck my ears I saw Jimmy and Gyp set off at full speed.

They returned both at odds, the one growling, the other calling his rival a bad bunyip dog, but both holding tightly by a large bird, Gyp having its head, Jimmy the legs.

It proved to be something between a turkey and a pheasant, and from its look it promised to be good eating, for which purpose it was handed over to Ti-hi's care.

The leader now bore off a little to our left, the result being that we once more struck the river, to find it a large swift stream, but not an attractive place for travellers, since from that one spot where we stood beneath the shelter of some trees I counted at least twenty crocodiles floating slowly down, with the protuberances above their eyes just visible, and here and there at least thirty more lying about on the muddy banks.

Towards evening, as we were journeying slowly on, Jimmy came running back to fetch me, and catching me by the hand he led me through some bushes to where a thickly wooded park-like stretch of land began, and motioning me to be silent and follow him he crept from tree to tree, till, having reached what he considered to be a satisfactory position, he pointed upward, and from behind the tree where we were ensconced I looked among the branches far overhead, and for the first time saw one of those wonderfully plumaged creatures—the birds of paradise.

I could have stopped there for long, gazing at the beautiful creatures with their fountain-like plumage of pale gold, but time would not permit of my lagging behind, and to Jimmy's great disgust I hurried back, and determined that no object should lead me away from the great aim of our journey.

The turkey was ample as a meal for us, but we wanted food for our followers, so as to husband our flour and biscuits. Birds were all very well, but we wanted to kill something more substantial, and for a long time past we had seen no sign of deer, though traces of buffalo were pretty frequent in spots where they had made a peculiar track down to the river, evidently going regularly to quench their thirst.

The sight of the buffalo tracks formed the subject of a discussion. Fresh meat was wanted for our followers, who made very light of birds, and one of these animals would have been invaluable to us just then; but the doctor decided that it would not be prudent to follow them, they being rather dangerous beasts, and therefore, though the meat would have been so useful both for present use and to dry in the sun, we gave up the idea of trying to obtain any, preferring to trust to finding deer, and continued our journey.

We had gone very little farther, and I was just about to propose to the doctor that we should venture as far as the river and try for some fish, when there was an alarm given by the native who was leading, and in an instant loads were thrown down and every man sought refuge in a tree.

We did not understand the natives' words, but their actions were easy enough to read, and all followed their example, the doctor and I getting up into the same tree, one which forked very low down, and we were just in safety when we heard a cry, and saw that Jack Penny was in difficulties. He too had climbed part of the way into a tree, when he had slipped, and in spite of all his efforts he could not at first contrive to get back; and this was just as a rushing noise was heard, that I thought must be a herd of buffalo, but, directly after, a drove of small wild pig came furiously charging down.

My attention was divided between the sight of the pigs and Jack Penny, whose long legs kept dropping down, and then being spasmodically snatched up.

I burst into a roar of laughter, and Jimmy, who was standing, spear in hand, upon a branch, holding on by another, danced with excitement and delight.

"Pull yourself right up, Jack," I shouted, and I had hard work to make my voice heard above the grunting and squealing.

"I can't," he yelled back.

"Then kick out at the little brutes," I shouted; and just then he lowered himself to the full length of his arms, swung to and fro, and half-a-dozen pigs rushed at him, but he had gained impetus, and just as they made a dash at him he swung his legs up, and clung with them to a branch.

"Hurrah!" I shouted; and then a sharp squeal uttered by one unfortunate pig as Jimmy drove his spear through it as it passed beneath his feet, and the sharp report of the doctor's piece, brought me to my senses.

The scene had been so comical, especially as regarded Jack Penny, that I had forgotten that I was letting several good dinners slip away, and I had just time to get a quick shot at one of the pigs which was stamping his hoof and grunting defiantly at Jack Penny, before the whole drove, including one that had received an arrow from Ti-hi's bow, swept by us as hurriedly as they came, and were gone.

"Not hurt, are you, Jack?" I said, preparing to jump.

"Keep your place," cried the doctor; "they may come back."

"Well, I shall have a better shot at them," I said.

"You foolish boy!" cried the doctor. "Why, the boars would rip you to pieces."

I returned to my place at this, and it was fortunate that I did so, for directly after, as if in the wildest of haste, the pig drove came dashing back, to stop as hastily as they came up, and stand snapping, tossing their heads, grunting, squealing, and at times literally barking at us.

A couple of shots which laid low one of their party seemed, however, to scare them, and they dashed on once more, and hardly had they gone twenty yards before there was a loud thud and Jack Penny fell from the branch, where he had been clinging, flat upon his back.

"Oh my!" he cried, as he sat up and looked about. "I couldn't hold on any longer. It's lucky they are gone."

"Look out!" I cried, swinging myself down, dropping my gun, and pulling my hatchet from my belt; but Jack would have fared badly if he had depended on me.

For the little boar that had been wounded by an arrow, had dropped, apparently dying, when its companions swept by the second time, but it had fierce life enough left in it to take advantage of Jack Penny's helpless condition, and leaping up it charged at him, its tusks glistening, and the foam tossed from its snapping jaws falling upon its sides.

A bullet would have given the fierce beast its quietus, but the doctor would not fire for fear of hitting Jack, and he sat with his gun raised waiting for an opportunity.

Jack saw his danger and rolled himself over, trying vainly the while to drag his axe from his belt. Then just as the furious little boar was dashing at him, I saw something black dart down from above; there was a rush, a squeal, and the boar was literally pinned to the earth, while Jimmy stood grinning and staring from the doctor to me and back, as if asking to be complimented upon his feat. For it really was a feat. He had jumped fully ten feet to the ground spear in hand, and literally thrown himself upon the little boar.

"A magnificent jump, Jimmy," I cried.

"Jimmy de boy to jump," he said, complacently. "Pig, pig kill Mass Jack Penny, Jimmy no spear um."

"Yes, I 'spect I should have ketched it pretty warmly," said Jack, gathering himself up. "Oh, I say, I did come down such a bump, Joe Carstairs. It seemed to shake my back joints all to pieces."

"Jimmy spear um lil pig, pig," said the black.

"Yes, and I'll give you my knife for it," said Jack, taking out his great clasp-knife. "It's a real good one, Jimmy, and I wouldn't have parted with it for a deal."

"Jimmy got knife," said the black, with a contemptuous look. "Jimmy don't want knife."

"Well, then, what shall I give you?" said Jack.

"Tickpence," said he, grinning; "give Jimmy tickpence."

"Why, what for?" I cried. "What are you going to do with *tick* pence?"

"Spend um," said Jimmy; "black fellow spend money, money. Give Jimmy all a tickpence."

"But there's nowhere to spend it," I said.

"Nev mind, Jimmy spend tickpence all a same. Give Jimmy tickpence."

Jack had not a single coin about him, neither had I, but fortunately the doctor had one, which he handed to Jack, who gave it to the delighted black, and it was forthwith thrust into the pocket of the curtailed trousers, after which he strutted about, leaving the other blacks to perform the duty of dressing the pigs.

Chapter Sixteen
How Jimmy was taken very bad indeed

This sudden supply of food necessitated our making camp where we were, and cutting the meat up into strips to dry, while, apparently on the principle of making their hay while the sun shone, the blacks lit a fire and had a tremendous feast, both Jack Penny and I laughing heartily to see the solemn face of Jimmy as he devoted himself to the task of storing up an abundance of food, ready for emergencies.

At our table, as the doctor called it, we contented ourselves with the turkey-like bird, which was delicious, but we tasted the wild pig, a piece of which, fairly well roasted, was brought to us in the most solicitous manner by Ti-hi, who smiled contentedly as he saw us begin to partake thereof.

We set it aside, though, as soon as the black had gone, for the doctor pronounced it strong and musky, and Jack Penny behaved very rudely, according to the ordinary etiquette of the dinner table, and exclaimed:

"Oh, law!"

It was a glorious sunset, and the place where we were encamped, as we styled it, was once more beneath a huge tree. For a time I was listening to the birds' screams and cries from the forest, and then all at once they ceased, and a long-drawn howl, which recalled the horrors of our night-watch, arose from a distance. Then the sun sank, and darkness began to come on very quickly. First the sky paled and a star or two began to twinkle, then all above us was of a deep intense purple, studded and encrusted with points of dazzling light, and, like the doctor, tired out with loss of rest, I began to yawn.

For our evenings were not devoted to amusements. Our day only had two divisions, that for work and that for rest. As soon as the arduous toil of the day was over, and we had partaken of food, we were ready for sleep; so this time Jack Penny was set to watch with Ti-hi and Gyp, and we lay down on a bough-made bed.

One moment I was lying on my back gazing up at the stars, and first thinking of my mother and how anxious she must be as to how I was getting on; then wondering where my father was likely to be, and whether we were going to work in the best way to find him; the next moment I was dreaming that Gyp had run after and caught a wild man of the woods by the tail, and had dragged him into camp, howling dismally.

It did not fit into my dream that wild men of the woods were not likely to be possessed of tails for Gyp to tug, and if they were, that they would have striven to crush the dog by one blow of the hand; my dream arranged itself, and the howling was continued as I started up, all wakefulness, and saw a dark figure bending over me and looking colossal as seen against the ruddy light of the fire.

"Is that you, doctor?" I said.

"Yes, Joe; wake up. I want you."

"What's the matter—has that horrible thing come again?"

"No," he said; "the black is very bad."

"What! old Jimmy?" I cried.

"Yes. That is he howling."

I jumped up with a curious sensation of suffocation at my chest, for, startled from a deep sleep into wakefulness, it occurred to me that something dreadful was going to happen, and that we were to lose the true-hearted, merry, boyish companion of so many years. Like a flash there seemed to come back to me the memory of dozens of expeditions in which he had been my faithful comrade, and this was like a death-blow to our hopes, for, in spite of his obstinacy and arrogance, Jimmy would have laid down his life to serve me.

"Let us go to him, doctor," I said. "Make haste!"

Our way to the black lay past the camp fire, where Jack Penny was sitting with Ti-hi, and the former spoke excitedly as we drew near:

"I say, doctor, do make haste and give him a dose of something to do him good, or else put him out of his misery."

"Jack!" I said in disgust.

"Well, he's awful bad, you know, and he ought to have something. Mind how you go to him. I went just now and he began hitting at my legs with his waddy, and then he poked at Gyp with his spear for going up to smell him."

"He won't hurt me," I said sadly; and as another doleful cry came from among the bushes, I led the way to where the poor fellow lay, horribly swollen and writhing in agony.

Two of the blacks were watching him, and from what we could make out it seemed that Jimmy had alarmed them by his restlessness, and that they had fetched him back when he ran some distance and fell, and laid him where he now was, in too much agony to stir.

"What is the matter with him, doctor?" I said excitedly, as I went down on one knee and took the poor fellow's hand, which he grasped convulsively, and laid flat directly upon his chest—at least that is to say, nearly.

"I hardly know yet, my lad," said the doctor. "Perhaps he has eaten some poisonous berry. You know how he tastes every wild fruit we pass."

"And will it—will it—"

I could say no more, for something seemed to choke my voice, and I looked up imploringly in the doctor's eyes.

"Oh! no, Joe, my lad," he said kindly, "not so bad as that."

"Jimmy bad as that—Jimmy bad as that," moaned the poor fellow; and as just then Jack Penny threw some light twigs upon the fire, the blaze showed me the swollen and distorted countenance of my poor companion, and a strange chill of apprehension came over me.

We watched by him all night, but he grew worse towards morning, and at last he lay apparently stupefied, free from pain, but as if the berry, or whatever it was that he had swallowed, had rendered him insensible.

Of course, continuing our journey was out of the question, so all we could do was to make the rough brushwood pallet of the sufferer more comfortable by spreading over it a blanket, and I did little else but watch by it all the day.

I felt hurt two or three times by the rough, unfeeling manner in which the doctor behaved towards the black, and I could not help thinking that if Jimmy had been a white man the treatment would have been different.

This worried me a good deal, for it seemed so different to the doctor's customary way; but I took comfort from the fact that poor Jimmy was as insensible to pain as he was to kindness, and in this state of misery I hardly left him all day.

Towards evening the doctor, who had spent the time overhauling and cleaning our guns and pistols, came to me and insisted upon my going to Jack Penny, who had just got a good meal ready.

"But I am not a bit hungry, doctor," I cried.

"Then go and eat against you are," he said. "Lay in a moderate store, and don't," he added meaningly, "don't eat more than is good for you."

I looked at him wonderingly, and got up without a word, feeling more hurt and annoyed with him than ever, and the more so as he looked at me with a peculiar smile as he twisted a stout cane about in his hands.

"How's Jimmy?" said Jack Penny.

"Dying," I said sadly, as I took my seat before him.

"Oh! I say, not so bad as that, Joe Carstairs! It takes a lot to kill a fellow like Jimmy. He'll come all right again. Here, set to and have a good feed. You must want it awfully."

"I can't eat," I said bitterly. "I liked poor old Jimmy. A better fellow never breathed. He saved your life yesterday."

"Ah! that he did," said Jack; "and it's all right. The doctor says—Hullo! what's that?"

I started to my feet, for a horrible scream rang through the woods from the direction where poor Jimmy lay; and a pang shot through me as I felt that it was a new throe being suffered by my poor black comrade—comrade soon to be no more.

Chapter Seventeen
How the Doctor gave Jimmy his Physics

I could not move for a few moments, the terrible cry and the shrieks that followed seemed to rob me of all power; but overcoming this paralysing feeling at last, I ran towards where poor Jimmy lay, the thought flashing upon my mind that the doctor must be performing some operation to try and save the poor fellow's life.

I was quite right, as I found when I reached the spot, followed by all the little camp: the doctor was performing an operation, and the Australian was upon his knees now, his feet then, capering about, and appealing for mercy.

For the instrument with which the doctor was performing his operation was the stout cane I had previously seen in his hand, one that he had cut in the jungle, and then sent me away so as to spare my feelings and keep me from witnessing the painful sight.

To my utter astonishment Jimmy was apparently free from all traces of his late ailment, and catching sight of me he bounded to me, getting behind me to avoid the hail of blows that the doctor was showering upon his unprotected person.

"Doctor!" I shouted.

"The dose to be repeated," he said, "when necessary," and he reached round me with the cane, giving Jimmy two or three very sharp cuts. "See how this takes down the swelling. For outward application only. One dose nearly certain to cure."

"What are you doing?" I cried.

"Doing? Performing a wonderful cure. Hasn't Jimmy here been horribly ill, and alarmed the whole camp?"

Every time he could he gave Jimmy a smart cut, and the black shrieked with pain.

"How are you now, my man?" he said mockingly.

"Jimmy quite as well. Ever so better. All rightums. Tank you better," yelled the black, and he sheltered himself again behind my back.

"Doctor," I said, surprised and angry at what seemed horrible cruelty.

"Give him some more?" he said laughing. "Of course I will," and he tried to reach round me, but I caught hold of the cane, and Jimmy took advantage of the cessation of hostilities for a moment to run for some distance and then climb up a tree, in one of the higher branches of which he settled himself like a monkey, and sat rubbing himself and looking down at the danger from which he had escaped.

"There, Joe," said the doctor, laughing; "it has made me hot. That's as good a cure as the Queen's physician could have made."

"How could you be so brutal to the poor wretch?" I said indignantly.

"Brutal! Ha! ha! ha! My indignant young hero!" he cried. "Here are you going to take up the cudgels in the rascal's behalf. Don't you see there was nothing the matter with the artful black ruffian."

"Nothing the matter!" I said. "Why, wasn't he dangerously ill?"

"Dangerously full," said the doctor, clapping me on the shoulder. "I was obliged to give him a lesson, Joe, and it will do him good for all our trip. I suspected the rascal from the very first, but I have studied medicine long enough to know how easy it is to be deceived by appearances; so I gave Master Jimmy the benefit of the doubt, and treated him as if he was really very ill, till I had made assurance doubly sure, and then I thrashed him."

"What! do you really mean, doctor—" I began.

"It could not very well have happened with an Englishman, Joe. With Master Jimmy there, it was different."

"But was he not very ill?"

"You saw him run and climb that tree; you heard how he yelled. Now what do you think? Could a dying man do that?"

"N–no," I faltered. "What does it all mean, then?"

"Pig!" said the doctor, smiling; "the gluttonous dog ate till he could not stir. He had as much as anybody else, and then waited his chance, and when every one was lying down he began upon the store of dried strips."

"Jimmy terribull sorry, Mass Joe," came from up the tree.

"He behaved like a boa constrictor, and then alarmed us all horribly instead of confessing the truth. Why, my dear boy, do you suppose I should have been so cruel to a sick man?"

"You black rascal!" I cried, looking up at Jimmy, who howled like a dog.

"Jimmy come down now! Never do so no more."

"Only let me have a turn at you," I said, and he immediately began to climb higher.

"Here, you come down, sir," I shouted.

For answer he climbed higher and higher till he was pretty well out of sight among the small branches in the top of the tree.

"All right!" I said, "I can wait;" and I walked away with the doctor, horribly annoyed at the waste of time, but wonderfully relieved at matters being no worse.

I never knew, but I suspect that Jimmy stopped in the top of the tree till it was dark and then slunk down and hid himself amongst the bushes close up to the watch-fire.

At all events he was busy the next morning working away as if nothing had been wrong overnight. He showed himself to be most active in putting things straight, making up the loads, and every now and then glancing furtively first at one of us and then at the other.

"Oh, I do like Jimmy, that I do," said Jack Penny to me, and then he threw himself down and began to laugh heartily, shutting his eyes and rolling himself gently to and fro till he declared that he felt better, and got up.

"I don't care about laughing when I'm standing up," he said seriously, "it waggles my back so."

When breakfast time came, for we had a seven or eight mile walk first in the cool of the early morning, we made a halt and the rations were served out by the doctor, who gave me a look and handed each black his portion in turn, but omitted Jimmy.

The latter stood disconsolately looking on for some minutes in the hope that he was to be remembered after all; but when he saw everybody busy at work eating and himself utterly neglected, he walked slowly away some distance from where we were seated and, laying his head against the trunk of a tree, let out a series of the most unearthly howls.

"Oh, I say!" exclaimed Jack Penny.

"Pleasant," said the doctor, going on with his breakfast; and seeing that he was observed, and that his howls were having some effect, Jimmy displayed the utter childlike disposition of a savage by redoubling his cries.

"If he don't stop directly I shall go and talk to him with this," I said, snatching up a stick.

"How—aw—ooo!" cried Jimmy, and I jumped to my feet, when he became silent, and I resumed my place.

Jimmy watched us eagerly for a few minutes, when, left half starved himself, and unable to bear the neglect when others were enjoying themselves, the howls burst out again followed by a self-commiserating— "Poor Jimmy, Mass Joe not care poor Jimmy never now."

No one took any notice, and we went on eating grilled turkey and damper and drinking coffee, and all the time I was rather enjoying my importance and the fact of being able to control, boy as I was, a stout powerful fellow like Jimmy and make him as obedient as a dog.

"Poor old Jimmy cut handums. Ebber so sorry, poor Jimmy. Go and die himself. Haw—ow!"

"I say," said Jack Penny, "he couldn't dye himself any blacker, could he, Joe Carstairs?"

"Have some more coffee, Joe?" said the doctor aloud. "Here, give me a piece more turkey."

"Poor Jimmy go starve a deff," was the next that met our ears, and it had such an effect upon Jack Penny that some of his coffee got into his windpipe and he choked and coughed and laughed till he was obliged to lie down.

"If I was to cough much like that I should break my back," he said, sitting up and wiping his eyes. "Poor old Jimmy? I do like him. He *is* a one."

Jimmy stood watching the disappearing food, then he sat down. Then he lay at full length; but no one took the slightest notice, for the blacks were selfishly busy, and we were keeping up the punishment for the false alarm to which our follower had subjected us.

At last this attack upon Jimmy's tenderest part—his appetite—grew to be more than he could bear, and he sat up in the squatting attitude so much affected by savages.

"Ah!" he exclaimed dolefully, "poor black fellow—poor Jimmy!" and this started Jack Penny off laughing once more, which so exasperated Jimmy that he sprang up as sharply as if stung, and ran in a rage to where his black companions were eating their food.

"Here, hi! you black fellow, Jimmy done wid him. Jimmy gib boomerang. You no fro down wallaby."

He held out his curious hard-wood weapon to Ti-hi, who took it, gazing at him wonderingly, while Jimmy glanced at us to see if we were about to relent and give him some breakfast.

"Jimmy going," he said at last, loud enough for us to hear; but we paid no heed.

"Jimmy going; nebber come back no more," he said in a louder voice; but no one turned a head.

"Jimmy go jump river. Big bunyip crocodile come eat poor Jimmy. All um very sorry. No see poor Jimmy not nev more."

He glanced at us again, but we were laughing over our breakfast, though not so busy but that we were able to see the black fold his arms and stalk away, evidently under the impression that we should start up and arrest him; but no one moved.

"Big water bunyip glad get black fellow," he said, as loudly as he could, and with a scornful look at us.

"Here, suppose we go," said the doctor, rising.

"Go?" said Jack, getting up slowly, "where to?"

"To see Jimmy feed the crocodiles. Come along, lads."

Jimmy stopped short with his jaw dropped, and nearly beside himself with rage. He seemed to be completely staggered at our cool way of taking things, and at last he ran off like the wind, rushed back again with his eyes flashing, and slapping his legs as he darted upon Ti-hi, waddy in hand.

"Gib boomerang Jimmy, black tief fellow," he roared. "Take a boomerang. Jimmy boomerang. Tief fellow tole a boomerang."

Snatching it from Ti-hi's hand he made believe to strike him with the curious weapon and then rushed off with it into the bush.

"Well, Joe," said the doctor, "do you think the crocodiles will dine on blackbird?"

I shook my head.

"What do you say, Jack Penny, eh?"

"Jimmy won't jump in, I know," drawled Jack.

"You're right," said the doctor; "he'll come back before long hungry as a hunter, and regularly tamed down or I'm no judge of character."

"Yes," I said, "and he'll bring back something he has killed so as to try and make friends. That's how he always did at home."

"Well," said Jack Penny solemnly, "I hope he will. I like Jimmy, he makes me laugh, and though it hurts my back I like laughing. It does me good. I never used to have anything to laugh at at home. Father used to laugh when he kicked me, but it never seemed funny to me, and I never used to laugh at that."

"Well, Jack Penny, I dare say the black will give you something to laugh at before long, for I don't suppose it will be long before he is back."

Chapter Eighteen
How I nearly had an Arrow to drink

We were soon on the way towards the interior again, and the doctor and I had set to work trying to obtain some information from Ti-hi, and also from Aroo, another intelligent looking follower who had been one of the prisoners made by the captain of the burnt schooner.

It was hard work, but we were daily getting to understand more and more of the commoner words of conversation, and by degrees we managed to make out that the reason why we had not come upon any native village was that the nearest was still many days' journey distant, but that if we changed our course and went down to the sea-shore we should soon find signs of occupation.

But I felt that this would be of no use, for if my father had been anywhere on the coast he must have come in contact sooner or later with one or other of the trading vessels, whose captains, even if they could not bring him away on account of his being a prisoner, would certainly have reported somewhere that they had seen a white captive, and the news must have spread.

"He must be right in the interior somewhere," I said; "and I'm sure we can't do better than keep on."

"I think you are right, Joe," said the doctor thoughtfully.

"I feel sure I am," I said. "I don't expect to find him directly; but I mean to go on trying till I do."

"That's the way to find anybody," said Jack Penny. "You're sure to find 'em if you keep on like that. Come along."

Jack went off; taking great strides as if he expected to be successful at once; but he did not keep up the pace long, but hung back for me to overtake him, saying:

"I say, Joe Carstairs; does your back ever ache much?"

"No," I said; "very little. Only when I'm very tired."

"Ah! you ain't got so much back as I have," he said, shaking his head. "When you've got as much as I have you'll have the back-ache awfully, like I do. I say, I wonder where old Jimmy has got to."

"He's close at hand somewhere," I said. "Depend upon it he has not gone far. If the truth were known," I continued, "he's walking along abreast of us, just hidden in the bushes."

"Think so?" said Jack dubiously.

"I'm about sure of it," I replied.

"I ain't," said Jack. "I'm afraid he's gone right away back; and we've offended him so that we sha'n't see him any more."

"You keep your opinion, Jack, and I'll keep to mine. I say, I wonder what that noise is!"

"Noise! Birds," said Jack.

"No, no! That dull murmur. There, listen!"

"Wind in the trees."

"No, I'm sure it is not!" I exclaimed. "There! it is gone now. It is like far-off thunder."

"Water," said the doctor, who had closed up with us unperceived. "I've been listening to it, and it sounds to me like a waterfall. Depend upon it we shall find that the river comes down over some pile of rocks, and if we were clear of the forest and could take a good look round we should find that the country is growing mountainous on ahead."

It seemed during the next day's journey that the doctor was right, for we were certainly ascending, the land growing more rugged and toilsome, but at the same time far more beautiful and full of variety. In place of always journeying on through thick forest or park-like stretches, we now found our way was among stony ridges and long heavy slopes, with here and there a lovely valley, so full of beauty that I used to think to myself that perhaps we should find my father had built himself a hut in some such place as this, and was patiently going on with his collecting.

We had seen nothing of Jimmy for three days, and though I suspected him of being close at hand, and coming to our camp at night stealthily in search of food, it really began to appear as if he had left us for good, when an adventure towards evening showed us who was correct in his surmise.

"I don't think much of the doctor's waterfall," Jack said to me, in his dry drawling way.

"Why, we haven't seen it!" I replied.

"No, nor we ain't going to, seemingly. It's wind amongst the trees."

"Don't be so obstinate," I said, listening intently to hear the heavy thunderous murmur still, now I listened for it, though I had not seemed to notice it before.

"There ain't no waterfall," he replied, "or we should have seen it before now."

"Perhaps the shape of the land keeps us from getting near it, or perhaps the wind drives the sound away."

"Or perhaps the sound drives the wind away, or perhaps the— Look out, Joe, look out!"

Jack Penny leaped aside nimbly, and I followed his example, hardly escaping, while the man in front of me, less quick in his motion consequent upon his having a load upon his head, was sent flying by a great slate-coloured buffalo which had suddenly charged us from behind a clump of trees where it had been lying.

It all happened so quickly that I had not time to think of my gun, while the doctor was fifty yards behind, and could not have fired had he been able to see, for fear of hurting us.

The great beast had stopped for a moment after sending our bearer flying, and then, seeing him down, snorted a little, lowered his head, and would doubtless have tossed and trampled him to death had there not suddenly come a whirring whizzing noise from some bushes in a hollow on our right, when something struck the buffalo a heavy blow upon the muzzle, making it turn up its head, utter a furious roar, and charge at the bushes.

This was my opportunity, and taking a quick aim I fired, and heard the bullet strike with a heavy thud, when the buffalo seemed to drop upon its knees on the steep slope, and literally turned a somersault, crashing with a tremendous noise into some trees; and then, to my astonishment, rising again and going off at a lumbering gallop.

It did not go far, for just then there was the sharp crack of the doctor's piece, and once more the buffalo fell heavily, to lie struggling, while, to my astonishment I saw a familiar black figure bound out of the bushes, catch up the boomerang he had thrown, and then race after the buffalo, which he reached just as the doctor also came up and put it out of its misery by a merciful shot in the head.

"Jimmy killum! Jimmy boomerang killum!" shouted the black, dancing on the prostrate beast, while Jack and I were busy helping the poor bearer to his feet, and making sure that though stunned he was not seriously hurt.

"No," said the doctor. "No bones broken. It's wonderful what some of these savage races will bear."

He ceased his examination and gave the poor fellow a friendly clap on the shoulder, while, after lying down for a time in the new camping-ground, close up to the welcome supply of meat, the injured man was sufficiently recovered to sit up, and eat his share of roast buffalo flesh.

Some delicious steaks which we cooked proved very welcome to us by way of a change, but we did not commence without a few words with Master Jimmy, who was all smiles and friendliness now with everybody, till the doctor said, pointing to the abundant supply of meat:

"No more bad illness, Jimmy. You are not to eat much."

"Jimmy won't eat not bit!" he cried viciously. "Go in a bush and starve a deff."

"There, sit down and eat your supper!" said the doctor sternly; "and no more nonsense, please."

The black looked at him in a sidelong fashion, and his fingers played with the handle of his waddy, which was behind him in his waistband, and then he quailed beneath the doctor's steady gaze, and sat down humbly by the camp fire to cook and eat what was really a moderate quantity for an Australian black.

Next morning we were off at daybreak, our way lying up a narrow ravine for a short distance, and then between a couple of masses of rock, which seemed to have been split apart by some earthquake; and directly we were through here the dull humming buzz that we had heard more or less for days suddenly fell upon our ears with a deep majestic boom that rose at times, as the wind set our way, into a deafening roar.

I looked triumphantly at Jack Penny, but he only held his head higher in the air and gave a sniff, lowering his crest directly after to attend to his feet, for we were now in a complete wilderness of rocks and stones, thrown in all directions, and at times we had regularly to climb.

"It is useless to bring the men this way," the doctor said, after a couple of hours' labour; but as he spoke Ti-hi called a halt and pointed in a different direction, at right angles to that which we had so far followed, as being the one we should now take.

The sun had suddenly become unbearable, for we were hemmed in by piled-up stones, and its heat was reflected from the brightly glistening masses, some of which were too hot even to be touched without pain, while the glare was almost blinding wherever the rocks were crystalline and white.

"I say, is that a cloud?" said Jack Penny, drawing our attention to a fleecy mass that could be seen rising between a couple of masses of rock.

"Yes!" cried the doctor eagerly, as he shaded his eyes from the sun's glare; "a cloud of spray. The falls are there!"

"Or is it the wind you can see in the trees?" I said, with a look at Jack Penny.

"Get out!" retorted that gentleman. "I didn't say I was sure, and doctor isn't sure now."

"No, not sure, Penny," he said; "but I think I can take you to where water is coming down."

We felt no temptation to go on then, and willingly followed our guides, who pointed out a huge mass of overhanging rock right in the side of the ravine, and here we gladly halted, in the comparatively cool shade, to sit and partake of some of the buffalo strips, my eyes wandering dreamily to right and left along the narrow valley so filled with stones.

I was roused from my thoughts about the strangeness of the place we were in and the absence of trees and thick bush by the doctor proposing a bit of a look round.

"We are getting up among the mountains, Joe," he said; "and this means more difficult travelling, but at the same time a healthier region and less heat."

"Oh, doctor!" I said, wiping my forehead.

"Why, it couldn't be any hotter than it is out there!" said Jack.

"Come with us, then, and let's see if we can find a fresh way out. Perhaps we may hit upon a pass to the open country beyond. At all events let's go and see the falls."

We took our guns, leaving all heavy things with the blacks, who were settling themselves for a sleep.

The sun's heat almost made me giddy for the first hundred yards, and either my eyes deceived me or Jack Penny's long body wavered and shook.

But we trudged laboriously on over and among masses of rock, that seemed to be nearly alive with lizards basking in the sun, their curious coats of green and grey and umber-brown glistening in the bright sunshine, and looking in some cases as if they were covered with frosted metal as they lay motionless upon the pieces of weatherworn stone.

Some raised their heads to look at us, and remained motionless if we stopped to watch them, others scuffled rapidly away at the faintest sound, giving us just a glimpse of a quivering tail as its owner disappeared down a crevice almost by magic.

"Don't! don't fire!" cried the doctor, as Jack suddenly levelled his piece.

"Why not?" he said in an ill-used tone. "I daresay they're poison and they ain't no good."

The object that had been his aim was an ash-grey snake, rather short and thick of form, which lay coiled into the figure of a letter S, and held its head a few inches from the rock on which it lay.

"If you wish to kill the little vipers do it with a stick, my lad. Every charge of powder may prove very valuable, and be wanted in an emergency."

"I say," said Jack Penny, dropping the butt of his piece on the rock, leaning his arms upon it, and staring at the speaker. "You don't think we are likely to have a fight soon, do you?"

"I hope not," said the doctor; "but we shall have to be always on the alert, for in a land like this we never know how soon danger may come."

"I say, Jack," I whispered, "do you want to go back?"

"No: I don't want to go back," he said with a snort. "I don't say I ain't afraid. P'r'aps I am. I always thought our place lonely, but it was nothing to these parts, where there don't seem to be no living people at all."

"Well, let's get on," said the doctor, smiling; and we threaded our way as well as we could amongst the chaotic masses of stones till we were stopped short by a complete crack in the stony earth, just as if the land had been dragged asunder.

As we stood on the brink of the chasm, and gazed down at the bottom some hundred feet below, we could see that it was a wild stony place, more sterile than that we had traversed. In places there were traces of moisture, as if water sometimes trickled down, and where this was the case I could see that ferns were growing pretty freely, but on the whole the place was barrennesss itself.

It seemed to have a fascination though for Jack Penny, who sat down on the edge and dangled his long legs over the rock, amusing himself by throwing down pieces of stone on to larger pieces below, so as to see them shatter and fall in fragments.

"Snakes!" he said suddenly. "Look at 'em. See me hit that one." He pitched down a large piece of stone as he spoke, and I saw something glide into a crevice, while another reptile raised itself up against a piece of rock and fell back hissing angrily.

We were so high up that I could not tell how big these creatures were, but several that we noticed must have been six or seven feet long, and like many vipers of the poisonous kinds, very thick in proportion.

I daresay we should have stopped there amusing ourselves for the next hour, pitching down stones and making the vipers vicious; but our childish pursuit was ended by the doctor, who clapped Jack on the shoulder.

"Come, Jack," he said, "if we leave you there you'll fall asleep and topple to the bottom."

Jack drew up his legs and climbed once more to his feet, looking very hot and languid, but he shouldered his piece and stepped out as we slowly climbed along the edge of the chasm for about a quarter of a mile, when it seemed to close up after getting narrower and narrower, so that we continued our journey on what would have been its farther side had it not closed.

Higher and higher we seemed to climb, with the path getting more difficult, save when here and there we came upon a nice bare spot free from stones, and covered with a short kind of herb that had the appearance of thyme.

But now the heat grew less intense. Then it was comparatively cool, and a soft moist air fanned our heated cheeks. The roar of the falls grew louder, and at any moment we felt that we might come upon the sight, but we had to travel on nearly half a mile along what seemed to be a steep slope. It was no longer arid and barren here, for every shelf and crevice was full of growth of the most vivid green. For a long time we had not seen a tree, but here tall forest trees had wedged their roots in the cracks and crevices, curved out, and then shot straight up into the air.

The scene around was beautiful, and birds were once more plentiful, dashing from fruit to flower, and no doubt screaming and piping according to their wont, but all seemed to be strangely silent, even our own voices sounded smothered, everything being overcome by the awful deep loud roar that came from beyond a dense clump of trees.

We eagerly pressed forward now, ready, however, to find that we had a long distance to go, and the doctor leading we wound our way in and out, with the delicious shade overhead, and the refreshing moist air seeming to cool our fevered faces and dry lips.

"Why, we're walking along by the very edge," said Jack Penny suddenly. "This is the way;" and stepping aside he took about a dozen steps and then the undergrowth closed behind him for the moment, but as we parted it to follow him we caught sight of his tall form again and then lost it, for he uttered a shrill "Oh!" and disappeared.

"Doctor! quick!" I cried, for I was next, and I sprang forward, to stop appalled, for Jack was before me clinging to a thin sapling which he had caught as he fell, and this had bent like a fishing-rod, letting him down some ten feet below the edge of an awful precipice, the more terrible from the fact that the river seemed to be rushing straight out into the air from a narrow ravine high upon our right, and to plunge down into a vast rocky basin quite a couple of hundred feet below.

As I caught sight of Jack Penny's face with its imploring eyes I was for the moment paralysed. He had tight hold of the tree, which was only about half the thickness of his own thin wrists, and he was swaying up and down, the weight of his body still playing upon the elastic sapling.

"I can't hold on long, Joe Carstairs," he said hoarsely. "I'm such a weight; but I say I ain't a bit afraid, only do be quick."

The doctor had crept to my side now, and he reached out his hand to grasp Jack, but could not get hold of him by a couple of feet.

"Can't you reach?" the poor fellow gasped.

"No, not yet," the doctor said sharply; and his voice seemed quite changed as he took in the position; and I saw him shudder as he noted, as I had done, that if Jack fell it would be into the foaming basin where the water thundered down.

"Be quick, please," panted Jack. "I can't do nothing at all; and I don't—think—I could swim—down there."

"Don't look down," roared the doctor, though even then his voice sounded smothered and low.

Jack raised his eyes to ours directly, and I seemed to feel that but for this he would have been so unnerved that he would have loosed his hold.

"Now," cried the doctor, "the tree's too weak for you to cling to it with your legs. Swing them to and fro till we catch hold of you."

Jack looked at me with a face like ashes; but he obeyed, and it was horrible to see the sapling bend and play like a cart-whip with the weight upon it. Each moment I expected it to snap in two or give way at the roots; but no: it held fast, and Jack swung to and fro, and danced up and down over the awful gulf till he was within our reach.

"Now!" shouted the doctor to me. "Both together."

I did as he did, clutched at Jack's legs as they swung up to us; held on; and then we threw ourselves back, dragging with all our might.

"Let go! let go!" roared the doctor to Jack.

"I daren't, not yet," he cried, with his head hidden from us, that and his body being over the gulf, while we had his legs over the edge of the rock.

"But the tree is drawing you away from us," shouted the doctor. "Let go, I say."

All this time it was as though Jack Penny were made of india-rubber, for as we pulled his legs it was against something elastic, which kept giving and drawing us back.

For a few moments it seemed doubtful whether we should save him, for our hold was hastily taken and none of the best, and I felt the cold perspiration gathering in my hands and on my brow. Then just as I felt that I must give way, and the doctor's hard panting breathing sounded distant and strange through the singing in my ears, our desperate tugging prevailed over even the wild clutch of one who believed himself in deadly peril. Jack's hands relaxed, and we all fell together amongst the bushes, but safe.

No one spoke, and the dull sound of panting was heard even amidst the roar of the falling waters. Then the doctor got up, looking fierce and angry, and seizing Jack by the collar he gave him a shake.

"Look here," he said. "I'll have no more of it. Next time you get into danger, you may save yourself."

"Thank ye, doctor," said Jack, sitting up and rocking himself softly. "I might just as well have gone as be treated like this. You might have taken hold of a fellow's clothes, both of you. You've about tore the flesh off my bones."

The doctor turned away to look at the great waterfall, evidently amused by Jack's dry drawling speech; and I sat and looked at my companion, while he looked at me, and spoke out so as to make me hear above the roar of the torrent.

"I say, Joe Carstairs, I didn't seem to be very much frightened, did I?"

"No," I said. "You bore it very bravely."

"Mean it?"

"Of course," I said.

"That's right; because I did feel awfully queer, you know. I don't mind that though so long as I didn't show it."

"How did you manage to get into such a pickle?" I said.

"Oh, I don't know," he drawled, still rubbing himself gently. "I was wandering forward to get a good look at the waterfall, and then my legs seemed to go down. I only had time to grip hold of that tree, and then I was swinging about. That's all. Let's have a look at the water, though, all the same."

We followed the doctor, going cautiously along till we found him standing gun in hand gazing from a bare spot right out at the huge tumbling body of water, which made the very rocks on which we stood tremble and vibrate as it thundered down.

In one spot, half-way down what looked to be a terribly gloomy chasm, a broad beam of sunlight shone right across the foam and fine spray that rose in a cloud, and from time to time this was spanned by a lovely iris, whose colours looked more beautiful than anything of the kind that I had before seen.

I could have stood for hours gazing at the soft oily looking water as it glided over the piled-up rocks, and watched it breaking up into spray and then plunge headlong into the chaos of water below; but the doctor laid his hand upon my shoulder and pointed upwards, when, leading the way, he climbed on and on till we were beyond the rocks which formed the shelf over which the water glided, and here we found ourselves at the edge of a narrow ravine, along which the stream flowed swiftly from far beyond our sight to the spot where it made its plunge.

We were in comparative quiet up here, the noise of the fall being cut off by the rocks, which seemed to hush it as soon as we had passed.

"Let us get back, my lads," the doctor said then; "I don't think we shall advance our business by inspecting this grand river;" and so leaving the water-worn smooth rock of the ravine, we retraced our steps, and at last, hot and fainting almost with the heat, reached the little camp, where our black followers were eagerly looking out for our return.

"Where's Jimmy?" I said as I glanced round; but no one knew, and supposing that he had gone to hunt something that he considered good to eat I took no further notice then, though the doctor frowned, evidently considering that he ought to have been in camp. Gyp was there though, ready to salute his master, who lay down at once, as he informed me in confidence, to rest his back.

We were only too glad to get under the shelter of the great overhanging rock, which gave us comparative coolness, situated as it was beneath a hill that was almost a mountain, towering up in successive ledges to the summit.

The walk, in spite of the excitement of the adventure, had given us an excellent appetite, and even Jack Penny ate away heartily, looking self-satisfied and as complacent as could be.

"Why, what are you laughing at, Jack?" I said, as I happened to look up.

"I was only smiling," he whispered, "about my accident."

"Smiling—at that!" I exclaimed. "Why, I should have thought you would have been horrified at the very thought of it."

"So I should if I had been a coward over it, Joe Carstairs; but I wasn't—now was I?"

"Coward! No," I said, "of course not. Here, fill my cup with water."

We were sitting pretty close to the edge of our shelter, which really might have been termed a very shallow cave, some twenty feet above the level; and as I spoke I held out the tin pannikin towards Jack, for the heat had made me terribly thirsty. The next moment, though, something struck the tin mug and dashed it noisily out of my hand, while before I could recover from my astonishment, the doctor had dragged me backwards with one hand, giving Jack Penny a backhander on the chest with the other.

"Arrows!" he whispered. "Danger! There are savages there below."

Chapter Nineteen
How we were besieged, and I thought of Birnam Wood

I believe the doctor saved us from dangerous wounds, if not from death, for, as he threw himself flat, half a dozen arrows struck the roof of our shelter, and fell pattering down amongst us as we lay.

"Here, quick! pass these packages forward," the doctor whispered; and we managed to get the blacks' loads between us and the enemy, making of the packages a sort of breastwork, which sheltered us while we hauled forward some pieces of stone, arrow after arrow reaching this extempore parapet, or coming over it to strike the roof and fall back.

The natives with us understood our plans at once, and eagerly helped, pushing great pieces of stone up to us, so that in about a quarter of an hour we were well protected, and the question came uppermost in my mind whether it was not time to retaliate with a charge of shot upon the cowardly assailants, who had attacked us when we were so peacefully engaged.

We had time, too, now to look round us and lament that our force was so much weakened by the absence of Jimmy and Aroo, who had gone to fetch more water.

"They will be killed," I said, and I saw Ti-hi smile, for he had evidently understood my meaning. He shook his head too, and tried to make me understand, as I found afterwards, that Aroo would take care of himself; but we left off in a state of the greatest confusion.

Being then well sheltered we contrived loopholes to watch for our enemies, and Ti-hi pointed out to me the place from whence the arrows were shot every time the enemy could see a hand.

The spot he pointed to as that in which our assailants lay was where a patch of thick growth flourished among some stones, about fifty yards along the rocky pass in the direction in which we had come, and as I was intently watching the place to make out some sign of the enemy, and feeling doubtful whether the black was right, I saw a slight movement and the glint of a flying arrow, which struck the face of the rock a few feet above my head, and then fell by Jack Penny's hand.

"Mind," I said, as he picked it up; "perhaps it is poisoned."

Ti-hi was eagerly watching my face, and as I spoke he caught the arrow from Jack's hand, placed it against his arm, and then closed his eyes and pretended to be dead; but as quickly came to life again, as several more arrows struck the rock and fell harmlessly among us. These he gathered together all but one, whose point was broken by coming in contact with the rock, and that he threw away.

After this he carefully strung the bow that he always, like his fellows, carried, and looked eagerly at the doctor, who was scanning the ground in front of us with his little double glass.

"I don't like the look of things, my lads," he said in a low voice, and his countenance was very serious as he spoke. "I intended for ours to be a peaceable mission, but it seems as if we are to be forced into war with two men absent."

"Shall we have to shoot 'em?" said Jack Penny excitedly.

"I hope not," said the doctor, "for I should be sorry to shed the blood of the lowest savage; but we must fight in defence of our lives. We cannot afford to give those up, come what may."

Ti-hi fitted an arrow to the string of his short, strong bow, and was about to draw it, but the doctor laid his hand upon him and checked him, to the savage warrior's great disgust.

"No," said the doctor, "not until we are obliged; and then I shall try what a charge of small shot will do."

We were not long in finding out that it was absolutely necessary to defend ourselves with vigour, for the arrows began to fall thickly—thickly enough, indeed, to show us that there were more marksmen hidden among the trees than the size of the clump seemed to indicate from where we crouched.

I was watching the patch of trees very intently when I heard a sharply drawn inspiration of breath, and turning I saw the doctor pulling an arrow from the flannel tunic he wore.

"As doctors say, Joe," he whispered with a smile, "three inches more to the right and that would have been fatal."

I don't know how I looked, but I felt pale, and winced a little, while the doctor took my hand.

The force of habit made me snatch it away, for I thought he was going to feel my pulse. I fancied for the moment that it must be to see whether I was nervous, and the blood flushed to my cheeks now, and made me look defiant.

"Why, Joe, my lad, what is it?" he said quietly. "Won't you shake hands?"

"Oh! yes," I cried, placing mine in his, and he gave it a long, firm grip.

"I ought," he said, after a pause, "to have said more about the troubles, like this one, which I might have known would arise, when we arranged to start; but somehow I had a sort of hope that we might make a peaceful journey, and not be called upon to shed blood. Joe, my lad, we shall have to fight for our lives."

"And shoot down these people?" I said huskily.

"If we do not, they will shoot us. Poor wretches, they probably do not know the power of our guns. We must give them the small shot first, and we may scare them off. Don't you fire, my lad; leave it to me."

I nodded my head, and then our attention was taken up by the arrows that kept flying in, with such good aim that if we had exposed ourselves in the least the chances are that we should have been hit.

The doctor was on one side of me, Jack Penny on the other, and my tall young friend I noticed had been laying some cartridges very methodically close to his hand, ready for action it seemed to me; but he had not spoken much, only looked very solemn as he lay upon his chest, kicking his legs up and sawing them slowly to and fro.

"Are we going to have to fight, Joe Carstairs?" he whispered.

"I'm afraid so," I replied.

"Oh!"

That was all for a few minutes, during which time the arrows kept coming in and striking the roof as before, to fall there with a tinkling sound, and be collected carefully by Ti-hi and his companions, all of whom watched us with glowing eyes, waiting apparently for the order to be given when they might reply to the shots of the enemy.

"I say, Joe Carstairs," said Jack, giving me a touch with his long arm.

"Yes; what is it?" I said peevishly, for his questions seemed to be a nuisance.

"I don't look horribly frightened, do I?"

"No," I said; "you look cool enough. Why?"

"Because I feel in a horrid stew, just as I did when a lot of the black fellows carried me off. I was a little one then."

"Were you ever a little one, Jack!" I said wonderingly.

"Why, of course I was—a very little one. You don't suppose I was born with long legs like a colt, do you? The blacks came one day when father was away, and mother had gone to see after the cow, and after taking all the meal and bacon they went off, one of them tucking me under his arm, and I never made a sound, I was so frightened, for I was sure they were going to eat me. I feel something like I did then; but I say, Joe Carstairs, you're sure I don't show it?"

"Sure! Yes," I said quickly. "If we have to shoot at these savages shall you take aim at them?"

"All depends," said Jack coolly. "First of all, I shall fire in front of their bows like the man-o'-war's men do. If that don't stop 'em I shall fire at their legs, and if that don't do any good then I shall let 'em have it right full, for it'll be their own fault. That's my principle, Joe Carstairs; if a fellow lets me alone I never interfere with him, but if he begins at me I'm nasty. Here, you leave those arrows alone, and—well, what's the matter with you?"

This was to Gyp, who was whining uneasily as if he scented danger, and wanted to run out.

"Down, Gyp, down!" said his master; and the dog crouched lower, growling, though, now as a fresh arrow flashed in from another part.

The doctor started and raised his gun to take aim at the spot from whence this shot had come, for one of the savages had climbed up and reached a ledge above where we were. In fact this man's attack made our position ten times more perilous than it was before.

But the doctor did not fire, for Ti-hi, without waiting for orders, drew an arrow to its head, the bow-string gave a loud twang, and the next instant we saw a savage bound from the ledge where he had hidden and run across the intervening space, club in one hand, bow in the other, yelling furiously the while.

The doctor was about to fire, and in the excitement of the moment I had my piece to my shoulder, but before he had come half-way the savage turned and staggered back, Ti-hi pointing triumphantly to an arrow sticking deep in the muscles of the man's shoulder.

There was a loud yelling as the wounded savage rejoined his companions, and our own men set up a triumphant shout.

"That's one to us," said Jack Penny drily. "I think I shall keep the score."

The doctor looked at me just at this time and I looked back at him; and somehow I seemed to read in his eyes that he thought it would be the best plan to let the blacks fight out the battle with their bows and arrows, and I felt quite happy in my mind for the moment, since it seemed to me that we should get out of the difficulty of having to shed blood.

But directly after I coloured with shame, for it seemed cowardly to want to do such work by deputy and to make these ignorant people fight our battle; while after all I was wrong, for the doctor was not thinking anything of the kind. In fact he knew that we would all have to fight in defence of our lives, and when a flight of about twenty arrows came whizzing and pattering over our heads and hurtled down upon the stony floor, I knew it too, and began to grow cool with the courage of desperation and prepared for the worst.

"Here, Jack Penny," I whispered, "you'll have to fight; the savages mean mischief."

"All right!" he replied in a slow cool drawling way, "I'm ready for them; but I don't know whether I can hit a man as he runs, unless I try to make myself believe he's a kangaroo."

The yelling was continued by our enemies, and as far as I could tell it seemed to me that there must be at least thirty savages hiding amongst the rocks and trees, and all apparently thirsting for our blood.

"It seems hard, doctor," I said bitterly. "They might leave us alone."

"I'm afraid they will think that they would have done better in leaving us," said the doctor gloomily, "for I don't mean them to win the day if I can help it."

I could not help staring at the doctor: his face looked so stern and strange till, catching my eye, he smiled in his old way, and held out his hand.

"We shall beat them off, Joe," he said gently. "I would have avoided it if I could, but it has become a work of necessity, and we must fight for our lives. Be careful," he added sternly. "It is no time for trifling. Remember your father, and the mother who is waiting for you at home. Joe, my boy, it is a fight for life, and you must make every shot tell."

For the moment I felt chilled with horror; and a sensation of dread seemed to paralyse me. Then came the reaction, with the thought that if I did not act like a man I should never see those I loved again. This, too, was supplemented, as it were, by that spirit of what the French call *camaraderie*, that spirit which makes one forget self; and thinking that I had to defend my two companions from the enemy I raised the barrel of my piece upon the low breastwork, ready to fire on the first enemy who should approach.

"Look," said Ti-hi just then, for he was picking up scraps of our tongue; and following his pointing finger I made out the black bodies of several savages creeping to posts of vantage from whence they would be able to shoot.

"Take care," said the doctor sternly, as an arrow nearly grazed my ear. "If one of those arrows gives ever so slight a wound it may prove fatal, my lad; don't expose yourself in the least. Ah! the game must begin in earnest," he said partly under his breath.

As he spoke he took aim at a man who was climbing from rock to rock to gain the spot from which the other had been dislodged. Then there was a puff of white smoke, a roar that reverberated amongst the rocks, and the poor wretch seemed to drop out of sight.

The doctor's face looked tight and drawn as he reloaded, and for a moment I felt horrified; but then, seeing a great brawny black fellow raise himself up to draw his bow and shoot at the part where Jack Penny was crouching, and each time seem to send his arrow more close to my companion, I felt suddenly as if an angry wave were sweeping over my spirit, and lay there scowling at the man.

He rose up again, and there was a whizz and a crack that startled me.

"I say," drawled Jack Penny, "mind what you're after. You'll hit some one directly."

He said this with a strange solemnity of voice, and picking up the arrow he handed it to one of the blacks.

"That thing went right through my hair, Joe Carstairs," he continued. "It's making me wild."

I hesitated no longer, but as the great savage rose up once more I took a quick aim and fired just as he was drawing his bow.

The smoke obscured my sight for a few moments, during which there was a furious yelling, and then, just as the thin bluish vapour was clearing off, there was another puff, and an echoing volley dying off in the distance, for Jack Penny had also fired.

"I don't know whether I hit him," he answered; "but he was climbing up there like t'other chap was, and I can't see him now."

In the excitement of the fight the terrible dread of injuring a fellow creature now seemed to have entirely passed away, and I watched one savage stealing from bush to bush, and from great stone to stone with an eagerness I could not have believed in till I found an opportunity of firing at him, just as he too had reached a dangerous place and had sent his first arrow close to my side.

I fired and missed him, and the savage shouted defiance as my bullet struck the stones and raised a puff of dust. The next moment he had replied with a well-directed arrow that made me wince, it was so near my head.

By this time I had reloaded and was taking aim again with feverish eagerness, when all at once a great stone crashed down from above and swept the savage from the ledge where he knelt.

I looked on appalled as the man rolled headlong down in company with the mass of stone, and then lay motionless in the bottom of the little valley.

"Who is it throwing stones?" drawled Jack slowly. "That was a big one, and it hit."

"That could not have been an accident," said the doctor; "perhaps Aroo is up there."

"I only hope he is," I cried; "but look, look! what's that?"

I caught at the doctor's arm to draw his attention to what seemed to be a great thickly tufted bush which was coming up the little valley towards us.

"Birnam wood is coming to Dunsinane," said the doctor loudly.

"Is it?" said Jack Penny excitedly. "What for? Where? What do you mean?"

"Look, look!" I cried, and I pointed to the moving bush.

"Well, that's rum," said Jack, rubbing his nose with his finger. "Trees are alive, of course, but they can't walk, can they? I think there's some one shoving that along."

"Why, of course there is," I said.

"Don't fire unless you are obliged," exclaimed the doctor; "and whatever you do, take care. See how the arrows are coming."

For they were pattering about us thickly, and the blacks on our side kept sending them back, but with what result we could not tell, for the savages kept closely within the cover.

It was now drawing towards evening, and the sun seemed hotter than ever; the whole of the sultry ravine seemed to have become an oven, of which our cavern shelter was the furnace. In fact the heat was momentarily, from the sun's position, and in spite of its being so long past the meridian, growing more and more intense.

Jack Penny had of late grown very silent, but now and then he turned his face towards me with his mouth open, panting with heat and thirst, as uneasily as his dog, whose tongue was hanging out looking white and dry.

"Is there any water there?" said the doctor suddenly, as he paused in the act of reloading.

"Not a drop," I said, dismally.

"Oh! don't say that," groaned Jack Penny. "If I don't have some I shall die."

"It will be evening soon," said the doctor in a husky voice, "and this terrible heat will be over. Keep on firing when you have a chance, my lads, but don't waste a shot. We must read them such a lesson that they will draw off and leave us alone."

But as he spoke, so far from the loss they had sustained having damped the ardour of the enemy, they kept on sending in the arrows more thickly, but without doing us—thanks to our position and the breastwork—the slightest harm.

The sun sank lower, but the rock where we were seemed to grow hotter, the air to be quivering all along the little valley, and as the terrible thirst increased so did our tortures seem to multiply from the fact that we could hear the heavy dull thunderous murmur away to our right, and we knew that it was cool, clear, delicious water, every drop of which would have given our dried-up mouths and parched throats relief.

At one time I turned giddy and the whole scene before me seemed to be spinning round, while my head throbbed with the pain I suffered, my tongue all the time feeling like a piece of dry leather which clung to the roof of my mouth.

And still the firing was going steadily on, each sending a bullet straight to its mark whenever opportunity occurred; but apparently without effect, for in the midst of all this firing and confusion of shouts from the enemy and defiant replies from our people, the arrows went to and fro as rapidly as ever.

If it had not been for the sound of the falling water I believe I could have borne the thirst far better; but no matter how the fighting went, there was always the soft deep roar of the plashing water tantalising us with thoughts of its refreshing draughts and delicious coolness when laving our fevered heads.

I grew so giddy at times that I felt that I should only waste my shot if I fired, and refrained, while, gaining experience and growing bolder by degrees, the savages aimed so that every shot became dangerous, for they sent them straight at a mass of rock before us some ten or a dozen yards, and this they struck and then glanced off, so that we were nearly hit three times running.

Stones were set up at once upon our right as a protection, but this only saved us for a time. The savages had found out the way to touch us, and before many minutes had elapsed *ricochet* shots were coming amongst as again.

"I can hardly see them, Joe," whispered the doctor suddenly; "my eyes are dizzy with this awful thirst. We must have water if we are to live."

He ceased speaking to catch me by the arm, and point to the bush that had been so long stationary in one place that I had forgotten it.

"What's that, my lad?" he whispered; "is that bush moving, or are my eyes playing me false. It must be on the move. It is some trick. Fire at once and stop it, or we shall be taken in the flank."

I raised my gun as I saw the bush moving slowly on towards us, now coming a yard or two and then stopping; but I was so giddy and confused that I lowered it again, unable to take aim. This took place again and again, and at last I lay there scanning as in a nightmare the coming of that great green bush.

The doctor was watching with bloodshot eyes the enemy on his own side, Jack Penny was busy on the other, and the command of this treacherous advancing enemy was left to my gun, which seemed now to have become of enormous weight when I tried to raise it and take aim.

"It's all a dream—it is fancy," I said to myself, as I tried to shade my eyes and steady my gaze; but as I said this the bush once more began to glide on, and the black patch I saw beneath it must, I felt, be the leg of the savage concealed behind.

Chapter Twenty
How Jimmy turned up a Trump

Even then I could not shoot, but remained staring, helplessly fascinated for a few minutes by the coming danger. At last, though, I turned to Ti-hi, leaning back and touching him where he crouched, busily seizing upon the arrows that came in his way and sending them back.

He crept up to me directly and I pointed to the bush.

His eyes glistened, and bending forward he drew an arrow to the head, and was about to send it winging into the very centre of the bush when we suddenly became aware of some strange excitement amongst the savages, who undoubtedly now caught sight of the bush for the first time and sent a flight of arrows at it.

The effect of this was that he who had been making use of it for a shield suddenly darted from behind it and made for our shelter.

"Aroo, Aroo!" exclaimed the men with us, yelling with delight, while to cover his escape we all fired at the savages, who had come out of their concealment, but only to dart back again, for one after the other three large stones came bounding down the mountain side, scattering the enemy to cover, and the duel once more began, with our side strengthened by the presence of a brave fighting man, and refreshed, for Aroo had his water calabash slung from his shoulders, containing quite a couple of quarts, which were like nectar to us, parched and half-dying with thirst.

Its effects were wonderful. The heat was still intense; but after the refreshing draught, small as it was, that we had imbibed, I seemed to see clearly, the giddy sensation passed off, and we were ready to meet the attack with something like fortitude.

We could think now, too, of some plans for the future, whereas a quarter of an hour before there had seemed to be no future for us, nothing but a horrible death at our enemies' hands.

Ti-hi contrived to make us understand now that as soon as the sun had gone down, and it was dark, he would lead us away to the river side and then along the gorge, so that by the next morning we could be far out of our enemies' reach, when they came expecting to find us in the cave.

His communication was not easy to comprehend, but that this was what he meant there could be no doubt, for we all three read it in the same way.

Encouraged then by this hope we waited impatiently for the going down of the sun, which was now slowly nearing the broad shoulder of a great hill. Another half-hour and it would have disappeared, when the valley would begin to fill with shadows, darkness—the tropic darkness—would set in at once, and then I knew we should have to lose no time in trying to escape.

But we were not to get away without an attack from the enemy of a bolder nature than any they had yet ventured upon.

For some little time the arrow shooting had slackened and we watched anxiously to see what it meant, for there was evidently a good deal of excitement amongst the enemy, who were running from bush to stone, and had we been so disposed we could easily have brought three or four down.

But of course all we wished for was freedom from attack, and in the hope that they were somewhat disheartened, and were perhaps meditating retreat, we waited and withheld our fire.

Our hopes were short-lived though, for it proved that they were only preparing for a more fierce onslaught, which was delivered at the end of a few minutes, some twenty savages bounding along the slope war-club in hand, two to fall disabled by a mass of stone that thundered down from above.

We fired at the same moment and the advance was checked, the savages gathering together in a hesitating fashion, when *crash, crash,* another mass of rock which had been set at liberty far up the hillside came bounding down, gathering impetus and setting at liberty an avalanche of great stones, from which the savages now turned and fled for their lives, leaving the valley free to a single black figure, which came climbing down from far up the steep slope, waddy in hand; and on reaching the level advanced towards us in the fast darkening eve, looking coolly to right and left to see if any enemy was left, but without a single arrow being discharged.

A minute later he was looking over our breastwork into the shallow cave, showing his teeth, which shone in the gloom as he exclaimed:

"Black fellow dreffle hungry. Give Jimmy somefin eat. All gone now."

Chapter Twenty One
How we retreated and were
caught in a Tropic Storm

Our black companion was quite right. The enemy had indeed gone, and the time had come for us to get beyond their reach, for all at once it seemed to grow dark, and we stood farther out of our shelter, glad to free our limbs from the cramping positions in which they had been for so long.

The doctor handed to each of us some chips of dried meat, bidding us eat as we walked. The bearers were well provided, and starting at once, with Ti-hi to lead and Aroo to cover our retreat, we stepped lightly off.

Our blacks knew well enough what was required of them now as to our baggage, and every package was taken from the breastwork, shouldered or placed upon the head, and, watchful and ready to use our arms, we soon left the scene of the fight behind.

The New Guinea savage Ti-hi as we called him, that being the nearest approach I can get to his name, followed very much the course we had taken early in the day when we sought the waterfall, but left it a little to our left and struck the river some few hundred yards above, pausing for a few minutes for his men to take breath, and then pointing out the course he meant to take.

It was a perilous-looking place, enough to make anyone shiver, and there was a murmur amongst the blacks as they looked down at what seemed to be a mere shelf or ledge of rock low down near the black hurrying water of the river, which seemed to be covered with flowing specks of gold as the brilliant stars were reflected from the smooth rushing stream.

Where we were to descend the water seemed to be about thirty feet below, but the rocky side of the river bed ran sheer up quite fifty feet as far as we could make out in the darkness, and I did not wonder at the murmur we heard.

But Ti-hi's voice rose directly, now pleading softly in his own tongue, now in tones of command, and the murmur trailed off into a few mutterings which resulted in the men beginning to descend.

"They were grumbling about having to go down there, weren't they, Joe Carstairs," said Jack Penny in a whisper.

"Yes," I said.

"And 'nough to make 'em," he said. "I don't like it; even Gyp don't like it. Look at him, how he's got his tail between his legs. I say, can't we wait till daylight?"

"And be shot by poisoned arrows, Penny?" said the doctor quietly. "Come: on with you! I'm sure you're not afraid?"

"Afraid! What! of walking along there?" said Jack, contemptuously. "Not likely. Was I afraid when I hung over the waterfall?"

"Not a bit, my lad; nor yet when you so bravely helped us to defend ourselves against the savages," said the doctor quietly. "Come along. I'll go first."

The blacks were all on ahead save Aroo and Jimmy, who followed last, I being next to the doctor, and Jack Penny and his dog close behind me. We had to go in single file, for the ledge was not above a yard wide in places, and it was impossible to avoid a shiver of dread as we walked slowly along, assuming a confidence that we did not feel.

The path rose and fell—rose and fell slightly in an undulating fashion, but it did not alter much in its width as we journeyed on for what must have been quite a mile, when we had to halt for a few minutes while the bearers readjusted their loads. And a weird party we looked as we stood upon that shelf of rock, with the perpendicular side of the gorge towering straight up black towards the sky, the summit showing plainly against the starry arch that spanned the river, and seemed to rest upon the other side of the rocky gorge fifty yards away. And there now, close to our feet, so close that we could have lain down and drunk had we been so disposed, rushed on towards the great fall the glassy gold-speckled water.

I was thinking what an awful looking place it was, and wondering whether my father had ever passed this way, when Jack Penny made me jump by giving me a poke with the barrel of his gun.

"Don't do that," I said angrily, for I felt that I might have slipped, and to have fallen into that swiftly gliding water meant being borne at headlong speed to the awful plunge down into the basin of foam into which I had looked that day.

"Oh, all right!" whispered Jack. "I only wanted to tell you that it must be cramp."

"What must be cramp?" I replied.

"Don't speak so loud, and don't let the doctor hear you," whispered Jack. "I mean in one of my legs: it will keep waggling so and giving way at the knee."

"Why, Jack!" I said.

"No, no," he whispered hastily, "it ain't that. I ain't a bit afraid. It's cramp."

"Well, if you are not afraid," I whispered back, "I am. I hope, Jack, I may never live to be in such an awful place again."

"I say, Joe Carstairs, say that once more," whispered Jack excitedly.

"I hope I may never be—"

"No, no, I don't mean that. I mean the other," whispered Jack.

"What, about being afraid?" I said. "Well, I'm not ashamed to own it. It may be cramp, Jack Penny, but I feel as if it is sheer fright."

"Then that's what must be the matter with my leg," said Jack eagerly, "only don't let's tell the doctor."

"Ready behind there?" said the latter just then.

"Yes," I said, "quite ready;" and I passed the word to Jimmy and Aroo, who were close to me.

"Let's get on then," said the doctor in a low voice. "I want to get out of this awful gorge."

"Hooray!" whispered Jack Penny, giving me such a dig with his elbow that for the second time he nearly sent me off the rocky shelf. "Hooray! the doctor's frightened too, Joe Carstairs. I ain't ashamed to own it now."

"Hist!" whispered the doctor then, and slightly raised as was his voice it seemed strangely loud, and went echoing along the side of the chasm.

Going steadily on at once we found the shelf kept wonderfully the same in width, the only variation being that it dipped down close to the rushing water at times, and then curved up till we were fifteen or twenty feet above the stream. With the walls on either side of the river, though, it was different, for they gradually rose higher and higher till there was but a strip of starry sky above our heads, and our path then became so dark that but for the leading of the sure-footed blacks we could not have progressed, but must have come to a halt.

I was wondering whether this gorge would end by opening out upon some plain, through its being but a gap or pass through a range of hills, but concluded that it would grow deeper and darker, and bring us face to face with a second waterfall, and I whispered to the doctor my opinion; but he did not agree with me.

"No," he said, "the gorge is rising, of course, from the way in which the river rushes on, but there can be no waterfall this way or we should hear it. The noise of the one behind us comes humming along this rocky passage so plainly that we should hear another in the same way. But don't talk, my lad. Look to your footsteps and mind that we have no accident. Stop!" he exclaimed, then, "Halt!"

I did not know why he called a halt just then in that narrow dangerous place, but it seemed that he heard a peculiar sound from behind, and directly after Aroo closed up, to say that the enemy were following us, for he had heard them talking as they came, the smooth walls of the rocks acting as a great speaking-tube and bearing the sounds along.

"That's bad news, my lad," said the doctor, "but matters might be worse. This is a dangerous place, but it is likely to be far more dangerous for an attacking party than for the defenders. Our guns could keep any number of enemies at a distance, I should say. Better that they should attack us here than out in the open, where we should be easy marks for their arrows."

"I do wish they'd leave us alone," said Jack Penny in an ill-used tone. "Nobody said anything to them; why can't they leave off?"

"We'll argue out that point another time, Jack Penny," said the doctor. "Only let's get on now."

"Oh, all right! I'm ready," he said, and once more our little party set forward, the doctor and I now taking the extreme rear, with the exception that we let Aroo act as a scout behind, to give warning of the enemy's near approach.

And so we went on in the comparative darkness, the only sounds heard being the hissing of the swiftly rushing water as it swept on towards the fall, and the dull deep roar that came booming now loudly, now faintly, from where the river made its plunge.

Twice over we made a halt and stood with levelled pieces ready to meet an attack, but they only proved to be false alarms, caused by our friends dislodging stones in the path, which fell with a hollow sullen plunge into the rushing water, producing a strange succession of sounds, as of footsteps beating the path behind us, so curiously were these repeated from the smooth face of the rock.

Hiss-hiss, rush-rush went the water, and when we paused again and again, so utterly solemn and distinct were the sounds made by the waterfall and the river that I fancied that our friend Aroo must have been deceived.

"If the savages were pursuing us," I said, "we should have heard them by now."

"Don't be too satisfied, my dear boy," said the doctor. "These people have a great deal of the animal in them, and when they have marked down their prey they are not likely to leave the track till the end."

I did not like the sound of that word, "end." It was ominous, but I held my tongue.

"As likely as not," continued the doctor, "the enemy are creeping cautiously along within a couple of hundred yards of where we stand, and—"

"I say," cried Jack Penny eagerly, "it's rather cold standing about here; hadn't we better make haste on?"

"Decidedly, Penny," said the doctor. "Forward!"

"Yes, let's get forward," I said, and the doctor suddenly clapped his hand over my mouth and whispered:

"Hush! Look there!"

"I can't see anything," I said, after a long gaze in the direction by which we had come.

"Can you see just dimly, close to where that big star makes the blur in the water, a light-coloured stone?"

"Yes."

"Watch it for a minute."

I fixed my eyes upon the dimly-seen rock, just where quite a blaze of stars flecked the black water with their reflections, but for a time I saw nothing. I only made my eyes ache, and a strong desire came upon me to blink them very rapidly. Then all at once the stone seemed darker for a moment, and then darker again, as if a cloud had come between the glinting stars and the earth.

It was so plain that a couple of the savages had glided by that stone that we felt it would be best to remain where we were for the present, awaiting the attack that we knew must follow.

"We are prepared now," whispered the doctor, "and if we must fight it would be better to fight now than have to turn suddenly and meet an attack on our rear."

The result was that we remained watching through the next painful hour, guns and bows ready for the first oncoming of the savages; but with terrible distinctness there was the washing sound of the river hissing past the rocks, and the rising and falling musical roar of the distant cascade—nothing more!

Then another hour of silence in that awful chasm passed away, with the expectation of being attacked every moment keeping our nerves upon the stretch.

How different it all seemed, what a change from the peaceful life at home! There I had led a happy boyish life, with the black for my companion; sometimes he would disappear to live amongst his tribe for a few weeks, but he always returned, and just after breakfast there would be his merry black face eagerly watching for my coming to go with him to "kedge fis" in some fresh creek or water-hole that he had discovered; to hunt out wallabies or some other of the hopping kangaroo family peculiar to the land. Jimmy had always some fresh expedition on the way, upon which we started with boy-like eagerness. But now all at once, consequent upon my determination, my course of life had been changed, and it seemed that, young as I was, all the work that fell to my hand was man's work. Yesterday I was a boy, now I was a man.

That was my rather conceited way of looking upon matters then, and there was some ground for my assumption of manliness; but if excuse be needed let me say in my defence that I was suddenly cast into this career of dangerous adventure, and I was very young.

Some such musings as the above, mixed up with recollections of my peaceful bed-room at home, and the gentle face that bent over me to kiss me when I was half asleep, were busy in my brain, when the doctor said softly:

"This seems to be such a strong place, Joe, my lad, that I hardly like leaving it; but we must get on. Go forward and start them. Tell them to be as quiet as possible."

His words seemed full of relief, and I started round to obey him, glad to have an end to the terrible inaction, when, to my utter astonishment, I found Jack Penny, who was behind me, sitting with his legs dangling over the edge of the rocky shelf, and apparently within an inch or two of the water, while his shoulders were propped against the side of the chasm; his rifle was in his lap and his chin buried in his breast—fast asleep!

"Jack!" I whispered softly, utterly astounded that any one could sleep at a time like that; but he did not hear me.

"Jack!" I said again, and laid my hand upon his shoulder, but without result.

"Jack!" I said, giving him an impatient shove.

"Get out!" he mumbled softly; and Gyp, whom I had not seen before, resented this interference with his master by uttering a low growl.

"Down, Gyp!" I said. "Here, Jack; wake up!" I whispered, and this time I gave him a kick in the leg.

"I'll give you such a wunner, if you don't be quiet!" he growled. "Let me alone, will yer!"

"Jack! be quiet!" I whispered, with my lips to his ear. "The savages are close at hand!"

"Who cares for the savages?" he grumbled, yawning fearfully. "Oh! I am so sleepy. I say, I wish you'd be quiet!"

"Wake up!" I said, shaking him; and Gyp growled again.

"Shan't!" very decidedly.

"Wake up directly, Jack! Jack Penny, wake up!"

"Shan't! Get out!"

"Hist!" whispered the doctor from behind me.

"Wake up!" I said again, going down on one knee so that I could whisper to him.

Snore!

It was a very decided one, and when I laid my gun down and gave a tug at him, it was like pulling at something long and limp, say a big bolster, that gave way everywhere, till in my impatience I doubled my fist and, quite in a rage, gave him, as his head fell back, a smart rap on the nose.

I had previously held him by the ears and tapped the back of his head against the rock without the slightest effect; but this tap on the nose was electric in its way, for Jack sprang up, letting his gun fall, threw himself into a fighting attitude, and struck out at me.

But he missed me, for when his gun fell it would have glided over the edge of the rocky shelf into the stream if I had not suddenly stooped down and caught it, the result being that Jack's fierce blow went right over my head, while when I rose upright he was wide awake.

"I say," he said coolly, "have I been asleep?"

"Asleep! yes," I whispered hastily. "Here, come along; we are to get forward. How could you sleep?"

"Oh, I don't know!" he said. "I only just closed my eyes. Why, here's somebody else asleep!"

Sure enough Jimmy was curled up close to the rock, with his hands tucked under his arms, his waddy in one fist, a hatchet in the other.

Jack Penny was in so sour a temper at having been awakened from sleep, and in so rude a way, that he swung one of his long legs back, and then sent it forward.

"Don't kick him!" I said hastily; but I was too late, for the black received the blow from Jack's foot right in the ribs, and starting up with his teeth grinding together, he struck a tremendous blow with his waddy, fortunately at the rock, which sent forth such an echoing report through the gully that the doctor came hurriedly to our side.

"What is it?" he said in an anxious whisper.

"Big bunyip hit Jimmy rib; kick, bangum, bangum!" cried the black furiously. "Who kick black fellow? Bash um head um! Yah!"

He finished his rapidly uttered address by striking a warlike attitude.

"It's all right now," I whispered to the doctor. "Come along, Jimmy;" and taking the black's arm I pushed him on before me, growling like an angry dog.

"All right!" the doctor said. "Yes, for our pursuers! Get on as quickly as you can."

I hurried on now to the front, giving Ti-hi his order to proceed, and then signing to the bearers to go on, I was getting back past them along the narrow path, and had just got by Jimmy and reached Jack Penny, when there was a flash, and a rattling echoing report as of twenty rifles from where the doctor was keeping guard.

I knew that the danger must be imminent or he would not have fired, and passing Jack Penny, who was standing ready, rifle in hand, I reached the doctor just as there was another flash and roar echoing along the gully.

"That's right, my lad!" he whispered; "be ready to fire if you see them coming while I reload."

I knelt down, resting my elbow on my knee, and found it hard work to keep the piece steady as I waited to see if the savages were coming on.

I had not long to wait before I distinctly saw a couple of dimly-seen figures against the surface of the starlit water. I fired directly, and then again, rising afterwards to my feet to reload.

"Now, back as you load, quickly!" whispered the doctor, and he caught Aroo by the shoulder and drew him back as half a dozen arrows came pattering against the rock over our head and fell at our feet.

"Back!" whispered the doctor quietly; "we must keep up a running fight."

"Here, hold hard a minute!" said Jack Penny aloud; "I must have a shot at 'em first."

"No: wait!" cried the doctor. "Your turn will come."

Jack Penny uttered a low growl in his deep bass voice, which was answered by Gyp, who was getting much excited, and had to be patted and restrained by angry orders to lie down before he would consent to follow his master in the hurried retreat we made to where Ti-hi and his men were waiting for us. Here we found the shelf had widened somewhat, and some pieces of rock that had fallen offered shelter from an attack.

As we joined them the men, who had laid down their loads, prepared to discharge a volley of arrows, but they were stopped, as it would have been so much waste.

For the next six hours, till the stars began to pale, ours was one continuous retreat before the enemy, who seemed to grow bolder each time we gave way and hurried along the edge of the river to a fresh halting-place.

We fired very seldom, for it was only waste of ammunition, and the darkness was so great that though they often sent a volley of arrows amongst us, not one of our party was hurt.

It was a fevered and exciting time, but fortunately we were not called upon to suffer as we had during the attack upon the cave. Then we were maddened almost by the heat and thirst. Now we had ample draughts of cool refreshing water to fly to from time to time, or to bathe our temples where the shelf was low.

The savages made no attempts at concealing their presence now, and we could hear a loud buzz of excited voices constantly in our rear, but still they did not pursue us right home, but made rushes that kept us in a constant state of excitement and, I may say, dread.

"Do you think they will get tired of this soon, doctor?"

I said, just at daybreak, when I found the doctor looking at me in a strange and haggard way.

"I can't say, my lad," he whispered back. "We must hope for the best."

Just then Ti-hi came from the front to sign to us to hurry on, and following him we found that he had hit upon a place where there was some hope of our being able to hold our own for a time.

It was extremely fortunate, for the coming day would make us an easy mark, the pale-grey light that was stealing down having resulted in several arrows coming dangerously near; and though there were equal advantages for us in the bodies of our enemies becoming easier to see, we were not eager to destroy life, our object, as I have before said, being to escape.

We followed Ti-hi, to find that the narrow shelf slowly rose now higher and higher, till at the end of a couple of hundred yards it gained its highest point of some five-and-twenty feet above the river; while to add to the advantage of our position, the rock above the path stretched over it like the commencement of some Titan's arch, that had been intended to bridge the stream, one that had either never been finished, or had crumbled and fallen away.

In support of this last fanciful idea there were plenty of loose rocks and splinters of stones that had fallen from above, mingled with others whose rounded shapes showed that they must have been ground together by the action of water.

I did not think of that at the time, though I had good reason to understand it later on.

The position was admirable, the ledge widening out considerably; we were safe from dropping arrows, and we had only to construct a strong breastwork, some five feet long, to protect us from attack by the enemy. In fact in five minutes or so we were comparatively safe; in ten minutes or a quarter of an hour our breastwork was so strengthened that we began to breathe freely.

By this time it was morning, but instead of its continuing to grow light down in the ravine, whose walls towered up on either side, the gathering light seemed suddenly to begin to fade away. It grew more obscure. The soft cool refreshing morning breeze died away, to give place to a curious sultry heat. The silence, save the rushing of the river, was profound, and it seemed at last as if it was to be totally dark.

"What does this mean, doctor?" I said, as I glanced round and noted that the sombre reflection from the walls of the chasm gave the faces of my companions a ghastly and peculiar look.

"A storm, my lad," he said quietly. "Look how discoloured the water seems. There has been a storm somewhere up in the mountains, I suppose, and now it is coming here."

"Well, we are in shelter," I said, "and better off than our enemies."

"What difference does that make?" grumbled Jack Penny in ill-used tones. "They can't get wet through, for they don't wear hardly any clothes. But, I say, ain't it time we had our breakfast? I've given up my night's rest, but I must have something to eat."

"Quick! look out, my lads! look out!" cried the doctor, as there was a loud yelling noise from the savages, whom we could plainly see now coming along the narrow path, while almost simultaneously there was a vivid flash of lightning that seemed to blind us for the time, and then a deafening roar of thunder, followed so closely by others that it was like one rolling, incessant peal.

Chapter Twenty Two
How high the Water came

The coming of the storm checked the furious onslaught of our black enemies, but it was only for the moment. Setting thunder, lightning, and the deluging rain at defiance, they came rushing on, shouting and yelling furiously, and we were about to draw trigger, reluctantly enough, but in sheer desperation, when a volley of arrows checked them for a time, while, resuming what seemed to be a favourite means of warring upon his enemies, Jimmy commenced hurling masses of stone at the coming foes.

Checked as they were, though, it was only for a while; and we were compelled to fire again and again, with fresh assailants taking the places of those who fell. The thunder pealed so that the reports of our pieces seemed feeble, more like the crack of a cart-whip, and their flashes were as sparks compared with the blinding lightning, which darted and quivered in the gorge, at times seeming to lick the walls, at others plunging into the rushing, seething stream, into which the rain poured in very cataracts down the rocky sides.

We should have ceased in very awe of the terrible battle of the elements, but in self-defence we were driven to fight hard and repel the continued attacks of the enemy, who, growing more enraged at our resistance, came on once more in a determined fashion, as if meaning this time to sweep us before them into the rushing stream.

But for the bravery of our black companions our efforts would have been useless, and we should certainly have been driven back by the fierce savages, who advanced up the path, sprang upon the stone breastwork, and would have dashed down upon us regardless of our firearms, but Ti-hi and Aroo cast aside their bows at this final onslaught, and used their war-clubs in the most gallant manner. Jimmy, too, seemed to be transformed into as brave a black warrior as ever fought; and it was the gallant resistance offered that checked the enemy and made them recoil.

The falling back of the foremost men, who were beaten and stunned by the blows they had received, drove their companions to make a temporary retreat, and enabled us to reload; but ere we could seem to get breath, one who appeared to be a chief rallied them, and two abreast, all that the path would allow, they came charging up towards us once again.

Then there was a dead pause as the thunder crashed overhead once more, and then seemed to be continued in a strange rushing sound, which apparently paralysed the attacking party, who hesitated, stopped short about a third of the way up the narrow slope that led to our little fort, and then with a shriek of dismay turned and began to retreat.

I stared after them, wondering that they should give way just at a time when a bold attack would probably have ended in our destruction; but I could make out nothing, only that the noise of the thunder still seemed to continue and grow into a sound like a fierce rush. But this was nothing new: the thunder had been going on before, and that and the blinding lightning the enemy had braved. Our defence had had no effect upon them, save to make them attack more fiercely. And yet they were now in full retreat, falling over each other in their haste, and we saw two thrust into the swift river.

"Yah, ah!—big bunyip water, water!" roared Jimmy just then, clapping me on the shoulder; and, turning sharply, I saw the meaning of the prolongation of the thunder, for a great wave, at least ten feet high, ruddy, foaming, and full of tossing branches, came rushing down the gorge, as if in chase of our enemies, and before I had more than time to realise the danger, the water had leaped by us, swelling almost to our place of refuge, and where, a minute before, there had been a rocky shelf—the path along which we had come—there was now the furious torrent tearing along at racing speed.

I turned aghast to the doctor, and then made as if to run, expecting that the next moment we should be swept away; but he caught me by the arm with a grip like iron.

"Stand still," he roared, with his lips to my ear. "The storm—high up the mountains—flood—the gorge."

Just then there was another crashing peal of thunder, close upon a flash of lightning, and the hissing rain ceased as if by magic, while the sky began to grow lighter. The dull boom of the tremendous wave had passed too, but the river hissed and roared as it tore along beneath our feet, and it was plain to see that it was rising higher still.

The noise was not so great though, now, that we could not talk, and after recovering from the appalling shock of the new danger we had time to look around.

Our first thought was of our enemies, and we gazed excitedly down the gorge and then at each other, Jack Penny shuddering and turning away his head, while I felt a cold chill of horror as I fully realised the fact that they had been completely swept away.

There could not be a moment's doubt of that, for the ware spread from rocky wall to rocky wall, and dashed along at frightful speed.

We had only escaped a similar fate through being on the summit, so to speak, of the rocky path; but though for the moment safe, we could not tell for how long; while on taking a hasty glance at our position it was this: overhead the shelving rock quite impassable; to left, to right, and in front, the swollen, rushing torrent.

The doctor stood looking down at the water for a few moments, and then turned to me.

"How high above the surface of the water were we, do you think, when we came here?"

"I should say about twenty-five feet?"

"Why, we ain't four foot above it now; and—look there! it's a rising fast. I say, Joe Carstairs, if I'd known we were going to be drowned I wouldn't have come."

"Are you sure it is rising?" said the doctor, bending down to examine the level—an example I followed—to see crack and crevice gradually fill and point after point covered by the seething water, which crept up slowly and insidiously higher and higher even as we watched.

"Yes," said the doctor, rising to his feet and gazing calmly round, as if to see whether there was any loophole left for escape; "yes, the water is rising fast; there can be no doubt of that."

Just then Gyp, who had been fierce and angry, snapping and barking furiously at the savages each time they charged, suddenly threw up his head and uttered a dismal howl.

"Here, you hold your noise," cried Jack Penny. "You don't hear us holler, do you? Lie down!"

The dog howled softly and crouched at his master's feet, while Jack began to take off his clothes in a very slow and leisurely way. First he pulled off his boots, then his stockings, which he tucked methodically, along with his garters, inside his boots. This done he took off his jacket, folded it carefully, and his shirt followed, to be smoothed and folded and laid upon the jacket.

And now, for the first time I thoroughly realised how excessively thin poor Jack Penny was, and the reason why he so often had a pain in his back.

It seemed a strange time: after passing through such a series of dangers, after escaping by so little from being swept away, and while in terrible danger from the swiftly-rising waters, but I could not help it—Jack's aspect as he sat there coolly, very coolly, clothed in his trousers alone, was so ludicrous that I burst out laughing, when Jimmy joined in, and began to dance with delight.

"What are you larfin at?" said Jack, half vexed at my mirth.

"At you," I said. "Why, what are you going to do?"

"Do!" he said. "Why, swim for it. You don't suppose I'm going to try in my clothes?"

My mirth died out as swiftly as it came, for the doctor laid his hand upon my arm and pressed it silently, to call my attention to our black followers, who were laying their bows and arrows regularly in company with their waddies, each man looking very stern and grave.

They showed no fear, they raised no wild cry; they only seemed to be preparing for what was inevitable; and as I saw Ti-hi bend over and touch the water easily with his hand, and then rise up and look round at his companions, saying a few words in their tongue, the chill of horror came back once more, for I knew that the group of savages felt that their time had come, and that they were sitting there patiently waiting for the end.

Chapter Twenty Three
We await our Fate

I glanced from the blacks to the doctor, to see that he was intently gazing up the gorge where the rushing water came seething down, and I read in his face that he could not see the slightest hope.

I looked at Jack Penny, who was deeply intent upon a little blue anchor that some bush shepherd had tattooed upon his thin white arm.

Then I turned to Jimmy, whose quick dark eyes were busy inspecting his toes, those on the right foot having hold of his war-club, which he was holding out for Gyp to smell.

He alone of the party did not seem to realise the fact that the end was so near.

"Can we do anything, doctor?" I said at last in a low awe-stricken voice.

He gazed at me tenderly and held out his hand to press mine, when I laid it in his grasp.

"No, my lad," he said, "nothing. I have tried mentally to see a way out of our peril, but I can see none. Unless the water sinks we are lost! Joe, my lad, you must act like a man!"

"I'll try, doctor," I said in a choking voice; and as I spoke, once more there seemed to rise up before me our quiet peaceful home near Sydney, with its verandah and flowers and the simply furnished pretty rooms, in one of which sat my mother, waiting for tidings of her husband and son.

I could not help it, but clasped my hands together uttering a despairing cry. For it seemed so hard to give up hope when so young and full of health and strength. Even if it had been amidst the roar and turmoil of the storm it would not have seemed so bad, or when the great flood wave came down; but now, in these calm cool moments, when there was nothing to excite, nothing to stir the blood, and, above all, just when the sky was of a dazzling blue, with a few silvery clouds floating away in the rear of the storm, while the sun shone down gloriously, it seemed too hard to bear.

I gazed eagerly at the water, to see that it was nearly a foot higher, and then I joined the doctor in searching the rock with my eyes for a place where we might find foothold and clamber beyond the reach of the rushing torrent; but no, there seemed no spot where even a bird could climb, and in despair I too began to strip off some of my clothes.

"Are you going to try to swim?" said the doctor gravely.

I nodded.

"That's right," he said. "I shall do the same. We might reach some ledge lower down."

He said that word *might* with a slow solemn emphasis that made me shudder, for I knew he felt that it was hopeless; but all the same he granted that it was our duty to try.

The doctor now bent down over the water, and I could see that it was rising faster than ever.

All at once Jimmy seemed to rouse himself, throwing up his waddy with his foot and catching it in his hand.

"No water go down," he said. "Mass Joe, Mass Jack, doctor, an all a let get up higher; no get wet. Top along get drown, die, and bunyip pull um down an eat um!"

"I'm afraid escape is impossible, Jimmy," I said sadly.

"No know what um say!" cried the black impatiently.

"Can't get away," I said.

"No get way! Waitum, waitum! Jimmy—Jimmy see!"

He went to the edge of the shelf and dipped one foot in the water, then the other, worked his toes about, and then, after a contemptuous look at the blacks, who were calmly awaiting their fate, he looked up at the face of the rock beyond the curving over abutment, and, reaching up as high as he could, began to climb.

It did not seem to occur to him at first that if he were able to escape no one else would be, and he tried twice with a wonderful display of activity, which resulted merely in his slipping back.

Then he tried elsewhere in two places, but with the same result, and after a few more trials he came to me and stood rubbing the back of his head, as if puzzled at his being so helpless and beaten at every turn.

"Get much, too much water, Mass Joe!" he said. "What um going to do?"

I shook my head sadly, and went to where the doctor was watching the progress of the rushing river as it rose inch by inch—cracks and points of rock that we had before noticed disappearing entirely, till the flowing earth-stained surface was but a few inches below the ledge where we were grouped, waiting for the time when we should be swept away.

In spite of the knowledge that at most in an hour the ledge would be covered I could not help watching the rushing stream as it dashed along. It was plain enough to me now why the sides of the gorge were so smooth and regular, for the action of the water must have been going on like this for many ages after every storm, and, laden as the waters were with masses of wood and stone, with pebbles and sand, the scouring of the rocks must have been incessant.

Then my thoughts came back to our horrible position, and I looked round in despair, but only to be shamed out of any frantic display of grief by the stoical calmness with which all seemed to be preparing to meet their fate.

Still the water rose steadily higher and higher inch by inch, and I could see that in a very few minutes it would be over the ledge.

I was noting, too, that now it was so near the end, my companions seemed averse to speaking to me or each other, but were evidently moody and thoughtful; all but Jimmy, who seemed to be getting excited, and yet not much alarmed.

I had gone to the extreme edge of the ledge, where the water nearly lapped my feet, and gazing straight up the gorge at the sunlit waters, kept backing slowly up the slope, driven away as the river rose, when the black came to me and touched my shoulder.

"Poor black fellow there going die, Mass Joe. Not die yet while: Jimmy not go die till fin' um fader. Lot o' time; Jimmy not ready die—lot o' time!"

"But how are we to get away, Jimmy? How are we to escape?"

"Black fellow hab big tink," he replied. "Much big tink and find um way. Great tupid go die when quite well, tank you, Mass Joe. Jimmy black fellow won't die yet? Mass Joe hab big swim 'long o' Jimmy. Swim much fass all down a water. Won't die, oh no! Oh no!"

There was so much hope and confidence in the black's manner and his broken English that I felt my heart give a great throb; but a sight of the calm resignation of my companions damped me again, till Jimmy once more spoke:

"Mass Joe take off closums. Put long gun up in corner; come and fetch um when no water. Big swim!"

Many had been the times when Jimmy and I had dashed into the river and swum about by the hour together; why not then now try to save our lives in spite of the roughness of the torrent and the horrors of the great fall I knew, too, that the fall must be at least two or three miles away, and there was always the possibility of our getting into some eddy and struggling out.

My spirits rose then at these thoughts, and I rapidly threw off part of my clothes, placing my gun and hatchet with the big knife, all tied together, in a niche of the rock, where their weight and the shelter might save them from being washed away.

As I did all this I saw the doctor look up sadly, but only to lower his head again till his chin rested upon his breast; while Jack Penny stared, and drew his knees up to his chin, embracing his legs and nodding his head sagely, as if he quite approved of what I was doing.

The only individual who made any active demonstration was Gyp, who jumped up and came to me wagging his tail and uttering a sharp bark or two. Then he ran to the water, snuffed at it, lapped a little, and threw up his head again, barking and splashing in it a little as he ran in breast-high and came back, as if intimating that he was ready at any moment for a swim.

The doctor looked up now, and a change seemed to have come over him, for he rose from where he had been seated and took my hand.

"Quite right, my lad," he said; "one must never say despair. There's a ledge there higher up where we will place the ammunition. Let's keep that dry if we can. It may not be touched by the water; even if we have to swim for our lives the guns won't hurt—that is, if they are not washed away."

It was as if he had prepared himself for the worst, and was now going to make strenuous efforts to save himself and his friends, after we had taken such precautions as we could about our stores.

Jimmy grinned and helped readily to place the various articles likely to be damaged by water as high as we could on ledges and blocks of stone, though as I did all this it was with the feeling that we were never likely to see the things again.

Still it was like doing one's duty, and I felt that then, of all times, was the hour for that.

So we worked on, with many a furtive glance at the water, which kept on encroaching till it began to lap the feet of our black companions.

But they did not stir; they remained with their positions unaltered, and still the water advanced, till the highest point of the ledge was covered, and Gyp began whining and paddling about, asking us, as it were, with his intelligent eyes, whether we did not mean to start.

"Hi! Gyp, Gyp!" shouted Jimmy just then; "up along, boy; up along!" and he patted the top of one of the stones that we had used for a breastwork.

The dog leaped up directly, placing himself three feet above the flood, and stood barking loudly.

"Yes, we can stand up there for a while," said the doctor, "and that will prolong the struggle a bit. Here, come up higher!" he cried, making signs to our black companions, who after a time came unwillingly from their lower position, splashing mournfully through the water, but evidently unwilling even then to disobey their white leader.

They grouped themselves with us close up to the breastwork, where we stood with the water rising still higher, and then all at once I felt that we must swim, for a fresh wave, the result probably of some portion of the flood that had been dammed up higher on the river course, swept upon us right to our lips, and but for the strength of our stone breastwork we must have been borne away.

As it was, we were standing by it, some on either side, and all clinging together. We withstood the heavy wrench that the water seemed to give, and held on, the only one who lost his footing being Jack Penny, who was dragged back by the doctor as the wave passed on.

"Enough to pull your arms out of the socket," whined Jack dolefully. "I say, please don't do it again. I'd rather have to swim."

Higher and higher came the water, icily cold and numbing. The wave that passed was succeeded by another, but that only reached to our waists, and when this had gone by there was the old slow rising of the flood as before till it was as high as our knees. Then by degrees it crept on and on till I was standing with it reaching my hips.

A fearful silence now ensued, and the thought came upon me that when the final struggle was at hand we should be so clasped together that swimming would be impossible and we must all be drowned.

And now, once more, with the water rising steadily, the old stunned helpless feeling began to creep over me, and I began to think of home in a dull heavy manner, of the happy days when I had hardly a care, and perhaps a few regrets were mixed with it all; but somehow I did not feel as if I repented of coming, save when I thought that my mother would have two sorrows now when she came to know of her loss.

Then everything seemed to be numbed; my limbs began to feel helpless, and my thoughts moved sluggishly, and in a half dreamy fashion I stood there pressed against, the rock holding tightly by the doctor on one side, by Jimmy on the other, and in another minute I knew that the rising water would be at my lips.

I remember giving a curious gasp as if my breath was going, and in imagination I recalled my sensations when, during a bathing expedition, I went down twice before Jimmy swam to my help and held me up. The water had not touched my lips—it was only at my chest, but I fancied I felt it bubbling in my nostrils and strangling me; I seemed to hear it thundering in my ears; there was the old pain at the back of my neck, and I struggled to get my hands free to beat the water like a drowning dog, but they were tightly held by my companions, how tightly probably they never knew. Then I remember that my head suddenly seemed to grow clear, and I was repeating to myself the words of a familiar old prayer when my eyes fell upon the surface of the water, and I felt as if I could not breathe.

The next minute Gyp was barking furiously, as he stood upon his hind legs resting his paws upon his master's shoulders, and Jimmy gave a loud shout.

"All a water run away, juss fass now," and as he spoke it fell a couple of inches, then a couple more, so swiftly, indeed, that the terrible pressure that held us tightly against the stones was taken off pound by pound, and before we could realise the truth the water was at my knees.

Ten minutes later it was at my feet, and before half an hour had passed we were standing in the glorious sunshine with the rocky ledge drying fast, while the river, minute by minute, was going down, so that we felt sure if no storm came to renew the flood it would be at its old level in a couple of hours' time.

We were dripping and numbed by the icy water; but in that fierce sunshine it was wonderful how soon our wrung-out garments dried; and warmth was rapidly restored to our limbs by rocks that soon grew heated in the torrid rays.

"Big bunyip got no more water. All gone dis time," said Jimmy calmly. "Poor black fellows tink go die. No die Jimmy. Lots a do find um fader all over big country. Water all gone, Jimmy cunning—artful, not mean die dis time. Bunyip not got 'nuff water. Give Jimmy something eat. Ready eat half sheep and damper. Give Jimmy some eat."

We all wanted something to eat, and eagerly set to work, but soaking damper was not a very sumptuous repast; still we feasted as eagerly as if it had been the most delicious food, and all the time the water kept going down.

Chapter Twenty Four
How the Doctor took me in Hand

It is surprising how elastic the mind is in young people, and my experience has shown me that there is a great deal of resemblance between the minds of savages and those of the young.

In this case we had all been, I may say, in a state of the most terrible despair one hour. The next, our black companions were laughing and chattering over their wet damper, and Jimmy was hopping about in the highest of glee, while I must confess to a singular feeling of exhilaration which I showed in company with Jack Penny, who, after resuming his garments, seemed to have been seized with the idea that the proper thing to do was to go round from one to another administering friendly slaps on the shoulder accompanied by nods and smiles.

I used to wish that Jack Penny would not smile, for the effect upon his smooth boyish countenance was to make him look idiotic. When the doctor smiled there was a grave kindly benevolent look in his fine heavily-bearded massive face. When Jimmy smiled it was in a wholesale fashion, which gave you an opportunity of counting his teeth from the incisors right back to those known as wisdom-teeth at the angles of his jaws. He always smiled with all his might and made me think of the man who said he admired a crocodile because it had such a nice open countenance.

Jimmy had a nice open countenance and a large mouth; but it in no respect resembled a crocodile's. His regular teeth were white with a china whiteness, more than that of ivory, and there was a genuine good-tempered look about his features which even the distortion produced by anger did not take away. It was only the rather comic grotesqueness seen sometimes in the face of a little child when he is what his mother calls a naughty boy, and distends his mouth and closes his eyes for a genuine howl.

But Jack Penny had a smile of his own, a weak inane sickly smile that irritated instead of pleasing you, and made you always feel as if you would like to punch his head for being such a fool, when all the time he was not a fool at all, but a thoroughly good-hearted, brave, and clever fellow—true as steel—steel of the very elastic watch-spring kind, for the way in which he bent was terrible to see.

So Jack Penny went about smiling and slapping people's backs till it was time to go, and we all watched the cessation of the flood with eagerness.

The doctor, in talking, said that it was evident that this gorge ran right up into quite a mountainous region acting as a drain to perhaps a score of valleys which had been flooded by the sudden storm, and that this adventure had given us as true an idea of the nature of the interior we were about to visit as if we had studied a map.

Down went the water more and more swiftly till, as I was saying to the doctor how grand it must have been to see the flood rolling over the great fall, we saw that the rocky ledge along which we had come and that on the other side of our little haven of safety were bare and drying up, being washed perfectly clean and not showing so much as a trace of mud.

"Let us get on at once," the doctor said; "this is no road for a traveller to choose, for the first storm will again make it a death-trap."

So here we were rescued, and we started at once, every one carefully avoiding the slightest reference to the fate of our pursuers, while in the broad light of day, in place of looking terrible, the chasm was simply grand. The cool rolling water seemed to bring with it a soft sweet breeze that made us feel elastic, and refreshed us as we trudged along at an ordinary rate, for there was no fear now of pursuit.

So with one or two halts we walked on all day till I felt eager to get out from between the prison-like walls to where the trees were waving, and we could hear the voices of the birds. Here there was nothing but stone, stone as high as we could see.

It was a great drawback our not being able to converse with the bearers, but we amended this a little every hour, for Ti-hi struggled hard to make us understand how much he knew about the place and how he knew that there were such floods as this from time to time.

We managed to learn from him, too, that we should not escape from the gorge that night, and to our dismay we had to encamp on a broad shelf when the sun went down; but the night proved to be clear and calm, and morning broke without any adventure to disturb our much-needed rest.

The gorge had been widening out, though, a great deal on the previous evening, and by noon next day, when we paused for a rest after a long tramp over constantly-rising ground, we were beyond risk from any such storm as that which had nearly been our destruction, but as we rested amid some bushes beside what was a mere gurgling stream, one of several into which the river had branched, Ti-hi contrived to make us understand that we were not in safety, for there were people here who were ready to fight and kill, according to his words and pantomimic action, which Jimmy took upon himself to explain.

For days and days we journeyed on finding abundance of food in the river and on its banks by means of gun and hook and line. The blacks were clever, too, at finding for us roots and fruit, with tender shoots of some kind of grassy plant that had a sweet taste, pleasantly acid as well, bunches of which Jimmy loved to stick behind him in his waistband so that it hung down like a bushy green tail that diminished as he walked, for he kept drawing upon it till it all was gone.

Now and then, too, we came upon the great pale-green broad leaves of a banana or plantain, which was a perfect treasure.

Jimmy was generally the first to find these, for he was possessed of a fine insight into what was good for food.

"Regular fellow for the pot," Jack Penny said one day as Jimmy set up one of his loud whoops and started off at a run.

This was the first time we found a plantain, and in answer to Jimmy's *cooey* we followed and found him hauling himself up by the large leaf-stalks, to where, thirty feet above the bottom, hung, like a brobdignagian bunch of elongated grapes, a monstrous cluster of yellow plantains.

"I say, they ain't good to eat, are they?" said Jack, as Jimmy began hacking through the curved stalk.

"Yup, yup! hyi, hyi!" shouted Jimmy, tearing away so vigorously at the great bunch that it did not occur to him that he was proceeding in a manner generally accredited to the Irishman who sawed off a branch, cutting between himself and the tree.

The first knowledge he, and for the matter of fact we, had of his mistake, was seeing him and the bunch of bananas, weighing about a hundredweight, come crashing down amongst the undergrowth, out of a tangle of which, and the huge leaves of the plantain tree, we had to help our black companion, whose first motion was to save the fruit.

This done he began to examine himself to see how much he was hurt, and ended by seizing my axe and bounding back into the jungle, to hew and hack at the tree till we called him back.

"Big bunyip tree! Fro black fellow down," he cried furiously. "Got um bana, though!" he exclaimed triumphantly, and turning to the big bunch he began to separate it into small ones, giving us each a portion to carry.

"I say, what's these?" said Jack Penny, handling his bunch with a look of disgust.

"Bananas," I said. "Splendid fruit food."

"How do you know?" said Jack sourly. "There's none in your garden at home."

"My father has often told me about them," I replied. "They are rich and nutritious, and—let's try."

I ended my description rather abruptly, for I was thirsty and hungry as well, and the presence of a highly flavoured fruit was not to be treated with contempt.

I cut off one then, and looking at Jack nodded, proceeded to peel it, and enjoyed the new sweet vegetable butter, flavoured with pear and honey, for the first time in my life.

"Is it good?" said Jack, dubiously.

"Splendid," I said.

"Why, they look like sore fingers done up in stalls," he said. "I say, I don't like the look of them."

"Don't have any, then," I said, commencing another; while every one present, the doctor included, followed my example with so much vigour that Jack began in a slow solemn way, peeling and tasting, and making a strange grimace, and ending by eating so rapidly that the doctor advised a halt.

"Oh, all right!" said Jack. "I won't eat any more, then. But, I say, they are good!"

There was no likelihood of our starving, for water was abundant, and fruit to be found by those who had such energetic hunters as the blacks. So we proceeded steadily on, hoping day by day either to encounter some friendly tribe, or else to make some discovery that might be of value to us in our search.

And so for days we journeyed on, hopeful in the morning, dispirited in the heat of the day when weary. Objects such as would have made glad the heart of any naturalist were there in plenty, but nothing in the shape of sign that would make our adventure bear the fruit we wished. If our object had been hunting and shooting, wild pig, deer, and birds innumerable were on every hand. Had we been seeking wonderful orchids and strangely shaped flowers and fruits there was reward incessant for us, but it seemed as if the whole of the interior was given up to wild nature, and that the natives almost exclusively kept to the land near the sea-shore.

The doctor and I sat one night by our watch-fire talking the matter over, and I said that I began to be doubtful of success.

"Because we have been all over the country?" he replied, smiling.

"Well, we have travelled a great way," I said.

"Why, my dear boy, what we have done is a mere nothing. This island is next in size to Australia. It is almost a continent, and we have just penetrated a little way."

"But I can't help seeing," I said, "that the people seem to be all dwellers near the sea-coast."

"Exactly. What of that?" he replied.

"Then if my poor father were anywhere a prisoner, he would have been sure to have found some means of communicating with the traders if he had not escaped."

"Your old argument, Joe," he said. "Are you tired of the quest?"

"Tired? No!" I cried excitedly.

"Then recollect the spirit in which we set about this search. We said we would find him."

"And so we will: my mind is made up to find him—if he be living," I added mournfully.

"Aha!" said the doctor, bending forward and looking at me by the light of the burning wood, "I see, my fine fellow, I see. We are a bit upset with thinking and worry. Nerves want a little tone, eh? as we doctors say. My dear boy, I shall have to feel your pulse and put you to bed for a day or two. This is a nice high and dry place: suppose we camp here for a little, and—"

"Oh no, no, doctor," I cried.

"But I say, Oh yes, yes. Why, Joe, you're not afraid of a dose of physic, are you? You want something, that's evident. Boys of your age don't have despondent fits without a cause."

"I have only been thinking a little more about home, and—my poor father," I said with a sigh.

"My dear Joe," said the doctor, "once for all I protest against that despondent manner of speaking. 'My poor father!' How do you know he is poor? Bah! lad: you're a bit down, and I shall give you a little quinine. To-morrow you will rest all day."

"And then?" I said excitedly.

"Then," he said thoughtfully—"then? Why, then we'll have a fishing or a shooting trip for a change, to do us both good, and we'll take Jack Penny and Jimmy with us."

"Let's do that to-morrow, doctor," I said, "instead of my lying here in camp."

"Will you take your quinine, then, like a good boy?" he said laughingly.

"That I will, doctor—a double dose," I exclaimed. "A double dose you shall take, Joe, my lad," he said; and to my horror he drew a little flat silver case out of his pocket, measured out a little light white powder on the blade of a knife into our pannikin, squeezed into it a few drops of the juice of a lemon-like fruit of which we had a pretty good number every day, filled up with water, and held it for me to drink.

"Oh, I say, doctor!" I exclaimed, "I did not think I should be brought out here in the wilderness to be physicked."

"Lucky fellow to have a medical man always at your side," he replied. "There, sip it up. No faces. Pish! it wasn't nasty, was it?"

"Ugh! how bitter!" I cried with a shudder.

"Bitter? Well, yes; but how sweet to know that you have had a dose of the greatest medicine ever discovered. There, now, lie down on the blanket near the fire here, never mind being a little warm, and go to sleep."

I obeyed him unwillingly, and lay attentively watching the doctor's thoughtful face and the fire. Then I wondered whether we should have that savage beast again which had haunted our camp at our first starting, and then I began to dose off, and was soon dreaming of having found my father, and taken him in triumph back to where my mother was waiting to receive us with open arms.

Chapter Twenty Five
How I was disposed to find
Fault with my best Friend

When I unclosed my eyes it was bright morning and through an opening in the trees opposite to where I lay I gazed upon the dazzling summit of a mountain of wonderfully regular shape. As I lay there it put me in mind of a bell, so evenly rounded were the shoulders, and I was thinking whether it would be possible to clamber up it and inspect the country from its summit, when the doctor came up.

"Ah! Joe," he said; "and how are the spirits this morning?"

"Spirits?" I said wonderingly, for my sleep had been so deep that I had forgotten all about the previous evening. "Oh, I'm quite well;" and springing up I went to the stream by which we were encamped to bathe my face and hands, coming back refreshed, and quite ready for the breakfast that was waiting.

"Let's see," said the doctor. "I promised an expedition did I not?"

"Yes: hunting or fishing," I said eagerly, though I half repented my eagerness directly after, for it seemed as if I did not think enough about the object of our journey.

"I've altered my mind," said the doctor. "We've been travelling for days in low damp levels; now for a change what do you say to trying high ground and seeing if we can climb that mountain? What do you say, Penny?"

"Won't it make our backs ache a deal?" he said, gazing rather wistfully up at the glittering mountain.

"No doubt, and our legs too," the doctor replied. "Of course we shall not try to ascend the snowy parts, but to get as far as the shoulder; that will give us a good view of the lay of the country, and it will be something to climb where perhaps human foot has never trod before."

There was something fascinating enough in this to move Jack Penny into forgetfulness of the possibility of an aching back; and after getting in motion once more, we followed our black bearers for a few miles, and then giving them instructions where to halt—upon a low hill just in front—we struck off to the left, the doctor, Jack Penny, Jimmy, and the dog, and at the end of half an hour began the ascent.

So slight was the slope that we climbed I could hardly believe it possible how fast we had ascended, when at the end of a couple of hours we sat down to rest by a rill of clear intensely cold water that was bubbling amongst the stones. For on peering through a clump of trees I gazed at the most lovely landscape I had seen since I commenced my journey. Far as eye could reach it was one undulating forest of endless shades of green, amidst which, like verdant islands, rose hill and lesser mountain.

I could have stopped and gazed at the scene for hours had not the doctor taken me by the arm.

"Rest and food, my lad," he said; "and then higher up yet before we settle to our map making and mark out our future course."

Jimmy was already fast asleep beneath a rock, curled up in imitation of Gyp, while Jack Penny was sitting with his back against a tree, apparently studying his legs as he rubbed his hands up and down them gently, to soften and make more pliable the muscles.

"Tain't time to go on yet, is it?" he said with a dismal glance up at us.

"No, no, Penny; we'll have a good rest first," said the doctor; and Jack uttered a profound sigh of relief.

"I am glad," he said, "for I was resting my back. I get up against a small tree like this and keep my back straight, and that seems to make it stronger and stiffer for ever so long."

"Then take my advice, Penny; try another plan, my lad. You have grown too fast."

"Yes, that's what father always said," replied Jack, beginning with a high squeak and rumbling off into a low bass.

"You are then naturally weak, and if I were you I should lie flat down upon my back every time we stopped. You will then get up refreshed more than you think for."

"But you wouldn't lie flat like that when you were eating your victuals, would you? I ain't Jimmy."

"No, but you could manage that," I said; and Jack Penny nodded and lay down very leisurely, but only to spring up again most energetically and uttering a frightened yell.

Gyp and Jimmy uncoiled like a couple of loosened springs, the former to utter a series of angry barks, and the latter to spring up into the air suddenly.

"Where de bunyip—where de big bunyip? Jimmy kill um all along."

He flourished his waddy wildly, and then followed Gyp, who charged into the wood as the doctor and I seized our guns, ready for action.

Then a fierce worrying noise took place for a few moments in amongst the bushes, and then Jimmy came bounding out, dragging a small snake by the tail, to throw it down and then proceed to batter its head once again with his waddy, driving it into the earth, though the reptile must already have ceased to exist.

"Killum dead um!" cried Jimmy, grinning with triumph. "Jimmy killum headums; Gyp killums tail."

"I wish you'd look, doctor, and see if he bit me," said Jack, speaking disconsolately. "I lay down as you told me, and put my head right on that snake."

"Don't you know whether it bit you?" said the doctor anxiously.

"No, not the least idea," said Jack, shaking his head. "I think it must have bit me, I was so close."

"I don't believe it did," I said. "Why, you must have known."

"Think so?" said Jack dismally. "I say, doctor, is it best, do you think, to lie right down?"

"Yes, if you look first to see whether there is danger from snakes. There, lie down, my lad, and rest."

Jack obeyed him very reluctantly, and after Gyp and Jimmy had both re-curled themselves, the doctor and I lay down to talk in a low voice about our prospects, and then as I lay listening to his words, and wondering whether I should ever succeed in tracing out my father, all seemed to become blank, till I started up on being touched.

"Had a good nap?" said the doctor. "Then let's get on again."

We started once more, with the ground now becoming more difficult. Trees were fewer, but rocks and rugged patches of stony soil grew frequent, while a pleasant breeze now played about our faces and seemed to send vigour into our frames.

Gyp and the black were wonderfully excited, bounding about in front of us, and even Jack Penny stepped out with a less uncertain stride.

Higher we climbed and higher, and at every pause that we made for breath the beauty of the great country was more impressed upon me.

"What a pity!" exclaimed the doctor, as we halted at last upon a rugged corner of the way we were clambering, with the glistening summit far above our heads, while at our feet the wild country looked like some lovely green garden.

"What is a pity?" I said wonderingly, for the scene, tired and hot as I was, seemed lovely.

"That such a glorious country should be almost without inhabitant, when thousands of our good true Englishmen are without a scrap of land to call their own."

"Hey, hi!" cried Jack Penny excitedly. "Look out! There's something wrong."

Jimmy and the dog had, as usual, been on ahead; but only to come racing back, the former's face full of excitement, while the dog seemed almost as eager as the black.

"Jimmy find um mans, find. Quiet, Gyp; no make noise."

"Find? My father?" I cried, with a curious choking sensation in my throat.

"No; no findum fader," whispered Jimmy. "Get um gun. Findum black fellow round a corner."

"He has come upon the natives at last, doctor," I said softly. "What shall we do?"

"Retreat if they are enemies; go up to them if they are friendly," said the doctor; "only we can't tell which, my lad. Ours is a plunge in the dark, and we must risk it, or I do not see how we are to get on with our quest."

"Shall we put on a brave face and seem as if we trusted them then?" I said.

"But suppose they're fierce cannibals," whispered Jack Penny, "or as savage as those fellows down by the river? Ain't it rather risky?"

"No more risky than the whole of our trip, Penny," said the doctor gravely. "Are you afraid?"

"Well, I don't know," drawled Jack softly. "I don't think I am, but I ain't sure. But I sha'n't run away. Oh, no, I sha'n't run away."

"Come along then," said the doctor. "Shoulder your rifle carelessly, and let's put a bold front upon our advance. They may be friendly. Now, Jimmy, lead the way."

The black's eyes glittered as he ran to the front, stooping down almost as low as if he were some animal creeping through the bush, and taking advantage of every shrub and rock for concealment.

He went on, with Gyp close at his heels, evidently as much interested as his leader, while we followed, walking erect and making no effort to conceal our movements.

We went on like this for quite a quarter of a mile, and the doctor had twice whispered to me that he believed it was a false alarm, in spite of Jimmy's cautionary movements, and we were about to shout to him to come back, when all at once he stopped short behind a rugged place that stood out of the mountain slope, and waved his waddy to us to come on.

"He has come upon them," I said, with my heart beating faster and a curious sensation of sluggishness attacking my legs.

"Yes, he has found something," said the doctor; and as I glanced round I could see that Jack Penny had my complaint in his legs a little worse than I. But no sooner did he see that I was looking at him than he snatched himself together, and we went on boldly, feeling a good deal encouraged from the simple fact that Gyp came back to meet us wagging his tail.

As we reached the spot where Jimmy was watching, he drew back to allow us to peer round the block of stone, saying softly:

"Dat's um. Black fellow just gone long."

To our surprise there were no natives in the hollow into which we peered, but just beyond a few stunted bushes I could see smoke arising, so it seemed, and the black whispered:

"Black fellow fire. Cookum damper. Roastum sheep's muttons."

"But there is no one, Jimmy," I said.

"Jus' gone long. Hear Jimmy come long. Run away," he whispered.

"That is no fire," said the doctor, stepping forward. "It is a hot spring."

"Yes, yes, much big fire; go much out now. Mind black fellow; mind spear killum, killum."

"Yes, a hot spring, and this is steam," said the doctor, as we went on to where a little basin of water bubbled gently, and sent forth quite a little pillar of vapour into the air; so white was it that the black might well have been excused for making his mistake.

"Jimmy run long see where black fellow gone. Cookum dinner here. Eh! whar a fire?" he cried, bending down and poking at the little basin with the butt of his spear before looking wonderingly at us.

"Far down in the earth, Jimmy," said the doctor.

"Eh? Far down? Whar a fire makum water boils?" cried the black excitedly; and bending down he peered in all directions, ending by thrusting one hand in the spring and snatching it out again with a yell of pain.

"Is it so hot as that, Jimmy?" I said.

"Ah, roastum hot, O!" cried Jimmy, holding his hand to his mouth. "Oh! Mass Joe, doctor, stop. Jimmy go and find black fellow."

We tried very hard to make the black understand that this was one of Nature's wonders, but it was of no avail. He only shook his head and winked at us, grinning the while.

"No, no; Jimmy too cunning-artful. Play trickums. Make fool o' Jimmy. Oh, no! Ha! ha! Jimmy cunning-artful; black fellow see froo everybody."

He stood shaking his head at us in such an aggravating way, after all the trouble I had been at to show him that this was a hot spring and volcanic, that I felt ready to kick, and I daresay I should have kicked him if he had not been aware of me, reading my countenance easily enough, and backing away laughing, and getting within reach of a great piece of rock, behind which he could dodge if I grew too aggressive.

I left Jimmy to himself, and stood with the doctor examining the curious steaming little fount, which came bubbling out of some chinks in the solid rock and formed a basin for itself of milky white stone, some of which was rippled where the water ran over, and trickled musically along a jagged crevice in the rocky soil, sending up a faint steam which faded away directly in the glowing sunshine.

"I say," said Jack Penny, who had crouched down beside the basin, "why, you might cook eggs in this."

"That you might, Penny," said the doctor.

"But we ain't got any eggs to cook," said Jack dolefully. "I wish we'd got some of our fowls' eggs—the new-laid ones, you know. I don't mean them you find in the nests. I say, it is hot," he continued. "You might boil mutton."

"Eh! whar a mutton? Boil mutton?" cried Jimmy, running up, for he had caught the words.

"At home, Jimmy," I said, laughing. The black's disgust was comical to witness as he tucked his waddy under one arm, turned his nose in the air, and stalked off amongst the rocks, in the full belief that we had been playing tricks with him.

He startled us the next moment by shouting:

"Here um come! Gun, gun, gun!"

He came rushing back to us, and, moved by his evidently real excitement, we took refuge behind a barrier of rock and waited the coming onslaught, for surely enough there below us were dark bodies moving amongst the low growth, and it was evident that whatever it was, human being or lower animals, they were coming in our direction fast.

We waited anxiously for a few minutes, during the whole of which time Jimmy was busily peering to right and left, now creeping forward for a few yards, sheltered by stones or bush, now slowly raising his head to get a glimpse of the coming danger; and so careful was he that his black rough head should not be seen, that he turned over upon his back, pushed himself along in that position, and then lay peering through the bushes over his forehead.

The moving objects were still fifty yards away, where the bush was very thick and low. Admirable cover for an advancing enemy. Their actions seemed so cautious, too, that we felt sure that we must be seen, and I was beginning to wonder whether it would not be wise to fire amongst the low scrub and scare our enemies, when Jimmy suddenly changed his tactics, making a sign to us to be still, as he crawled backwards right past us and disappeared, waddy in hand.

We could do nothing but watch, expecting the black every moment to return and report.

But five minutes', ten minutes' anxiety ensued before we heard a shout right before us, followed by a rush, and as we realised that the black had come back past us so that he might make a circuit and get round the enemy, there was a rush, and away bounding lightly over the tops of the bushes went a little pack of a small kind of kangaroo.

It was a matter of moments; the frightened animals, taking flying leaps till out of sight, and Jimmy appeared, running up panting, to look eagerly round.

"Whar a big wallaby?" he cried. "No shoot? No killum? Eh? Jimmy killum one big small ole man!"

He trotted back as he spoke, and returned in triumph bearing one of the creatures, about equal in size to a small lamb.

This was quickly dressed by the black, and secured hanging in a tree, for the doctor would not listen to Jimmy's suggestion that we should stop and "boil um in black fellow's pot all like muttons;" and then we continued our climb till we had won to a magnificent position on the shoulder of the mountain for making a careful inspection of the country now seeming to lie stretched out at our feet.

A more glorious sight I never saw. Green everywhere, wave upon wave of verdure lit up by the sunshine and darkening in shadow. Mountains were in the distance, and sometimes we caught the glint of water; but sweep the prospect as we would in every direction with the glass it was always the same, and the doctor looked at me at last and shook his head.

"Joe," he said at last, "our plan appeared to be very good when we proposed it, but it seems to me that we are going wrong. If we are to find your father, whom we believe to be a prisoner—"

"Who is a prisoner!" I said emphatically.

"Why do you say that?" he cried sharply, searching me with his eyes.

"I don't know," I replied dreamily. "He's a prisoner somewhere."

"Then we must seek him among the villages of the blacks near the sea-shore. The farther we go the more we seem to be making our way into the desert. Look there!" he cried, pointing in different directions; "the foot of man never treads there. These forests are impassable."

"Are you getting weary of our search, doctor?" I said bitterly.

He turned upon me an angry look, which changed to one of reproach.

"You should not have asked me that, my lad," he said softly. "You are tired or you would not have spoken so bitterly. Wait and see. I only want to direct our energies in the right way. The blacks could go on tramping through the country; we whites must use our brains as well as our legs."

"I—I beg your pardon, doctor!" I cried earnestly.

"All right, my lad," he said quietly. "Now for getting back to camp. Where must our bearers be?"

He adjusted the glass and stood carefully examining the broad landscape before us, till all at once he uttered an exclamation, and handed the glass to me.

"See what you make of that spot where there seems to be a mass of rock rising out of the plain, and a thin thread of flashing water running by its side. Yonder!" he continued, pointing. "About ten miles away, I should say."

I took the glass, and after a good deal of difficulty managed to catch sight of the lump of rock he had pointed out. There was the gleaming thread of silver, too, with, plainly seen through the clear atmosphere and gilded by the sun, quite a tiny cloud of vapour slowly rising in the air.

"Is that another hot spring, doctor?" I said, as I kept my glass fixed upon the spot; "or—"

"Our blacks' fire," said the doctor. "It might be either; or in addition it might be a fire lit by enemies, or at all events savages; but as it is in the direction in which we are expecting to find our camp, and there seem to be no enemies near, I am in favour of that being camp. Come: time is slipping by. Let's start downward now."

I nodded and turned to Jack Penny, who all this while had been resting his back by lying flat upon the ground, and that he was asleep was proved by the number of ants and other investigating insects which were making a tour all over his long body; Gyp meanwhile looking on, and sniffing at anything large, such as a beetle, with the result of chasing the visitor away.

We roused Jack and started, having to make a détour so as to secure Jimmy's kangaroo, which he shouldered manfully, for though it offered us no temptation we knew that it would delight the men in camp.

The descent was much less laborious than the ascent, but it took a long time, and the sun was fast sinking lower, while as we approached the plains every few hundred yards seemed to bring us into a warmer stratum of air, while we kept missing the pleasant breeze of the higher ground.

If we could have made a bee-line right to where the smoke rose the task would have been comparatively easy, but we had to avoid this chasm, that piled-up mass of rocks, and, as we went lower, first thorny patches of scrub impeded our passage, and lower still there was the impenetrable forest.

I was getting fearfully tired and Jack Penny had for a long time been perfectly silent, while Jimmy, who was last, took to uttering a low groan every now and then, at times making it a sigh as he looked imploringly at me, evidently expecting me to share his heavy load.

I was too tired and selfish, I'm afraid, and I trudged on till close upon sundown, when it occurred to me that I had not heard Jimmy groan or sigh for some time, and turning to speak to him I waited till he came up, walking easily and lightly, with his spear acting as a staff.

"Why, Jimmy; where's the kangaroo?" I said.

"Wallaby ole man, Mass Joe?" he said, nodding his head on one side like a sparrow.

"Yes; where is it?"

"Bad un!" he said sharply. "Jimmy smell up poo boo! Bad; not good a eat. No get camp a night. Jimmy fro um all away!"

"Thrown it away!" I cried.

"Yes; bad ums. Jimmy fro um all away!"

"You lazy humbug!" I said with a laugh, in which he good-humouredly joined.

"Yess—ess—Jimmy laze humbug! Fro um all away."

"But I say, look here, Jimmy!" I said anxiously, "what do you mean?"

"Light fire here; go asleep! Findum camp a morning. All away, right away. Not here; no!"

He ended by shaking his head, and I called to the doctor:

"Jimmy says we shall not find the camp!" I said hastily; "and that we are going wrong."

"I know it," he said quietly; "but we cannot get through this forest patch, so we must go wrong for a time, and then strike off to the right."

But we found no opportunity of striking off to the right. Everywhere it was impenetrable forest, and at last we had to come to a halt on the edge, for the darkness was black, and to have gone on meant feeling our way step by step.

Chapter Twenty Six
How I got into serious Difficulties

It is not a pleasant place to pass a night, on the ground at the edge of a vast forest, inhabited by you know not what noxious beasts, while if you light a fire to scare them off you always do so with the idea that in scaring one enemy you may be giving notice to a worse where he may find you to make a prisoner or put you to death.

However we determined to risk being seen by savages, the more readily that we had gone so far now without seeing one, and in a short time a ruddy blaze was gilding the forest edge and the great sparks were cracking around the trees.

We had calculated upon being back at camp that night, so we had eaten all our food, and now, as we sat there by the fire hungry and tired, I began to think that we might have done worse than cut off the kangaroo's tail before Jimmy had thrown it away.

Poor Jimmy! He too seemed to be bitterly regretting the idleness that had made him give up his self-imposed task, and the dismal hungry looks he kept giving me from time to time were ludicrous in the extreme.

"Never mind, Joe," said the doctor smiling; "tighten your belt, my lad, and get to sleep. That's the best way to forget your hunger. You'll be sure to begin dreaming about feasts."

The doctor was right; I lay hungrily awake for a short time, and then dropped off to sleep, to dream of delicious fruits, and cooking, and the smell of meat burning, and I awoke with a start to find that there was a very peculiar odour close to my nose, for a piece of wood must have shot a spark of its burning body into the shaggy head of poor Jimmy, who was sleeping happily unconscious, while a tiny scrap of wood was glowing and the hair sending forth curls of smoke.

I jumped up, seized Jimmy by the hair, and crushed out the spark, awaking that worthy so sharply that he sprang up waddy in hand, caught me by the throat, and threw me back, swinging his war-club over his head to strike a tremendous blow.

He saw who it was in time and dropped his weapon.

"What a fool, Jimmy, yes! What a fool Jimmy sleep. Pull Jimmy hair, jig jag. Hallo! What a want?"

It took some time to make him understand what had been wrong, but even when he did comprehend he seemed to be annoyed with me for waking him out of a pleasant dream, probably about damper and mutton, for the saving of so insignificant a thing as his hair, which would have soon grown again.

Jimmy lay down again grumbling, but was soon asleep, and on comparing notes with the doctor I found I was so near my time for taking my turn at watching and keeping up the fire that I exchanged places with him.

As is often the case, the troubles and depressing influences of the night departed with the day, and setting out very hungry, but by no means in bad spirits, we soon found a more open part, where the forest was beginning to end, and after about three hours' walking we reached our little camp, where we had no difficulty in satisfying our cravings, our ordinary food being supplemented by a great bunch of plantains which one of the blacks had found and saved for us.

After a good rest, during which the doctor and I had talked well over our future course, we determined to go right on as we had come for another four days and then to strike due south to hit the shore, always supposing that we encountered nothing fresh to alter our plans.

"And I'm sure we shall," I said to myself, for somehow, I cannot tell you why—and perhaps after all it was fancy—I felt sure that we should not be long now before we met with some adventure.

I did not like to say anything of this kind to the doctor, for I felt that if I did he would laugh at me; but I took the first opportunity I could find of confiding in Jack Penny.

He looked down at me and then seemed to wave himself to and fro, looking at me in a curious dreamy fashion.

"Do you think that? do you feel like as if something is going to happen?"

"Yes," I said hastily. "I don't ask you to believe it but I cannot help thinking something about my curious feelings."

"Oh! I believe you," he said eagerly. "Oh! I quite believe you, Joe Carstairs. I used to feel like that always on mornings when I woke up first, and so sure as I felt that way father used to be going to lick me, and he did. I should put fresh cartridges in my gun if I was you. I'll keep pretty close to you all day and see you through with it anyhow."

But Jack Penny did not keep his word, for somehow as we were journeying on in the heat of the day looking eagerly for a spring or river to make our next halting-place we were separated. I think it was Jack's back wanted a rest. Anyhow I was steadily pushing on within shouting distance of my companions, all of whom had spread out so as to be more likely to hit upon water.

It was very hot, and I was plodding drowsily along through a beautiful open part dotted with large bushes growing in great clumps, many of which were covered with sweet smelling blossoms, when just as I was passing between a couple of the great clumps which were large enough to hide from me what lay beyond, I stopped utterly paralysed by the scene some fifty yards in front.

For there in the bright sunshine stood a boy who might have been about my own age intently watching something just beyond some bushes in his front, and the moment after a small deer stepped lightly out full in my view, gazed round, and then stooped its graceful head to begin browsing.

The boy, who was as black as ebony and whose skin shone in the sun, seemed to have caught sight of the deer at the same moment as I, for he threw himself into position, poising the long spear he carried, resting the shaft upon one hand and bending himself back so that he might get the greatest power into his throw.

I had seen Jimmy plant himself in the same position hundreds of times, and, surprised as I was at coming upon this stranger, whose people were probably near at hand, I could not help admiring him as he stood there a thorough child of nature, his body seeming to quiver with excitement for the moment and then becoming perfectly rigid.

My eye glanced from the boy to the deer and back again, when a slight movement to my right caught my attention and I stood paralysed, for in a crouching attitude I could see a second black figure coming up, war-club in hand, evidently inimically disposed towards the young hunter.

"And he may belong to a friendly set of people," I thought. "It is Jimmy!"

"No: it was not Jimmy, but one of the bearers—Ti-hi," I thought.

"No: it was a stranger!"

Just then the boy drew himself back a little more, and as I saw the stooping figure, that of a big burly savage, stealthily creeping on, I realised his intention, which was to wait till the boy had hurled his spear and then leap upon him and beat him to the ground.

I made no plans, for all was the work of moments. I saw the spear leave the boy's hand like a line of light in the sunshine; then he turned, alarmed by some sound behind him, saw the savage in the act of leaping upon him, uttered a shrill cry of fear, and ran somewhat in my direction, and at the same moment my gun made a jump up at my shoulder and went off.

As the smoke rose I stood aghast, seeing the boy on my left crouching down with a small waddy in his hand and the great black savage prone on his face just to my right.

"I've killed him!" I exclaimed, a chill of horror running through me; but as I thought this I brought my piece to the ready again, for the savage leaped to his feet and turned and ran into the bush at a tremendous pace.

From habit I threw open the breech of my gun without taking my eyes from the boy, and, thrusting my hand into my pouch, I was about to place a fresh ball cartridge in its place when I found that I had drawn the right trigger and discharged the barrel loaded with small shot, a sufficient explanation of the man being able to get up and run away.

I remained standing motionless as soon as I had reloaded, the boy watching me intently the while and looking as if he was either ready to attack or flee according to circumstances. Friendly advance there was none, for he showed his white teeth slightly and his eyes glittered as they were fixed upon mine.

Suddenly I caught sight of the deer lying transfixed by the boy's spear, and without a word I walked quietly to where the little animal lay, the boy backing slowly and watchfully from me, but holding his waddy ready for a blow or to hurl at me, it seemed, if I ventured to attack.

I wanted to make friends, and as soon as I reached the dead deer I stooped down, holding my gun ready though, and taking hold of the spear, drew it out and offered it to the young hunter.

He understood my motion, for he made a couple of steps forward quickly, but only to draw back uttering an angry ejaculation, and raise his waddy in a threatening way.

"He thinks I want to trap him," I said to myself; and taking the spear in regular native style, as Jimmy had taught me, I smiled and nodded, tossed it in the air, and let it drop a few yards away with the shaft upright and towards his hands.

I pointed to it and drew back a few yards, when, quick as some wild animal, he made two or three bounds, caught up the spear, poised it, and stood as if about to hurl it at me.

It was not a pleasant position, and my first impulse was to raise my gun to my shoulder; but my second was to stand firm, resting on my piece, and I waved my hand to him to lower the spear.

The boy hesitated, uttered a fierce cry, and stamped one foot angrily; but I waved my hand again, and, thrusting my hand into my pocket, pulled out a ring of brass wire, such as we carried many of for presents to the savages, and I tossed it to him.

I saw the boy's eyes glitter with eagerness, but he was too suspicious to move, and so we stood for some minutes, during which I wondered whether my companions had heard the report of my gun, and if so whether they would come up soon. If they did I was sure they would alarm the boy, who seemed as suspicious as some wild creature and shook his spear menacingly as soon as I took a step forward.

A thought struck me just then as I saw a red spot glisten on a leaf, and stepping forward I saw another and another, which I pointed to, and then again at a continuous series of them leading towards the dense bush.

I took a few more steps forward when the boy suddenly bounded to my side as if he realised that I had saved his life and that he was bound to try and save me in turn.

He uttered some words fiercely, and, catching my arm, drew me back, pointing his spear menacingly in the direction taken by the great savage, and in response to his excited words I nodded and smiled and yielded to his touch.

We had not taken many steps before he stopped short to stand and stare at me wonderingly, saying something the while.

Then he touched me, and as I raised my hand to grasp his he uttered a fierce cry and pointed his spear at me once more, but I only laughed—very uncomfortably I own—and he lowered it slowly and doubtfully once again, peering into my eyes the while, his whole aspect seeming to say, "Are you to be trusted or no?"

I smiled as the best way of giving him confidence, though I did not feel much confidence in him—he seemed too handy with his spear. He, however, lowered this and looked searchingly at me, while I wondered what I had better do next. For this was an opportunity—here was a lad of my own age who might be ready to become friends and be of great service to us; but he was as suspicious and excitable as a wild creature, and ready to dash away or turn his weapons against me at the slightest alarm.

It was very hard work to have to display all the confidence, but I told myself that it was incumbent upon me as a civilised being to show this savage a good example, and generally I'm afraid that I was disposed to be pretty conceited, as, recalling the native words I had picked up from our followers, I tried all that were available, pointing the while to the deer and asking him by signs as well if he would sell or barter it away to me for food.

My new acquaintance stared at me, and I'm afraid I did not make myself very comprehensible. One moment he would seem to grasp my meaning, the next it appeared to strike him that I must be a cannibal and want to eat him when I made signs by pointing to my mouth. At last, though, the offer of a couple of brass rings seemed to convince him of my friendliness, and he dragged the little deer to me and laid it at my feet.

After this we sat down together, and he began chattering at a tremendous rate, watching my gun, pointing at the spots upon the leaves, and then touching himself, falling down, and going through a pantomime as if dying, ending by lying quite stiff with his eyes closed, all of which either meant that if I had not fired at the big black my companion would have been killed, or else that I was not on any consideration to use my thunder-and-lightning weapon against him.

I did not understand what he meant, and he had doubtless very little comprehension of what I tried to convey; but by degrees we became very good friends, and he took the greatest of interest in my dress, especially in my stout boots and cartridge-belt. Then, too, he touched my gun, frowning fiercely the while. My big case-knife also took up a good deal of his attention and had to be pulled out several times and its qualities as a cutter of tough wood shown.

After this he drew my attention to his slight spear, which, though of wood, was very heavy, and its point remarkably sharp and hard. In spite of its wanting a steel point I felt no doubt of its going through anything against which it was directed with force.

He next held out his waddy to me to examine. This was a weapon of black-looking wood, with a knob at the end about the shape of a good-sized tomato.

I took hold of the waddy rather quickly, when it must have struck the boy that I had some hostile intention, for he snatched at it, and for the moment it seemed as if there was a struggle going on; then I felt a violent blow from behind, as if a large stone had fallen upon my head, and that was all.

Chapter Twenty Seven
How I found that I had a Fellow-Prisoner

I have had a good many headaches in my time, but nothing to compare with the fearful throbbing, that seemed as if I were receiving blow after blow upon my temples, when I began to come to myself.

I was stupefied and confused, and it took a long time before I recovered sufficiently to comprehend my position. By degrees, though, I was able to bear my eyes unclosed for sufficiently long at a time to see that I was in some kind of hut, and as I realised all this it seemed that I must be still a prisoner, and that all my long journeying since was only a dream.

I began wondering where Jimmy could be, and the doctor, and Jack Penny, and then my head throbbed so violently that I closed my eyes, feeling at the same time that I had no arms, no legs, nothing but an inanimate body, and a head that ached with terrible violence as I lay there half-stunned.

After a time I must have grown a little more collected, for I awoke to the fact that I was tightly bound with twisted grass, hand and foot; that I was certainly in a hut, quite a large hut, built of bamboo and mats; and that behind me the light shone in, and somewhere close by the sound arose as of a person sleeping heavily.

I tried to turn round, but the movement caused such intense pain that I desisted for a time, till my anxiety to know more about my position forced me to make a fresh effort, and I swung myself over, making my head throb so that I gladly closed my eyes, while I wrenched my arms and wrists, that were tied behind my back so harshly that I became quite aware of the fact that I had limbs, as well as an inert body and a throbbing head.

When I could unclose my eyes again I saw that it was getting near sundown, and that the sunshine was lighting up the limbs of the great trees beneath which the native village to which I had been brought was built. From where I lay I looked across a broad opening, around which was hut after hut, with its open door facing towards the centre.

There was very little sign of life around, but twice in the distance I saw a black figure come out of the doorway of a hut and disappear amongst the trees, but it was some time before I could make out from whence the heavy breathing came that I had heard.

As far as I could judge it was from some one just outside the entrance to the hut where I lay, but no one was visible, and it seemed to me that if I could untie the rope that held my wrists and legs there was nothing to prevent my walking out and making my escape.

I had just come to this conclusion when there was a rustling noise as of a stick passing over twigs and leaves, and a spear fell down across the doorway.

The next instant I saw a black arm and shoulder come forward, the spear was picked up, and the black arm disappeared. Then there was a shuffling sound, as of some one settling down in a fresh position, and all was silent, for the heavy breathing had ceased.

"That's my guard," I said to myself, "and he has been, asleep!"

Simple words, but they sent a throb of joy through me, and I began to wonder where the doctor was, and what Jack Penny was doing.

Then I thought about Jimmy, and that as soon as I was missed he would be sure to hunt me out.

My head began to throb once more horribly, but by degrees the fit died off, and I found myself thinking again of escape.

"How foolish of me not to have had a dog!" I thought. "Why, if I had had one like Gyp he would have tracked me out by this time."

"They'll find me out sooner or later," I said to myself; "so I need not regret being without a dog. But suppose the savages should attack our little party and make them prisoners too."

This was quite a new idea to me. The doctor and I had thought out a good many possibilities; but that we, who had come in search of one who was a prisoner, should be ourselves made captives, hardly ever occurred to me.

"That would be a sorry end to our voyage," I thought, and I lay gazing out across the open space, wondering in a dreamy misty way whether my poor father had been attacked and captured as I had been, and whether I should be kept a prisoner, and have to live for the rest of my life among savages.

My head was not so painful then, and I began to feel that if it would only leave off aching and my poor mother would not be so troubled at this second loss, such a life would be better than being killed, especially as there would always be the chance of escape.

I think I must have sunk into a sort of doze or half stupor just then, for the scene at which I lay gazing grew dim, and it seemed to me that it must all have been a dream about my meeting with that black boy; and once more I suppose I slept.

How long I slept I cannot tell, but I can recall being in a confused dream about home, and going with Jimmy to a neighbour's sheep-run, where there was a dog, and Jimmy coaxed him away with a big piece of meat, which he did not give to the dog, but stuck on the end of his spear and carried it over his shoulder, with the animal whining and snuffling about, but which was to be reserved until several wallabies had been hunted out, for that was the aim of the afternoon.

It seemed very tiresome that that dog should be snuffling about me, and scratching and pawing at me, and I was about to tell Jimmy to give the poor brute the meat and let him go, when his cold nose touched my face, and I started awake, trembling in every limb.

The darkness was intense, and for some minutes, try how I would, I could not think.

All sorts of wild fancies rushed through my brain, and I grew more and more confused; but I could not think—think reasonably, and make out where I was and what it all meant.

The past seemed to be gone, and I only knew that I was there, lying with my arms and legs dead and my head throbbing. There seemed to be nothing else.

Yes there was—my dream.

It all came with a flash just where it left off, and Jimmy had coaxed the dog away, and it was here annoying me. But why was it dark?

There was dead silence then, following upon the light pattering sound of some animal's feet, and with my brain rapidly growing clearer I began to arrange my thoughts I had even got so far as to recollect dropping off asleep, and I was concluding that I had slept right on into the darkness of night, when there was the pattering of feet again, and I knew now that it was no fancy, for some animal had touched me, though it was not likely to be the dog that Jimmy had coaxed away to go wallaby hunting.

There was a curious snuffling noise now, first in one part of the hut, then in another.

Some animal, then, must have come into the hut, and this, whatever it was, had been touching and had awakened me. What could it be? I wondered, as I tried to think what creature was likely to be prowling about in the darkness.

It could not be a wild pig, and my knowledge of animal life taught me that it was not likely to be any one of the cat family, for they went so silently about, while the pattering steps of this creature could be plainly heard.

We had encountered nothing in our journey that suggested itself as being likely, and I was beginning to perspire rather profusely with something very much like utter fright, when I heard the creature, whatever it was, come close up and begin snuffling about my legs.

"It's coming up to my face," I thought with a chill of horror seeming to paralyse me, or I am certain that I should have called for help.

So there I lay numbed and helpless, not knowing what to expect, unless it was to be seized by the throat by some fierce beast of prey, and perhaps partly devoured before I was dead.

I tried to shriek out, but not a sound came. I tried to move my arms; to kick out at the creature; but arms and legs had been bound so long that the circulation as well as sensation had ceased, and I lay like a mass of lead, able to think acutely, but powerless to stir a limb.

The snuffling noise went on; came to my chest, to my throat, to my face; and I could feel the hot panting breath of the creature, smell the animal odour of its skin; and then, when the dread seemed greater than I could bear, I felt a moist nose touch my face.

Another moment and I felt that the intruder would be burying its fangs in my throat, and still I could not stir—could not utter sound, but lay like one in a trance.

Suddenly the animal began to tear at my chest with its claws, giving three or four sharp impatient scratchings alternately with its feet, and though I could not see, I could realise that the creature was standing with its forepaws on my chest.

Then it was right upon me, with its muzzle at my throat, snuffing still, and then it touched my face with its nose again and uttered a low whine.

That sound broke the spell, for I can call it nothing else, and I uttered the one word:

"Gyp!"

It was magical in its effects, for the faithful beast it was, and uttering a low cry of delight he began nuzzling about my face, licking me, pawing me, and crouching closer to me, as all the while he kept up a regular patting noise with his tail.

My speech had returned now, and with it a feeling of shame for my cowardice, as I thought it then, though I do not think so hardly about it now.

"Gyp, you good old dog!" I whispered. "And so you've found me out!"

I suppose he did not understand my words, but he liked the sound of my voice, for he continued his eager demonstrations of delight, many of which were exceedingly unwelcome. But unwelcome or no I could not help myself, and had to lie there passive till, apparently satisfied that enough had been done, Gyp crouched close to me with his head upon my breast.

For a time I thought he was asleep, and thoroughly enjoying the consolation of his company in my wretched position, I lay thinking of the wonderful instinct of the animal, and of his training to be silent, for in spite of the excitement of our meeting he had not barked once.

But Gyp was not asleep, for at the slightest sound outside he raised his head quickly, and in the deep silence I could hear the great hairy ears give quite a flap as he cocked them up.

As the noise died away or failed to be repeated, he settled down again with his head upon my breast till some fresh sound arose—a distant cry in the forest, or a voice talking in some neighbouring hut, when he would start up again, and once uttered a low menacing growl, which made me think what an unpleasant enemy he would be to a bare-legged savage.

Once more Gyp uttered a low growl; but after that he lay with his head upon my breast, and I could feel his regular breathing. Then he lifted a paw and laid it by his nose, but evidently it was not a comfortable position, and he took it down. And there we lay in that black silence, while I wished that dog could speak and tell me where my friends where; whether they had sent him, or whether his own instinct had led him to hunt me out. Whichever way it was, I felt a curious kind of admiration for an animal that I had before looked upon as a kind of slave, devoted to his master, and of no interest whatever to anyone else.

"Poor old Gyp!" I thought to myself, and I wished I could pat his head.

I kept on wishing that I could pay him that little bit of kindness; and then at last I seemed to be stroking his shaggy head, and then it seemed that I was not free to do it, and then all at once it seemed to be morning, with the sun shining, and plenty of black fellows passing and repassing to the huts of what was evidently a populous village.

It all looked very bright and beautiful, I thought, seen through the open door, but I was in great pain. My head had pretty well ceased to throb, but there was a dull strange aching in my arms and legs. My shoulders, too, seemed as if they had been twisted violently, and I was giddy and weak for want of food.

"Prisoner or no prisoner they sha'n't starve me," I said half aloud; and I was about to shout to a tall savage who was going by spear on shoulder, when I suddenly recollected Gyp and looked sharply round for the dog, but he was not to be seen.

For the moment I wondered whether I had not made a mistake and dreamed all about the dog; but no, it was impossible, everything was too vivid, and after lying thinking for a few minutes I called to the first black who came near.

He stopped short, came to the door, thrust in his head and stared at me, while, for want of a better means of expressing myself, I opened my mouth and shut it as if eating.

He went away directly, and I was about to shout to another when the first one came back with a couple more, all talking excitedly, and evidently holding some discussion about me.

This ended by two of them going away, leaving the other to stand watching.

He was a fine stalwart looking fellow, black as Jimmy, but of a different type of countenance, and his hair was frizzed and stuck out all round, giving his head the aspect of being twice the size of nature.

As soon as the others had gone he stooped down over me, turning me roughly on my face so as to examine my bound hands.

He wrenched my shoulders horribly in doing this, but it did not seem to hurt my hands in the least, and he finished by unfastening the cords of twisted grass and making me sit up.

This I did, but with great pain, my arms hanging helplessly down by my sides.

The men soon returned, and to my great delight one had a gourd and the other some plantains, which they put down before me in a morose, scowling way.

I bent towards the gourd, which I believed to contain water; but though I tried to take it with my hands I could not move either, and I turned my eyes up pitifully to my captors.

The man who had unloosed me said something to his companions, one of whom bent down, lifted my right hand, and let it fall again. The second man followed suit with my left, and I saw before they dropped them again that they were dark and swollen, while as to use, that seemed to be totally gone.

The man who had remained with me took hold of the gourd and held it to my lips in a quick angry fashion, holding it while I drank with avidity every drop, the draught seeming to be more delicious than anything I had ever before tasted.

Setting it aside he looked down at me grimly, and then in a laughing contemptuous way one of the others picked up and roughly peeled a plantain, holding it out to me to eat.

It was not sumptuous fare, cold water and bananas, but it was a most delicious and refreshing repast; while to make my position a little more bearable one of the men now undid the grass cord that was about my ankles, setting them free.

The act probably was meant kindly, but when, soon after, they left the cabin, after setting me up and letting me fall again, my wrists and ankles began to throb and ache in the most unbearable way, somewhat after the fashion of one's fingers when chilled by the cold and the circulation is coming back.

As I sat making feeble efforts to chafe the swollen flesh I became aware that though unbound I was not to be trusted, for fear of escape, and that to prevent this a broad-shouldered black with his hair frizzed into two great globes, one on either side of his head, had been stationed at the hut door.

When he came up, spear in hand, I saw that he was tattooed with curious lines across his chest and back, similar lines marking his arms and wrists, something after the fashion of bracelets.

He looked in at me attentively twice, and then seated himself just outside the entrance, where he took his waddy from where it was stuck through his lingouti or waistband, drew a sharp piece of flint from a pouch, and began to cut lines upon his waddy handle in the most patient manner.

He had been busily at work for some time, when there was a great sound of shouting and yelling, which seemed greatly to excite the people of the village, for dozens came running out armed with clubs and spears, to meet a batch of about a dozen others, who came into the opening fronting my prison, driving before them another black, who was struggling with them fiercely, but compelled by blows and pricks of spears to keep going forward.

Then three men ran at him with grass cords and seized him, but he drove his head fiercely into one and sent him flying, kicked the second, and then attacked the other with his fists, regular English fashion, and I knew now who it was, without hearing the shout the new prisoner uttered and the language he applied to his captors.

Another pair approached, but he drove them back at once, and probably feeling' pretty well satisfied that his enemies did not want to spear him, he stuck his doubled fists in his sides and went slowly round the great circle that had collected, strutting insultingly, as if daring them to come on, and ending by striding into the middle of the circle and squatting down, as if treating his foes with the most profound contempt.

"Poor old Jimmy!" I exclaimed, proud even to admiration of the black's gallant bearing. "Who would call him a coward now!"

For a time Jimmy was untouched, and sat upon his heels with his wrists upon his knees and his hands dangling down, but evidently watchfully on the look-out for an attack. I felt so excited as I sat there that I forgot my own pain, and had I been able to move I should have made a dash and run to my old companion's side; but I was perfectly helpless, and could only look on, feeling sure that sooner or later the blacks would attack Jimmy, and if he resisted I shuddered for his fate.

Sure enough, at the end of a consultation I saw a rush made at the waiting prisoner, who started up and fought bravely; but he seemed to disappear at once, the little crowd heaving and swaying here and there, and ending by seeming to group itself under a tall tree, from which they at last fell away, and then it was that my heart began to beat less painfully and I breathed more freely, for there was Jimmy bound to the tree trunk, grinning and chattering at his captors, and evidently as full of fight as ever.

I sank down upon my elbow with a sigh of relief, for I felt that had they meant to kill my black companion they would have done it at once instead of taking the trouble to bind him to the tree.

And now, oddly enough, while I could hear Jimmy calling his captors by all the absurd and ugly names he could invent, the pain and aching seemed to come back into my wrists and ankles, making me groan as I sat and clasped them, a little use having begun to creep back into my arms.

As I rubbed my aching limbs I still had an eye on Jimmy, interest in his fate making me think little about my own; and as I watched now the black, now the savages grouped about armed with spear and club, I saw that his dangerous position had so excited Jimmy that he was quite reckless. He had no means of attack or defence left save his tongue, and this he began to use in another way.

He had abused his captors till he had exhausted his list of available words, and now in token of derision he gave me another instance to study of the childish nature of even a grown-up savage. For, tied up helplessly there, he put out his tongue at his enemies, thrust it into his cheeks, and displayed it in a variety of ways.

Jimmy was possessed of a very long tongue, unusually large for a human being, and this he shot out, turned down, curled up at the end, and wagged from side to side as a dog would his tail. At the same time he contorted and screwed his face up into the most hideous grimaces, elongating, flattening, and working his countenance as easily as if it had been composed of soft wax, till at times his aspect was perfectly hideous.

Every moment I expected to see a spear thrown or the savages rush at Jimmy with their clubs; but they retained their composure, simply gazing at him, till Jimmy grew weary, and, full of contempt, shouting out something about poor black fellow dingoes, and then shutting his eyes and pretending to go to sleep.

My guard was, like me, so intent upon the scene that he did not hear a slight rustling noise in the darker corner of the hut.

Chapter Twenty Eight
How I had a Visitor in the Night

The sufferings I had gone through and the excitement must have made me in a feverish state, so that, though I heard the faint noise again and again, I began to look upon it as dreaming, and nothing which need trouble me. Even the sight of Jimmy bound to the tree, and now hanging forward with his head sidewise, did not seem to disturb me. It, too, appeared part of a dream, and my eyes kept closing, and a peculiar hot sensation running over my face.

Then this passed off and my brain grew clear, and it was not a dream, but real, while the thought now began to torment me, that as the savages were conferring together it must be about how they should put poor Jimmy to death.

There was the faint noise again, and I glanced at the savage who was my guard, but he had not heard it apparently, for he was chipping and carving away at the handle of his waddy, only looking up from time to time at his fellows with their prisoner.

I wanted to turn myself round and look in the direction whence the sound came, for I felt now that it was no fancy, but that Gyp had been really with me, and that this was he forcing his way to my side again.

I could not turn, though, without giving myself great pain, for now my wrists and ankles were fearfully swollen and tender, so I lay still, waiting and wondering why the dog was so long.

Then the rustling ceased altogether, and I was beginning to think that the dog had failed to get through and would come round to the front, when there was a faint rustle once more, and I was touched on the shoulder.

But it was not by Gyp's paw; it was a small black hand laid upon me; while, on looking up, there in the dim light was the face of the boy I had encountered on the previous day, or whenever it was that I was struck down.

He showed his teeth and pointed to the savage on guard, laying his hand upon my lips as if to stay me from making any sound. Then he looked at my wrists and ankles, touching them gently, after which he laid his hand very gently on the back of my head, and I knew now why it was that I was suffering such pain.

For, lightly as he touched me, it was sufficient to send a keen agony through me, and it was all I could do to keep from crying out.

The boy saw my pain, and looked at me half wonderingly for a few moments before stooping low and whispering in my ear.

I felt so sick from the pain that I paid little heed to his words; but whisper or shout it would have been all the same, I could not have understood a word.

So faint and strange a sensation came over me that all seemed dim, and when I once more saw clearly I was alone and the crowd of blacks had disappeared, taking with them Jimmy—if it had not all been a dream due to my feverish state.

Just then, however, a couple of blacks came up with the boy straight to the door of the hut, and while the latter stood looking on, the men applied a roughly made plaster of what seemed to be crushed leaves to my head, and then examined my wrists and feet, rubbing them a little and giving me intense pain, which was succeeded by a peculiar, dull warm sensation as they pressed and kneaded the joints.

While they were busy the boy went off quickly, and returned with a handful of plum-like fruit, one of which he placed to my dry lips, and I found its acid juice wonderfully refreshing.

They all left me soon after, and I saw the boy go and join a tall, peculiar-looking savage, who was marked with tattoo lines or paint in a way different to the rest, and these two talked together for a long while, gesticulating and nodding again and again in my direction, as if I was the subject of their discourse.

The effect of the attention to my injuries was to produce a sensation of drowsiness, resulting in a deep sleep, which must have lasted a very long time, for when I awoke it was in the dark, and I was not startled now on hearing the snuffling noise and feeling myself touched by Gyp, who, after silently showing his pleasure, lay down with his head upon my chest once more, and seemed to go to sleep.

I made an effort to raise my hand to stroke him, but the pain was too great, and soon after it was I who went to sleep, not Gyp, and when I awoke it was daybreak and the dog was gone.

I was better that morning, and could take more interest in all that went on. I saw the tall, peculiar-looking savage go by the hut door at a distance, and I saw the boy go up to him and pass out of sight.

Soon after a couple of blacks brought me some food and water, of which I partook eagerly.

Later on the boy came with the same two men as on the previous day, and my head was once more dressed and my limbs chafed.

Then I was left alone, and I lay watching once more the savages coming and going in a slow deliberate way. I noticed that there were a good many women and children, but if ever they attempted to come in the direction of the hut where I lay they were angrily driven back.

Some of the women appeared to be occupied in domestic work, preparing some kind of bread, others busily stripped the feathers from some large birds brought in by men who seemed to have been hunting.

I noticed all this feeling calm and restful now, and I was lying wondering whether Jack Penny and the doctor would find out where I was, when I heard a scuffling noise, which seemed to come from a hut where there was a crowd of the people standing.

Then there was a repetition of the scene I had previously witnessed, Jimmy being brought out, kicking, struggling, and full of fight.

The blacks seemed to want to drag him to the tree where I had seen him tied, but to this Jimmy objected strongly. The way in which he butted at his captors, and kicked out like a grasshopper, would have been most laughable had I not been anxious, for I felt sure that it would result in his hurting some one, and being rewarded with a blow on the head or a spear thrust.

I grew so excited at last as the struggle went on that I waited till there was a moment's pause when Jimmy and his captors were drawing breath for a fresh attack, and shouted with all my might—

"Jimmy! be quiet!"

My guard, for there was still one at the door, jumped up and stared in, while Jimmy and his captors looked in my direction.

Jimmy was the first to break silence by shouting loudly: "Mass Joe! Mass Joe!"

"Here!" I shouted back; but I repented the next moment, for Jimmy uttered a yell and made a bound to run towards where he had heard the sound.

The result was that one savage threw himself down before the prisoner, who fell headlong, and before he could recover, half a dozen of the blacks were sitting upon him.

My heart seemed to stand still, and I felt that poor Jimmy's end had come, but to my delight I could see that our captors were laughing at the poor fellow's mad efforts to escape, and I shouted to him once again:

"Be quiet! Lie still!"

There was no answer, for one of the men was sitting on Jimmy's head; but he ceased struggling, and after a while the blacks rose, circled about him with their spears, and a couple of them began to push my companion towards the tree to which he had before been bound.

"Jimmy no fight?" he shouted to me.

"Not now," I shouted back. "Wait."

"All rightums," cried Jimmy: "but gettum waddy back, gibs um bang, bang—knockum downum—whack, whack—bangum, bangum!"

This was all in a voice loud enough for me to hear, as the poor fellow allowed his captors to bind him to the tree, after which he hung his head and pretended or really did go to sleep.

Towards evening I saw the blacks take Jimmy some food, and some was brought to me; and as I sat up and ate and drank I saw the strangely-marked savage and the boy come into the centre of the space by the huts, and lie down near Jimmy, who behaved a good deal after the fashion of some captured beast, for he raised his head now and then, utterly ignoring those who were around, and staring straight before him. But in his case it was not right away toward the forest, but in the direction of the hut where I was confined, and even at the distance where I lay I could read the eagerness in the black's countenance as he waited to hear me speak.

It was getting fast towards sundown, and I was wondering how long they would leave Jimmy tied up to the tree, and fighting hard to get rid of an idea that kept coming to me, namely, that the savages were feeding us and keeping us for an object that it made me shudder to think about, when I noted a little excitement among the people. There was some loud talking, and directly after about a dozen came to my prison and signed to me to get up.

I rose to my knees and then tried to stand, but my ankles were still so painful that I winced. By a stern effort, though, I stood up, and a sturdy black on either side took my arms and hurried me to a tree close by the one where Jimmy was tied.

As we crossed the opening I saw the boy and the tall painted savage standing by the door of a hut on one side, the latter holding a long spear tasselled with feathers, and I supposed him to be the chief, or perhaps only the doctor or conjuror of the village.

Jimmy's delight knew no bounds. He shouted and sang and laughed, and then howled, with the tears running down his cheeks.

"Hi, yup! Jimmy glad as big dingo dog for mutton bones!" he cried. "How quite well, Mass Joe? Jimmy so glad be with you. Seems all over again, Mass Joe, and Jimmy knock all black fellow up and down—make um run, run. Whatum, Mass Joe—legs?"

"Only with being tied up so tightly, Jimmy. They're getting better. My head is the worst."

"Head um worse, Mass Joe! Show Jimmy black debble hurt um head. Jimmy whack um, whack um too much can't say kangaroo."

"No, no! wait a bit, Jimmy," I said, as the blacks bound me to the tree. "We must watch for our time."

"Watch?" said Jimmy; "watch? Doctor got um watch clock. Tick, tick, tick!"

"Where is the doctor?" I said.

"Jimmy don't know little bitums. Doctor go one way. Mass Jack-Jack Penny-Penny, one way find Mass Joe. Jimmy-Jimmy, go one way find Mass Joe. Jimmy-Jimmy find um. Hooray! Nebber shall be slabe!"

"I hope not, Jimmy," I said, smiling. "So the doctor and Jack Penny and you all went to find me, and you were seized by the blacks?"

"Dats um—all lot take um way," cried Jimmy. "Only Jimmy find Mass Joe. Come along a black fellow. All jump atop Jimmy. Jimmy fight um, kick um—play big goose berry strong black fellow. Too much big coward big. Topper, topper, Jimmy head um. Go sleep um. Bring um here."

"Too many of them, and they hit you on the head and stunned you?"

"Hiss! 'tunned Jimmy. Hiss! 'tunned Jimmy. Send um all asleep. Topper head."

"Never mind the topper they gave you, Jimmy. We'll escape and find our friends."

"Don't know um," said Jimmy dolefully. "Bad good black fellow got no muttons—no grub—no wallaby. Eat Mass Joe—eat Jimmy."

"Do you think they are cannibals, Jimmy?" I said excitedly.

Jimmy opened his mouth and his eyes very wide and stared at me.

"I say, do you think they are cannibals? How stupid! Do you think they eat man?"

"Yes; 'tupid, 'tupid. Eat man, lot o' man. Bad, bad. Make um sick, sick."

I turned cold, for here was corroboration of my fear. This was why they were treating us well instead of killing us at once; and I was turning a shuddering look at the circle of black faces around me when Jimmy exclaimed:

"Sha'n't ums eat Jimmy. No, no. Jimmy eat a whole lot fust. No eat Mass Joe. Jimmy killum killum all lot."

I stood there tightly bound, talking from time to time to the black, happier in mind at having a companion in my imprisonment, and trying to make him understand that our best policy was to wait our time; and then when our captors were more off their guard we could perhaps escape.

"No good 't all," said Jimmy, shaking his head. "Go eat um, Mass Joe, poor Jimmy. Make up fat um—fat um like big sheep. No run at all, catch fas'."

"Not so bad as that, Jimmy," I said, laughing in spite of my position at the idea of being made so fat that we could neither of us run.

Just then there was a movement among our captors, and having apparently satisfied themselves with a long inspection of their prisoners they were evidently about to take us back to our prisons.

"Jimmy gib all big kick?" said the black.

"No, no," I cried, "go quietly."

"Jimmy come 'long Mass Joe?" he said next.

"If they will let you," I replied; "but if they will not, go back to your own place quietly."

"Mass Joe no kind poor Jimmy," he whimpered. "Want kick um. Mass Joe say no."

"Wait till I tell you, Jimmy," I replied. "Now go quietly."

He made an attempt to accompany me, but the blacks seized him sharply and led him one way, me the other; and as the sun set and the darkness began to come on, I lay in my hut watching the boy and the tall painted chief talking earnestly together, for I could not see Jimmy's prison from inside my own.

I felt lighter of heart and more ready to take a hopeful view of my position now that my sufferings from my injuries were less, and that I had a companion upon whom I could depend. But all the same I could not help feeling that my position was a very precarious one. But when I was cool and calm I was ready to laugh at the idea about cannibalism, and to think it was the result of imagination.

"No," I said to myself as I lay there, "I don't think they will kill us, and I am certain they will not eat us. We shall be made slaves and kept to work for them—if they can keep us!"

As I lay there listening to the different sounds made in the village dropping off one by one in the darkness, I grew more elate. I was in less pain, and I kept recalling the many instances Jimmy had shown me of his power to be what he called "cunning-artful." With his help I felt sure that sooner or later we should be able to escape.

Drowsiness began to creep over me now, and at last, after listening to the hard breathing of the spear-armed savage whose duty it was to watch me, I began to wonder whether Gyp would come that night.

"I hope he will," I said to myself. "I'll keep awake till he does."

The consequence of making this determination was that in a very few minutes after I was fast asleep.

Just as before I was wakened some time in the night by feeling something touch me, and raising my arm for the first time made the faithful beast utter low whines of joy as I softly patted his head and pulled his ears, letting my hand slip lower to stroke his neck, when my fingers came in contact with the dog's collar, and almost at the same moment with a stiff scrap of paper.

For a moment my heart stood still. Then, sitting up, I caught the dog to me, holding his collar with both hands, touching the paper all the while, but afraid to do more lest the act should result in disappointment.

At last I moved one hand cautiously and felt the paper, trembling the while, till a joyous throb rose to my lips, and I rapidly untied a piece of string which tightly bound what was evidently a note to the dog's collar.

Gyp whined in a low tone, and as I loosened him, grasping the note in my hand, I knew that he gave a bit of a skip, but he came back and nestled close to me directly.

I needed no thought to know that the note was from the doctor, who must be near. Perhaps, too, Gyp had been night after night with that same note, and I had been too helpless to raise a hand and touch his neck where it had been tied.

The doctor was close by, then. There was help, and I would once more be free to get back safe to my dear mother.

I stopped there and said half aloud:

"Not yet—safe to try once more to find him."

What was I to do?

I could not read the note. I opened it and moved my fingers over it as a blind person would, but could not feel a letter, as I might have known.

What was I to do?

Gyp would be going back. The letter would be gone, while the doctor might not know but what it had been lost.

What should I do?

There was only one thing, and that was to tie my handkerchief, my torn and frayed silk handkerchief, tightly to the dog's collar.

"He will know that I am here, and alive," I said to myself. "I wish I could send him word that Jimmy is here as well."

I tried hard to think of some plan, but for a long time not one would come.

"I have it!" I said at last; and rapidly taking off the handkerchief I tied two knots fast in one corner.

"Perhaps he will understand that means two of us," I said; and I was about to fasten it to the dog's collar, when there was a noise outside as of some one moving, and Gyp dashed away from me and was gone.

"Without my message," I said to myself in tones of bitter disappointment, as all became silent again.

To my great joy, though, I heard a faint panting once more, and Gyp touched my hand with his wet nose.

"I'll be safe this time," I remarked, as I rapidly secured and tied the knotted handkerchief, ending by fondling and caressing the dog, I was so overjoyed.

"Go on, dear old Gyp," I cried softly; "and come back to-morrow night for an answer. There, good-bye. Hush! don't bark. Good-bye!"

I patted him, and he ran his nose into my breast, whining softly. Then after feeling the handkerchief once more, to be sure it was safe, I loosened the dog and he bounded from me. I heard a rustling in the corner, and all was silent, while I lay there holding the note tightly in my pocket and longing for the day to come that I might read all that my friends had to say.

Chapter Twenty Nine
How I heard English spoken here

I suppose I must have dropped asleep some time, but it seemed to me that I was lying awake watching for the daylight, which seemed as if it would never come. Then I dropped soundly asleep and slept some hours, for when I opened my eyes with a start there was one of the blacks leaning over me with some cords in his hands, with which he seemed to be about to bind me; but a shout outside took his attention, and he went out, leaving me trembling with anxiety and crushing the note in my hand.

It was broad daylight with brilliant sunshine without, but my prison was windowless, and where I lay was in the shadow, save where here and there a pencil of light shone through the palm-leaf thatch and made a glowing spot upon the floor.

Every moment I expected to see my guard back again, or I might be interrupted, I knew, by the coming of some one with food. I dared not then attempt to read for some time, since it seemed like too great a risk of losing words that were inexpressibly precious.

At last all seemed so still but the buzz and hum of distant voices that I determined to venture, and undoing my hot hand I unfolded the little scrap of paper, upon which, written closely but clearly, were the following words—

"*As we are so near a village of the blacks, and you have not returned, I have concluded that you have been made a prisoner. Gyp found your scent and went off, returning after many hours' absence; so I write these lines to bid you be of good heart, for we shall try by stratagem to get you away.*"

Then there was this, evidently written the next day:

"*Gyp has been again and brought back the above lines which I tied to his collar. If you get them tie something to the dog's collar to show you are alive and well. Poor Jimmy went in search of you, but has not returned.*"

"Tie something to the dog's collar to show you are alive and well!" I said to myself over and over again, as I carefully secreted the scrap of paper—a needless task, as, if it had been seen, no one would have paid any heed to it. "And I have tied something to the dog's collar and they will come, the doctor and Jack Penny, with the blacks, to-night to try and save me, and I shall escape."

I stopped here, for the words seemed to be wild and foolish. How could they rescue me, and, besides, ought I not to feel glad that I was here among the natives of the island? What better position could I be in for gaining information about my father?

I lay thinking like this for long, and every hour it seemed that my injured head and my cut wrists and ankles were healing. The confused feeling had passed away, leaving nothing but stiffness and soreness, while the message I had received gave me what I wanted worst—hope.

I did not see Jimmy that day, for he was not brought out, neither was I taken to the tree, but I saw that the savage who brought me food had a double quantity, and to prove that some of it was meant for my fellow-prisoner I soon afterwards heard him shout:

"Mass Joe come have 'nana—come have plantain 'nana."

This he repeated till I uttered a low long whistle, one which he had heard me use scores of times, and to which he replied.

An hour after he whistled again, but I could not reply, for three or four of the blacks were in the hut with me, evidently for no other purpose than to watch.

That night I lay awake trembling and anxious. I wanted to have something ready to send back by the dog when it came at night, but try how I would I could contrive nothing. I had no paper or pencil; no point of any kind to scratch a few words on a piece of bark—no piece of bark if I had had a point.

As it happened, though I lay awake the dog did not come, and when the morning came, although I was restless and feverish I was more at rest in my mind, for I thought I saw my way to communicate a word or two with the doctor.

I was unbound now, and therefore had no difficulty in moving about the hut, from whose low roof, after a good deal of trying, I at last obtained a piece of palm-leaf that seemed likely to suit my purpose. This done, my need was a point of some kind—a pin, a nail, the tongue of a buckle, a hard sharp piece of wood, and I had neither.

But I had hope.

Several different blacks had taken their places at the door of my hut, and I was waiting patiently for the one to return who sat there carving his waddy handle. When he came I hoped by some stratagem to get hold of the sharp bit of flint to scratch my palm-leaf.

Fortunately towards mid-day this man came, and after a good look at me where I lay he stuck his spear in the earth, squatted down, took out his flint and waddy, and began once more to laboriously cut the zigzag lines that formed the ornamentation.

I lay there hungrily watching him hour after hour, vainly trying to think out some plan, and when I was quite in despair the black boy, whom I had not seen for many hours, came sauntering up in an indifferent way to stand talking to my guard for some minutes, and then entered the hut to stand looking down at me.

I was puzzled about that boy, for at times I thought him friendly, at others disposed to treat me as an enemy; but my puzzled state was at an end, for as soon as I began to make signs he watched me eagerly and tried to comprehend.

I had hard work to make him understand by pointing to the savage outside, and then pretending to hack at my finger as if carving it. Jimmy would have understood in a moment, but it was some time before the boy saw what I meant. Then his face lit up, and he slowly sauntered away, as if in the most careless of moods, poising his spear and throwing it at trees, stooping, leaping, and playing at being a warrior of his tribe, so it seemed to me, till he disappeared among the trees.

The sun was sinking low, but he did not return. I saw him pass by with the tall painted warrior, and then go out of sight. My food had been given me, but I had not seen Jimmy, though we had corresponded together by making a few shrill parrot-like whistles. Night would soon be upon me once again, and when Gyp came, if he did come, I should not be ready.

I was just thinking like this when there was a slight tap close by me, and turning quickly I saw a sharp-pointed piece of stone upon the beaten earth floor, and as I reached out my hand to pick it up a piece of white wood struck me on the hand, making a sharp metallic sound.

I felt that there was danger, and half threw myself over my treasures, looking dreamily out at the entrance and remaining motionless, as my guard entered to stare round suspiciously, eyeing me all over, and then going slowly back.

I breathed more freely, and was thinking as I saw him settle down that I might at any time begin to try and carve a word or two, and in this mind I was about to take the piece of wood from beneath me when the savage swung himself round and sprang into the hut in a couple of bounds.

He had meant to surprise me if I had been engaged upon any plan of escape, but finding me perfectly motionless he merely laughed and went back.

Directly after, another savage came up and took his place, and I eagerly began my task.

Very easy it sounds to carve a few letters on a piece of wood, but how hard I found it before I managed to roughly cut the words "All Well," having selected these because they were composed of straight lines, which mine were not. Still I hoped that the doctor would make them out, and I hid my piece of flint and my wooden note and waited, meaning to keep awake till the dog came.

But I had been awake all the previous night, and I fell fast asleep, till Gyp came and roused me by scratching at my chest, when in a dreamy confused way I found and took something from the dog's collar and tied my note in its place, falling asleep directly after from sheer exhaustion.

It was broad daylight when I awoke, and my first thought was of my message, when, thrusting my hand into my breast, a curious sensation of misery came over me as my hand came in contact with a piece of wood, and it seemed that I had been dreaming and the dog had not come.

I drew out the flat piece of white wood, but it was not mine. The doctor, probably having no paper, had hit upon the same plan as I.

His words were few.

"Be on the alert. We shall come some night."

I thrust the wooden label beneath the dust of the floor, scraped some more earth over it, and already saw myself at liberty, and in the joy of my heart I uttered a long parrot-like whistle, but it was not answered.

I whistled again, but there was no reply; and though I kept on making signals for quite an hour no response came, and the joyousness began to fade out of my breast.

Twice over that morning I saw the tall savage who was so diabolically painted and tattooed go by, and once I thought he looked very hard at my hut; but he soon passed out of my sight, leaving me wondering whether he was the chief, from his being so much alone, and the curious way in which all the people seemed to get out of his path.

Once or twice he came near enough for me to see him better, and I noticed that he walked with his eyes fixed upon the ground in a dreamy way, full of dignity, and I felt certain now that he must be the king of these people.

The next day came and I saw him again in the midst of quite a crowd, who had borne one of their number into the middle of the inclosure of huts, and this time I saw the tall strange-looking savage go slowly down upon his knees, and soon after rise and motion with his hands, when everyone but the boy fell back. He alone knelt down on one side of what was evidently an injured man.

The blacks kept their distance religiously till the painted savage signed to them once more, when they ran forward and four of their number lifted the prostrate figure carefully and carried it into a hut.

"I was right," I said to myself with a feeling of satisfaction. "I was right the first time. It is the doctor, and he ought to have come to my help when I was so bad."

Two days, three days passed, during which I lay and watched the birds that flitted by, saw the people as they came and went, and from time to time uttered a signal whistle; but this had to be stopped, for on the afternoon of the third day a very tall savage entered hurriedly in company with my guard and half a dozen more, and by signs informed me that if I made signals again my life would be taken.

It was very easy to understand, for spears were pointed at me and war-clubs tapped me not very lightly upon the head.

As soon as I was left alone I sat thinking, and before long came to the conclusion that this was probably the reason why I had not heard any signal from Jimmy, who had perhaps been obstinate, and consequently had been treated with greater severity.

I longed for the night to come that I might have some fresh message from the doctor, but somehow I could not keep awake, anxious as I was, and I was sleeping soundly when a touch awoke me with a start.

I threw up my hands to catch Gyp by the collar, but to my consternation I touched a hand and arm in the darkness, and there was something so peculiar in the touch, my hand seeming to rest on raised lines of paint, that I turned cold, for I knew that one of the savages was bending over me, and I felt that it must mean that my time had come.

I should have called out, but a hand was laid over my lips and an arm pressed my chest, as a voice whispered in good English:

"Run, escape! You can't stay here!"

"Who is it?" I whispered back, trembling with excitement. "I know!" I added quickly; "you are the tall savage—the doctor!"

"Yes—yes!" he said in a low dreamy tone. "The tall savage! Yes—tall savage!"

"But you are an Englishman!" I panted, as a terrible thought, half painful, half filled with hope, flashed through my brain.

"Englishman! yes—Englishman! Before I was here—before I was ill! Come, quick! escape for your life! Go!"

"And you?"

He was silent—so silent that I put out my hands and touched him, to make sure that he had not gone, and I found that he was resting his head upon his hands.

"Will you go with me to my friends?" I said, trembling still, for the thought that had come to me was gaining strength.

"Friends!" he said softly; "friends! Yes, I had friends before I came—before I came!"

He said this in a curious dreamy tone, and I forced the idea back. It was impossible, but at the same time my heart leaped for joy. Here was an Englishman dwelling among the savages—a prisoner, or one who had taken up this life willingly, and if he could dwell among them so could my father, who must be somewhere here.

"Tell me," I began; but he laid his hand upon my lips.

"Hist! not a sound," he said. "The people sleep lightly; come with me."

He took my hand in his and led me out boldly past a black who was lying a short distance from my hut, and then right across the broad opening surrounded by the natives' dwellings, and then through a grove of trees to a large hut standing by itself.

He pressed my hand hard and led me through the wide opening into what seemed to be a blacker darkness, which did not, however, trouble him, for he stepped out boldly, and then I heard a muttering growl which I recognised directly.

"Hush, Jimmy!" I whispered, throwing myself upon my knees. "Don't speak."

"Jimmy not a go to speak um," he said softly. "Mass Joe come a top."

"Go," said my companion. "Go quick. I want to help—I—the fever—my head—help."

There was another pause, and on stretching out my hand I found that my guide was pressing his to his forehead once again.

"He has lived this savage life so long that he cannot think," I felt as, taking his hand, I led him to the opening, through which he passed in silence, and with Jimmy walking close behind he led us between a couple more huts, and then for a good hour between tall trees so close together that we threaded our way with difficulty.

My companion did not speak, and at last the silence grew so painful that I asked him how long it would be before daybreak.

"Hush!" he said. "Listen! They have found out."

He finished in an excited way, repeating hastily some native words before stooping to listen, when, to my dismay, plainly enough in the silence of the night came the angry murmur of voices, and this probably meant pursuit—perhaps capture, and then death.

Chapter Thirty
How I talked with my new Friend

As I heard the sound of the pursuit a horrible sensation of dread came over me. I felt that we must be taken, and, in addition, vague ideas of trouble and bloodshed floated through my brain, with memories of the fight in the gorge, and I shuddered at the idea of there being more people slain.

The effect was different upon Jimmy, the distant cries seeming to excite him. He stopped every now and then to jump from the ground and strike the nearest tree a tremendous blow with a waddy he had obtained from our guide.

The latter checked him, though, laying a hand upon his arm as he said to me, after listening intently:

"You don't want to fight. These people are too strong. You must escape."

"But you will come with us?" I said once more, with the vague fancy coming back that this was he whom I sought, but terribly changed.

He said something in reply in the savage tongue, stopped, and then went on.

"I forget—I don't know. I am the doctor—a savage—what did you say?"

"Come with us," I whispered, and he bent his head in the dark; but my words seemed to have no effect upon him, one idea seeming to be all that he could retain, for he hurried me on, grasping my arm tightly, and then loosed it and went on in front.

Jimmy took his place, gripping my arm in turn, and, whispering, showed his power of observation by saying:

"Much good him. No black fellow. Talk like Mass Joe some time. Jimmy tink um Mass Joe fader got dust in head. Don't know know."

"Oh no! impossible, Jimmy," I whispered back with emotion. "It cannot be my father."

"No fader? All um white fellow got mud mud in head. Can't see, can't know know. No Mass Joe fader?"

"No, I am sure it is not."

"Then um white fellow. No black fellow. Tupid tupid. Don't know at all. No find wallaby in hole. No find honey. No kedge fis. Tupid white fellow all a same, mud in um head."

"He seems strange in his head," I said.

"Yes. Iss mad mad. No wash um head clean. Can't tink straight up an down ums like Jimmy."

"But he is saving us," I said. "Taking us to our friends."

"Jimmy no know. Jimmy tink doctor somewhere right long—big hill. Gib black white fellow topper topper make um tink more."

"No, no," I whispered, for he had grasped his waddy and was about to clear our guide's misty brain in this rough-and-ready way. "Be quiet and follow him."

Just then our guide stopped and let me go to his side.

"Fever—my head," he said softly, and as if apologising. "Can't think."

"But you will come with us?" I said. "My friend the doctor will help you. You shall help us. You must not go back to that degraded life."

"Doctor!" he said, as if he had only caught that word. "Yes, the doctor. Can't leave the people—can't leave him."

"Him!" I said; "that boy?"

"Hush! come faster." For there were shouts and cries behind, and he hurried us along for some distance, talking rapidly to me all the while in the savages' tongue, and apparently under the impression that I understood every word, though it was only now and then that I caught his meaning, and then it was because they were English words.

After catching a few of these I became aware, or rather guessed, that he was telling me the story of his captivity among these people, and I tried eagerly to get him to speak English; but he did not seem to heed me, going on rapidly, and apparently bent on getting us away.

I caught such words as "fever—prisoner—my head—years—misery—despair—always—savage—doctor"—but only in the midst of a long excited account which he said more to himself. I was at last paying little heed to him when two words stood out clear and distinctly from the darkness of his savage speech, words that sent a spasm through me and made me catch at his arm and try to speak, but only to emit a few gasping utterances as he bent down to me staring as if in wonder.

The words were "fellow-prisoner;" and they made me stop short, for I felt that I had really and providentially hit upon the right place after all, and that there could be only one man likely to be a fellow-prisoner, and that—my poor father.

It was impossible to flee farther, I felt, and leave him whom I had come to seek behind.

Then common sense stepped in and made me know that it was folly to stay, while Jimmy supplemented these thoughts by saying:

"Black fellow come along fas. Mass Joe no gun, no powder pop, no chopper, no knife, no fight works 'tall."

"Where is he?" I said excitedly, as I held the arm of our guide.

"Blacks—coming after us."

He talked on rapidly in the savage tongue and I uttered a groan of despair.

"What um say, Mass Joe?" whispered Jimmy excitedly. "Talk, talk, poll parrot can't say know what um say. Come along run way fas. Fight nunner time o," he added. "Black fellow come along."

He caught my arm, and, following our guide, we hurried on through the darkness, which was so dense that if it had not been for the wonderful eyesight of my black companion—a faculty which seemed to have been acquired or shared by our guide—I should have struck full against the trunk of some tree. As it was, I met with a few unpleasant blows on arm or shoulder, though the excitement of our flight was too great for me to heed them then.

I was in despair, and torn by conflicting emotions: joy at escaping and at having reached the goal I had set up, misery at having to leave it behind just when I had found the light. It might have been foolish, seeing how much better I could serve him by being free, but I felt ready to hurry back and share my father's captivity, for I felt assured that it must be he of whom our guide spoke.

We were hurrying on all this time entirely under the guidance of the strange being who had set us free, but not without protests from the black, who was growing jealous of our guide and who kept on whispering:

"No go no farrer, Mass Joe, Jimmy fine a doctor an Mass Jack Penny. Hi come along Jimmy now."

He was just repeating this in my ear when we were hurrying on faster, for the sounds of our pursuers came clear upon the wind, when our guide stopped short and fell back a few paces as a low angry growl saluted him from the darkness in front and he said something sharply to us in the native tongue.

His words evidently meant "Fall back!" but I had recognised that growl.

"Gyp!" I cried; and the growling changed to a whining cry of joy, and in an instant the dog was leaping up at my face, playfully biting at my hands, and then darting at Jimmy he began the same welcoming demonstrations upon the black.

"Mass Joe, Mass Joe, he go eat up black fellow. Top um away, top um away."

"It's only his play, Jimmy," I said.

"Him eat piece Jimmy, all up leggum," cried the black.

"Here, Gyp!" I cried, as the dog stopped his whining cry of pleasure, but growled once more. "Here," I said, "this is a friend. Pat his head, sir, and —, where is he, Jimmy?"

"Black white fellow, Mass Joe?"

"Yes, yes, where is he?"

"Gone 'long uder way. Run back fas fas. Fraid o Gyp, Gyp send um way."

"Stop him! Run after him! He must not go," I cried.

I stopped, for there was a low piping whistle like the cry of a Blue Mountain parrot back at home.

"Jack Penny!" I gasped, and I answered the call.

"Iss, yes, Mass Jack Penny," cried Jimmy, and Gyp made a bound from my side into the darkness, leaving us alone.

We heard the crash and rustle of the underwood as the dog tore off, and I was about to follow, but I could not stir, feeling that if I waited our guide might return, when, in the midst of my indecision, the whistle was repeated, and this time Jimmy answered.

Then there was more rustling, the dog came panting back; and as the rustling continued there came out of the darkness a sound that made my heart leap.

It was only my name softly uttered, apparently close at hand, and I made a bound in the direction, but only to fall back half-stunned, for I had struck myself full against a tree.

I just remember falling and being caught by some one, and then I felt sick, and the darkness seemed filled with lights.

But these soon died out, and I was listening to a familiar voice that came, it appeared, from a long way off; then it came nearer and nearer, and the words seemed to be breathed upon my face.

"Only a bit stunned," it said; and then I gasped out the one word:

"Doctor!"

"My dear Joe!" came back, and— well, it was in the dark, and we were not ashamed: the doctor hugged me to his heart, as if I had been his brother whom he had found.

Chapter Thirty One
How we made further Plans

"Why, Joe, my lad," he said at last, in a voice I did not recognise, it was so full of emotion, "you've driven me half-wild. How could you get in such a fix?"

"Jimmy get in big fix," said an ill-used voice. "Nobody glad to see Jimmy."

"I'm glad to feel you," drawled a well-known voice. "I can't see you. How are you, Joe Carstairs? Where have you been?"

"Jack, old fellow, I'm glad!" I cried, and I grasped his hands.

"That will do," said the doctor sternly. "Are the savages after you, Joe?"

"Yes, in full pursuit, I think," I said. "But my guide. I can't leave him."

"Your guide? Where is he?"

"I don't know. He was here just now. He brought us here."

"Jimmy-Jimmy say um goes back along," said the black. "He no top, big fright. Gyp bite um."

"One of the blacks, Joe?" said the doctor.

"No, no!" I said, so excited that I could hardly speak coherently. "A white man—a prisoner among the blacks—like a savage, but—"

"No, no," said Jimmy in a disgusted tone; "no like savage black fellow-fellow. Got a dust in head. No tink a bit; all agone."

"His mind wanders, being a prisoner," I stammered. "He is with the blacks—a prisoner—with my father."

"What?" cried the doctor.

"He has a fellow-prisoner," I faltered. "I am not sure—it must be—my father!"

"Mass Joe find um fader all along," said the black. "Jimmy find um too."

"Be silent!" cried the doctor. "Do I understand aright, Joe, that your father is a prisoner with the people from whom you have escaped?"

"Yes—I think so—I am not sure—I feel it is so," I faltered.

"Humph!"

"Have you seen him?"

"No," I said. "I did not know he was there till I was escaping."

"Jimmy see um. All rightums. Find Mass Joe fader."

"You saw him, Jimmy?" I panted.

"Iss. Yes, Jimmy see him. Big long hair beard down um tummuck."

"You have seen him—the prisoner?" said the doctor.

"Yes; iss Jimmy see um. Shut up all along. Sittum down, um look at ground all sleep, sleep like wallaby, wallaby."

"He means the poor fellow who helped us to escape," I said sadly.

"Jimmy see Mass Joe fader," cried the black indignantly. "Jimmy take um right long show um."

"The man who brought us here?"

"No, no, no, no!" cried Jimmy, dancing with vexation. "Not, not. Jimmy see um Mass Joe fader sit all along. See froo hole. Big long beard down um tummuck—long hair down um back. Um shake um head so, so. Say 'hi—hi—ho—hum. Nev see home again. Ah, my wife! Ah, my boy!'"

"You heard him say that, Jimmy?" I cried, catching him by the arm.

"Jimmy sure, sure. Jimmy look froo hole. Den fro little tone an hit um, and den black fellow come along, and Jimmy lay fas' sleep, eye shut, no move bit."

"He has seen him, Joe," cried the doctor. "He could not have invented that."

There was a low whining growl here again from Gyp, and Jack Penny drawled:

"I say, sha'n't we all be made prisoners if we stop here?"

"Quick!" said the doctor; "follow me."

"And our guide?" I cried.

"We must come in search of him another time. If he has been with the blacks for long he will know how to protect himself."

I was unwilling to leave one who had helped us in such a time of need; but to stay meant putting ourselves beyond being able to rescue my father, if it were really he who was our guide's fellow-prisoner. The result, of course, was that I followed the doctor, while a snuffling whine now and then told us that Gyp was on in front, and, in spite of the darkness, leading the way so well that there seemed to be no difficulty.

"Where are we going?" I said, after a pause, during which we had been listening to the cries of the savages, which appeared to come from several directions.

"To our hiding-place," said the doctor. "Jimmy found it before we lost him, and we have kept to it since, so as to be near you."

"But how did you know you were near me?" I said.

"Through Gyp first. He went away time after time, and I suspected that he had found you, so one day we followed him and he led us to the village."

"Yes?" I said.

"Then we had to wait. I sent messages to you by him; and at last I got your answer. To-night we were coming again to try and reach you, perhaps get you away. We meant to try. I should not have gone back without you, my lad," he said quietly.

The cries now seemed distant, and we went slowly on through the darkness—slowly, for the trees were very close and it required great care to avoid rushing against them; but the doctor seemed to have made himself acquainted with the forest, and he did not hesitate till all at once the shouts of the blacks seemed to come from close by upon our right, and were answered directly from behind us.

"A party of them have worked round," whispered the doctor. "Keep cool. They cannot know we are so near. Hist! crouch down."

We were only just in time, for hardly had we crouched down close to the ground than the sound of the savages pushing forward from tree to tree was heard.

I could not understand it at first, that curious tapping noise; but as they came nearer I found that each man lightly tapped every tree he reached, partly to avoid it, by the swinging of his waddy, partly as a guide to companions of his position.

They came closer and closer, till it seemed that they must either see or touch us, and I felt my heart beat in heavy dull throbs as I longed for the rifle that these people had taken from me when they made me prisoner.

I heard a faint rustle to my right, and I knew it was Jimmy preparing for a spring. I heard a slight sound on my left just as the nearest savage uttered a wild cry, and I knew that this was the lock of a gun being cocked. Then all was silent once more.

Perhaps the savages heard the faint click, and uttered a warning, for the tapping of the trees suddenly ceased, and not the faintest sound could be heard.

This terrible silence lasted quite five minutes. It seemed to me like an hour, and all the while we knew that at least a dozen armed savage warriors were within charging distance, and that discovery meant certain captivity, if not death.

I held my breath till I felt that when I breathed again I should utter a loud gasp and be discovered. I dared not move to bury my face in my hands or in the soft earth, and my sensations were becoming agonising, when there was a sharp tap on a tree, so near that I felt the ground quiver. The tap was repeated to right and left, accompanied by a curious cry that sounded like "Whai—why!" and the party swept on.

"A narrow escape!" said the doctor, as we breathed freely once more. "Go on, Gyp. Let's get to earth; we shall be safer there."

I did not understand the doctor's words then, but followed in silence, with Jack Penny coming close up to me whenever he found the way open, to tell me of his own affairs.

"My back's a deal better," he whispered. "I've been able to rest it lately—waiting for you, and it makes it stronger, you know, and—"

"Silence, Penny!" said the doctor reprovingly, and Jack fell back a few feet; and we travelled on, till suddenly, instead of treading upon the soft decayed-leaf soil of the forest, I found that we were rustling among bushes down a steep slope. Then we were amongst loose stones, and as the darkness was not quite so dense I made out by sight as well as by the soft trickling sound, that a little rivulet was close to our feet.

This we soon afterwards crossed, and bidding me stoop the doctor led the way beneath the dense bushes for some little distance before we seemed to climb a stony bank, and then in the intense darkness he took me by the shoulders and backed me a few steps.

"There's quite a bed of branches there," he said aloud. "You can speak out, we are safe here;" and pressing me down I sat upon the soft twigs that had been gathered together, and Jack Penny came and lay down beside me, to talk for a time and then drop off to sleep, an example I must have followed. For all at once I started and found that it was broad daylight, with the loud twittering song of birds coming from the bushes at the entrance of what seemed to be a low-roofed extensive cave, whose mouth was in the shelving bank of a great bluff which overhung a silvery-sounding musical stream.

Some light came in from the opening; but the place was made bright by the warm glow that came from a kind of rift right at the far end of the cave, and through this was also wafted down the sweet forest scents.

"Jimmy's was a lucky find for us," said the doctor, when I had partaken of the food I found they had stored there, and we had talked over our position and the probability of my belief being correct. "It is shelter as well as a stronghold;" and he pointed to the means he had taken to strengthen the entrance, by making our black followers bind together the branches of the tangled shrubs that grew about the mouth.

In the talk that ensued it was decided that we would wait a couple of days, and then go by night and thoroughly examine the village. Jimmy would be able to point out the hut where my father was confined, and then if opportunity served we would bring him away, lie hidden here for a few days till the heat of the pursuit was over, and then escape back to the coast.

I would not own to the doctor that I had my doubts, and he owned afterwards to me that his feeling was the same. So we both acted as if we had for certain discovered him of whom we came in search, and waited our time for the first venture.

It was dangerous work hunting for food at so short a distance from the village, but our black followers, aided by Jimmy, were very successful, their black skins protecting them from exciting surprise if they were seen from a distance, and they brought in a good supply of fish every day simply by damming up some suitable pool in the little stream in whose bank our refuge was situated. This stream swarmed with fish, and it was deep down in a gully between and arched over by trees. The bows and arrows and Jimmy's spear obtained for us a few birds, and in addition they could always get for us a fair supply of fruit, though not quite such as we should have chosen had it been left to us. Roots, too, they brought, so that with the stores we had there was not much prospect of our starving.

In fact so satisfactory was our position in the pleasant temperate cave that Jack Penny was in no hurry to move.

"We're just as well here as anywhere else," he said; "that is, if we had found your father."

"And got him safe here," he added after a pause.

"And the black chaps didn't come after us," he said after a little more thought.

"And your mother wasn't anxious about you," he said, after a little more consideration.

"You'll find such a lot more reasons for not stopping, Jack Penny," I said, after hearing him out, "that you'll finish by saying we had better get our work done and return to a civilised country as soon as we can."

"Oh, I don't know!" said Jack slowly. "I don't care about civilised countries: they don't suit me. Everybody laughs at me because I'm a bit different, and father gives it to me precious hard sometimes. Give me Gyp and my gun, and I should be happy enough here."

"Don't talk like that, Jack," I said in agony, as I thought of him who had helped me to escape, and of the prisoner he had mentioned, and whom the black professed to have seen. "Let's get our task done and escape as soon as we can. A savage life is not for such as we."

That day we had an alarm.

Our men had been out and returned soon after sunrise, that being our custom for safety's sake. Then, too, we were very careful about having a fire, though we had no difficulty with it, for it burned freely, and the smoke rose up through the great crack in the rock above our heads, and disappeared quietly amongst the trees. But we had one or two scares: hearing voices of the blacks calling to each other, but they were slight compared to the alarm to which I alluded above.

The men, I say, were back, having been more successful than usual — bringing us both fish and a small wild pig. We had made a good meal, and the doctor and I were lying on the armfuls of leafy boughs that formed our couch, talking for the twentieth time about our plans for the night, when all at once, just as I was saying that with a little brave effort we could pass right through the sleepy village and bring away the prisoner, I laid my hand sharply on the doctor's arm.

He raised his head at the same moment, for we had both heard the unmistakable noise given by a piece of dead twig when pressed upon by a heavy foot.

We listened with beating hearts, trying to localise the very spot whence the sound came; and when we were beginning to breathe more freely it came again, but faint and distant.

"Whoever it was has not found out that we are here," I whispered.

The doctor nodded; and just then Jack Penny, who had been resting his back, sat up and yawned loudly, ending by giving Jimmy, who was fast asleep, a sounding slap on the back.

I felt the cold perspiration ooze out of me as I glanced at the doctor. Then turning over on to my hands and knees I crept to where Jimmy was threatening Jack with his waddy in much anger, and held up my hand.

The effect was magical. They were silent on the instant, but we passed the rest of that day in agony.

"I'm glad that we decided to go to-night," the doctor said. "Whoever it was that passed must have heard us, and we shall have the savages here to-morrow to see what it meant."

The night seemed as if it would never come, but at last the sun went down, and in a very short time it was dark.

Our plans were to go as near as we dared to the village as soon as darkness set in, place our men, and then watch till the savages seemed to be asleep, and then, by Jimmy's help, seek out my father's prison, bring him away to the cave, and there rest for a day or two, perhaps for several, as I have said. But the events of the day had made us doubtful of the safety of our refuge; and, after talking the matter over with the doctor, we both came to the conclusion that we would leave the latter part of our plan to take care of itself.

"First catch your hare, Joe!" said the doctor finally. "And look here, my lad; I begin to feel confident now that this prisoner is your father. We must get him away. It is not a case of *try*! We *must*, I say; and if anything happens to me—"

"Happens to you!" I said aghast.

"Well; I may be captured in his place!" he said smiling. "If I am, don't wait, don't spare a moment, but get off with your prize. I don't suppose they will do more than imprison me. I am a doctor, and perhaps I can find some favour with them."

"Don't talk like that, doctor!" I said, grasping his hand. "We must hold together."

"We must release your father!" he said sternly. "There, that will do."

Chapter Thirty Two
How we heard a Black Discussion
and did not understand

The rescue party consisted of the doctor, Ti-hi, and myself, with Jimmy for guide. Jack Penny was to take command of the cave, and be ready to defend it and help us if attacked or we were pursued. At the same time he was to have the bearers and everything in readiness for an immediate start, in case we decided to continue our flight.

"I think that's all we can say, Penny," said the doctor in a low grave voice, as we stood ready to start. "Everything must depend on the prisoners. Now be firm and watchful. Good-bye."

"I sha'n't go to sleep," said Jack Penny. "I say, though, hadn't you better take Gyp?"

"Yes, yes; take Gyp!" I said; "he knows the way so well."

"Jimmy know a way so well, too!" said the black. "No take a dog—Gyp!"

But we decided to take the dog, and creeping down into the bed of the rivulet we stood in the darkness listening, shut-in, as it were, by the deep silence.

"Forward, Jimmy!" said the doctor, and his voice sounded hollow and strange.

Gyp uttered a whine—that dog had been so well trained that he rarely barked—ran quickly up the further bank of the rivulet; Jimmy trotted after him, waddy in hand; the doctor went next, I followed, and Ti-hi brought up the rear.

One minute the stars were shining brightly over us, the next we were under the great forest trees, and the darkness was intense.

"Keep close to me, my lad," the doctor whispered; and I followed him by the ear more than by the eye; but somehow the task grew easier as we went on, and I did not once come in contact with a tree.

By the way Gyp took us I don't suppose it was more than six miles to the savages' village; and though we naturally went rather slowly, the excitement I felt was so great that it seemed a very little while before Jimmy stopped short to listen.

"Hear um talkum talkum," he whispered.

We could neither of us hear a sound, but I had great faith in Jimmy's hearing, for in old times he had given me some remarkable instances of the acuteness of this sense.

"Jimmy go first see!" he whispered; and the next minute we knew that we were alone with Ti-hi, Jimmy and the dog having gone on to scout.

"I detest having to depend upon a savage!" muttered the doctor; "it seems so degrading to a civilised man."

"But they hear and see better than we do."

"Yes," he said; "it is so."

There we waited in that dense blackness beneath the trees, listening to the faintest sound, till quite an hour had elapsed, and we were burning to go on, when all at once Ti-hi, who was behind us, uttered a faint hiss, and as we turned sharply a familiar voice said:

"All rightums! Jimmy been round round, find um Mass Joe fader!"

"You have found him?" I cried.

"Not talk shouto so!" whispered Jimmy. "Black fellow come."

"But have you found him?" I whispered.

"Going a find um; all soon nuff!" he replied coolly. "Come long now."

He struck off to the right and we followed, going each minute more cautiously, for we soon heard the busy hum of many voices—a hum which soon after developed into a loud chatter, with occasional angry outbursts, as if something were being discussed.

Jimmy went on, Gyp keeping close to his heels now, as if he quite understood the importance of not being seen. We had left the dense forest, and were walking in a more open part among tall trees, beneath which it was black as ever, but outside the stars shone brilliantly, and it was comparatively light.

The voices seemed so near now that I thought we were going too far, and just then Jimmy raised his hand and stopped us, before what seemed to be a patch of black darkness, and I found that we were in the shadow cast by a long hut, whose back was within a yard or so of our feet.

Jimmy placed his lips close to my ear, then to the doctor's, and to each of us he whispered:

"Soon go sleep—sleep. Find Mass Joe fader, and go away fast. All top here Jimmy go see."

I quite shared with the doctor the feeling of helpless annoyance at having to depend so much on the black; but I felt that he was far better able to carry out this task than we were, so stood listening to the buzz of voices, that seemed now to arise on every hand.

From where we stood we could see a group of the savages standing not thirty yards from us, their presence being first made plain by their eager talking, and I pressed the doctor's arm and pointed.

"Yes," he whispered; "but we are in the shadow."

From huts to right and left we could hear talking, but that in front of us was silent, and I began wondering whether it was the one that had been my prison. But it was impossible to tell, everything seemed so different in the faint light cast by the stars. I could not even make out the tree where Jimmy had been tied.

All at once a sensation as of panic seized me, for the group of blacks set up a loud shout, and came running towards where we were.

I was sure they saw us, and with a word of warning to the doctor I turned and should have fled but for two hands that were laid upon my shoulders, pressing me down, the doctor crouching likewise.

At first I thought it was Jimmy, but turning my head I found that it was Ti-hi, whose hand now moved from my shoulder to my lips.

I drew a breath full of relief the next moment, for in place of dashing down upon us the blacks rushed into the hut behind which we were standing, crowding it; and there was nothing now but a wall of dried and interwoven palm leaves between us and our fierce enemies.

Here a loud altercation seemed to ensue, angry voices being heard; and several times over I thought there was going to be a fight. I could not comprehend a word, but the tones of voice were unmistakably those of angry men, and it was easy to tell when one left off and another began.

We dared not stir, for now it seemed to be so light that if we moved from the shadow of the hut we should be seen, while the fact of one of us stepping upon a dead twig and making it snap would be enough to bring half the village upon us, at a time when we wanted to employ strategy and not force.

The burst of talking in the hut ended all at once, and there was a dead silence, as if those within were listening intently.

We held our breath and listened too, trembling with excitement, for all at once we heard a voice utter a few words, and then there was a faint sound of rustling, with the cracking noise made by a joint, as if some one had risen to a standing position.

Were the savages coming round to our side and about to leap upon us? Perhaps they were even then stealing from both ends; and my heart in the terrible excitement kept on a heavy dull throb, which seemed to beat right up into my throat.

The moments passed away, though, and at last I began to breathe more freely. It was evident that the savages had quitted the hut.

In this belief I laid my hand upon the doctor's arm, and was about to speak, when close by us, as it seemed, but really from within the wall of the hut, there came the low muttering of a voice, and I knew that some one had been left behind.

The doctor pressed my hand, and I shivered as I felt how narrow an escape we had had.

We wanted, of course, to move, but it seemed impossible, and so we stayed, waiting to see if the black had made any discovery.

After what seemed to me an interminable time I heard a slight rustling sound, and almost at the same moment there was a hand upon my arm, and directly after a warm pair of lips upon my ear:

"Jimmy no find um fader yet! Take um out o' place place! Put um somewhere; no know tell!"

I placed my lips to his ear in turn and whispered that there was some one left in the hut.

"Jimmy go see," he said softly; and before I could stay him he was gone.

"What is it?" whispered the doctor; and I told him.

The doctor drew his pistol—I heard him in the darkness—and grasped my arm, as if to be ready for flight; but just then I heard a voice in the hut which made me start with joy. Then there was a rustling sound, and Jimmy came round the corner of the hut.

"All rightums!" he whispered. "Find somebody's fader!"

"You here again, my boy!" whispered a familiar voice.

"Yes!" I said, catching the speaker's arm; and then, "Doctor," I said, "this is the prisoner who saved me—and set Jimmy free!"

"Doctor!" said the poor fellow in a low puzzled voice, as if his mind were wandering. "Yes, I am the doctor! They made me their doctor when— the fever—when—oh! my boy, my boy! why did you come back?" he cried excitedly, as if his brain were once more clear.

"To fetch you and—the other prisoner!" I said.

"Mr Carstairs?" he said earnestly. "Hush, hush! They are coming back—to kill me, perhaps! I must go."

He slipped away from us before we could stop him, and while we were debating as to whether we had not better rush in and fight in his defence, the savages crowded into the hut, and once more there was a loud buzz of voices.

These were checked by one deeper, slower, and more stern than the others, which were silenced; and after a minute or two, we heard our friend the Englishman respond in a deprecating voice, and apparently plead for mercy.

Then the chief savage spoke again in stern tones, there was a buzz of voices once more, and the savages seemed to file out and cross the opening towards the other side of the village.

We dared not move, but remained there listening, not knowing but that a guard might have been left; but at the end of a minute or two our friend was back at our side, to say excitedly:

"I want to help you, but my head—I forget—I cannot speak sometimes—I cannot think. It is all dark here—here—in my mind. Why have you come?"

"We are friends," said the doctor. "Where is Mr Carstairs?"

"Carstairs?—Mr Carstairs?" he said. "Ah—"

He began to speak volubly in the savage tongue now, tantalising me so that I grasped his arm, exclaiming fiercely:

"Speak English. Where is my father?"

I could hardly see his face, but there was light enough to tell that he turned towards me, and he stopped speaking, and seemed to be endeavouring to comprehend what I said.

"My father—the prisoner," I said again, with my lips now to his ear.

"Prisoner? Yes. At the great hut—the chief's hut—"

He began speaking again volubly, and then stopped and bent his head.

"At the chief's hut?" said the doctor excitedly. "Wait a moment or two to give him time to collect himself, then ask him again."

The poor dazed creature turned to the doctor now, and bent towards him, holding him by the arm this time.

"Chief's hut? Yes: right across. There."

He pointed in the direction the savages seemed to have taken, and from whence we could hear the voices rising and falling in busy speech.

My heart leaped, for we knew now definitely where he whom we sought was kept, and the longing, impatient sensation there came upon me to be face to face with him was so strong that I could hardly contain myself.

"Let us get round there at once," I whispered, "Here, Jimmy."

There was no answer: Jimmy had crept away.

Chapter Thirty Three
How I nearly made a terrible Mistake

We tried several times over to get our friend to speak, but the result was only a voluble burst of words in a tongue we could not comprehend, while all the time he seemed to be aware of his failing, and waved his hands and stretched them out to us as if begging us to forgive him for his weakness.

"Let him be, Joe," whispered the doctor at last; "we may excite him by pressing him. Let him calm himself, and then perhaps he can speak."

I felt as if it was resigning myself to utter despair, and it seemed that our attempt that night was to be in vain, when Jimmy suddenly popped up among us once more.

"'Long here," he whispered, and we were about to follow him when our friend stopped us.

"No; this way," he said, and he pointed in the opposite direction.

"No, no! 'long here way," said Jimmy excitedly. "Much lot black fellow that way."

"Never mind," I whispered; "let's follow him."

"Jimmy find Mass Joe fader right 'long this way," cried the black. "Not go 'long other way."

"Where is my father?"

"Big hut over 'cross," said Jimmy.

"Let's get round this way to it then," I whispered. "Come along."

The doctor was already in advance, following our guide, and after striking the earth a heavy blow with his waddy to get rid of his anger, Jimmy followed me, not able to understand that we could get to the opposite point by going round one way as readily as by the other.

It was very slow work and we had to labour hard, holding the bushes and trees so that they should not fly back upon those who followed us; but by dint of great care we got round at last to what, as far as I could judge, was the far side of the village, our principal guide being the sound of voices which came to us in a dull murmur that increased as we drew nearer, and at last we found ourselves similarly situated as to position, being at the back of another large hut.

Here we waited, listening to the buzz of voices, till I wondered in my impatience what they could be discussing, and longed to ask our guide, but feared lest I should confuse him, now that perhaps he was about to do us good service if left alone.

I was glad that I had kept quiet the next minute, for the doctor laid his hand upon my shoulder and whispered in my ear:

"There is no doubt about it, my lad. We have reached the right spot. Your father is a prisoner in this very hut, and the savages are discussing whether they will keep him here or take him away."

"What shall we do?" I whispered back in agony, for it seemed so terrible to have come all these hundreds of miles to find him, and then to sit down, as it were, quite helpless, without taking a step to set him free.

"We can do nothing yet," he replied, "but wait for an opportunity to get him away."

"Can you not make some plan?" I whispered back.

"Hist!"

He pressed my hand, for I had been growing louder of speech in my excitement, and just then there was a fresh outburst of voices from within the hut, followed by the trampling of feet and loud shouting, which seemed to be crossing the village and going farther away.

"They have taken the prisoner to—"

Our companion said the first words excitedly, and then stopped short.

"Where?" I exclaimed aloud, as I caught at his arm.

He answered me in the savage tongue, and with an impatient stamp of the foot I turned to the doctor.

"What can we do?" I said. "It makes me wish to be a prisoner too. I should see him, perhaps, and I could talk to him and tell him that help was near."

"While you shut up part of the help, and raised expectations in his breast, that would perhaps result in disappointment," replied the doctor. "We must wait, my lad, wait. The savages are excited and alarmed, and we must come when their suspicions are at rest."

"What do you mean?" I said. "Do you mean to go back to-night without him?"

"Not if we can get him away," he said; "but we must not do anything mad or rash."

"No, no, of course not," I said despairingly; "but this is horrible: to be so close to him and yet able to do nothing!"

"Be patient, my lad," he whispered, "and speak lower. We have done wonders. We have come into this unknown wild, and actually have found that the lost man is alive. What is more, we have come, as if led by blind instinct, to the very place where he is a prisoner, and we almost know the hut in which he is confined."

"Yes, yes. I know all that," I said; "but it is so hard not to be able to help him now."

"We are helping him," said the doctor. "Just think: we have this poor half-dazed fellow to glean some information, and we have a hiding-place near, and—Look out!"

I turned my piece in the direction of the danger, for just then a member of our little expedition, who had been perfectly silent so far, uttered a savage growl and a fierce worrying noise.

Simultaneously there was a burst of shouts and cries, with the sound of blows and the rush of feet through the bush.

For the next few minutes there was so much excitement and confusion that I could hardly tell what happened in the darkness. All I knew was that a strong clutch was laid upon my shoulders, and that I was being dragged backwards, when I heard the dull thud of a blow and I was driven to the ground, with a heavy body lying across me.

I partly struggled out of this position, partly found myself dragged out, and then, in a half-stunned, confused fashion, I yielded, as I was dragged through the dark forest, the twigs and boughs lashing my face horribly.

I had kept tight hold of my gun, and with the feeling strong upon me that if I wished to avoid a second captivity I must free myself, I waited for an opportunity to turn upon the strong savage who held me so tightly in his grasp and dragged me through the bush in so pitiless a manner.

He had me with his left hand riveted in my clothes while with his right hand, I presumed with a war-club, he dashed the bushes aside when the obstacles were very great.

My heart beat fast as I felt that if I were to escape I must fire at this fierce enemy, and so horrible did the act seem that twice over, after laying my hand upon my pistol, I withdrew it, telling myself that I had better wait for a few minutes longer.

And so I waited, feeling that, after all, my captivity would not be so bad as it was before, seeing that now I should know my father was near at hand.

"I can't shoot now," I said to myself passionately; "I don't think I'm a coward, but I cannot fire at the poor wretch, and I must accept my fate."

My arm dropped to my side, and at that moment my captor stopped short.

"No hear um come 'long now," he said.

"Jimmy!" I cried; and for a moment the air seemed full of humming, singing noises, and if I had not clung to my companion I should have fallen.

Chapter Thirty Four
How Jimmy and I were hunted like Beasts

"Jimmy!" I panted, as soon as I had recovered myself to find that the black was feeling me all over in the darkness.

"Not got no knock um chops, no waddy bang, no popgun ball in um nowhere," he whispered.

"No Jimmy, I'm not wounded," I said. "I thought you were one of the black fellows."

"No, no black fellow—no common black fellow sabbage," he said importantly. "Come long fas, fas."

"But the doctor and the prisoner and Ti-hi?" I said.

"All run way much fas," said Jimmy. "Gyp, Gyp, see black fellow come long much, for Jimmy do and nibblum legs make um hard hard. Gib one two topper topper, den Jimmy say time um way, take Mass Joe. Come long."

"But we must go and help the doctor," I said.

"Can't find um. All go long back to big hole. Hidum. Say Mass Joe come back long o' Jimmy-Jimmy."

It seemed probable that they would make for our hiding-place, but I was very reluctant to go and leave my friends in the lurch, so I detained Jimmy and we sat listening, the black making me sit down.

"Rest um leggums," he said. "Run much fas den."

We stayed there listening for what must have been the space of half an hour, and during that time we could hear the shouting and rapping of trees of the blacks as they were evidently searching the bush, but there was no sound of excitement or fighting, neither did it seem to me that there were any exulting shouts such as might arise over the capture of prisoners.

This gave me hope, and in the belief that I might find my companions at the hiding-place I was about to propose to Jimmy that we would go on, when he jumped up.

"No stop no longer. Black fellow come along fas. Get away."

The noises made by the blacks were plainly coming nearer, and I sprang to my feet, trying to pierce the darkness, but everywhere there were the dimly-seen shapes of trees so close that they almost seemed to lower and their branches to bear down upon our heads; there was the fresh moist scent of the dewy earth and leaves, and now and then a faint cry of some bird, but nothing to indicate the way we ought to go.

I turned to Jimmy.

"Can you tell where the cave is?" I said.

"No: Jimmy all dark," he answered.

"Can't you tell which way to go?"

"Oh yes um," he whispered. "Jimmy know which way go."

"Well, which?" I said, as the shouts came nearer.

"Dat away where no black fellow."

"But it may be away from the cave," I said.

"Jimmy don't know, can't help along. Find cave morrow nex day."

There was wisdom in his proposal, which, awkwardly as it was shaped, meant that we were to avoid the danger now and find our friends another time.

"Mass Joe keep long close," he whispered. "Soon come near time see along way Mass doctor and Mass Jack Penny-Penny."

We paused for a moment, the black going down on his knees to lay his head close to the ground so as to make sure of the direction where the savages were, and he rose up with anything but comfortable news.

"All round bout nearer, come 'long other way."

Just then I gave a jump, for something touched my leg through a great rent in my trousers. It felt cold, and for the moment I thought it must be the head of a serpent; but a low familiar whine undeceived me, and I stooped down to pat the neck of Jack Penny's shaggy friend.

"Home, Gyp!" I said. "Home!"

He understood me and started off at once, fortunately in the direction taken by Jimmy, and after a long toilsome struggle through the bush, the more arduous from the difficulty we experienced in keeping up with the dog, we at last reached a gully at the bottom of which we could hear the trickling of water.

"All right ums," said Jimmy quickly, and plunging down through the bushes he was soon at the bottom, and went upon his knees to find out which way the stream ran.

He jumped up directly, having found that by the direction the water ran we must be below the cave, always supposing that this was the right stream.

Down in the gully the sounds of pursuit grew very faint, and at last died out, while we waded at times, and at others found room upon the shelving bank to get along, perhaps for a hundred yards unchecked; then would come a long stretch where the gully was full of thick bushes, and here our only chance was to creep under them, wading the while in the little stream, often with our bodies bent so that our faces were close to the water.

Gyp trotted cheerfully on as I plashed through the water, stopping from time to time to utter a low whine to guide us when he got some distance ahead, and I often envied the sagacious animal his strength and activity, for beside him at a time like this I seemed to be a *very* helpless creature indeed.

Two or three times over I grasped the black's arm and we stopped to listen, for it seemed to me that I could hear footsteps and the rustling of the bushes at the top of the gully far above our heads; but whenever we stopped the noise ceased, and feeling at last that it was fancy I plodded on, till, half dead with fatigue, I sank down on my knees and drank eagerly of the cool fresh water, both Jimmy and the dog following my example.

At last, though I should not have recognised the place in the gloom, Jimmy stopped short, and from the darkness above my head, as I stood with the stream bubbling past my legs, I heard the unmistakable click of a gun cock.

"Jack!" I whispered. "Jack Penny!"

"That'll do," he whispered back. "Come along. All right! Have you got him?"

"Whom?" I said, stumbling painfully up into the cave, where I threw myself down.

"Your father."

"No," I said dismally, "and we've lost the doctor and Ti-hi. Poor fellows, I'm afraid they are taken. But, Jack Penny, we are right. My father is a prisoner in the village."

"Then we'll go and fetch him out, and the doctor too. Ti-hi can take care of himself. I'd as soon expect to keep a snake in a wicker cage as that fellow in these woods; but come, tell us all about it."

I partook, with a sensation as if choking all the while, of the food he had waiting, and then, as we sat there waiting for the day in the hope that the doctor might come, I told Jack Penny the adventures of the night, Jimmy playing an accompaniment the while upon his nose.

Chapter Thirty Five
How Jack Penny fired a straight Shot

There was no stopping Jimmy's snoring. Pokes and kicks only intensified the noise, so at last we let him lie and I went on in a doleful key to the end.

"Oh, it ain't so very bad after all!" said Jack Penny, in his slow drawl. "I call it a good night's work."

"Good, Jack?"

"Yes. Well, ain't it?" he drawled. "Why, you've got back safe, and you don't know that the doctor won't get back, and you've done what you came to do—you've found your father."

"But—but suppose, Jack Penny," I said, "they—they do him some injury for what has passed."

"'Tain't likely," drawled Jack. "They've kept him all this time, why should they want to—well, kill him—that's what you're afraid of now?"

"Yes," I said sadly.

"Gammon! 'tain't likely. If you'd got an old kangaroo in a big cage, and the young kangaroo came and tried to get him away you wouldn't go and kill the old kangaroo for it?"

"No, no," I said.

"Of course not. I didn't mean to call your father an old kangaroo, Joe Carstairs. I only meant it to be an instance like. I say, do kick that fellow for snoring so."

"It is of no use to kick him, poor fellow, and, besides, he's tired. He's a good fellow, Jack."

"Yes, I suppose he is," said Jack Penny; "but he's awfully black."

"Well, he can't help that."

"And he shines so!" continued Jack in tones of disgust. "I never saw a black fellow with such a shiny skin. I say, though, didn't you feel in a stew, Joe Carstairs, when you thought it was a black fellow lugging you off?"

"I did," I said; "and when afterwards—hist! is that anything?"

We gazed through the bushes at the darkness outside, and listened intently, but there was no sound save Jimmy's heavy breathing, and I went on:

"When afterwards I found it was the black I turned queer and giddy. Perhaps it was the effect of the blow I got, but I certainly felt as if I should faint. I didn't know I was so girlish."

Jack Penny did not speak for a few minutes, and I sat thinking bitterly of my weakness as I stroked Gyp's head, the faithful beast having curled up between us and laid his head upon my lap. I seemed to have been so cowardly, and, weary and dejected as I was, I wished that I had grown to be a man, with a man's strength and indifference to danger.

"Oh, I don't know," said Jack Penny suddenly.

"Don't know what?" I said sharply, as he startled me out of my thinking fit.

"Oh! about being girlish and—and—and, well, cowardly, I suppose you mean."

"Yes, cowardly," I said bitterly. "I thought I should be so brave, and that when I had found where my father was I should fight and bring him away from among the savages."

"Ah! yes," said Jack Penny dryly, "that's your sort! That's like what you read in books and papers about boys of fifteen, and sixteen, and seventeen. They're wonderful chaps, who take young women in their arms and then jump on horseback with 'em and gallop off at full speed. Some of 'em have steel coats like lobsters on, and heavy helmets, and that makes it all the easier. I've read about some of them chaps who wielded their swords—they never swing 'em about and chop and stab with 'em, but wield 'em, and they kill three or four men every day and think nothing of it. I used to swallow all that stuff, but I'm not such a guffin now."

There was a pause here, while Jack Penny seemed to be thinking.

"Why, some of these chaps swim across rivers with a man under their arm, and if they're on horseback they sing out a battle-cry and charge into a whole army, and everybody's afraid of 'em. I say, ain't it jolly nonsense Joe Carstairs?"

"I suppose it is," I said sadly, for I had believed in some of these heroes too.

"I don't believe the boy ever lived who didn't feel in an awful stew when he was in danger. Why, men do at first before they get used to it. There was a chap came to our place last year and did some shepherding for father for about six months. He'd been a soldier out in the Crimean war and got wounded twice in the arm and in the leg, big wounds too. He told me that when they got the order to advance, him and his mates, they were all of a tremble, and the officers looked as pale as could be, some of 'em; but every man tramped forward steady enough, and it wasn't till they began to see their mates drop that the want to fight began to come. They felt savage, he says, then, and as soon as they were in the thick of it, there wasn't a single man felt afraid."

We sat in silence for a few minutes, and then he went on again:

"If men feel afraid sometimes I don't see why boys shouldn't; and as to those chaps who go about in books killing men by the dozen, and never feeling to mind it a bit, I think it's all gammon."

"Hist! Jack Penny, what's that?" I whispered.

There was a faint crashing noise out in the forest just then, and I knew from the sound close by me that the black who was sharing our watch must have been lifting his spear.

I picked up my gun, and I knew that Jack had taken up his and thrown himself softly into a kneeling position, as we both strove to pierce the darkness and catch sight of what was perhaps a coming enemy.

As we watched, it seemed as if the foliage of the trees high up had suddenly come into view. There was a grey look in the sky, and for the moment I thought I could plainly make out the outline of the bushes on the opposite side of the gully.

Then I thought I was mistaken, and then again it seemed as if I could distinctly see the outline of a bush.

A minute later, and with our hearts beating loudly, we heard the rustling go on, and soon after we could see that the bushes were being moved.

"It is the doctor," I thought; but the idea was false, I knew, for if it had been he his way would have been down into the stream, which he would have crossed, while, whoever this was seemed to be undecided and to be gazing about intently as if in search of something.

When we first caught a glimpse of the moving figure it was fifty yards away. Then it came to within forty, went off again, and all the time the day was rapidly breaking. The tree tops were plainly to be seen, and here and there one of the great masses of foliage stood out quite clearly.

Just then the black, who had crept close to my side, pointed out the figure on the opposite bank, now dimly-seen in the transparent dawn.

It was that of an Indian who had stopped exactly opposite the clump of bushes which acted as a screen to our place of refuge, and stooping down he was evidently trying to make out the mouth of the cave.

He saw it apparently, for he uttered a cry of satisfaction, and leaping from the place of observation he stepped rapidly down the slope.

"He has found us out," I whispered.

"But he mustn't come all the same," said Jack Penny, and as he spoke I saw that he was taking aim.

"Don't shoot," I cried, striking at his gun; but I was too late, for as I bent towards him he drew the trigger, there was a flash, a puff of smoke, a sharp report that echoed from the mouth of the cave, and then with a horrible dread upon me I sprang up and made for the entrance, followed by Jack and the blacks.

It took us but a minute to get down into the stream bed and then to climb up amongst the bushes to where we had seen the savage, and neither of us now gave a thought of there being danger from his companions. What spirit moved Jack Penny I cannot tell. That which moved me was an eager desire to know whether a horrible suspicion was likely to be true, and to gain the knowledge I proceeded on first till I reached the spot where the man had fallen.

It was a desperate venture, for he might have struck at me, wounded merely, with war-club or spear; but I did not think of that: I wanted to solve the horrible doubt, and I had just caught sight of the fallen figure lying prone upon its face when Jimmy uttered a warning cry, and we all had to stoop down amongst the bushes, for it seemed as if the savage's companions were coming to his help.

Chapter Thirty Six
How the Doctor found a Patient
ready to his hand

We waited for some minutes crouched there among the bushes listening to the coming of those who forced their way through the trees, while moment by moment the morning light grew clearer, the small birds twittered, and the parrots screamed. We could see nothing, but it was evident that two if not three savages were slowly descending the slope of the ravine towards where we were hidden. The wounded man uttered a low groan that thrilled me and then sent a cold shudder through my veins, for I was almost touching him; and set aside the feeling of horror at having been, as it were, partner in inflicting his injury, there was the sensation that he might recover sufficiently to revenge himself upon us by a blow with his spear.

The sounds came nearer, and it was now so light that as we watched we could see the bushes moving, and it seemed to me that more of this horrible bloodshed must ensue. We were crouching close, but the wounded man was moaning, and his companions might at any moment hear him and then discovery must follow; while if, on the other hand, we did not resist, all hope of rescuing my poor father would be gone.

"We must fight," I said to myself, setting my teeth hard and bringing my gun to bear on the spot where I could see something moving. At the same time I tried to find where Jack Penny was hiding, but he was out of sight.

At the risk of being seen I rose up a little so as to try and get a glimpse of the coming enemy; but though the movement among the bushes was plain enough I only caught one glimpse of a black body, and had I been disposed to shoot it was too quick for me and was gone in an instant.

They were coming nearer, and in an agony of excitement I was thinking of attempting to back away and try to reach the cave, when I felt that I could not get Jack Penny and the black to act with me unless I showed myself, and this meant revealing our position, and there all the time were the enemy steadily making their way right towards us.

"What shall I do?" I said to myself as I realised in a small way what must be the feelings of a general who finds that the battle is going against him. "I must call to Jack Penny."

"*Cooey!*" rang out just then from a little way to my right, and Jimmy looked up from his hiding-place.

"Is Carstairs there?" cried the familiar voice of the doctor, and as with beating heart I sprang up, he came staggering wearily towards me through the clinging bushes.

"My dear boy," he cried, with his voice trembling, "what I have suffered on your account! I thought you were a prisoner."

"No!" I exclaimed, delighted at this turn in our affairs. "Jimmy helped me to escape. I say, you don't think I ran away and deserted you?"

"My dear boy," he cried, "I was afraid that you would think this of me. But there, thank Heaven you are safe! and though we have not rescued your father we know enough to make success certain."

"I'm afraid not," I said hastily. "The savages have discovered our hiding-place."

"No!"

"Yes; and one of them was approaching it just now when Jack Penny shot him down."

"This is very unfortunate! Where? What! close here?"

I had taken his hand to lead him to the clump of bushes where the poor wretch lay, and on parting the boughs and twigs we both started back in horror.

"My boy, what have you done?" cried the doctor, as I stood speechless there by his side. "We have not so many friends that we could afford to kill them."

But already he was busy, feeling the folly of wasting words, and down upon his knees, to place the head of our friend, the prisoner of the savages, in a more comfortable position before beginning to examine him for his wound.

"Bullet—right through the shoulder!" said the doctor in a short abrupt manner; and as he spoke he rapidly tore up his handkerchief, and plugged and bound the wound, supplementing the handkerchief with a long scarf which he wore round the waist.

"Now, Ti-hi! Jimmy! help me carry him to the cave."

"Jimmy carry um all 'long right way; put um on Jimmy's back!" cried my black companion; and this seeming to be no bad way of carrying the wounded man in such a time of emergency, Jimmy stooped down, exasperating me the while by grinning, as if it was good fun, till the sufferer from our mistake was placed upon his back, when he exclaimed:

"Lot much heavy-heavy! Twice two sheep heavy. Clear de bush!"

We hastily drew the boughs aside, and Jimmy steadily descended the steep slope, entered the rivulet, crossed, and then stopped for a moment beneath the overhanging boughs before climbing to the cabin.

"Here, let me help you!" said the doctor, holding out his hand.

"Yes," said Jimmy, drawing his waddy and boomerang from his belt; "hold um tight, um all in black fellow way."

Then, seizing the boughs, he balanced the wounded man carefully, and drew himself steadily up step by step, exhibiting wonderful strength of muscle, till he had climbed to the entrance of the cave, where he bent down and crawled in on hands and knees, waiting till his burden was removed from his back, and then getting up once more to look round smiling.

"Jimmy carry lot o' men like that way!"

We laid the sufferer on one of the beds of twigs that the savages had made for us, and here the doctor set himself to work to more securely bandage his patient's shoulder; Jack Penny looking on, resting upon his gun, and wearing a countenance full of misery.

"There!" said the doctor when he had finished. "I think he will do now. Two inches lower, Master Penny, and he would have been a dead man."

"I couldn't help it!" drawled Jack Penny. "I thought he was a savage coming to kill us. I'm always doing something. There never was such an unlucky chap as I am!"

"Oh, you meant what you did for the best!" said the doctor, laying his hand on Jack Penny's shoulder.

"What did he want to look like a savage for?" grumbled Jack. "Who was going to know that any one dressed up—no, I mean dressed down—like that was an Englishman?"

"It was an unfortunate mistake, Penny; you must be more careful if you mean to handle a gun."

"Here, take it away!" said Jack Penny bitterly. "I won't fire it off again."

"I was very nearly making the same mistake," I said, out of compassion for Jack Penny—he seemed so much distressed. "I had you and Ti-hi covered in turn as you came up, doctor."

"Then I'm glad you did not fire!" he said. "There, keep your piece, Penny; we may want its help. As for our friend here, he has a painful wound, but I don't think any evil will result from it. Hist, he is coming to!"

Our conversation had been carried on in a whisper, and we now stopped short and watched the doctor's patient in the dim twilight of the cavern, as he unclosed his eyes and stared first up at the ceiling and then about him, till his eyes rested upon us, when he smiled.

"Am I much hurt?" he said, in a low calm voice.

"Oh, no!" said the doctor. "A bullet wound—not a dangerous one at all."

To my astonishment he went on talking quite calmly, and without any of the dazed look and the strange habit of forgetting his own tongue to continue in that of the people among whom he had been a prisoner for so long.

"I thought I should find you here," he said; "and I came on, thinking that perhaps I could help you."

"Help us! yes, of course you can! You shall help us to get Mr Carstairs away!"

"Poor fellow; yes!" he said softly, and in so kindly a way that I crept closer and took his hand. "We tried several times to escape, but they overtook us, and treated us so hard that of late we had grown resigned to our fate."

I exchanged glances with the doctor, who signed to me to be silent.

"It was a very hard one—very hard!" the wounded man continued, and then he stopped short, looking straight before him at the forest, seen through the opening of the cave.

By degrees his eyelids dropped, were raised again, and then fell, and he seemed to glide into a heavy sleep.

The doctor motioned us to keep away, and we all went to the mouth of the cave, to sit down and talk over the night's adventure, the conversation changing at times to a discussion of our friend's mental affection.

"The shock of the wound has affected his head beneficially, it seems," the doctor said at last. "Whether it will last I cannot say."

At least it seemed to me that the doctor was saying those or similar words from out of a mist, and then all was silent.

The fact was that I had been out all night, exerting myself tremendously, and I had now fallen heavily asleep.

Chapter Thirty Seven
How we passed through a great Peril

It was quite evening when I woke, as I could see by the red glow amongst the trees. I was rested but confused, and lay for some minutes thinking, and wondering what had taken place on the previous day.

It all came back at once, and I was just in the act of rising and going to see how our poor friend was, when I felt a hand press me back, and turning I saw it was Jack Penny, who was pointing with the other towards the entrance of the cave.

"What is it?" I whispered; but I needed no telling, for I could see that a group of the blacks were on the other side of the ravine, pointing in the direction of the bushes that overhung our refuge, and gesticulating and talking together loudly.

They know where we are then, I thought; and glancing from one to the other in the dim light I saw that my opinion was shared by the doctor and our black followers, who all seemed to be preparing for an encounter, taking up various places of vantage behind blocks of stone, where they could ply their bows and arrows and make good use of their spears.

Just then the doctor crept towards me and placed his lips to my ear:

"They have evidently tracked us, my lad," he said; "and we must fight for it. There is no chance beside without we escape by the back here, and give up the object of our search."

"We must fight, doctor!" I said, though I trembled as I spoke, and involuntarily glanced at Jack Penny, wondering even in those critical moments whether he too felt alarmed.

I think now it was very natural: I felt horribly ashamed of it then.

Whether it was the case, or that Jack Penny was only taking his tint from the greeny reflected light in the cavern, certainly he looked very cadaverous and strange.

He caught my eye and blew out his cheeks, and began to whistle softly as he rubbed the barrel of his gun with his sleeve.

Turning rather jauntily towards the doctor he said softly:

"Suppose I am to shoot now, doctor?"

"When I give the order," said the latter coldly.

"There won't be any mistake this time?"

"No," said the doctor, quietly; "there will not be any mistake this time!"

He stopped and gazed intently at the savages, who were cautiously descending towards the stream, not in a body but spread out in a line.

"Fire first with large shot," he said softly. "If we can frighten them without destroying life we will. Now creep each of you behind that clump of stones and be firm. Mind it is by steadily helping one another in our trouble that we are strong."

I gave him a quick nod—it was no time for speaking—and crept softly to my place, passing pretty close to where our friend lay wounded and quietly asleep.

The next minute both Jack Penny and I were crouched behind what served as a breastwork, with our pieces ready, the doctor being on our left, and the blacks, including Jimmy, right in front, close to the mouth of the cave.

"We must mind and not hit the blacks!" whispered Jack. "I mean our chaps. Lie down, Gyp!"

The dog was walking about in an impatient angry manner, uttering a low snarl now and then, and setting up the hair all about his neck till in the dim light he looked like a hyena.

Gyp turned to his master almost a reproachful look, and then looked up at me, as if saying, "Am I to be quiet at a time like this?"

Directly after, though, he crouched down with his paws straight out before him and his muzzle directed towards the enemy, ready when the struggle began to make his teeth meet in some one.

The savages were all the time coming steadily on lower and lower down the bank, till suddenly one of them stopped short and uttered a low cry.

Several ran to his side at once, and we could see them stoop down and examine something among the bushes, talking fiercely the while.

"They've found out where our friend was wounded, Jack Penny," I said.

"Think so?" he said slowly. "Well, I couldn't help it. I didn't mean to do it, I declare."

"Hist!" I whispered; and now my heart began to beat furiously, for the blacks, apparently satisfied, began to spread out again, descended to the edge of the little stream, and then stopped short.

If I had not been so excited by the coming danger I should have enjoyed the scene of this group of strongly-built naked savages, their jetty black, shining skins bronzed by the reflections of orange and golden green as the sun flooded the gorge with warm light, making every action of our enemies plain to see, while by contrast it threw us more and more into the shade.

They paused for a few moments at the edge of the stream, so close now that they could touch each other by simply stretching out a hand; and it was evident by the way all watched a tall black in the centre of the line that they were waiting his orders to make a dash up into the cave.

Those were terrible minutes: we could see the opal of our enemies' eyes and the white line of their teeth as they slightly drew their lips apart in the excitement of waiting the order to advance. Every man was armed with bow and arrows, and from their wrists hung by a thong a heavy waddy, a blow from which was sufficient to crush in any man's skull.

"They're coming now," I said in a low voice, the words escaping me involuntarily. And then I breathed again, for the tall savage, evidently the leader, said something to his men, who stood fast, while he walked boldly across the stream beneath the overhanging bushes, and one of these began to sway as the chief tried to draw himself up.

I glanced at the doctor, being sure that he would fire, when, just as the chief was almost on a level with the floor of the cave, there was a rushing, scratching noise, and the most hideous howling rose from just in front of where I crouched, while Gyp leaped up, with hair bristling, and answered it with a furious howl.

The savage dropped back into the water with a tremendous splash, and rushed up the slope after his people, not one of them stopping till they were close to the top, when Jimmy raised his grinning face and looked round at us.

"Um tink big bunyip in um hole, make um all run jus fas' away, away."

He had unmistakably scared the enemy, for they collected together in consultation, but our hope that they might now go fell flat, for they once more began to descend, each one tearing off a dead branch or gathering a bunch of dry ferns as he came; and at the same moment the idea struck Jack Penny and me that they believed some fierce beast was in the hole, and that they were coming to smoke it out.

The blacks came right down into the rivulet, and though the first armfuls of dry wood and growth they threw beneath the cave mouth went into the water, they served as a base for the rest, and in a very short time a great pile rose up, and this they fired.

For a few moments there was a great fume, which floated slowly up among the bushes, but very soon the form of the cavern caused it to draw right in, the opening at the back acting as a chimney. First it burned briskly, then it began to roar, and then to our horror we found that the place was beginning to fill with suffocating smoke and hot vapour, growing more dangerous moment by moment.

Fortunately the smoke and noise of the burning made our actions safe from observation, and we were thus able to carry our wounded right to the back, where the air was purer and it was easier to breathe.

It was a terrible position, for the blacks, encouraged by their success, piled on more and more brushwood and the great fronds of fern, which grew in abundance on the sides of the little ravine, and as the green boughs and leaves were thrown on they hissed and spluttered and sent forth volumes of smoke, which choked and blinded us till the fuel began to blaze, when it roared into the cave and brought with it a quantity of hot but still breathable air.

"Keep a good heart, my lads," said the doctor. "No, no, Penny! Are you mad? Lie down! lie down! Don't you know that while the air high up is suffocating, that low down can be breathed?"

"No, I couldn't tell," said Jack Penny dolefully, as he first knelt down and then laid his head close to the ground. "I didn't know things were going to be so bad as this or I shouldn't have come. I don't want to have my dog burned to death."

Gyp seemed to understand him, for he uttered a low whine and laid his nose in his master's hand.

"Burned to death!" said the doctor in a tone full of angry excitement. "Of course not. Nobody is going to be burned to death."

Through the dim choking mist I could see that there was a wild and anxious look in the doctor's countenance as he kept going near the mouth of the cave, and then hurrying back blinded and in agony.

We had all been in turn to the narrow rift at the end through which we had been able to see the sky and the waving leaves of the trees, but now all was dark with the smoke that rolled out. This had seemed to be a means of escape, but the difficulty was to ascend the flat chimney-like place, and when the top was reached we feared that it would only be for each one who climbed out to make himself a mark for the savages' arrows.

Hence, then, we had not made the slightest attempt to climb it. Now, however, our position was so desperate that Jimmy's proposal was listened to with eagerness.

"Place too much big hot," he said. "Chokum-chokum like um wallaby. Go up."

He caught hold of the doctor's scarf of light network, a contrivance which did duty for bag, hammock, or rope in turn, and the wearer rapidly twisted it from about his waist.

"Now, Mas' Jack Penny, tan' here," he cried; and Jack was placed just beneath the hole.

Jack Penny understood what was required of him, and placing his hands against the edge of the rift he stood firm, while Jimmy took the end of the doctor's scarf in his teeth and proceeded to turn him into a ladder, by whose means he might get well into the chimney-like rift, climb up, and then lower down the scarf-rope to help the rest.

As I expected, the moment Jimmy caught Jack Penny's shoulders and placed one foot upon him my companion doubled up like a jointed rule, and Jimmy and he rolled upon the floor of the cave.

At any other time we should have roared with laughter at Jimmy's disgust and angry torrent of words, but it was no time for mirth, and the doctor took Jack Penny's place as the latter drawled out:

"I couldn't help it; my back's so weak. I begin to wish I hadn't come."

"Dat's fine," grunted Jimmy, who climbed rapidly up, standing on the doctor's shoulders, making no scruple about planting a foot upon his head, and then we knew by his grunting and choking sounds that he was forcing his way up.

The moment he had ceased to be of use the doctor stood aside, and it was as well, for first a few small stones fell, then there was a crash, and I felt that Jimmy had come down, but it only proved to be a mass of loose stone, which was followed by two or three more pieces of earth and rock.

Next came a tearing sound as of bushes being broken and dragged away, and to our delight the smoke seemed to rush up the rift with so great a current of air that fresh breath of life came to us from the mouth of the cave, and with it hope.

In those critical moments everything seemed dream-like and strange. I could hardly see what took place for the smoke, my companions looking dim and indistinct, and somehow the smoke seemed to be despair, and the fresh hot wind borne with the crackling flames that darted through the dense vapour so much hope.

"Ti-hi come 'long nextums," whispered Jimmy; and the black ran to the opening eagerly, but hesitated and paused, ending by seizing me and pushing me before him to go first.

"No, no," I said; "let's help the wounded man first."

"Don't waste time," said the doctor angrily. "Up, Joe, and you can help haul."

I obeyed willingly and unwillingly, but I wasted no time. With the help of the doctor and the scarf I had no difficulty in climbing up the rift, which afforded good foothold at the side, and in less than a minute I was beside Jimmy, breathing the fresh air and seeing the smoke rise up in a cloud from our feet.

"Pull!" said the doctor in a hoarse whisper that seemed to come out of the middle of the smoke.

Jimmy and I hauled, and somehow or another we got Jack Penny up, choking and sneezing, so that he was obliged to lie down amongst the bushes, and I was afraid he would be heard, till I saw that we were separated from the savages by a huge mass of stony slope.

Two of the black bearers came next easily enough, and then the scarf had to be lowered down to its utmost limits.

I knew why, and watched the proceedings with the greatest concern as Jimmy and one of the blacks reached down into the smoky rift and held the rope at the full extent of their arms.

"Now!" said the doctor's voice, and the two hardy fellows began to draw the scarf, with its weight coming so easily that I knew the doctor and one of the blacks must be lifting the wounded man below.

Poor fellow, he must have suffered the most intense agony, but he did not utter a sigh. Weak as he was he was quite conscious of his position, and helped us by planting his feet wherever there was a projection in the rift, and so we hauled him up and laid him on the sand among the bushes, where he could breathe, but where he fainted away.

The rest easily followed, but not until the doctor had sent up every weapon and package through the smoke. Then came his turn, but he made no sign, and in an agony of horror I mastered my dread, and, seizing the scarf, lowered myself down into the heat and smoke.

It was as I feared; he had fainted, and was lying beneath the opening.

My hands trembled so that I could hardly tie a knot, but knowing, as I did, how short the scarf was, I secured it tightly round one of his wrists and called to them to haul just as Jimmy was coming down to my help.

He did not stop, but dropped down beside me, and together we lifted the fainting man, called to them to drag, and he was pulled up.

"Here, ketch hold," came from above the next moment in Jack Penny's voice, and to my utter astonishment down came the end of the scarf at once, long before they could have had time to untie it from the doctor's wrist.

"Up, Jimmy!" I cried, as I realised that it was the other end Jack Penny had had the *nous* to lower at once.

"No: sha'n't go, Mass Joe Carstairs."

"Go on, sir," I cried.

"No sha'n't! Debble—debble—debble!" he cried, pushing me to the hole.

To have gone on fighting would have meant death to both, for the savages were yelling outside and piling on the bushes and fern fronds till they roared.

I caught the scarf then, and was half-hauled half-scrambled up, to fall down blinded and suffocated almost, only able to point below.

I saw them lower the scarf again, and after what seemed a tremendous time Jimmy's black figure appeared.

Almost at the same moment there were tongues of flame mingled with the smoke, and Jimmy threw himself down and rolled over and over, sobbing and crying.

"Burn um hot um. Oh, burn um—burn um—burn um!"

There was a loud roar and a rush of flame and smoke out of the rift, followed by what seemed to be a downpour of the smoke that hung over us like a canopy, just as if it was all being sucked back, and then the fire appeared to be smouldering, and up through the smoke that now rose slowly came the dank strange smell of exploded powder and the sounds of voices talking eagerly, but coming like a whisper to where we lay.

Chapter Thirty Eight
How the Doctor said "Thank You" in a very quiet Way

For some little time we did nothing but lie there blackened and half choked, blinded almost, listening to the sound that came up that rift, for the question now was whether the savages would know that we were there, or would attribute the roar to that of some fierce beast that their fire and smoke had destroyed.

The voices came up in a confused gabble, and we felt that if the blacks came up the rift we could easily beat them back; but if they came round by some other way to the rocky patch of forest where we were, our state was so pitiable that we could offer no defence.

Jimmy had been applying cool leaves to his legs for some minutes as we lay almost where we had thrown ourselves, seeming to want to do nothing but breathe the fresh air, when all at once he came to where the doctor and I now rested ourselves upon our elbows and were watching the smoke that came up gently now and rose right above the trees.

"Jimmy no hurt now. Roast black fellow," he said grinning. "Jimmy know powder go bang pop! down slow."

"Yes," said the doctor. "I was trying to get that last canister when I was overcome by the smoke, and just managed to reach the bottom of the rift. Who was it saved me?"

"Jimmy-Jimmy!" said the black proudly.

"My brave fellow!" cried the doctor, catching the black's hand.

"Jimmy come 'long Mass Joe. Haul Mass doctor up. Mass doctor no wiggle Jimmy 'gain, eat much pig."

The doctor did not answer, for he had turned to me and taken my hand.

"Did you come down, Joe?" he said softly.

"Of course I did," I replied quietly, though I felt very uncomfortable.

"Thank you!" he said quietly, and then he turned away.

"Black fellow hear powder bang," said Jimmy, grinning. "Tink um big bunyip. All go way now."

I turned to him sharply, listening the while.

"Yes: all go 'long. Tink bunyip. Kill um dead. No kill bunyip. Oh no!"

There was the sound of voices, but they were more distant, and then they seemed to come up the rift in quite a broken whisper, and the next moment they had died away.

"Safe, doctor!" I said, and we all breathed more freely than before.

The blacks had gone. Evidently they believed that the occupant of the cave had expired in that final roar, and when we afterwards crept cautiously round after a détour the next morning, it was to find that the place was all open, and for fifty yards round the bushes and tree-ferns torn down and burned.

The night of our escape we hardly turned from our positions, utterly exhausted as we were, and one by one we dropped asleep.

When I woke first it was sometime in the night, and through the trees the great stars were glinting down, and as I lay piecing together the adventures of the past day I once more fell fast asleep to be awakened by Jimmy in the warm sunlight of a glorious morning.

"All black fellow gone long way. Come kedge fis an fine 'nana."

I rose to my feet to see that the doctor was busy with his patient, who was none the worse for the troubles of the past day, and what was of more consequence, he was able to speak slowly and without running off into the native tongue.

We went down to the stream, Jack Penny bearing us company, and were pretty fortunate in cutting off some good-sized fish which were sunning themselves in a shallow, and Ti-hi and his companions were no less successful in getting fruit, so that when we returned we were able to light a fire and enjoy a hearty meal.

What I enjoyed the most, though, was a good lave in the clear cold water when we had a look at the mouth of the cave.

The doctor came to the conclusion that where we were, shut-in by high shelving sand rocks, was as safe a spot as we could expect, the more so that the blacks were not likely to come again, so we made this our camp, waiting to recruit a little and to let the black village settle down before making any farther attempt. Beside this there was our new companion—William Francis he told us his name was, and that he had been ten years a prisoner among the blacks. Until he had recovered from the effect of his unlucky wound we could not travel far, and our flight when we rescued my father must necessarily be swift.

It was terribly anxious work waiting day after day, but the doctor's advice was good—that we must be content to exist without news for fear, in sending scouts about the village at night, we should alarm the enemy.

"Better let them think there is no one at hand," said the doctor, "and our task will be the easier."

So for a whole fortnight we waited, passing our time watching the bright scaled fish glance down the clear stream, or come up it in shoals; lying gazing at the brightly plumed birds that came and shrieked and climbed about the trees above our heads; while now and then we made cautious excursions into the open country in the direction opposite to the village, and fortunately without once encountering an enemy, but adding largely to our store of food, thanks to the bows and arrows of our friends.

At last, one evening, after quietly talking to us sometime about the sufferings of himself and my father, Mr Francis declared himself strong enough to accompany our retreat.

"The interest and excitement will keep me up," he said; "and you must not wait longer for me. Besides, I shall get stronger every day, and—"

He looked from me to the doctor and then back, and passed his hand across his forehead as if to clear away a mist, while, when he began to speak again, it was not in English, and he burst into tears.

"Lie down and sleep," the doctor said firmly; and, obedient as a child, the patient let his head sink upon the rough couch he occupied and closed his eyes.

"It is as if as his body grew strong his mental powers weakened," said the doctor to me as soon as we were out of hearing; "but we must wait and see."

Then we set to and once more talked over our plans, arranging that we would make our attempt next night, and after studying the compass and the position we occupied we came to the decision that we had better work round to the far side of the village, post Mr Francis and two of the blacks there, with our baggage, which was principally food; then make our venture, join them if successful, and go on in retreat at once.

Chapter Thirty Nine
How we took a last look round, and found it was time to go

That next evening seemed as it would never come, and I lay tossing feverishly from side to side vainly trying to obtain the rest my friend recommended.

At last, though, the time came, and we were making our final preparations, when the doctor decided that we would just take a look round first by way of a scout.

It was fortunate that we did, for just as it was growing dusk, after a good look round we were about to cross the rivulet, and go through the cavern and up the rift back into camp, when I caught the doctor's arm without a word.

He started and looked in the same direction as I did which was right down the gully, and saw what had taken my attention, namely, the stooping bodies of a couple of blacks hurrying away through the bushes at a pretty good rate.

The doctor clapped his piece to his shoulder, and then dropped it once more.

"No!" he said. "I might kill one, but the other would bear the news. Fortunately they are going the other way and not ours. Quick, my lad! let's get back to camp and start."

"And they'll come back with a lot of their warriors to attack us to-night and find us gone!"

"And while they are gone, Joe, we will attack their place and carry off our prize!"

"If we only could!" I cried fervently.

"No *ifs*, Joe," he said smiling; "we *will!*"

It did not take us many minutes to reach the mouth of the cave, and as we entered I looked round again, to catch sight of another black figure crouching far up the opposite bank, at the foot of a great tree.

I did not speak, for it was better that the black should not think he had been seen, so followed the doctor into the cave, climbed the rift with him, and found all ready for the start.

"Black fellow all 'bout over there way!" said Jimmy to me in a whisper.

"How do you know?" I said quickly.

"Jimmy smell am!" he replied seriously. "Jimmy go look 'bout. Smell um black fellow, one eye peeping round um trees."

"Yes, we have seen them too," I said; and signing to him to follow, I found the doctor.

"The sooner we are off the better!" he said. "Now, Mr Francis, do you think you can lead us to the other side of the village, round by the north? the enemy are on the watch."

Mr Francis turned his head without a word, and, leaning upon a stout stick, started at once; and we followed in silence, just as the stars were coming out.

It seemed very strange calling this savage-looking being Mr Francis, but when talking with him during his recovery from his wound one only needed to turn one's head to seem to be in conversation with a man who had never been from his civilised fellows.

He went steadily on, the doctor next, and I followed the doctor; the rest of our little party gliding silently through the forest for quite three hours, when Mr Francis stopped, and it was decided to rest and refresh ourselves a little before proceeding farther.

The doctor had settled to leave Mr Francis here, but he quietly objected to this.

"No!" he said; "you want my help more now than ever. I am weak, but I can take you right to the hut where Carstairs is kept a prisoner. If you go alone you will lose time, and your expedition may—"

He stopped short and lay down upon the earth for a few minutes, during which the doctor remained undecided. At last he bent down and whispered a few words to his patient, who immediately rose.

Orders were then given to the blacks, who were to stay under the command of Jack Penny, and, followed by Jimmy, and leaving the rest of our party in the shade of an enormous tree, we set off once more.

The excitement made the distance seem so short that I was astounded when a low murmur told us that we were close to the village, and, stepping more cautiously, we were soon close up behind a great hut.

"This is the place," whispered Mr Francis. "He is kept prisoner here, or else at the great hut on the other side. Hist! I'll creep forward and listen."

He went down in a stooping position and disappeared, leaving us listening to the continuous talk of evidently a numerous party of the savages; and so like did it all seem to the last time, that no time might have elapsed since we crouched there, breathing heavily with excitement in the shade of the great trees that came close up to the huts.

It was a painful time, for it seemed that all our schemes had been in vain, and that we might as well give up our task, unless we could come with so strong a body of followers that we could make a bold attack.

I whispered once or twice to the doctor, but he laid his hand upon my lips. I turned to Jimmy, but he had crouched down, and was resting himself according to his habit.

And so quite an hour passed away before we were aware by a slight rustle that Mr Francis was back, looming up out of the darkness like some giant, so strangely did the obscurity distort everything near at hand.

"Here!" he said in a low voice; and bending down we all listened to his words, which came feebly, consequent upon his exertions.

"I have been to the far hut and he is not there!" he whispered. "I came back to this and crept in unobserved. They are all talking about an expedition that has gone off to the back of the cave—to destroy us. Carstairs is in there, bound hand and foot."

"My poor father!" I moaned.

"I spoke to him and told him help was near," continued Mr Francis; "and then—"

He muttered something in the savages' tongue, and then broke down and began to sob.

"Take no notice," the doctor whispered to me, as I stood trembling there, feeling as I did that I was only a few yards from him we had come to save, and who was lying bound there waiting for the help that seemed as if it would never come.

The doctor realised my feelings, for he came a little closer and pressed my hand.

"Don't be downhearted, my lad," he whispered; "we are a long way nearer to our journey's end than when we started."

"Yes!" I said; "but—"

"But! Nonsense, boy! Why, we've found your father. We know where he is; and if we can't get him away by stratagem, we'll go to another tribe of the blacks, make friends with them, and get them to fight on our side."

"Nonsense, doctor!" I said bitterly. "You are only saying this to comfort me."

"To get you to act like a man," he said sharply. "Shame upon you for being so ready to give up in face of a few obstacles!"

I felt that the rebuke was deserved, and drew in my breath, trying to nerve myself to bear this new disappointment, and to set my brain at work scheming.

It seemed to grow darker just then, the stars fading out behind a thick veil of clouds; and creeping nearer to the doctor I sat down beside where he knelt, listening to the incessant talking of the savages.

We were not above half-a-dozen yards from the back of the great hut; and, now rising into quite an angry shout, now descending into a low buzz, the talk, talk, talk went on, as if they were saying the same things over and over again.

I thought of my own captivity—of the way in which Gyp had come to me in the night, and wondered whether it would be possible to cut away a portion of the palm-leaf wall of the hut, and so get to the prisoner.

And all this while the talking went on, rising and falling till it seemed almost maddening to hear.

We must have waited there quite a couple of hours, and still there was no change. Though we could not see anything for the hut in front of us we could tell that there was a good deal of excitement in the village, consequent, the doctor whispered, upon the absence of a number of the blacks on the expedition against us.

At last he crept from me to speak to Mr Francis.

"It is of no use to stay longer, I'm afraid, my lad," he whispered; "unless we wait and see whether the hut is left empty when the expedition party comes back, though I fear they will not come back till morning."

"What are you going to do, then?" I said.

"Ask Francis to suggest a better hiding-place for us, where we can go to-night and wait for another opportunity."

I sighed, for I was weary of waiting for opportunities.

"Fast asleep, poor fellow!" he whispered, coming back so silently that he startled me. "Where's the black?"

I turned sharply to where Jimmy had been curled up, but he was gone.

I crept a little way in two or three directions, but he was not with us, and I said so.

"How dare he go!" the doctor said angrily. "He will ruin our plans! What's that?"

"Gyp!" I said, as the dog crept up to us and thrust his head against my hand. "Jack Penny is getting anxious. It is a signal for us to come back."

"How do you know?"

"We agreed upon it," I said. "He was to send the dog in search of us if we did not join him in two hours; and if we were in trouble I was either to tie something to his collar or take it off."

"Do neither!" said the doctor quietly. "Look! they are lighting a fire. The others must have come back."

I turned and saw a faint glow away over the right corner of the hut; and then there was a shout, and the shrill cries of some women and children.

In a moment there was a tremendous excitement in the hut before us, the savages swarming out like angry bees, and almost at the same moment the whole shape of the great long hut stood out against the sky.

"The village is on fire!" whispered the doctor. "Back, my boy! Francis, quick!"

He shook the sleeping man, whom all at once I could see, and he rose rather feebly. Then we backed slowly more and more in amongst the trees, seeing now that one of the light palm-leaf and bamboo huts was blazing furiously, and that another had caught fire, throwing up the cluster of slight buildings into clear relief, while as we backed farther and farther in amongst the trees we could see the blacks—men, women, and children—running to and fro as if wild.

"Now would be the time," said the doctor. "We might take advantage of the confusion and get your father away."

"Yes!" I cried excitedly. "I'm ready!"

"Stop for your lives!" said a voice at our elbow, and turning I saw Mr Francis, with his swarthy face lit up by the fire. "You could not get near the hut now without being seen. If you had acted at the moment the alarm began you might have succeeded. It is now too late."

"No, no!" I cried. "Let us try."

"It is too late, I say," cried Mr Francis firmly. "The village is on fire, and the blacks must see you. If you are taken now you will be killed without mercy."

"We must risk it," I said excitedly, stepping forward.

"And your father too."

I recoiled shuddering.

"We must get away to a place of safety, hide for a few days, and then try again. I shall be stronger perhaps then, and can help."

"It is right," said the doctor calmly. "Come, Joe. Patience!"

I saw that he was right, for the fire was leaping from hut to hut, and there was a glow that lit up the forest far and wide. Had anyone come near we must have been seen, but the savages were all apparently congregated near the burning huts, while the great sparks and flakes of fire rose up and floated far away above the trees, glittering like stars in the ruddy glow.

"Go on then," I said, with a groan of disappointment, and Mr Francis took the lead once more, and, the doctor following, I was last.

"But Jimmy!" I said. "We must not leave him behind."

"He will find us," said the doctor. "Come along."

There was nothing for me to do but obey, so I followed reluctantly, the glow from the burning village being so great that the branches of the trees stood up clearly before us, and we had no difficulty in going on.

I followed more reluctantly when I remembered Gyp, and chirruped to him, expecting to find him at my heels, but he was not there.

"He has gone on in front," I thought, and once more I tramped wearily on, when there was a rush and a bound and Gyp leaped up at me, catching my jacket in his teeth and shaking it hard.

Chapter Forty
How Jimmy cried "Cooee!" and why he called

"Why, Gyp," I said in a low voice, "what is it, old fellow?"

He whined and growled and turned back, trotting towards the burning village.

"Yes, I know it's on fire," I said. "Come along."

But the dog would not follow. He whined and snuffled and ran back a little farther, when from some distance behind I heard a rustling and a panting noise, which made me spring round and cock my gun.

"Followed!" I said to myself, as I continued my retreat, but only to stop short, for from the direction in which we had come I heard whispered, more than called, the familiar cry of the Australian savage, a cry that must, I knew, come from Jimmy, and this explained Gyp's appearance.

"*Cooey!*"

There it was again, and without hesitation I walked sharply back, Gyp running before me as he would not have done had there been an enemy near.

There was the panting and rustling again as I retraced my steps, with the light growing plainer, and in less than a minute I came upon Jimmy trudging slowly along with a heavy burden on his back, a second glance at which made me stop speechless in my tracks.

"Mass Joe! Jimmy got um fader. Much big heavy. Jimmy got um right fas'."

He panted with the exertion, for he tried to break into a trot.

I could do no more than go to his side and lay my trembling hands upon the shoulder of his burden—a man whom he was carrying upon his back.

"Go on!" I said hoarsely. "Forward, Gyp, and stop them!"

The dog understood the word "Forward," and went on with a rush, while I let Jimmy pass me, feeling that if he really had him we sought he was performing my duty, while all I could do was to form the rear-guard and protect them even with my life if we were pursued.

Either the dog was leading close in front or the black went on by a kind of instinct in the way taken by our companions. At any rate he went steadily on, and I followed, trembling with excitement, ten or a dozen yards behind, in dread lest it should not be true that we had succeeded after all.

The light behind us increased so that I could plainly see the bent helpless load upon our follower's back; but the black trudged steadily on and I followed, panting with eagerness and ready the moment Jimmy paused to leap forward and try to take his place.

The fire must have been increasing fast, and the idea was dawning upon me that perhaps this was a plan of the black's, who had set fire to one of the huts and then seized the opportunity to get the prisoner away. It was like the Australian to do such a thing as this, for he was cunning and full of stratagem, and though it was improbable the idea was growing upon me, when all at once a tremendous weight seemed to fall upon my head and I was dashed to the earth, with a sturdy savage pressing me down, dragging my hands behind me, and beginning to fasten them with some kind of thong.

For the moment I was half-stunned. Then the idea came to me of help being at hand, and I was about to *cooey* and bring Jimmy to my side, but my lips closed and I set my teeth.

"No," I thought, "he may escape. If any one is to be taken let it be me; my turn will come later on."

My captor had evidently been exerting himself a great deal to overtake me, and after binding me he contented himself by sitting upon my back, panting heavily, to rest himself, while, knowing that struggling would be in vain, I remained motionless, satisfied that every minute was of inestimable value, and that once the doctor knew of the black's success he would use every exertion to get the captive in safety, and then he would be sure to come in search of me.

Then I shuddered, for I remembered what Mr Francis had said about the people being infuriated at such a time, and as I did so I felt that I was a long way yet from being a man.

All at once my captor leaped up, and seizing me by the arm he gave me a fearful wrench to make me rise to my feet.

For some minutes past I had been expecting to see others of his party come up, or to hear him shout to them, but he remained silent, and stood at last hesitating or listening to the faint shouts that came from the glow beyond the trees.

Suddenly he thrust me before him, shaking his waddy menacingly. The next moment he uttered a cry. There was a sharp crack as of one war-club striking another, and then I was struck down by two men struggling fiercely. There were some inarticulate words, and a snarling and panting like two wild beasts engaged in a hard fight, and then a heavy fall, a dull thud, and the sound of a blow, as if some one had struck a tree branch with a club.

I could see nothing from where I lay, but as soon as I could recover myself I was struggling to my feet, when a black figure loomed over me, and a familiar voice said hoarsely:

"Where Mass Joe knife, cut um 'tring?"

"Jimmy!" I said. "My father?"

"Set um down come look Mass Joe. Come 'long fas. Gyp take care Jimmy fader till um come back again again."

As Jimmy spoke he thrust his hand into my pocket for my knife, while I was too much interested in his words to remind him that there was my large sheath-knife in my belt.

"Come 'long," he said as he set me free, and we were starting when he stopped short: "No; tie black fellow up firs'. No, can't 'top."

Before I knew what he meant to do he had given the prostrate black a sharp rap on the head with his waddy.

"Jimmy!" I said; "you'll kill him!"

"Kill him! No, makum sleep, sleep. Come 'long."

He went off at a sharp walk and I followed, glancing back anxiously from time to time and listening, till we reached the spot where he had set down his burden, just as the doctor came back, having missed me, and being in dread lest I had lost my way.

I did not speak—I could not, but threw myself on my knees beside the strange, long-haired, thickly-bearded figure seated with its back against a tree, while the doctor drew back as soon as he realised that it was my father the black had saved.

Chapter Forty One
How Jimmy heard the Bunyip speak, and it all proved to be "Big 'Tuff."

I Need not recount what passed just then. But few words were spoken, and there was no time for displays of affection. One black had seen and pursued Jimmy, and others might be on our track, so that our work was far from being half done even now.

"Can you walk, sir?" said the doctor sharply.

My poor father raised his face toward the speaker and uttered some incoherent words.

"No, no; he has been kept bound by the ankles till the use of his feet has gone," said Mr Francis, who had remained silent up to now.

"Can't walk—Jimmy carry um," said the black in a whisper. "Don't make noise—hear um black fellow."

"You are tired," said the doctor; "let me take a turn."

Jimmy made no objection, but bore the gun, while the doctor carried my father slowly and steadily on for some distance; then the black took a turn and bore him right to the place where our black followers were waiting, and where Jack Penny was anxiously expecting our return.

"I thought you wasn't coming back," he said as Jimmy set down the burden; and then in a doleful voice he continued, "I couldn't do that, my back's so weak."

But Ti-hi and his friends saw our difficulty, and cut down a couple of long stout bamboos whose tops were soon cleared of leaves and shoots. Two holes were made in the bottom of a light sack whose contents were otherwise distributed, the poles thrust through, and my poor father gently laid upon the sack. Four of us then went to the ends of the poles, which were placed upon our shoulders, and keeping step as well as we could, we went slowly and steadily on, Mr Francis taking the lead and acting as guide.

Our progress was very slow, but we journeyed steadily on hour after hour, taking advantage of every open part of the forest that was not likely to show traces of our passage, and obliged blindly to trust to Mr Francis as to the way.

It was weary work, but no one seemed to mind, each, even Jack Penny, taking his turn at the end of one of the bamboos; and when at last the morning broke, and the bright sunshine showed us our haggard faces, we still kept on, the daylight helping us to make better way till the sun came down so fiercely that we were obliged to halt in a dense part of the forest where some huge trees gave us shade.

Mr Francis looked uneasily about, and I caught his anxious gaze directed so often in different directions that I whispered to the doctor my fears that he had lost his way.

"Never mind, lad," replied the doctor; "we have the compass. Our way is south towards the coast—anywhere as long as we get beyond reach of the blacks. No, don't disturb him, let him sleep."

I was about to draw near and speak to my father, in whose careworn hollow face I gazed with something approaching fear. His eyes were closed, and now, for the first time, I could see the ravages that the long captivity had made in his features; but, mingled with these, there was a quiet restful look that made me draw back in silence from where the litter had been laid and join my companions in partaking of such food as we had.

Watch was set, the doctor choosing the post of guard, and then, lying anywhere, we all sought for relief from our weariness in sleep.

As for me, one moment I was lying gazing at the long unkempt hair and head of him I had come to seek, and thinking that I would rest like that, rising now and then to see and watch with the doctor; the next I was wandering away in dreams through the forest in search of my father; and then all was blank till I started up to catch at my gun, for some one had touched me on the shoulder.

"There is nothing wrong, my lad," said the doctor—"fortunately—for I have been a bad sentry, and have just awoke to find that I have been sleeping at my post."

"Sleeping!" I said, still confused from my own deep slumbers.

"Yes," he said; "every one has been asleep from utter exhaustion."

I looked round, and there were our companions sleeping heavily.

"I've been thinking that we may be as safe here as farther away," continued the doctor; "so let them rest still, for we have a tremendous task before us to get down to the coast."

Just then Jimmy leaped up staring, his hand on his waddy and his eyes wandering in search of danger.

This being absent, his next idea was regarding food.

"Much hungry," he said, "want mutton, want damper, want eatums."

The rest were aroused, and, water being close at hand in a little stream, we soon had our simple store of food brought out and made a refreshing meal, of which my father, as he lay, partook mechanically, but without a word.

The doctor then bathed and dressed his ankles, which were in a fearfully swollen and injured state. Like Mr Francis, he seemed as if his long captivity had made him think like the savages among whom he had been; while the terrible mental anxiety he had suffered along with his bodily anguish had resulted in complete prostration. He ate what was given to him or drank with his eyes closed, and when he opened them once or twice it was not to let them wander round upon us who attended to him, but to gaze straight up in a vague manner and mutter a few of the native words before sinking back into a stupor-like sleep.

I gazed at the doctor with my misery speaking in my eyes, for it was so different a meeting from that which I had imagined. There was no delight, no anguished tears, no pressing to a loving father's heart. We had found him a mere hopeless wreck, apparently, like Mr Francis, and the pain I suffered seemed more than I could bear.

"Patience!" the doctor said to me, with a smile. "Yes, I know what you want to ask me. Let's wait and see. He was dying slowly, Joe, and we have come in time to save his life."

"You are sure?" I said.

"No," he answered, "not sure, but I shall hope. Now let's get on again till dark, and then we'll have a good rest in the safest place we can find."

In the exertion and toil that followed I found some relief. My interest, too, was excited by seeing how much Mr Francis seemed to change hour by hour, and how well he knew the country which he led us through.

He found for us a capital resting-place in a rocky gorge, where, unless tracked step by step, there was no fear of our being surprised. Here there was water and fruit, and, short a distance as we had come, the darkness made it necessary that we should wait for day.

Then followed days and weeks of slow travel through a beautiful country, always south and west. We did not go many miles some days, for the burden we carried made our passage very slow. Sometimes, too, our black scouts came back to announce that we were travelling towards some black village, or that a hunting party was in our neighbourhood, and though these people might have been friendly, we took the advice of our black companions and avoided them, either by making a détour or by waiting in hiding till they had passed.

Water was plentiful, and Jimmy and Ti-hi never let us want for fruit, fish, or some animal for food. Now it would be a wild pig or a small deer, more often birds, for these literally swarmed in some of the lakes and marshes round which we made our way.

The country was so thinly inhabited that we could always light a fire in some shut-in part of the forest without fear, and so we got on, running risks at times, but on the whole meeting with but few adventures.

After getting over the exertion and a little return of fever from too early leaving his sick-bed of boughs, Mr Francis mended rapidly, his wound healing well and his mind daily growing clearer. Every now and then, when excited, he had relapses, and looked at us hopelessly, talking quickly in the savages' tongue; but these grew less frequent, and there would be days during which he would be quite free. He grew so much better that at the end of a month he insisted upon taking his place at one of the bamboos, proving himself to be a tender nurse to our invalid in his turn.

And all this time my father seemed to alter but little. The doctor was indefatigable in his endeavours; but though he soon wrought a change in his patient's bodily infirmities to such an extent, that at last my father could walk first a mile, then a couple, and then ease the bearers of half their toil, his mind seemed gone, and he went on in a strangely vacant way.

As time went on and our long journey continued he would walk slowly by my side, resting on my shoulder, and with his eyes always fixed upon the earth. If he was spoken to he did not seem to hear, and he never opened his lips save to utter a few words in the savage tongue.

I was in despair, but the doctor still bade me hope.

"Time works wonders, Joe," he said. "His bodily health is improving wonderfully, and at last that must act upon his mind."

"But it does not," I said. "He has walked at least six miles to-day as if in a dream. Oh, doctor!" I exclaimed, "we cannot take him back like this. You keep bidding me hope, and it seems no use."

He smiled at me in his calm satisfied way.

"And yet I've done something, Joe," he said. "We found him—we got him away—we had him first a hopeless invalid—he is now rapidly becoming a strong healthy man."

"Healthy!"

"In body, boy. Recollect that for years he seems to have been kept chained up by the savages like some wild beast, perhaps through some religious scruples against destroying the life of a white man who was wise in trees and plants. Likely enough they feared that if they killed such a medicine-man it might result in a plague or curse."

"That is why they spared us both," said Mr Francis, who had heard the latter part of our conversation; "and the long course of being kept imprisoned there seemed to completely freeze up his brain as it did mine. That and the fever and blows I received," he said excitedly. "There were times when—"

He clapped his hands to his head as if he dared not trust himself to speak, and turned away.

"Yes, that is it, my lad," said the doctor quietly; "his brain has become paralysed as it were. A change may come at any time. Under the circumstances, in spite of your mother's anxiety, we'll wait and go slowly homeward. Let me see," he continued, turning to a little calendar he kept, "to-morrow begins the tenth month of our journey. Come, be of good heart. We've done wonders; nature will do the rest."

Two days later we had come to a halt in a lovely little glen through which trickled a clear spring whose banks were brilliant with flowers. We were all busy cooking and preparing to halt there for the night. My father had walked the whole of the morning, and now had wandered slowly away along the banks of the stream, Mr Francis being a little further on, while Jimmy was busy standing beside a pool spearing fish.

I glanced up once or twice to see that my father was standing motionless on the bank, and then I was busying myself once more cutting soft boughs to make a bed when Jimmy came bounding up to me with his eyes starting and mouth open.

"Where a gun, where a gun?" he cried. "Big bunyip down 'mong a trees, try to eat Jimmy. Ask for um dinner, all aloud, oh."

"Hush! be quiet!" I cried, catching his arm; "what do you mean?"

"Big bunyip down 'mong stones say, 'Hoo! much hungry; where my boy?'"

"Some one said that?" I cried.

"Yes, 'much hungry, where my boy?' Want eat black boy; eat Jimmy!"

"What nonsense, Jimmy!" I said. "Don't be such a donkey. There are no bunyips."

"Jimmy heard um say um!" he cried, stamping his spear on the ground.

Just then I involuntarily glanced in the direction where my father stood, and saw him stoop and pick up a flower or two.

My heart gave a bound.

The next minute he was walking slowly towards Mr Francis, to whom he held out the flowers; and then I felt giddy, for I saw them coming slowly towards our camp, both talking earnestly, my father seeming to be explaining something about the flowers he had picked.

The doctor had seen it too, and he drew me away, after cautioning Jimmy to be silent.

And there we stood while those two rescued prisoners talked quietly and earnestly together, but it was in the savage tongue.

I need not tell you of my joy, or the doctor's triumphant looks.

"It is the beginning, Joe," he said; and hardly had he spoken when Jimmy came up.

"Not bunyip 'tall!" he said scornfully. "Not no bunyip; all big 'tuff! Jimmy, Mass Joe fader talk away, say, 'where my boy?'"

Chapter Forty Two
How I must wind up the Story

It was the beginning of a better time, for from that day what was like the dawn of a return of his mental powers brightened and strengthened into the full sunshine of reason, and by the time we had been waiting at Ti-hi's village for the coming of the captain with his schooner we had heard the whole of my father's adventures from his own lips, and how he had been struck down from behind by one of the blacks while collecting, and kept a prisoner ever since.

I need not tell you of his words to me, his thanks to the doctor, and his intense longing for the coming of the schooner, which seemed to be an age before it came in sight.

We made Ti-hi and his companions happy by our supply of presents, for we wanted to take nothing back, and at last one bright morning we sailed from the glorious continent-like island, with two strong middle-aged men on board, both of whom were returning to a civilised land with the traces of their captivity in their hair and beards, which were as white as snow.

Neither shall I tell you of the safe voyage home, and of the meeting there. Joy had come at last where sorrow had sojourned so long, and I was happy in my task that I had fulfilled.

I will tell you, though, what the captain said in his hearty way over and over again.

To me it used to be:

"Well, you have growed! Why, if you'd stopped another year you'd have been quite a man. I say, though I never thought you'd ha' done it; 'pon my word!"

Similar words these to those often uttered by poor, prejudiced, obstinate old nurse.

To Jack Penny the captain was always saying:

"I say, young 'un, how you've growed too; not uppards but beam ways. Why, hang me if I don't think you'll make a fine man yet!"

And so he did; a great strong six-foot fellow, with a voice like a trombone. Jack Penny is a sheep-farmer on his own account now, and after a visit to England with my staunch friend the doctor, where I gained some education, and used to do a good deal of business for my father, who is one of the greatest collectors in the south, I returned home, and went to stay a week with Jack Penny.

"I say," he said laughing, "my back's as strong as a lion's now. How it used to ache!"

We were standing at the door of his house, looking north, for we had been talking of our travels, when all at once I caught sight of what looked like a little white tombstone under a eucalyptus tree.

"Why, what's that?" I said.

Jack Penny's countenance changed, and there were a couple of tears in the eyes of the great strong fellow as he said slowly:

"That's to the memory of Gyp, the best dog as ever lived!"

I must not end without a word about Jimmy, my father's faithful companion in his botanical trips.

Jimmy nearly went mad for joy when I got back from England, dancing about like a child. He was always at the door, black and shining as ever, and there was constantly something to be done. One day he had seen the biggest ole man kangaroo as ever was; and this time there was a wallaby to be found; another the announcement that the black cockatoos were in the woods; or else it would be:

"Mass Joe, Mass Joe! Jimmy want go kedge fis very bad; do come a day."

And I? Well, I used to go, and it seemed like being a boy again to go on some expedition with my true old companion and friend.

Yes, friend; Jimmy was always looked upon as a friend; and long before then my mother would have fed and clothed him, given him anything he asked. But Jimmy was wild and happiest so, and I found him just as he was when I left home, faithful and boyish and winning, and often ready to say:

"When Mass Joe ready, go and find um fader all over again!"